Is she or isn't she?

She was perfection.

Her long hair was a mixture of golden brown, honey, and sun-kissed platinum. She held it back from her face with combs that sparkled in the dark and begged to be removed. She had to be tall because she was visible over the cars from her head to her sweetly curved breasts. Holy mammary glands, it was enough to turn a face man into a breast man.

She left the car, walking away on seemingly endless legs. Her tight skirt had a back vent that twitched open with each step to reveal a few inches of slender thigh. Good God, it was enough to turn a newly converted breast man into a leg man.

Her hair swayed from side to side in a way that could hypnotize a man and enslave him for life.

Vampire or mortal?

He had to know . . .

Avon Contemporary Romances by
Kerrelyn Sparks

VAMPS AND THE CITY
HOW TO MARRY A MILLIONAIRE VAMPIRE

Kerrelyn Sparks

VAMPS AND THE CITY

AVON BOOKS

An Imprint of HarperCollinsPublishers

AVON BOOKS
An Imprint of HarperCollins*Publishers*
10 East 53rd Street
New York, New York 10022-5299

Copyright © 2006 by Kerrelyn Sparks
ISBN-13: 978-0-06-075201-9
ISBN-10: 0-06-075201-7
www.avonromance.com

First Avon Books paperback printing: May 2006

Avon Trademark Reg. U.S. Pat. Off. and in Other Countries, Marca Registrada, Hecho en U.S.A.
HarperCollins® is a registered trademark of HarperCollins Publishers Inc.

Printed in the U.S.A.

10 9 8 7 6 5 4 3 2 1

To my son, Jonathan
and my daughter, Emily—
May you live long,
laugh loud,
and love deeply.
And may you never be pestered
by the sort of creatures
your mom writes about.

Acknowledgments

I'd like to acknowledge all those who ignited the blazing success of this vampire series. Wonderful readers and dedicated booksellers—thank you! I'd also like to thank all the editorial staff at HarperCollins, in particular, Senior Editor Erika Tsang. My gratitude to the art department for producing exquisite covers, and to the sales, publicity, and marketing departments for believing in my work. Thank you all!

I would never survive the long journey from page one to the end without my critique buddies: MJ Selle, Sandy Weider, Vicky Yelton, and Vicky Dreiling. Somewhere between the chicken lo mein and the eggrolls, they dish out great insight into characterization and conflict. My thanks to Paul Weider for helping me to create a very high-tech super spy. Thanks also to the members of West Houston, Northwest Houston, Rose City, Lake Country, and PASIC chapters of RWA for your continued support and encouragement. My heartfelt gratitude to agent Michelle Grajkowski and her heroic family.

And as always, my love and gratitude to my own hero and husband, Don.

Chapter 1

"**Eight-twenty** P.M., male Caucasian, five-foot-ten, 180 pounds, mid-twenties, leaving a white Honda Civic," Austin Erickson murmured into his mini-recorder. He adjusted the telescopic night lens on his binoculars and zoomed in on the subject across the parking lot. The guy didn't appear to be armed. More importantly, he was carrying a king-sized cup of gourmet coffee and a bag of doughnuts. Lucky bastard. Normally, that would be considered . . . well, normal. But this was the parking lot of the Digital Vampire Network. Nothing was normal here. Especially after sunset.

Austin exchanged his binoculars for a 35-mm camera and took another look at the guy. "Subject is human. He's going in."

The guy was taking breakfast inside DVN? Didn't he realize *he* could be breakfast? A shaft of light cut across the parking lot, then slowly disappeared as the door swung shut. It was dark once more. Austin had parked his black Acura in the shadowed corner of this lot in Brooklyn. The large warehouse that contained DVN was dark, all the windows blackened out. Only three letters, DVN, glowed in fluorescent red lights over the black-lacquered front door.

With a sigh, he dropped his camera on the passenger seat. He supposed the guy would be safe. Austin had been watching the vampire-owned television station for four nights now, and every night, several humans ventured inside. His conclusion—DVN actually employed a handful of mortals. Did the poor saps know they were working for demonic creatures? Were their minds being controlled? Maybe the vampires offered a great dental plan. Whatever their reasons for being there, as far as Austin could tell, all the humans left about five in the morning still alive and apparently in good health. It was strange, but then, there were a lot of strange things about the vampire world.

He had learned of their existence about six weeks ago when CIA operations officer Sean Whelan had transferred him to the Stake-Out team. Sean had explained what vicious killers these vampires were, so Austin was eager to protect the innocent. He had expected action, lots of action, ramming wooden stakes into nasty green creatures with rotting flesh and bumpy foreheads. Instead, he'd found himself staking out a television network where the vampires looked and acted too much like humans.

In fact, the only way Austin could tell a human from a vampire was to look through the 35-mm camera. Both the living and the undead showed up in a digital camera, but vampires could never appear in a 35-mm for the same reason they never showed up in a mirror. Their image could not be reflected.

He moved the 35-mm to the floor in front of the passenger seat. The rest of his equipment was there—night-vision goggles, digital camera with night lens, Glock with silver bullets, laptop, and his new favorite, his CV-3 video viewer. God, he loved working for the CIA. He had the coolest stuff.

He'd also been issued a box of wooden stakes. Made in China by a company that specialized in chopsticks. The box was sitting on the back seat of his car, open and ready for emergencies.

He opened his laptop on the passenger seat and typed in the secret frequency for receiving transmissions from DVN. The screen came into focus. Good, the vampire news was still on. And free for the taking. They naturally assumed no one could figure out their secret transmissions, and they didn't post guards around their facility. It was all indicative of what Austin considered their most obvious weakness. Their arrogance. He slipped in his ten-gigabyte thumb drive and began recording.

This was his mission—stake out DVN, acquire information, and most importantly, learn the whereabouts of Sean's daughter, who was being held prisoner. The last time they'd seen Shanna was eight days ago in Central Park. She'd been surrounded by an army of Scottish vampires. To Austin, she'd looked like a willing captive, but Sean insisted she was brainwashed. Terribly outnumbered, the Stake-Out team had been forced to retreat, leaving Shanna Whelan behind.

Sean was furious. He was staking out Roman Draganesti's townhouse every night, but so far, there was no sign of his daughter. He'd ordered Garrett to watch the Russian coven in Brooklyn. Alyssa was watching Romatech Industries. The new girl, Emma, was manning the office in Midtown and scouring police reports for anything that indicated vampire involvement. And Austin was watching DVN—the facility and the transmissions.

He slipped on his CV-3 video viewer. The special eyeglasses gave him a heads-up display that freed him from having to watch his computer screen. He could continue to scan the parking lot while DVN played on a virtual screen in front of his eyes.

According to the DVN newscaster, the Russian coven was in turmoil. Some of the male coven members were refusing to accept two females as masters. A civil war could erupt. Austin smiled to himself. Let the slimy vampires kill each other off.

He poured a cup of coffee from his thermos. Holy caffeine fix, he wished this was gourmet. And a few snacks would be nice. He should have confiscated that guy's doughnuts for evidence. While he drank, a commercial started. A sexy female claimed her yummy drink was low in cholesterol and blood sugar. *Blood Lite.*

Austin choked, spraying coffee all over his steering wheel before he managed to swallow. Sheesh, demon diet food? He grabbed an old napkin to wipe up the mess. Next was the vampire celebrity talk show, starring Corky Courrant. He eyed the hostess's chest. Those had to be implants.

His attention was diverted when a photo flashed on the screen next to Corky's head. A photo of Draganesti.

"You'll never believe it!" Corky exclaimed with a grin. "The most eligible bachelor in America is getting married! Yes, Roman Draganesti, coven master of East Coast vampires, billionaire inventor of synthetic blood and Fusion Cuisine, and CEO of Romatech Industries has announced his engagement. And you'll never believe who the lucky bride is! Stay tuned!"

Another commercial started, this one for a special vampire toothpaste, guaranteed to whiten your fangs or your money back. Austin wondered if there were vampire ladies at home, bawling their evil eyes out because superbachelor Roman Draganesti was marrying someone else. The whole thing sounded too weird. Could vampires actually fall in love? And where would they make their marriage vows? Surely, demons didn't go to church. And how could they promise "til death do you part" if they were already dead?

One thing was for sure. The bride had better not be Shanna Whelan. Sean would go ballistic. Literally. He'd probably detonate a truckload of C4 on the Upper East Side, where Draganesti's townhouse was located.

Corky's show came back on. Another photo was displayed.

"Oh, crap." Austin grimaced. It was a picture of Draganesti and Shanna Whelan together.

"Can you believe it?" Corky screeched. "Roman Draganesti is marrying a mortal!"

Holy matrimony. Austin pulled the CV-3 video viewer off and dropped it beside his laptop. This was the worst possible news. With a groan, he leaned forward and bumped his forehead against the steering wheel. Sean would want to retaliate. And there were only five agents on the Stake-Out team. They were too outnumbered to do anything overt. And they still didn't know where Shanna was. That damned Draganesti was hiding her.

Austin was too tense to sit in the car. He had to do something. The thumb drive was still recording, so he didn't need to stay put. He looked around the parking lot. There were thirty-seven cars, and most of them belonged to the undead. If he ran their plates, he could get their names and start compiling a database of known vampires.

He grabbed his digital camera and climbed out of the car. He was almost finished taking pictures of license plates when the bright flash of headlights ripped through the darkness. Another car was entering the lot. A black Lexus four-door sedan.

Keeping low, Austin darted from the cover of one car to the next until he had a clear view of where the Lexus had parked. He zoomed the camera lens onto the New York license plate and silently snapped.

The driver's door opened, and a tall male dressed in an expensive suit emerged. Austin took his picture. Then, the passenger door opened, and a young woman stepped out. *Young, my ass.* Austin gritted his teeth while he snapped her picture. She might dress like a teenager with her plaid skirt and fishnet hose, but if she were a vampire, she could be older than dirt.

Unfortunately, there was no way he could tell if they were alive or undead with the digital camera. He needed the 35-mm. He dashed back to his car, hugging the shadow of a tall brick wall. Then, he heard it. A third car door shutting. He edged around a large SUV and caught a glimpse of blond hair. The last time he'd seen Shanna, she'd been a blonde. Could it be? He inched closer, staying low. His mouth fell open. She wasn't Shanna.

She was perfection.

Holy moley. He'd always considered himself a face man, or more importantly, a man who gazed first into the eyes of a woman for a glimpse of her soul. Not possible with this one, for he could only see her profile. Her nose was petite and girlish, but her mouth wide and womanly. A dynamite combination, and it definitely lit his fuse. He took a few pictures.

Her long hair was a mixture of golden brown, honey, and sun-kissed platinum. She held it back from her face with combs that sparkled in the dark and begged to be removed. Hair that pretty deserved a few pictures.

He guessed she was about five-foot-nine. She had to be tall because she was visible over the cars from her head to her sweetly curved breasts. Holy mammary glands, it was enough to turn a face man into a breast man. Thank God for the zoom lens.

She left the car, walking away from him on seemingly endless legs. Her tight skirt had a back vent that twitched open with each step to reveal a few inches of slender thigh. Sheesh, it was enough to turn a newly converted breast man into a leg man.

But then, he noticed how her tight skirt outlined her hips and derrière. Holy honey buns. That was worth a picture or two. And certainly enough to turn a leg man into a connoisseur of fine booty.

Wait a minute. That blue business suit didn't look like something a vampire would wear. They usually went for a more flashy look. Of course! She might not be a vampire. She looked too vibrant to be undead. What if she was innocent and the two with her were vampires? They could be delivering her into a den of demons. *Dammit.* Not on his watch.

He straightened, then paused with a silent groan. *Idiot.* He was letting his dick do the thinking. The gorgeous woman wasn't a prisoner. She was walking toward the entrance of DVN with determination in her long-legged stride.

He had to know. Vampire or mortal—which was she? The threesome had reached the entrance of DVN. Austin rushed to his car, yanked open the door, and grabbed the 35-mm. He peered through the viewfinder. Total darkness. With a muttered curse, he removed the lens cap and raised the camera once more.

Nothing. The door to DVN was open, but no one was there. He lowered the camera. Now he could see the male holding the door open and the shorter woman going inside. They were definitely vampires. But what about the gorgeous blonde?

Shit! He'd missed her. He climbed into the car, wincing when his jeans cut into his swollen groin. She had to be human. He couldn't be this fired up over a dead demon. Could he?

Darcy Newhart came to an abrupt stop inside the lobby of DVN. She could hardly see the black and red décor, the room was so crowded. There had to be over fifty Vamps here, all jabbering with excitement. Good God, were they all seeking employment?

Gregori bumped into her from behind. "Sorry," he murmured, his gaze wandering about the room.

"I didn't expect so many." Her hands trembled as she made sure the combs were still holding back her long hair. She checked her leather portfolio one more time. Her neatly typed résumé was still there, looking the same as it had five minutes ago. How could she compete with so many? Who was she kidding? She would never get this job. The familiar tentacles of panic curled around her, squeezing the air from her lungs. She would never be free. She could never escape.

"Darcy," Gregori's sharp voice cut through the rising panic. He waited 'til she met his eyes, then he gave her the Look.

In the first year of her forced confinement, Gregori had become a good friend and pillar of support, repeatedly telling her, *This is the only world you have now. Deal with it.* Now, he only had to look at her to remind her to be strong. She nodded and squared her shoulders. "I'll be all right."

His brown eyes softened. "Yes, you will."

Maggie adjusted the pleats on her short plaid skirt. "I'm so nervous. What if I see Don Orlando? What will I say?"

"Don who?" Gregori asked.

"Don Orlando de Corazon," Maggie repeated his name in a reverent whisper. "He's the star of *As a Vampire Turns.*"

Gregori frowned. "That's why you came? To drool on the stars? I thought you wanted to give Darcy moral support."

"I do," Maggie insisted. "But then, I thought if Darcy can find a job, maybe I can, too. So I decided to audition for a soap opera."

"You want to be an actress?" Gregori asked.

"Oh, I don't know anything about acting. I just want to be with Don Orlando." Maggie clasped her hands to her chest and unleashed a long sigh. "He's the sexiest man on earth."

Gregori gave her a dubious look. "Okay. Good luck

with that. Excuse me." He grabbed Darcy's arm and
pulled her a few feet away. "You've got to help me.
The harem ladies are driving me crazy."

"Welcome to the club. I was ready for a padded cell
four years ago."

"I'm serious, Darcy."

She snorted. So was she. It had stretched her sanity
to the brink when she'd discovered the existence of
vampires. But for a modern woman to be forced to
live in a vampire harem and obey the dictates of a
master? It was more than she could bear.

She'd tried to escape once, but Connor had tracked
her down and teleported her back like a lost pet. Even
now, the humiliation curdled her stomach. Her new
master, Roman, had sat her down for a firm lecture.
She knew too much. The mortal world believed she
was dead. Because of her job on mortal television, her
face was recognizable to millions. She had to remain
hidden. But the good news was she would be safe
and sheltered within the confines of his harem. Roman
had explained it all calmly and gently, while she had
silently fumed and wanted to *scream*.

Trapped. For four long years. At least Roman's re-
cent engagement had put him in a good mood. He'd finally agreed to let her venture out into the world, as
long as it was the vampire world.

"I can't take it." Gregori gave her a desperate look.
Darcy knew he was already regretting his offer to
house Roman's newly rejected harem. "It took me a
week to move their luggage. Princess Joanna had
fifty-two boxes. And Cora Lee had so many trunks—"

"Thirty-four," Darcy muttered. "It's all those hoop
skirts she wears. They take up a lot of room."

"Room I don't have." Gregori dragged a hand

through his thick chestnut hair. "When I offered to take them in, I didn't realize they would come with so much crap. And they're acting like they plan to stay forever."

"I understand. I'm stuck there, too." Ten women squashed into two bedrooms, sharing one bathroom. It was a nightmare. But unfortunately, dealing with horror was nothing new to Darcy. "I'm sorry, Gregori, but I don't know how I can help you."

"You can show them how to get a life," he whispered. "Encourage them to be independent."

"They won't listen to me. They consider me an outsider."

"You can do it. Already Maggie is following your example." He lay a hand on her shoulder. "I have faith in you."

If only she had some in herself. There had been a time when she'd glowed with confidence. She took a deep breath. She needed that old Darcy back. She needed this job.

Gregori glanced at his watch. "I have an appointment in thirty minutes, so I'll catch up with you later." He looked around the room and grinned. "I think I see some babes I know."

Darcy smiled as he sauntered off. Gregori was such a charmer. She never would have survived without his friendship.

Maggie sidled up close, a frown creasing her youthful face. "There are so many people here. And they look more . . . dramatic than me."

"Don't worry. You look adorable." At the beginning of her confinement, Darcy had been shocked by the way the harem ladies dressed. Each one was trapped in an individual time warp, still clinging to the fashions they had experienced as mortals. She'd encouraged them to modernize their tastes, but only Maggie and Vanda had been willing to invent new looks for themselves. Maggie's usual attire was a short plaid skirt, fishnet hose, and a tight black sweater to highlight her generous bosom.

Darcy turned to face the reception desk. It seemed a mile away. Clutching her portfolio to her chest, she weaved through the crowd with Maggie close behind. The Vamps had gathered into groups, chatting and gesturing wildly with their hands. Darcy passed one group, noting the heavy makeup and clothes that showed too much skin. Sheesh. Whatever happened to manly men? She turned to check out the females instead.

"What happened to Gregori?" Maggie looked over the crowd, her eyes wide with worry. Her short stature made it easy for her to lose people.

Darcy spotted him with a group of women, each with hair dyed an unnatural color. They arched around him like a rainbow. When he smiled and spoke to them, they tittered with laughter.

"He's fine." Maybe those women thought green, blue, and pink hair was wild and wicked, but Darcy thought they looked more like a cuddly clan of Care Bears. *Hi! My name is TenderHeart Vamp. Do you need a hug?* She suppressed the image with a shudder. Good God, she'd been cooped up for way too long.

The receptionist was painting her fingernails a glossy blood red to match the highlights in her hair. "If you're here for the auditions, sign in and wait your turn." She pointed a wet nail at a clipboard.

Maggie studied the clipboard, her eyes growing wider. "Sweet Mary, I'll be number sixty-two."

"Yeah, it's like this every night." The receptionist blew on her fingernails. "But you won't have to wait very long."

"Okay." Maggie added her name on the bottom of the list.

"What about you?" The receptionist wrinkled her nose at Darcy's conservative business suit.

"I have an appointment with Sylvester Bacchus."

"Yeah, right. If you're here for an acting job, you'll have to wait your turn." The receptionist pointed at the clipboard.

Darcy pasted a smile on her face. "I'm a professional journalist, and Mr. Bacchus is expecting me. My name is Darcy Newhart."

The receptionist snorted to convey how underwhelmed she was, then checked a paper on her desk. Her mouth fell open. "No freakin' way."

"Excuse me?" Darcy asked.

"You're on the list, but . . ." The receptionist narrowed her eyes. "Are you sure you're Darcy Newhart?"

"Yes." Who else would she be? Darcy's smile withered away.

"Well, that's freakin' weird. I guess you might as well see him. Third door on the left."

"Thank you." Not a good start. Darcy squelched a feeling of doom. She rounded the desk and strode down the hall.

"You'd better knock first," the receptionist yelled in her nasal voice. "He may be in the middle of an audition."

Darcy glanced back. The receptionist was lolling back in her chair, wiggling fingers in the air while she admired her nail polish. Maggie gave Darcy an encouraging smile. She smiled weakly back, took a deep breath, and knocked on the door.

"Come in," a gruff voice hollered.

She entered the room and turned to close the door. Behind her, she heard a curious sound. A zipper?

She pivoted to face Sylvester Bacchus. He looked about fifty in mortal years, though there was no way she could estimate his age as a vampire. Mostly bald, he had embraced the condition by keeping the rest of his hair buzzed short. His moustache and beard were closely cropped and well-groomed, dark hair sprinkled with gray. His brown eyes immediately checked her out, focusing on her chest for far too long.

She lifted her leather portfolio to block his view. "How do you do? I'm—"

"You're new." His gaze drifted to her hips. "Not bad."

Her face heated up as she debated the long-range ramifications of starting a job interview by slapping the prospective employer in the face. Her dilemma was cut short when she noticed a blond head slowly rising from behind the desk.

"I'm sorry." Darcy retreated toward the door. "I didn't realize you were busy."

"No problem." Mr. Bacchus glanced at the blonde. "That'll be all, Tiffany. You can . . . polish my shoes another day."

She tilted her head. "You want me to do your shoes, too?"

"No," he grumbled. "Just come back in a week."

Darcy realized the zipper she'd heard was real. Good God, if this was how auditions were conducted, she needed to warn Maggie. She'd always been under the impression that vampires preferred vampire sex, a purely mental exercise that was considered superior to sloppy and sweaty mortal sex. Obviously, Mr. Bacchus possessed a more open mind. And a more open zipper.

Meanwhile, Tiffany had jumped to her feet and was pressing her hands to her plump breasts. "You mean I'm being recalled?"

"Sure." Mr. Bacchus patted her on the rump. "Off you go."

"Yes, Mr. Bacchus." Tiffany executed an amazing walk toward the door, managing to sway her hips and jiggle her breasts all at the same time. She leaned over to turn the door knob, jutting out her derrière and arching her back as if the act of opening a door could spiral her into fits of orgasmic ecstasy. She paused halfway out the door to toss a seductive smile back at Mr. Bacchus, then slithered down the hall.

Darcy kept her face carefully blank so her simmering anger wouldn't show. She should have known the Digital Vampire Network would adhere to archaic, chauvinistic rules of behavior. It was the same way throughout the vampire world. Most of the female Vamps were at least a hundred years old. Many were centuries old, so they didn't know about the advances mortal women had made. They didn't want to know. They were so sure their own world was vastly superior.

The end result was tragic. Female Vamps had no idea how poorly they were treated. They simply accepted their lot as normal. Darcy had told the harem ladies about the brave women who had suffered in order to obtain the vote. Her passionate tribute had been dismissed as ridiculous hogwash. No one voted for coven masters in the vampire world. How dreadfully plebian.

But this was the world she was stuck with. And since DVN was the only television network in the vampire world, it provided her only chance for the type of job she desperately wanted. And the independence she craved. So she had to be polite to Mr. Bacchus. Even if he was a sexist pig.

"Come on in. Don't be shy." Mr. Bacchus lounged back in his chair and propped his feet on the desk. "And shut the door, so we can have some privacy." He winked.

Darcy's eye twitched, and she prayed it hadn't looked like she was winking back. She shut the door and approached his desk. "I'm delighted to meet you, Mr. Bacchus. I'm Darcy Newhart, a professional television journalist." She removed the résumé from her portfolio and placed it on his desk. "As you can see—"

"What?" He lowered his feet to the floor. "You're Darcy Newhart?"

"Yes. You will notice on my résumé that I have—"

"But you're a woman."

Her eye twitched again. "Yes, I am, and as you can see"—she pointed to a section on her résumé—"I worked several years at a local news station here in the city—"

"Goddammit!" Mr. Bacchus pounded a fist onto his desk. "You were supposed to be a man."

"I assure you, I've been a female all my life."

"With a name like Darcy? Who the hell names a girl Darcy?"

"My mother did. She was very fond of Jane Austen—"

"Then why didn't she name you *Jane*? Shit." Mr. Bacchus leaned back in his chair to glower at the ceiling.

"If you could look at my résumé, you would see that I'm more than qualified for a position on the *Nightly News*."

"You're not qualified," he muttered. "You're a woman."

"I fail to see how my gender has anything to—"

He rocked forward suddenly, pinning her with a glare. "Have you ever seen a woman on the *Nightly News*?"

"No, but this would be an ideal opportunity for you to rectify that error." Oops. Poor choice of words.

"*Error?* Are you crazy? Women don't do the news."

"I did." She tapped a finger on her résumé.

He glanced down. "That's the mortal world. What the hell do they know? Their world's a mess." He crumbled up her paper and tossed it aside.

Darcy's heart fell into her stomach. "You could hire me for a month on a probationary status, so I could prove my ability—"

"No way. Stone would tear this place apart if I tried to pair him up with a female co-anchor."

"I understand. He's an excellent news anchor." Dull as a rock was more like it. "But Stone does all the stories, droning—I mean, talking for the entire thirty minutes."

"So?"

"The *Nightly News* would be more exciting and faster paced if you included reports from correspondents in the field. That was my specialty, and I would be delighted to—"

"I was considering doing that. And I was thinking about hiring you, but you turned out to be a woman."

Her heart dropped a few inches lower. "I fail to see—"

"News is serious business. We can't have females doing it. People would miss something important, 'cause they were looking at your perky little breasts."

Her shoulders slumped, taking her perky little breasts with them. This was it—the impenetrable wall of male vampire chauvinism, and once more, she'd slammed right into it. If only she could take a sledgehammer to it. Or a baseball bat to Mr. Bacchus's egg-shaped head. "I could work behind the scenes. I used to write my own—"

"You can write?"

"Yes."

"Can you be entertaining?"

"Yes." Her reports had been considered humorous.

He studied her. "You strike me as somewhat intelligent."

Her eye twitched. "Thank you."

"We're flooded every night with the flashy ones who want to be in front of the camera. Finding someone with intelligence and experience to work behind the scenes is a major problem."

"I'm very good at solving problems."

"Are you? Then I'll tell you what I really need at DVN." He leaned forward. "I need a big hit."

With a baseball bat? "You mean a new show?"

"Yeah." Mr. Bacchus stood and wandered toward a dry-erase board on the wall. "Do you realize that since DVN has been on the air, our lineup of shows has never changed?"

"Everyone loves your shows. Especially the soap operas."

"It's boring! Look at this." He pointed at the board where DVN's schedule was displayed. "Every freaking night, it's the same thing. We start at eight o'clock with the *Nightly News* with Stone Cauffyn. Then, at eight-thirty, it's *Live with the Undead,* our celebrity gossip magazine."

"With Corky Courrant. I saw her a few weeks ago at the Gala Opening Ball."

Mr. Bacchus pivoted toward her, his eyes wide. "You were invited to the ball?"

"Yes. I . . . used to be associated with Roman Draganesti."

"How?"

"I worked part time at Romatech." She'd refused to take an allowance from Roman, so Gregori had arranged for her to work in a back room at Romatech a few nights a week. Roman had okayed it, as long as no mortal ever saw her.

"Draganesti is one of our top sponsors." Mr. Bacchus watched her, scratching his beard. "How well do you know him?"

A blush crept up to her cheeks. "I . . . lived in his house."

"Really? You were in his harem?"

"I—you could say that." But she never would.

"Hmm." Mr. Bacchus's heated gaze wandered over her body. Clearly, her non-writing abilities were being reassessed.

She lifted her chin. "You were describing the schedule?"

"Oh, yeah." He turned back to the board. "In the nine o'clock slot, we have *As the Vampire Turns,* starring Don Orlando de Corazon. Then at ten, we have *All My Vampires,* and at eleven, *General Morgue.* But what happens at midnight?" He jabbed a finger at the dry-erase board.

Darcy frowned. There was nothing there. What *did*

come on at midnight? By then, she was usually at Romatech, immersed to her ears in boring paperwork.

"Nothing!" Mr. Bacchus yelled. "We start over again and repeat the whole damned schedule. It's pathetic! The midnight hour should be our greatest show ever, the *pièce de résistance*. But we have . . . nothing." He trudged back to his desk.

Darcy took a deep breath. This was her chance to show her true worth. "You need a new show, but not another soap opera."

"That's right." Mr. Bacchus paced behind his desk. "Maybe a cop show. A vampire cop. We could call it *Blood and Disorder*. That would be different. What do *you* think we should do?"

Gulp. She racked her brain. What had been the rage before her world had fallen apart? "How about a reality show?"

He whirled around to face her. "I like it! What could be more real than vampires? But what would be the premise?"

Her mind went completely blank. *Damn.* She sat in a chair and arranged her portfolio across her lap to buy herself some time. A reality show. What was real? The harem's new dilemma? "How about an expelled harem in need of a new master?"

"Not bad." Mr. Bacchus nodded. "Damned good, actually. Hey, wasn't Draganesti's harem just kicked out?"

"Yes. Corky did a feature about it on *Live with the Undead*." But none of the ladies had participated. It was too humiliating.

"You know, some of those harem ladies are famous. Could you get them to do the show?"

"I—I believe so."

"You know Draganesti really well, right?" Mr. Bacchus's mouth twisted with a knowing smirk. "Could you get him to rent us a big, fancy penthouse for the show? You know, one of those glitzy ones with a swimming pool on the roof."

"I—I suppose." Maybe Gregori could figure something out.

"It's gotta have a hot tub. Can't have a reality show without a hot tub."

"I understand."

"And you have experience in television?"

"Yes." Darcy glanced at the trash can that now held her neatly typed résumé. "I graduated in television journalism at the University of Southern California and worked in that region for several years before moving to New York and a position at Local Four News—"

"Fine, fine." Mr. Bacchus waved a hand to shut her up. "Look, I want this reality show. If you can get us a fancy location and guarantee that Draganesti's old harem will participate, then you've got a job. Director."

Her heart lurched. Director of a reality show? Okay. She could handle this. She had to. It was this or nothing.

"So can you do it? Deliver the penthouse and the harem?"

"Yes." She clenched her portfolio with a white-knuckled grip. "I'd be delighted." God help her.

"And don't forget the hot tub."

"I wouldn't dream of it."

"Great! I'll have an office ready for you tomorrow night. What do you want to call the show?"

Her mind raced, searching for a pithy title. *How to Dig Your Own Grave in Less than Five Minutes?*

"Well, the women will be selecting the perfect man to be their new master."

Mr. Bacchus perched on the corner of his desk and scratched at his beard. "*The Perfect Man?* Or *The Perfect Master?*"

Not exciting enough. Darcy closed her eyes briefly to concentrate. Maggie would think Don Orlando was the perfect man. What had she called him? "How about *The Sexiest Man on Earth?*"

"Excellent!" Mr. Bacchus grinned. "And call me Sly. It's short for Sylvester."

"Thank you . . . Sly."

"This has gotta be a hit. Not just an ordinary show, but one with twists and surprises."

"Yes, of course."

"Auditions will be easy. As you can see in the lobby, there'll be lots of male Vamps trying out for the show."

Darcy winced. Somehow her idea of the world's sexiest man didn't include makeup. "Do they all have to be Vamps?"

Sly snorted. "We're talking about the sexiest men on earth. Of course they'll be Vamps." He strode toward the door.

Of course. Darcy stood, gritting her teeth. Everyone knew vampires were superior in every way. A sudden idea sparked in her head. Why not put Sly's claim to the test?

She smiled as she walked toward the door. So her boss wanted the show to include some surprising twists? No problem.

She would deliver a doozy.

Chapter 2

Austin arrived early for the Stake-Out meeting, so he would have time to download the photos he'd taken the night before at DVN. He opened the unmarked door on the sixth floor of a federal office building. Most of the floor was occupied with Homeland Security, so no one realized he was actually CIA. Or that he was combating terrorists of the undead variety.

The Stake-Out team met every evening at seven before the sun went down and they moved on to their individual assignments. As he passed Sean Whelan's office, loud curses filtered through the walls. Great. Sean must be watching the DVN stuff Austin had emailed to his office. Definitely a good time to avoid the boss.

Austin hurried to the open area where he and the other teammates had their work stations. He wasn't surprised to find the place empty. They were all exhausted. He hadn't had a day or night off in weeks. He downloaded the pictures, then studied them on his monitor while the photo printer kicked into action. Lots of license plates. And lots of *her* in the blue suit, whoever she was. He'd waited 'til dawn, but had missed seeing her again. Dammit. She must have left while he'd gone to relieve himself. The price of too much coffee.

He yawned as he splayed his hands into his shaggy hair. Working nights made it hard to take care of mundane things like haircuts. And he still wasn't sleeping well during the day. The monitor blurred before his weary eyes. He needed coffee. He wandered to the break room.

"Good evening, Austin." Emma sat at the small round table, eating low-fat yogurt and looking bright-eyed and perky.

There should be a law against blatant cheerfulness in the workplace. Her neatly pressed yellow shirt reminded him that he looked like he'd slept in his wrinkled clothes. Except he hadn't slept much at all. He mumbled something and filled a coffee cup.

"You poor fellow, you look like shit," Emma continued with her crisp British accent.

He grunted, too tired to engage in verbal sparring. Besides, she always won. "Why are you here so early?"

She licked the last of her yogurt off her plastic spoon. "I wanted to get an early start on last night's police reports. I think I'm on to something."

"What?"

"In the last few months, there have been several calls to the police from Central Park. The caller reports seeing someone being attacked, but when the police arrive, they can't find anyone who knows anything."

Austin frowned. "That's not much. Could be pranksters."

"Or it could be real." Emma pointed her spoon at him to make her point. "And the people who called don't remember anything, because their memories were erased by vampires."

"I . . . suppose." Mind control was a vampire specialty. That was exactly why the Stake-Out team was so small. Everyone on the team needed a certain amount of psychic power in order to resist vampire control. There was no way to fight a creature if he could simply take over your mind. As far as Austin knew, he and Sean possessed the most power on the team.

"Think about it." Emma tossed her empty yogurt cup into the trash. Perfect aim, of course. She'd been working for MI6 when Sean had arranged for her transfer a week ago. "If you were a hungry vampire, wouldn't you troll for victims in a place like Central Park?"

"I suppose." Austin sipped his coffee.

"So I went there last night to look around."

He gulped. "You went by yourself?"

"Yes. You go on your stake-outs alone. Why shouldn't I?"

"Because hunting for vampires in Central Park is not a stake-out. You could have come across one of them."

She rolled her eyes. "That was the idea. Don't worry. I had a few stakes with me."

Austin snorted. "Haven't you been reading the reports? These vampires are super fast and strong."

She sauntered toward the fridge and removed a bottle of water. "I can take care of myself."

"I know." The one time he'd taken her on in a practice session, he'd found himself flat on his back with
stars swirling around his head. "But I don't think you
should go alone."

"Why not?" She unscrewed the bottle top. "They're
probably looking for lone females."

"Wait a minute. You're setting yourself up as bait?"

She shrugged one shoulder and took a sip of water.
"If I can draw one in, I'll kill him. That *is* our mission,
isn't it?"

"What if several of them gang up on you? It's way
too dangerous."

She sighed. "I shouldn't have told you." She cast
him an injured look. "I thought you would understand."

Dammit. He should tell her she was irresponsible
and crazy, but he hated being that blunt to a woman.
Besides, her vampire hunting sounded like something
he would do.

"Are you going to tell Sean?" she asked.

With their boss already livid over his daughter's upcoming marriage, Austin wasn't that big a glutton for
punishment. "I'll have to think about it. Did you see
any vampires last night?"

"Unfortunately, no."

"Good. There are only five of us, Emma. We can't
afford to lose you, so think before you play the hero."
He trudged back to his desk. Crazy woman, hunting
vampires all alone.

He sipped his coffee while he studied the pictures
on the screen. Speaking of vampires, who was the demon guy who had driven the gorgeous blonde to
DVN? Austin scanned the photos until he located the
black Lexus. He ran the license plate through the

system. The vehicle was registered to Gregori Holstein, address on the Upper West Side. Date of birth was 1964, which made him a very young vampire. Of course, vampires were probably adept at falsifying documents.

Austin wrote down Gregori's address, then did a credit search. The guy worked at Romatech Industries, not a big surprise. A lot of vampires worked there at night. The place manufactured artificial blood, which meant Gregori might not be a biter. That was good news. *She* wouldn't have to worry about him nibbling on her sweet little neck. If she was human.

The click of heels on linoleum warned him that Emma was approaching. She stopped in front of the photo printer and began looking at his pictures.

Maybe he'd been too hard on her. "Look, I know you have something personal against the vampires."

She shrugged one shoulder. "Where did you take these?"

"Parking lot at DVN. Last night."

"Lots of license plates." She set a stack of photos to the side. "I suppose all these cars belong to vampires."

"Most of them. Want to help me run the plates?"

"Love to." She picked up another bunch of photos.

"Emma, I won't tell Sean about Central Park, if you'll let me know whenever you go hunting again. I'll give you backup."

"That's super. Thank you." She gave him a brief smile, then resumed her study of his pictures. "These are very interesting."

"You recognize any of the cars?"

"No. But I recognize a woman's bum when I see one."

"What?"

"You must have twenty pictures of her legs and even more of her derrière. Who is she?"

Austin's nerves tensed, but he kept his face blank. He reached out his hand. "Those are personal. Give them to me."

"Doing personal business on company time? Shame on you." She set the pictures down and retrieved some more from the printer. "Oh, look. Boob shots. And the back of her head. Lovely hair."

"I said give them to me." Austin gritted his teeth and stared at the stack of pictures Emma had set down. They zipped across the table and stopped next to his keyboard.

Emma gasped. The photos in her hand tumbled to the table. She stepped back. "Oh, my God."

He wheeled his chair over to the printer and collected the photos she'd dropped.

"You're telekinetic," she whispered.

"Yeah. Big deal." He gathered the rest of the pictures from the printer, then pushed himself back to his computer.

"But it's brilliant! I didn't know you had such wicked powers. Oh no! Austin's powers." She chortled with laughter.

He groaned. "Very funny." He separated the pictures into two stacks—license plates and the girl in blue. "It's not like I earned the ability. I was born this way." Even his dad hadn't been able to squelch his abilities, though you had to give the guy credit for trying.

"How exciting." Emma grinned. "An international man of mystery, using his special powers to fight evil."

"Yeah, right." What could possibly be evil about *her?* After one last, lingering look at her stack of pictures, he stashed them in his desk drawer.

Emma crossed her arms and propped a hip against the worktable. "You're quite smitten with her, aren't you?"

"No." Was he? "I don't know who she is."

"The international man of mystery has a mystery woman? Super! Let's figure it out. Where did you take her pictures?"

"Outside DVN."

"Good heavens, Austin. She probably works there. That means she's a vampire."

"I don't think so. Romatech has lots of human employees. And DVN has some, too."

"Did you try the 35-millimeter on her?"

"No, I . . . didn't get a chance."

"Because you were too busy taking a hundred photos of her."

"I didn't take a hundred. Only about . . . sixty." Sheesh. He *was* smitten.

Emma lifted a dark brow and refrained from saying the obvious. "Was she alone?"

"No. She arrived with a male I have identified as Gregori Holstein, and an unknown female. They're both undead."

"So, she's traveling with two vampires to a vampire-owned television station? Austin, this is what we in the business refer to as a *clue.* The woman is a vampire."

"It's not proof." She had to be alive. She had to be.

Emma regarded him sadly. "You *are* smitten. And with the enemy, no less."

"We don't have proof that she's a vampire."

"Is she or isn't she? Only her hairdresser knows for sure." Emma gave him a wry smile. "She wouldn't show up in the mirror."

"Forget it. I doubt I'll ever see her again." He divided the license plate photos in half. "Let's get to work on these."

"There you are!" Sean Whelan strode toward them. "I need you in the conference room now. Garrett and Alyssa are already there."

"Yes, sir." Emma picked up a legal pad and pencil from her desk, then headed toward the conference room.

Austin checked quickly that there were no more pictures of *her* lying about. He followed his boss, wondering if he should convey condolences over Shanna's engagement to a fanged fiancé. Probably not. Sean's face was grim as he held open the door to the conference room. Austin entered quietly and sat in one of the chairs at the long oak table. He gave Garrett and Alyssa a brief nod. Emma greeted them personally. And cheerfully, of course. Austin yawned and wished he'd brought his coffee.

"Any news about your daughter?" Garrett asked as Sean closed the door.

Austin winced. He was beginning to think Garrett wasn't the sharpest guy around.

Sean stiffened and gave Garrett a cold stare. "Do *you* have anything positive to report?"

Garrett shifted in his chair, his clean-shaven cheeks reddening. "No, sir."

"I thought not." Sean stalked toward the head of the table. He grasped the leather back of the chair there, his grip so tight his knuckles showed white. "My daughter is still missing. What's more, that bastard

Draganesti has twisted her mind to the point she has agreed to marry him."

Alyssa and Emma gasped.

Garrett's mouth fell open. "But—but how do you know?"

"It was announced on DVN last night," Austin spoke quietly.

A strangled sound vibrated in Sean's throat as if he were suppressing another long litany of curses. He released the chair and began to pace about the room. "Obviously, time is running out. We have to find Shanna immediately, and the stake-outs are not getting us the information we need."

"We should check Draganesti's financial records," Emma suggested. "He may have rented or purchased another residence."

"Do it," Sean growled as he continued to pace.

Emma made a note on her legal pad.

"We need someone on the inside," Austin muttered.

"An informant?" Alyssa asked.

"No, an agent working undercover." Sean stopped at the head of the table and narrowed his eyes on Austin. "I was thinking the same thing. And I know how we can do it."

Silence pervaded the room as they all waited for Sean to elaborate. He began to pace again. "A month ago, I had Homeland Security contact businesses in the five boroughs and give them a list of names and businesses to look out for. One of those businesses was the Digital Video Network, the bogus name the vampires use for their network when dealing with humans."

Sean strode toward the door and paused. "Shortly before dawn, a female at DVN called the Stars of Tomorrow Casting Agency and left a message. Another call was made this afternoon to finalize the arrangements. Someone at DVN plans to use the agency's office tomorrow night to audition people for a reality show. The owner of the agency called Homeland Security to report the incident."

"The vampires are doing a reality show?" Alyssa asked.

Sean nodded. "Yes. And since they want to audition humans, it gives us the perfect chance to go in undercover."

"And infiltrate DVN," Austin whispered. His heartbeat quickened. He ought to volunteer. He might get to see *her* again.

"What kind of reality show? Is it like *The Bachelor?*" Emma exchanged a look with Alyssa. "With female contestants?"

Alyssa shuddered. "They could call it *Bride of Dracula.*"

"I bet it's more like a vampire *Survivor,*" Austin suggested. "They strand a group of humans on a deserted island with some hungry vampires, and see which one survives."

Alyssa grimaced. "That's terrible."

Sean rested a hand on the doorknob. "You're all wrong. They want men. Live men." He gave Austin and Garrett each a pointed look. "I need you two on that show."

Garrett turned pale. "Oh, God."

Oh, yes. "How do we get on?" Austin asked.

"It's all arranged. Just a minute. I have someone waiting outside in the hall." Sean left the room.

Silence descended. Alyssa gave the guys sympathetic looks.

"Well, here's your chance to be on the telly." Emma attempted a cheerful smile. "You might be famous."

"They might be dinner," Alyssa muttered.

Garrett sighed. "Why don't we just bomb them all and get it over with?"

Emma rolled her eyes. "Because we're not sure an explosion would actually kill them. Besides, there are innocent humans working at Romatech and DVN. And Shanna is with them, too."

Alyssa nodded. "This could be the best way to find her."

Austin remained quiet to disguise the fact that his heart was racing and his breathing more shallow. His first priority should be finding Shanna, but all he could think about was the possibility of seeing *her* again. *Shit.* What was wrong with him? Working undercover could be dangerous, and all he could think about was the mystery woman? There was a name for agents who allowed themselves to get distracted. *Deceased.*

Sean appeared at the door again, this time with a middle-aged woman in an expensive suit. "This is Ms. Elizabeth Stein."

The woman greeted them with a slight nod and an even slighter smile. Her dark hair was swept up into a bun, her slender frame held stiffly erect.

"Ms. Stein is the owner of the Stars of Tomorrow Casting Agency," Sean explained. "It's one of the most prestigious agencies in the city."

She lifted her chin and looked down her long nose at them. "*The* most prestigious agency."

"Of course." Sean motioned toward the men. "Will they do?"

She stepped forward and studied Garrett with narrowed eyes. "Striking. I'd love to sign him up."

Garrett smiled, baring his perfect white teeth. "Thank you, ma'am."

Ms. Stein withdrew some papers from her expensive valise. "You understand that I represent only the most promising actors and actresses in the city. I am highly selective."

"So are we," Austin muttered.

She turned and inspected him slowly. With the lift of an eyebrow, she sniffed. "He's not my type, but he'll do."

"What? I'm not striking?" Austin tried to look appalled. "My sensitive side is crushed." Or it would be, if he had one.

"Austin." Sean shot him a warning look. "Fill out the paperwork. And since you two will be working undercover, invent new names for yourselves."

Ms. Stein passed out the papers. "I suggest you select a name that would be appropriate for the stage or television."

Austin skimmed over the contract, then filled it out and signed it. "What kind of reality show is it?"

"I don't know a great deal about it, but it appears to be a competition." Ms. Stein slanted a doubtful look at Austin. "It's called *The Sexiest Man on Earth.*"

Emma let out a surprised laugh, then covered her mouth.

Austin gave her a lopsided smile. "You don't think I can win?"

"Not unless you introduce yourself to a razor and a comb, first." Ms. Stein picked up his contract with a disgusted look on her face. Then she smiled at Garrett as she gathered up his papers. "The auditions will begin at nine o'clock tomorrow evening at the Stars of Tomorrow Agency on Forty-fourth Street, two blocks from the Shubert Theatre. You should arrive early"— her gaze flickered back to Austin—"appropriately groomed and dressed."

"Thank you, Ms. Stein." Sean walked back to the door. "It is imperative that both these men get on the show."

Her eyes widened. "But there could be hundreds of suitable young men auditioning."

Sean glowered at her. "You don't understand, Ms. Stein. These men *must* get on the show. The security of our nation is at stake. The innocent people of our country are in grave danger."

She blinked. "From a reality show?"

"This is no ordinary reality show. These men will be in constant danger."

"Oh, my." She gave Garrett a worried look. "You—you'll be dealing with terrorists?"

Sean lowered his voice. "I'm sure you'll understand, Ms. Stein, that we're unable to divulge any more information."

Her face turned deathly pale. "I—I understand. I'll make sure your men are chosen."

"Fine, do that." Sean opened the door.

Ms. Stein glanced nervously at the two men and then at her papers. "Which one of you is going to be Garth Manly?"

"That's me." Garrett lifted a hand.

"Excellent. A very macho name. It suits you." She looked at Austin and frowned. "You need a decent haircut, Mr."—she glanced down at her papers— "Little Joe Cartwright?"

Alyssa and Emma snickered.

"Austin." Sean glowered at him.

He shrugged. "She said a name suitable for television."

Ms. Stein's frown deepened. "You must select another name."

"Hoss?"

She chewed on her red power lipstick.

"Adam?"

"Adam will do. And you, young man, should have a better attitude toward the performing arts." With a sniff, she left the room.

Sean went with her, leaving the teammates alone.

Garrett shook his head. "I can't believe this. A reality show?"

Austin shrugged. "Why should humans be the only ones with bad taste?"

"It sounds dumb to me," Garrett grumbled.

Alyssa smiled. "At least you have a good name."

"Garth Manly." Emma pursed her lips. "Ooh, it's so sexy."

Alyssa giggled, then abruptly stopped when Sean strode back into the room.

"All right." He pinpointed Austin with a stern look. "Ms. Stein is concerned about your . . . rumpled appearance. So, she's expecting you and Garrett at her agency in an hour. She's calling in an emergency hair stylist and wardrobe consultant."

Austin grimaced. "What about my stake-out?" He had hoped to see *her* again tonight. And have his 35-mm ready so he could discover the truth about her once and for all.

"Forget it," Sean answered. "Emma can record DVN from here."

Emma made another note on her legal pad. "I'll run those plates for you, too, Austin."

"Is this show really necessary?" Garrett lounged back in his chair. "Why don't we just break inside DVN during the day and gather information while the vampires are sleeping?"

Sean planted his palms on the table and leaned forward. "I want to know where my daughter is. I doubt it's written down on an invoice. You'll have to talk to the damned vampires and gain their trust. Working on this show will give you that opportunity. Am I clear?"

"Yes, sir." Austin's reply was echoed by Garrett.

"Good." Sean gave Austin a wry look. "You *do* need a haircut."

He ran a hand through his shaggy, thick hair. "Sheesh. I thought the poodle place was doing so well."

Emma snorted. "Apparently not."

"Take this seriously," Sean warned him. "My daughter's life is at stake. And you could get killed." His mouth twisted with a wry smile. "Or worse, you could become a star."

Chapter 3

"**Any luck convincing the ladies to be on the** show?" Gregori maneuvered his Lexus into the right lane on Broadway.

Darcy gazed out the car window at the bright lights and images that flashed across the buildings in Times Square. "No. Princess Joanna announced the show was disgraceful, and since the others follow her lead, they all refused to take part."

"Except Vanda," Maggie added from the back seat.

Darcy nodded. "She enjoys being a rebel."

"Well, keep trying." Gregori turned right onto Forty-fourth Street. "I'll find you the fancy penthouse. You just get the harem out of my apartment. Deal?"

"Deal." Darcy noted the lights of the Shubert Theatre. The Stars of Tomorrow Casting Agency was only two blocks away.

Gregori slanted a curious look her direction. "Why are you doing auditions at this agency instead of DVN?"

"I'm trying to keep it a secret from Sly. He wanted some surprises on the show, and I thought this would be a good one."

Gregori winced. "He might be angry that you're fouling up his show with lowly mortals."

"He might be," Darcy conceded. "At first. But then, I think his superiority complex will kick in. He'll be convinced the mortals can never advance past the first few rounds."

"But what if they do advance?" Gregori asked. "You could piss off a bunch of Vamps who think they're superior."

"Well maybe, they'll have to realize they're not so damned superior after all."

"Sheesh," Gregori muttered. "Look, I don't like their snotty attitude, either. I hate it when they look down their noses at my mortal mom. But that's the way it is. You can't fight it."

"Someone should. Look at what they're doing— running a television station with soaps like *All My Vampires* and *General Morgue*. They copy the mortals and claim to be superior to them at the same time. It's blatant hypocrisy, and I'm sick of it."

Gregori heaved a sigh. "I'm sorry you're unhappy, Darcy, but you gotta chill. It's not worth shooting yourself in the foot."

She gazed out the window. Gregori might have a point. This was the best job she could get, and she shouldn't let her anger destroy her chance at success. "Okay. I'll be careful."

"Good. Here we are." Gregori pulled over to double-park. "I'll be checking out rental sites for Roman's new restaurant. Just call me when you're done, and I'll come back."

Darcy touched his arm. "Thanks for everything."

She and Maggie left the car, went into the brown brick building, and waited in front of the elevator. Darcy realized that Maggie was being unusually quiet. Instead of her usual smile, she was frowning at the lit elevator button.

"Are you all right, Maggie?"

She sighed. "I didn't realize you hated us so much."

"I don't hate you! I never would have survived these last years if you hadn't been so kind to me."

Maggie turned toward her, anger flashing in her eyes. "Are you blind? Yes, I was nice. I felt sorry for you. But don't you see what you've done for me? When I met you I was still dressing like it was 1879. Sweet Mary, I was wearing a stupid bustle!"

"I have to admit, your tastes have improved."

"It's more than that. You gave me the nerve to try new things. You're so modern and strong and confident. I want to be like you. So, don't tell me that we all think we're superior."

"I'm sorry. I didn't realize . . ."

Maggie gave her a sad smile. "You've made my existence worthwhile again. I have great hopes for the future, now. Thanks to you."

Darcy's eyes misted with tears. "Thank you."

Maggie gave her a hug. "Everything happens for a purpose. I believe that, and you should, too. You're meant to be here now."

Darcy returned the hug. She wanted to tell Maggie she agreed, but the words wouldn't come. What purpose could she possibly have in the vampire world?

The elevator doors swooshed open, and a man stepped out. "Jeez, ladies. Get a room." He continued to mutter to himself as he left the lobby.

Darcy and Maggie released each other, then started to snicker as they stepped into the elevator. On the tenth floor, they found a middle-aged woman in an expensive suit waiting outside the agency. Darcy wished she could afford such a nice suit. She was wearing her blue one again for good reason. It was the only suit she owned. She'd lost everything when her life had turned into a nightmare.

The woman strode toward them. "I'm Ms. Elizabeth Stein, owner and director of the Stars of Tomorrow Casting Agency. Is one of you Miss Darcy?"

"I am." Smiling, Darcy extended her hand.

Ms. Stein shook her hand quickly as if she were afraid of catching a disease. Her face was pale, and her mouth pinched with stress. "Delighted to meet you, Miss Darcy."

Darcy let the error stand. She'd only left her first name on the phone message for fear that her complete name might trigger some memories. "This is my assistant, Margaret O'Brian."

Ms. Stein nodded briefly at Maggie, then clutched her hands together. "The lobby is filled with applicants. I thought you should avoid seeing them before the auditions. So, if you'll follow me?" She motioned jerkily toward an unmarked brown door.

Darcy and Maggie accompanied Ms. Stein. As they passed the glass entrance to the agency, Darcy noted that the lobby was indeed full. Great! She would have no problem finding suitable mortal men for the show.

Ms. Stein opened the unmarked door and gestured for them to enter. "This hallway will take us to the conference room."

Darcy and Maggie headed down the plain white hallway.

Ms. Stein rushed to catch up and squeezed past them. "This way." She turned right into a larger hallway, then halted in front of a set of double doors. She clenched her hands tightly, turning her bony knuckles white. "This is the conference room. I hope it will be satisfactory."

"I'm sure it will." Darcy smiled. "Thank you for allowing us to use your facilities."

"You're welcome." Ms. Stein opened the doors. "I'll give you a few minutes to settle in."

"Thank you." Darcy entered the room with Maggie, then heard the doors click shut behind her. It was a typical conference room—long table with leather-upholstered chairs. One wall had three large arched windows that overlooked Forty-fourth Street. The other walls were lined with autographed eight-by-ten glossies of Ms. Stein's successful clients.

Maggie glanced back at the closed doors. "She seemed awfully nervous."

"Yes." Darcy set her portfolio on the table. She was a bit nervous, too. "Thank you for helping me, Maggie."

"I didn't want to miss out on all the fun." Maggie had declined from participating on the reality show, because she still had hopes of getting on a soap. She'd been recalled for another audition in two weeks. In the meantime, she'd agreed to help Darcy as her assistant.

"I hope you didn't audition for Sly." Darcy remembered what services Tiffany had rendered in order to be recalled.

"No, I lucked out, and got the assistant director from *As the Vampire Turns*. She thought I'd be perfect for the show, and that means I'd be with Don Orlando." Maggie gazed out a window with a dreamy look. "We're destined to be together. I know it."

Darcy jumped when the cell phone inside her portfolio started to ring. It was a new phone, a gift from Gregori, so she'd be able to call him if she needed him.

Maggie drew close. "I wonder who's calling?"

"I don't know. Hardly anyone knows this number." Darcy fumbled in her portfolio and found the phone. "Hello?"

"Darcy!" Vanda's loud voice sounded frantic. "I'm coming over. Is it safe?"

"You mean you're teleporting? It's safe enough, but this isn't a good time." Darcy could hear screeching voices in the background. "Vanda? What's going on?"

"Is something wrong?" Maggie asked.

"I don't know." Darcy closed her phone when Vanda materialized in the room. "What are you doing here?"

Vanda looked around. "Great. You haven't started yet."

"You shouldn't be here," Darcy insisted. "You're the only one I have for the reality show, and you're not supposed to see the guys beforehand."

"Don't worry. I'll behave." Vanda adjusted the black whip she wore around her waist as a belt. "Besides, I had to get out of that apartment. It's a war zone."

"What happened?" Maggie asked.

"Everyone was grumbling at Cora Lee because her stupid hoop skirts take up all the closet space. Then Cora Lee said"—Vanda affected a southern accent—"I do declare the female form looks more beguiling in the corsets and hoop skirts of the Victorian era than any other style in the entire history of the world."

Darcy made a face. "If you enjoy being tortured."

"Right." Vanda ran a hand through her short, spiky,

purple hair. "Then, Maria Consuela said medieval gowns were much more attractive, and Cora Lee's hoop skirts could go to El Diablo."

"Sweet Mary and Joseph." Maggie crossed herself.

Vanda grinned. "Then, Lady Pamela Smythe-Worthing put on her snooty face and announced that the most elegant gowns ever created were the ones worn in Regency England. And that's when Cora Lee said that the high waistlines on Lady Pamela's gowns make her look as wide as the side of a barn."

Darcy winced. "And that's when the fight started?"

"Not quite. Lady Pamela screamed she was so dreadfully overset that she was flying into some boughs, or something like that. Then, she zipped over to the closet, grabbed one of Cora Lee's hoop skirts, and stuffed it into the fireplace."

"Oh, my!" Maggie pressed a hand to her chest. "And that's when the fight started?"

"Not quite. The skirt caught fire, but being a hoop skirt, it popped back out of the fireplace and landed on Princess Joanna's velvet cape."

Darcy gasped. "Not the red one lined in ermine? It's worth a fortune."

"That's the one." Vanda raised her hands dramatically. "And that's when all hell broke loose."

Maggie sighed. "That was Princess Joanna's favorite cape."

"I know," Vanda agreed. "And the really sad thing was that she was wearing it at the time."

"What?" Darcy squeaked. "Is she all right?"

"She's a little on the crispy side. But she'll be fine after a good day's sleep."

Darcy collapsed into a chair. "This is terrible! Those ladies are going to kill each other."

"I know. You've never seen the princess so steamed." Vanda snorted. "Or rather, she was smokin'."

The conference door opened, and Ms. Stein peeked inside. "Are you ready?" Her mouth fell open at the sight of Vanda. She glanced around the room, then looked behind her at the empty hall. "How—how did—I thought there were only two of you."

Darcy stood and smiled like nothing odd had happened. "This is Vanda Barkowski. She's my . . . second assistant."

Ms. Stein's eyes widened as she took in Vanda's purple hair and black spandex catsuit. "Okay. We, uh, we're ready to begin. My secretary, Michelle, will bring each candidate to you."

"Thank you, Ms. Stein." Darcy rounded the table so she would be facing the door.

Ms. Stein backed out of the room, closing the door.

Darcy took a seat at the center of the table, then removed a pad of paper and pen from her portfolio.

Vanda sat on her right. "So, we're looking for the most handsome men? That's easy. They're tall, dark, and mysterious."

"You mean like Don Orlando." Maggie sat on Darcy's left. "He would be my choice for the sexiest man on earth."

Vanda propped an elbow on the table. "What about you, Darcy? What do you think is sexy?"

"Well, let me think." She recalled her sunny, carefree days on the beaches of southern California. Which guys had made her heart rush like the pounding surf? "He would be intelligent, kind, honest, and have a bright sense of humor."

"Boring." Vanda yawned. "Tell us what he looks like."

Darcy narrowed her eyes, envisioning the perfect man. "He'd be tall with broad shoulders and golden skin bronzed by the sun. His hair would be blond, no, light brown, but with blond streaks, bleached by the sun. He'd have blue eyes that sparkle like a lake when the sun is setting. And his smile would be bright—"

"Let me guess," Vanda muttered. "Like the *sun?*"

Darcy grinned sheepishly. "Well, you asked. That's my idea of the perfect man."

Maggie shook her head. "Darlin', that's not a man. That's Apollo, the sun god."

Vanda snorted with laughter.

Apollo, the sun god? Darcy groaned. Maybe the perfect man was a myth, a false hope that would never see the light of day.

A knock sounded on the door. A young woman peeked in. "Hi, I'm Michelle." With her nice suit and her brown hair pulled back into a bun, it was obvious the secretary was emulating her boss. "Your first applicant is ready. Bobby Streisand."

Darcy picked up her pen to take notes, then froze. A tall woman with broad shoulders had entered the room. Her red evening gown sparkled with sequins. She flipped a red feather boa over one shoulder and struck a dramatic pose.

What? Darcy's mouth fell open. Didn't Ms. Stein know she was like the army—looking for a few good men? "I'm sorry, but we're looking for a male—"

"He *is* male," Vanda whispered.

Darcy blinked and looked more closely. *Oh, dear.*

Bobby sauntered toward them, his hips swaying in the tight red dress. "I'm all male, darling," he said in a deep, husky voice. "Would you like to hear me sing? My rendition of 'Memories' is guaranteed to make you cry." He set an eight-by-ten glossy autographed photo on the table and patted it gently. His red nail polish was an exact match to his dress.

Darcy stared at her, or him, for a moment. How could this happen? She'd made it clear that they were searching for the sexiest man on earth. "I—I'm afraid you won't be suitable for the role we have in mind."

Bobby's face crumbled. Sniffling, he drew a lace-trimmed hanky from the bosom of his evening gown. "It's always the same. People never understand me."

Darcy groaned inwardly. Shoot, now he was going to cry.

"I only want the chance to prove myself. Is that too much to ask?" Bobby dabbed at his eyes. "Why can't I be considered for a leading male role?"

"It might help if you dressed like a male," Vanda muttered.

"But I am male. I'm all male," Bobby insisted, then leaned toward Darcy. "Is my mascara running?"

"No, you look . . . great."

"Thank you." Bobby smiled sadly, his red lips trembling. "Don't worry about me." He held up a hand as if to ward off their sympathy. "Somehow, I will survive. I'll continue the struggle. After all, I'm an *artiste*. And I must never sacrifice my personal style."

"Of course not, Mr. Streisand. If I need someone with your . . . style, I'll be sure to give you a call."

Bobby raised the hanky high into the air, then yanked his arm down to clutch the hanky against his chest. "I thank you." He glided out the door.

Darcy shook her head. "It's gotta get better than this."

Michelle opened the door. "Chuckie—" She glanced at the clipboard and frowned. "Badabing."

"Must be a stage name," Maggie whispered.

A slim man sauntered into the room. His silk shirt was half unbuttoned to show off curly chest hair and three gold necklaces. He tossed his eight-by-ten glossy on the table. "Whoa!" He eyed them, his grin flashing a gold tooth. "I've never seen so many hot babes under one roof." He stepped back and struck a casual pose with one hip jutted to the side.

Darcy resisted a shudder. "Mr. . . . Badabing. Do you have any experience?"

He chuckled and rubbed at his thin moustache. The diamonds on his pinky ring glittered. "Hell, yeah. I've got all kinds of experience. What do you three ladies have in mind?" He winked.

Vanda leaned toward Darcy and whispered, "Can I kill him?"

"So." Chuckie tucked his thumbs under his belt. "If I win I'll be called the Sexiest Man on Earth?"

"You would need to be selected for the show first." Darcy collected his photo and slid it under her legal pad.

"Hey, if you want sexy, you've come to the right place." Chuckie rotated his narrow hips. "They don't call me Badabing for nothin'."

"Please, let me kill him," Vanda hissed.

Darcy was tempted to give her blessing. "I'm sorry, Mr. Badabing, but we won't be needing your services."

Chuckie snorted. "You don't know what you're missing."

Vanda smiled. "Neither do you."

With a sneer, Chuckie strode out the door.

Darcy's eye twitched. She rubbed her temple, trying to relieve the growing sense of doom.

Michelle opened the door. "This is Walter."

Walter strode into the room. He was a middle-aged man with thinning hair and a round belly. "How do you do?" He smiled as he set his photo down on the table.

He would never be considered sexy, but at least, he had good manners. Darcy smiled back. "Do you have any acting experience?"

"Sure do. For the last three years, I've been doing commercials for Captain Jake's Buffalo Wings." Walter's smile faltered when they didn't react. "You know, Captain Jake's Chicken? They've got the best buffalo wings in the city."

"I'm afraid we don't eat chicken," Maggie said.

"Oh, vegetarians, huh? Well, I sing and do this dance. Here, I'll show you." Walter proceeded to strut back and forth across the room, flapping his arms. Then, he began to sing. "I'm baked with herbs and spices, and come with tasty rices. I'm never fried, so you won't die. And you'll love my new low prices!"

Darcy's mouth fell open. Her friends were equally quiet.

Walter's grin glowed with pride. "Pretty awesome, huh? Of course, it looks even better when I wear the chicken costume. I've got it stashed in my car if you'd like to see it."

They continued to gape at him.

"Speechless, huh? I get that all the time."

Darcy's eye twitched again. "I'm afraid this isn't a musical reality show. But if we ever produce one, I'll remember you."

"Oh, okay." Walter's shoulders slumped. "Thank you, anyway." He trudged out the door, looking thoroughly henpecked.

Darcy tilted forward and plunked her forehead against the tabletop. "This is hopeless."

"Don't worry." Maggie patted her on the back. "There's a bunch more for us to see."

One hour and twenty applicants later, Walter the Dancing Chicken was starting to look really good.

Then, Michelle opened the door and emitted a long, dreamy sigh. "Garth Manly." She pressed a hand against her chest as he strode into the room.

More sighs came from Vanda and Maggie. They sagged in their seats. Darcy gave them a worried look. Maybe they'd drunk some blood past its expiration date. But no, they didn't appear to be suffering from indigestion. They were gazing blissfully at the new applicant.

He was all right, she supposed. Definitely the most handsome man they'd seen so far, though that wasn't saying much. His wavy, dark hair was brushed back from a tanned face. "Mr. Manly, do you have any acting experience?"

"Yes." He set his signed photo on the table, then took a wide stance. When he crossed his arms over his broad chest, his biceps bulged.

Maggie and Vanda sighed once again. Michelle remained at the door, rubbing her cheek against the doorframe.

"What kind of experience?" Darcy asked.

"Theater, mostly." He raised a dark brow. "Would you like to see me in action?"

"Oh, yes," Maggie breathed.

He bowed his head, apparently getting into character.

Vanda whispered, "Pick him. He's gorgeous."

Darcy hushed her.

Garth Manly lifted his chin and gazed over their heads. He raised his right hand. "To be, or not to be—"

"Could you turn around, please?" Maggie asked.

He looked surprised, then turned his back to them and started again. His right hand went up. "To be or not to be . . ."

Vanda and Maggie leaned forward, their eyes riveted to his buns of steel. Darcy had difficulty hearing his performance over their heavy breathing.

"Whether 'tis nobler—"

"Could you take off your shirt?" Vanda asked.

He swiveled to face them. "Excuse me?"

Darcy stifled a groan. She should have insisted on doing the interviews alone. "There'll be a hot tub," she explained. "We need to know if you look all right in a swimsuit."

"Oh, of course." He took off his black leather jacket and draped it on the back of the chair. As he unbuttoned his shirt, he glanced at them from under thick eyelashes and slowly smiled. "Do I get any music while I strip?"

Maggie giggled.

Darcy almost gagged.

Vanda skimmed a long purple fingernail over her bottom lip. "Tell me, Garth, do you have any experience in stripping?"

He gave her a smoldering look. "I prefer not to do it as a solo act."

Vanda dropped her hand to the neckline zipper of her slinky, black catsuit. "Oh, I'm definitely in the mood for a . . . duet."

Darcy slanted a glance to the side. Good Lord, Vanda was unzipping her catsuit. "Okay, that's enough.

Mr. Manly, could you wait in the lobby? We might need to see you again."

"Of course." With a knowing smile, he picked up his discarded clothes and left. Michelle stumbled after him.

Maggie turned to Darcy. "Why did you send him away? I thought he was perfect for the show."

"I believe he is," Darcy confessed, "but I had to get him out of here before Vanda stripped naked."

With a snort, Vanda zipped up her catsuit. "You're no fun."

"He'll be great, but he's only one," Darcy reminded them. "We need at least four more mortals, and we need to find them tonight."

"Okay." Vanda dragged a hand through her purple hair. "Let's get back to work."

After three more hours, Maggie was practicing writing Mrs. Don Orlando de Corazon on a sheet of paper, while Vanda was amusing herself by swiveling her chair in circles.

Darcy massaged her temples where tension was building. Good God, she'd forgotten how hard it was to find a decent man. No wonder she had remained single.

"Can we go home now?" Maggie asked. "I've never seen such a dreadful display of manhood."

"I know," Darcy agreed. "But we still need one more."

Michelle opened the door. With a smile, she announced, "This is our last applicant. Adam Cartwright."

He walked into the room. Darcy's mouth fell open. Tall, with long legs and broad shoulders, he moved with an understated grace as if he were conserving energy. His thick hair was shot through with golden streaks. His bronzed skin glowed with natural vitality.

He moved forward, scanning the room, then halted suddenly, his gaze fastened on Darcy.

His blue eyes widened. Darcy's breath caught, and she couldn't look away.

He stepped toward her. He cleared his throat, and she swore the sound rumbled in her own chest. "Miss Darcy?"

Was that deep, sexy voice coming from him? She willed herself to reply, but the words refused to come out. She licked her lips, thinking that might help, but then his blue gaze lowered to her mouth, and she forgot what to say.

"Darcy?" Maggie whispered.

His eyes focused on hers once again. Instantly, a flood of warmth surged through her. Warm like the sun beating down on her head. Warm like the sand between her toes. Good God, she hadn't felt this warm since that terrible night four years ago. She closed her eyes and relished the liquid heat as it poured through her veins. It was like being on the beach again with the surf pounding in her ears and the salty air tickling her nose. She could almost feel a volleyball in her hands, see the net in front of her, hear her sister laughing beside her.

"Darcy." Vanda nudged her with an elbow.

She opened her eyes with a jerk. He was still there, still staring at her. Slowly, he smiled. Oh my God, dimples. Her brain turned to mush.

"Are you all right, Darcy?" Maggie whispered.

She took a deep breath and managed a whisper. "Apollo."

Chapter 4

She was mortal.

Thank God! Austin slowly became aware that he was standing there with a dopey grin on his face. But why not? He'd found the mystery woman, and she was mortal. She had to be. He'd entered her mind so easily, and once there, her thoughts had burst forth like rays of sunshine. She was thinking about warm sand, beach volleyball, and her sister's laughter. No vampire would have thoughts like that.

And the other two women? The short one with dark hair was definitely a vampire. He recognized her from the parking lot at DVN. And he would bet the purple-haired one was undead, too. She had that flashy look and hungry gleam in her eye. His gaze barely flickered to the other two women, before returning to the lovely woman in blue. He kept his power carefully focused on her alone, so the other women wouldn't detect him.

She finally spoke, her voice a hushed whisper. "Apollo."

Huh? He cocked his head, trying to decipher her meaning. The images in her mind were still focused on the beach. She dreamed of the sun's warmth caressing her skin. Her face was flushed, her breasts rising with each rushed breath. He realized with a jolt that she'd look the same way if he were making love to her. A surge of blood careened toward his groin, and for a second, he visualized himself pulling her on top of the table and kissing her 'til her lips were swollen and red. And then he'd—what? He couldn't do anything with one, maybe two vampires in the room.

Why was she here with these two undead women? Was she a prisoner? Were they blackmailing her or threatening a member of her family in order to force her cooperation? The two women kept whispering and nudging her. Was she under their control? But Ms. Stein had told him Miss Darcy was the one in charge.

He needed more information. He needed to gain her trust. And staring at her with a big bulge in his pants was not the way to do it. He placed his photo on the table in front of her. Her smoky blue eyes glanced down, then back at his face.

"May I?" He pulled a black, leather-upholstered chair away from the table and sat, facing her.

Her thoughts flitted into his head. *He doesn't want to stand there and stare down at us like the other men. No, he's bringing himself down to my eye level. How kind and considerate.*

Kind and considerate? Sheesh, he was just hiding his erection. "How do you do, ladies? I'm . . . Adam Olaf Cartwright."

The purple-headed one wrinkled her nose. "Olaf?"

"Yes." Austin knew the most successful lies included as much of the truth as possible. "I was named

after my grandfather, Papa Olaf. Best fisherman in
Minnesota. My favorite memories are going fishing
with him." He caught some thoughts coming from the
beautiful Miss Darcy. *He loves his family. And the
outdoors. And the simple pleasures in life.*

The short one yawned. "You like killing fish?"

"I enjoy the process of fishing, the anticipation of
what could happen. If I don't need the fish for food, I put
them back in the water." He heard more thoughts, coming from Miss Darcy. *He's patient and compassionate.
And so gorgeous.* Holy moley, she really liked him.

The purple-headed one leaned toward her and whispered, "He's boring."

Austin knew Miss Darcy wasn't bored. He also realized the other women were simply calling her Darcy.
"May I know your names?"

"I guess so," the short one answered. "I'm Margaret Mary O'Brian, the assistant director. Everyone
calls me Maggie."

"Vanda Barkowski." The purple-headed one raised
a hand, displaying long purple fingernails.

He shifted his gaze back to the woman in blue.
"And you?"

She curled her fingers around her writing pen.
"Darcy."

"First name or last?"

"Last," she whispered, while the other two said,
"First." Her eye twitched, and her hands clenched the
pen more tightly.

"Which is it?" he asked softly. The poor girl was a
nervous wreck. Why? Was it because she was forced
to keep company with vampires?

She took a deep breath and set the pen down carefully
on the table. "Do you have any acting experience?"

He started to recite the list of lies he'd prepared, but changed his mind. "No, no experience at all."

He's an honest man. And intelligent. Her thoughts sifted into his head, followed by a flood of guilt from his own conscience. Honest? He wasn't even telling her his real name. And how intelligent could he be if he was auditioning for a reality show? Besides, these women didn't look or act like vicious killers. He'd questioned the other applicants as they'd left the conference room, and none of them reported being harmed in any way. Could it be true what Shanna had said? That there were actually two kinds of vampires— harmless ones and violent ones?

No, he wasn't ready to accept that yet. Even so, this seemed like a waste of time. Emma had the right idea. His abilities would be better spent in Central Park, hunting the vampires who attacked people and fed off them. And when he caught one of the creatures, he could interrogate it about Shanna.

"I'm afraid my audition was a mistake. I'm sorry I wasted your time." He gave Miss Darcy one last look as he stood. Poor beautiful sweetheart. Whoever she was, he wasn't giving up on her. She might be in danger and need his help. He'd start investigating her right away. He strode toward the door.

"Wait!"

He turned. She'd risen to her feet.

"You . . . you don't really need any experience. Or even any talent. This is a reality show."

He couldn't help but smile. And when she smiled shyly back, he knew he was lost. So what if it was a waste of time? Sean had ordered him to do the show.

She gave him a pleading look. "I'd like you to be on the show."

I'd like to kiss you senseless. "I can do that."

She heaved a sigh of relief and grinned. "Good."

Oh, it would be good. His gaze swept down to her hips, then back to her face. "More like excellent."

Her eyes widened. "I—we'll be in touch."

"I'm sure we will." He let out a long breath as he left the room. He had every intention of touching her. And very soon.

Darcy took a deep breath and willed her racing heart to calm down. Adam Olaf Cartwright—just the thought of him made her heart thump ridiculously fast. She reached for his photo with trembling fingers. Good God, you could see his dimples in the picture. And the beautiful turquoise blue of his eyes.

"Are you all right?" Maggie asked. "You could hardly speak."

"I—I had an itch in my throat."

"Really?" Vanda watched her with an amused expression. "I could have sworn that itch was further south."

Maggie huffed. "Sweet Mary! There's no need to be crude."

"No need to be in denial, either." Vanda stood and stretched. "Admit it, Darcy, you have the hots for that guy."

Darcy shook her head. "I'm just tired. We've been interviewing the dregs of manhood for over four hours."

"Dregs is right," Maggie yawned. "But you *are* flushed."

Darcy fanned herself with his photo. "It's hot in here."

"I'm not hot." Vanda looked at Maggie. "Are you hot?"

"No. Actually, I thought it was a little chilly in here."

"Enough, you two." Darcy spread all the photos on the table. "We need to pick the five best guys."

"Number one has to be Garth Manly." Maggie located his photo and handed it to Darcy.

"I agree. And number two should be"—Vanda reached for a photo. "Here he is—Apollo, the sun god."

Maggie snickered.

"His name is Adam." Darcy snatched the photo from Vanda. Adam as in the primeval man. A vision flitted through her head—Adam Olaf Cartwright, cavorting around the Garden of Eden wearing nothing but a loincloth. No, make that a fig leaf. A very large fig leaf. One that would blow away with the slightest breeze.

Sheesh! Was she so ridiculously shallow that she could be floored by a gorgeous body, handsome face with dimples, and pair of dazzling blue eyes? She glanced at his photo. Well, apparently, *yes.*

With a silent groan, she admitted this was more than instant lust. Adam Olaf Cartwright possessed more than a great exterior. She'd sensed his intelligence, kindness, honesty, and strength.

"You're blushing again," Maggie warned her gently.

Darcy sat down with a sigh. "It's an impossible situation. You know that."

"Maybe not." Vanda lounged back in her chair. "I've heard stories about ladies who keep a male mortal as a sex toy."

Darcy winced. "I could never do that."

"And that sort of relationship never lasts," Maggie added. "I'm sorry, Darcy. We'll stop teasing you about it."

"Good." She set the photos of Garth and Adam to the side, then rummaged through the remaining pictures. "What did you think about George Martinez and Nicholas Poulos?" She pulled out their pictures.

"They were okay." Maggie selected one more. "And this one was good, too. Seth Howard."

"Great. Then, we're done." Darcy dug in her portfolio for the cell phone. "I'll call Gregori, so he can pick us up." She reached him in his car, and he estimated he'd be there in fifteen minutes.

Vanda stood. "I'd better teleport home. I'm hungry, and Garth Manly is looking kinda yummy."

"Go." Darcy quickly handed her the phone. "Oh, and try to convince the other ladies to be on the show with you."

"I'll try." Vanda shrugged. "But if they've been fighting all this time, they're not going to be in a mood to listen."

"One more thing," Darcy continued. "Swear you won't tell them what we were doing tonight. It's supposed to be a surprise that there'll be mortals on the show."

Vanda wrinkled her nose. "How can it be a surprise? We can smell them a block away."

"I've got it covered." Darcy gathered the photos of all the rejected applicants into a neat stack. "When I was working at Romatech, they had this situation where a couple of vampires lost control and bit some of the mortal employees."

"Oh, I remember that," Maggie said. "Roman was furious."

Darcy nodded. "It totally blew his mission of making the world safe for mortals and vampires alike. And the fact that it was happening at his own business was very upsetting."

"What did he do?" Vanda asked.

"First, he offered free synthetic blood to all the vampire employees. It worked for a while, but then, the biting started again. Roman was afraid the mortals would sue and it would end up drawing attention to the vampire world. So, he developed a plastic anklet coated with some kind of chemical that completely masks a mortal's scent. It works like a vampire repellent. When the Vamps can no longer smell the mortals, they're no longer tempted to bite."

"You're going to use the anklets on the show?" Maggie asked.

"Yes. The mortals will be safe. And impossible to detect."

Vanda cocked her head as she considered. "Vamps can still detect a mortal by reading their minds."

"There will be no mind reading or mind control allowed on the show," Darcy announced. "It'll be included in the Vamp contracts. Otherwise, we could never run a fair contest."

"That makes sense." Vanda dialed Gregori's house. "I've gotta go. The smell of those men down the hall is making me ravenous." She paused, then spoke into the phone. "Lady Pamela, is that you? Keep talking, will you?"

Darcy held the phone until Vanda had completely vanished, then she stashed it in her portfolio.

There was a knock on the door, and Ms. Stein peeked in. She scanned the room. "Where—" She glanced back at the empty hallway. "I thought there were three of you."

"Yes." With a smile, Darcy quickly changed the subject. "We've made our decision. These are the five men we want." She held out the five autographed photos.

"Good." Ms. Stein inched forward to take the pictures.

"I have some instructions here and the contracts for them to sign." Darcy removed the papers from her portfolio.

Ms. Stein took them. "I'll give these to the poor—er, lucky men."

"Thank you. They'll need to return the signed contracts within five days so we can keep on schedule. If you don't mind, it would be easier for us if they returned them here. Maggie will come on the evening of the fifth day to collect them."

"Very well." Ms. Stein bustled out the door.

Darcy rounded the table. "We need an artist who can paint the portraits of all the male contestants. Do you think you can find a vampire artist for me?"

"I guess so. I'll look in the Black Pages."

"Good. Let me know when you find one. I have some special instructions for him."

Maggie's eyes widened. "Is this another surprise?"

Darcy smiled. "Could be."

The crowd in the waiting room had dwindled to about twenty anxious men. Austin figured those who left early had been openly rejected by Miss Darcy and her . . . friends. The situation grated on him. Why would an intelligent, beautiful woman like her hang out with vampires?

He edged toward the coffee pot and motioned with his head for Garrett to join him there. He poured some coffee into a Styrofoam cup, then fiddled with the pink and blue sugar packets while he waited.

Garrett stopped beside him and poured a cup of coffee.

"I think I'm in," Austin whispered. "How about you?"

"I think so." Garrett glanced back as a short, rotund guy who resembled a mountain troll walked by. "Lucky for us, the competition was pretty easy."

"You think?" Austin gritted his teeth. Didn't Garrett realize that Ms. Stein had manipulated the auditions to make them look good? "What did you think of the three . . . women?"

"They're definitely . . . you know."

All three of them? "No, the one in blue is normal." Stupendous was more like it, but she was definitely alive.

Garrett stirred some powdered creamer into his coffee. "I have to disagree."

Austin's nerves tensed. He lowered his voice. "I got into her mind. She was thinking about sunshine and beaches and family."

"Really? I couldn't get into any of their heads."

"You're not as strong as me. No offense."

"None taken. But even so, I could have sworn—" Garrett broke off when the mountain troll moved in for some coffee.

Austin raised his voice. "I don't believe we've met. I'm Adam Cartwright."

"Garth Manly." Garrett shook his hand.

"I'm Fabio Funicello," the mountain troll grunted as he emptied five sugar packets into his coffee.

"Nice to meet you." Austin sidled over to an empty corner of the room with Garrett close behind. "You were saying?"

Garrett looked around to make sure they couldn't be overheard. "When I was in the conference room, I could see my reflection in the windows overlooking the street."

"So?" A heavy stone settled in Austin's gut.

Garrett lowered his voice to a hushed whisper. "The ladies were not reflected. None of them were."

A chill skittered down Austin's back. Holy shit. "It . . . it's not positive proof. It could be a matter of the lighting, and where you were standing, and a bunch of other factors."

Garrett shrugged. "Maybe so, but I'm betting all three of them are . . . up the creek without a coffin."

Austin's stomach twinged. The coffee left a bitter taste in his mouth, and he set the cup down on a nearby table. It couldn't be true. "No, wait. Sean said a lady called this agency in the afternoon. During daylight. That had to be Darcy." She had to be alive.

"May I have your attention, please?" Ms. Stein's voice rang out, and the room grew silent. "Five men have been selected for *The Sexiest Man on Earth* reality show. If you've been chosen, please remain here so I can give you your contracts."

While she paused, the atmosphere in the room sizzled with tension. Men loosened their ties. Fists clenched with anticipation. Fabio climbed up on a chair so he could see.

"Garth Manly," Ms. Stein announced with a satisfied smile aimed at Garrett. Her smile faded as she hurried down the rest of the list. "Adam Cartwright, Nicholas Poulos, George Martinez, and Seth Howard. Congratulations."

While the room buzzed with shouts of excitement and groans of defeat, Austin leaned toward Garrett and whispered, "Call Sean. Tell him we're in."

Garrett nodded and pulled out his cell phone. Fabio hopped down from his chair with an angry grunt and waddled out the door. More disappointed men trudged out while the other three who were selected gathered around Ms. Stein. She gave them their paperwork, then strode toward Austin and Garrett.

Garrett completed his call to Sean and pocketed his phone.

"I suppose congratulations are in order." Ms. Stein regarded them sadly. "Here are your contracts."

"Thank you." Austin took his and glanced over it. "Ms. Stein, did you notice anything unusual about tonight?"

She made a sour face. "The whole evening was ridiculous. My character actors are very talented, but not at all suited for a contest called *The Sexiest Man on Earth.*"

"What can you tell me about Miss Darcy?" Austin asked. "Is that her last name?"

"I really don't know." Ms. Stein stepped closer. "Is this DVN a legitimate network? I've never heard of them."

"They're legit. Been in business for over five years."

"Hmm." Ms. Stein frowned as she handed Garrett a contract. "They seemed a little odd to me."

"Yeah," Garrett agreed. "That purple hair was a bit much."

She waved a hand in dismissal. "I work with creative people all the time. I'm used to that. No, it was the way they kept . . ."

"What?" Austin pressed.

"Well." Ms Stein looked around, then lowered her voice. "At first, there were just two of them. But then, there were three. And when I peeked in just a moment ago, there were only two again. I never saw that purple-headed one come or go, did you?"

Austin exchanged a glance with Garrett. Obviously, the purple-haired Vanda Barkowski was teleporting, which meant she was definitely a vampire. "Don't worry about it, Ms. Stein. I'm sure there's a simple explanation."

She huffed. "I'm not stupid, Mr. . . . . Cartwright."

Garrett touched her shoulder. "Try not to let this upset you, ma'am. We have everything under control."

She smiled at Garrett. "Thank God our nation's security is in capable hands like yours."

But not mine? "I'll be going now." Austin nodded at Ms. Stein and Garrett. "Good night."

While Austin waited for an elevator, he punched in the number for information on his cell phone. "Digital Video Network in Brooklyn." He removed a notepad from his jacket pocket and jotted down the number. "Thank you."

He waited 'til he was out of the building and walking down the busy sidewalk before he made the next call.

"This is DVN," a receptionist answered with a nasal voice. "If you're not digital, you can't be seen."

Well, that made sense . . . if you were undead. "That's a catchy phrase."

"It's lame, but I have to say it whenever I answer the phone. So, what do you want?"

"My name is . . . Damien, and I have a message here to call, let me see . . . shit, I can't make out this handwriting. Darcy something. She's the new director of that reality show."

"Oh, you mean Darcy Newhart?"

Bingo. "Yeah, that's it. Is she in?"

"Not at the moment." The receptionist paused. "She'll be here tomorrow night for sure. Are you going to audition?"

"Yeah, I thought I would."

"Well, open call is tomorrow night and Friday night, starting at ten o'clock. You'd better get here early. We're expecting a huge turnout."

"I'll do that. Thanks." Austin pocketed his phone. *Darcy Newhart.* He was making progress. He climbed into his car and drove to the office. Emma was there, going over police reports while DVN played on her computer screen.

He went straight to his desk and did a search on Darcy Newhart. A list of newspaper reports came up. He stared at the headlines, stunned. "Local Reporter Missing," "Where's Darcy?," "Reporter feared Murdered."

Austin's fingers felt numb as he clicked on the first report. *Date: October 31, 2001.* Four years ago on Halloween. He'd been stationed in Prague during that time. *Place: Fangs of Fortune Vampire Club in Greenwich Village.* A joint where kids pretended they were vampires. Some of the kids remembered seeing Darcy and her cameraman leave through the back exit. Darcy was never seen again.

This was bad. Austin clicked on the next report. Three days later, and Darcy was still missing. The cameraman had shown up, hiding at Battery Park and suffering from exposure. He'd been admitted to Shady Harbor Mental Hospital, babbling that Darcy had been abducted by vampires.

This was really bad. Austin's grip on the mouse tightened as he clicked on the last report. A picture of Darcy appeared on the screen. She looked the same as she did now, but then, as young as she was, four years might not make much of a difference. Two weeks had passed since she'd disappeared. Her body had never been found, but a bloody knife had been discovered outside the club, along with a pool of her blood. Authorities had decided she was most likely dead.

Dead? But that would mean she was now a vampire.

Chapter 5

Austin completed his research on Darcy Newhart.
She was born in San Diego, the oldest of three daughters. At the time of her disappearance, she was twenty-eight years old. Had she continued to age, or was she stuck at twenty-eight for all eternity?

He switched his investigation to her two companions. The name Vanda Barkowski came up with zilch, but he located a birth certificate for a Margaret Mary O'Brian in 1865. Her parents had emigrated from Ireland during the potato famine. Maggie was the eighth child of twelve, though only seven of them had lived past the age of ten. Poor girl had had a tough life. Hopefully, it was better for her now.

Holy zombies, what was he thinking? She was a vampire. Synthetic blood had only been around for eighteen years. She'd existed for a long time by attacking humans. He shouldn't be feeling any compassion for these monsters.

Sunshine shot through the window blinds, creating

streaks of light across his desk. He wandered to the
window to look out. The sidewalks were bustling with
early morning commuters; the streets filled with de-
livery trucks and vans. And Darcy—was she watching
the sunrise or was she hidden away, dead to the
world?

He gathered up his notes and photos, then drove to
the television station in Queens where Darcy had
worked. After flashing his badge, he listened to the
manager talk for an hour about Darcy. Everyone
there had loved her. Some still clung to the hope that
she was alive. Austin promised to do his best to solve
the mystery of her disappearance and left with a box
of copied videotapes of Darcy's old newscasts. He
stashed the box in the trunk and drove to his apartment in Greenwich Village.

He settled on the couch with a beer and a sandwich
and began watching Darcy's old reports. He'd expected it to be boring, but she made him smile and
laugh with the crazy situations she got herself into. He
was watching her attempt an interview with a pregnant hippo at the Bronx Zoo when he finally fell
asleep.

And dreamed of Darcy.

When he woke, the television greeted him with
static and snow. He turned the TV and VCR off, noticing the time. Six-forty in the evening. Crap. He'd be
late to the seven o'clock nightly meeting. He called
the office, but Sean surprised him by telling him to
take a few days off.

"Have you signed the contract yet?" Sean asked.

"No sir. I'll take care of that." Austin hung up and
dug through his papers 'til he located the contract
from DVN. An odd paragraph caught his eye. Why

not ask Darcy about it? After all, he knew where she would be tonight.

The auditions at DVN were scheduled to begin at ten P.M., so Austin arrived at nine. He slid two stakes into an inside pocket of his jacket. That and the silver crucifix under his shirt would have to suffice for protection.

He hesitated outside the entrance. The letters DVN glowed in neon over his head. *Act normal,* he warned himself. *You don't know vampires exist. You're a dumb innocent.* Yeah, and he felt like a sheep meandering into a lion's den.

He pushed open the door and entered. The lobby décor was dramatic, done in shades of black and red. A few men lounged in red leather chairs. They looked at him and sniffed. He strode toward the receptionist desk. The girl was well coordinated with the room, dressed in black with a red scarf around her neck. Even her hair was dyed black with bright red highlights. She was sharpening her red-painted nails with an emery board.

"Good evening."

Without glancing up, she pointed at a clipboard. "If you're here for the auditions, sign in," she began with a nasal voice.

"I'm here to see Darcy Newhart."

She looked up and sniffed. "What are you doing here?"

"I need to see Darcy Newhart. It's a business matter." He showed her the brown envelope in his hand.

"But you're a—" She snapped her mouth shut, apparently realizing she shouldn't admit that she wasn't as alive as he was. "Uh, sure. Her office is down the hall. Fifth door on the right, just before you get to the recording studios."

"Thank you." Austin proceeded down the hall, aware that every vampire in the lobby was staring at his back. He knocked on the door. No answer.

"Miss Newhart?" He cracked the door. No one there, though the papers on her desk indicated she'd been there recently. He slipped inside and closed the door. It was a small office—no windows, old desk, old computer. The two chairs facing the desk looked like they'd been retired from an old hotel.

His wandering gaze snagged on a large paper cup on her desk. It had an opaque plastic cover snapped on top with a straw stuck in the hole. He picked it up. It was almost empty. And icy cold. That was good. What vampire would want his blood cold? He lifted the cup to his nose and sniffed. Chocolate? There was another flavor he wasn't sure of, but the chocolate was definitely there. He grinned. She had to be alive. Still, he should have a taste, just to be sure. He started to peel off the cover.

The door opened. Darcy Newhart strode inside, then stopped short. Her mouth fell open. His did, too, and he didn't even have the excuse of being surprised. But he'd forgotten how strongly she affected him. His physical reaction was immediate, causing his heart to race and his groin to swell.

Her hair was loose about her shoulders. She was dressed in khaki slacks and a blue T-shirt that molded perfectly to her breasts. The shirt was devoid of any pithy sayings like *Hot Babe,* which would have been ridiculously redundant in her case.

"Good evening." He focused on her face, so he would stop ogling her gorgeous body.

"Hello." Her cheeks flushed a becoming pink. She slowly shut the door. "This is a bit of a surprise,

Mr. Cartwright." Her gaze landed on the cup in his hand, and her face turned pale.

"Sorry." He shoved the cover back on and set the cup on her desk. "It sure smelled good. Chocolate milkshake?"

"Not exactly. I—" She rushed forward, grabbed the cup, and dropped it in the trash. "I'm . . . lactose intolerant. Would you like something to drink, Mr. Cartwright?" She motioned toward the door. "I could get you—"

"I'm fine. Thank you." He smiled, trying to put her at ease. "Since we'll be working together, why don't you call me Adam?"

"Okay." She slipped past him and around the desk. "What can I do for you . . . Adam?"

"It's about the contract." He opened the clasp envelope and removed the papers.

"Shouldn't you have your agent help you with that?"

"Frankly, it has Ms. Stein confused, too." At least, Austin figured it would. He turned to page six and pointed at the tiny print at the bottom of the page. "Here it is. *DVN will assume no liability for injuries incurred during the term of employment. This includes loss of blood, puncture wounds, and fatalities.*"

He glanced up at Darcy. Her face had turned deathly pale. "It seems a bit extreme, don't you think?"

She tucked her hair behind her ear with trembling fingers. "It's fairly standard for DVN. They like to cover all the bases. People tend to sue over the most trivial of things these days."

"I wouldn't call puncture wounds or fatalities trivial."

She waved a hand in the air. "Anything could happen.

We'll be filming in a huge penthouse. You could fall down a flight of stairs, or trip on a rug and—"

"Fall on a fork?"

"Excuse me?"

"Puncture wounds, Miss Newhart. How exactly do you expect me to be punctured?" *With a pair of fangs?*

Her eye twitched. "I agree the wording is a bit unusual, but the intent is clear. DVN cannot be held responsible for any injuries that may occur during the show."

"Are you going to require us to do anything dangerous?"

"No, of course not. Believe me, Mr. Cartwright, I'm going to great lengths to insure your safety."

"You're concerned for our safety?"

"Of course. I hate to see innocent mort—people get hurt."

She'd almost said *mortals,* which seemed a bit odd since she was a mortal herself. Wasn't she? Dammit, this indecision had to end. "You're a kind person, Miss Newhart." He took her hand in his. Her fingers were cold.

"Thank you." Her gaze dropped to their joined hands. "But I'm not the one you need to impress. There will be a panel of five female judges deciding the outcome of the contest."

He enveloped her hand with both of his. "I'm not interested in your five judges or the contest."

Her gaze jerked up. "You don't want to be in the show? Please don't let the wording in the contract dissuade you."

He slipped two fingers around her wrist. "Do you think I could win something called *The Sexiest Man on Earth*?"

"I—I think you have a sporting chance. And it would certainly look good for your acting career, don't you think?"

He pressed his fingertips into the soft skin of her wrist. "I really don't want to be seen as a sex toy." *Except by you.*

"I understand. I would feel the same way." Her cheeks blushed. "But you haven't heard the latest news. Our producer, Mr. Bacchus, has just announced that the winner will receive a million dollars! Surely that will convince you to do the show?"

"Not really." He concentrated on his fingertips. Yes, there! Wasn't that a pulse?

She frowned at him. "I don't understand. If you're not interested in winning the title or the prize money, then why are you asking questions about the contract?"

Yes! That was definitely a pulse. It was throbbing rapidly against his fingertips. At last, positive proof. Darcy Newhart was alive. *Alive!*

"Mr. Cartwright?" She pulled her hand from his grip and regarded him with a puzzled look. "Why are you here?"

He smiled slowly. "Miss Newhart, I'm here because of you."

She inhaled sharply and moved back a step. "Mr. Cartwri—"

"I thought you agreed to call me Adam."

"I—I did, but you may have gotten the wrong—"

"And then, normally, you would reciprocate by inviting me to call you Darcy. Don't you think?"

"Normally, perhaps, but this isn't exactly normal—"

"You're right." He stepped closer. "There's something special happening here. I feel it. Don't you?"

Her eyes widened. She looked nervous, and for a moment, he wondered if he was pushing her too fast. Her agitated state could be caused by desire or by fear.

She moistened her lips. "I . . ."

"Is that a yes?" He touched her neck.

"I—" Her gaze dropped to his mouth, and she licked her lips again. "I don't think it's wise for us to—I mean, I'm the director."

"Then, direct me." He curled his hand around the back of her neck. Her hair was soft against his skin. "Tell me what to do." God, he wanted to kiss her. But was he pushing too fast? Just a peek into her mind, that's all it would take. Just a peek.

It was so easy. His invasion swept in like a breeze, and her mind simply unfurled like a dazzling white sail. He caressed her thoughts. She was warm with desire. Desire for him. *Apollo, the sun god.*

He pulled back, surprised. She thought he was like a god? Holy performance anxiety, that was a tough image to live up to.

Her face flushed. She looked so hot and delicious, he shoved all his doubts away. She *did* desire him. He'd felt it in her mind. And that was enough to make him feel as powerful as any man-made god.

Her eyes flickered shut. "I can't . . ."

"You can't kiss me?" He touched his lips lightly on the corner of her mouth.

A tremor skittered down her body. "I can't . . . resist." She grabbed his shoulders.

Wow, she did want him. He planted his mouth firmly on hers, plying and molding her lips with his own. He pulled her tight, and her hands delved into his hair, tugging him closer.

He invaded her mouth. Jesus, she let him in. She was feeling this, too, this powerful hunger. How could two relative strangers be so damned desperate for each other? It was more than physical desire; it was a hunger from the soul.

Her tongue entwined with his, leaving the faint taste of chocolate. Oh, she was sweet. Sweet all over. His hands skimmed down her back and encircled her waist. He pulled her forward against his erection. With a moan, she melted against him.

He nibbled kisses down her throat, then back up to her ear. His hands spread over her rump, pressing into her skin and grinding her hips against his groin.

"Darcy," he whispered in her ear. "I knew it. The minute I saw you. I knew we belonged together."

Her hands clutched his shoulders, then with a painful groan, she pushed him away. "No!"

He stepped back. "What? What's wrong?"

Breathing heavily, she crossed her arms. "I . . . I'm sorry."

"Don't be sorry. I'm not sorry."

Her face crumpled. "I can't. I can't let this happen."

"Sweetheart, it already has."

"No!" She took a deep, shaky breath, and her face cleared into a stony mask. "We have to keep this professional. I need this job."

"I wouldn't do anything to jeopardize it. I would never harm you in any way."

She shook her head, hugging herself tighter.

"Darcy, if you need anything, please tell me. I could help you."

She remained silent, frowning as if she was engaged in a private struggle. Finally, she spoke. "If you truly wish to help, you'll agree to be in the show."

"Fine, I'll do it." He grabbed a pen off her desk and signed the contract. Risking puncture wounds or death was worth it. "I mean it, Darcy. If you're in trouble, if any . . . thing is threatening you or frightening you, I want you to let me know."

She swallowed. "I'm fine."

She wasn't fine. She was a mortal living among vampires. He needed to gain her trust so she would confide in him.

"I'm conducting more auditions in a few minutes. I need some time to prepare."

She wanted him to leave. Sensitive guy that he was, he could take a hint. "Maybe we can meet later for a cup of coffee."

Her smile was resigned and weary. "I appreciate that, but I have no idea how long these auditions will take."

"Tomorrow night?"

She straightened the papers on her desk. Though she tried to conceal it, the trembling of the papers gave proof that her hands were shaky. "I have more auditions tomorrow."

"Saturday night?" He had no pride.

"I have a wedding to go to."

"Not yours, I hope."

"No, definitely not. But they're a lovely couple." A sad, wistful look crossed her face. "I think they'll be very happy."

"Anyone I know?"

"I doubt you'd know Roman or Shanna."

He froze his face to hide the shock. Holy shit, the engagement had only been announced a few days ago. How could he tell Sean the wedding was this Saturday night? "I've never heard of them. Which one is your friend, the bride or the groom?"

"I—I've known the groom for several years. But I consider the bride a friend, too."

"Do you need a date?" The uncomfortable look on her face told Austin he was pushing too hard. "Sorry, I shouldn't invite myself. One of those big, fancy church weddings, huh?"

Her cheeks reddened as she fumbled through a stack of papers on her desk. "You—you'll need to have your portrait done. I left the information with Ms. Stein, but I have a copy here." She grabbed a Post-it stack and jotted down the address. Then, she tore off the note and handed it to him.

She obviously didn't want to discuss a vampire wedding. He'd have to let it go for now or she would suspect. His fingers brushed against hers as he took the note and instantly, desperately, he yearned to hold her in his arms. "Darcy."

For just a few seconds, her eyes responded with an expression of pain and longing, then she blinked and turned away. "We can't allow ourselves to . . . to lose control again."

How the hell was she going to stop him? Her attraction to him was out in the open. He wasn't going to ignore it, not when he felt the same way. "I'll keep in touch." He pocketed the note and left.

On the drive home, he called the number on the note and made an appointment to have his portrait done. The artist only worked at night, so Austin assumed he was a vampire.

He started to dial Sean's number, then stopped. How could he tell Sean about the wedding? Sean would use all his resources to discover the time and place of the ceremony. And then, he'd order the team to attack with crossbows, shooting wooden arrows at everyone in sight. And Darcy was going to be there. What if she was injured or killed? And all because he had passed on the information to Sean. How could he live with himself if Darcy was harmed?

She actually thought Shanna and Roman made a lovely couple. How could a mortal say that? But she knew them both. Maybe she was right. Austin had seen Roman and Shanna together in Central Park. They had been hugging each other and seemed genuinely happy.

Shanna had tried to convince the Stake-Out team that Roman was a good man. He'd invented the synthetic blood that was saving millions of human lives. And according to Shanna, he was encouraging thousands of vampires to give up real blood for the synthetic kind, thus protecting humans from attack. Sean had dismissed all her statements as the result of brainwashing, but now, Austin wasn't so sure.

Holy shit, what a mess. Austin gripped the steering wheel. For the first time in his career, he was sorely tempted to withhold vital information from his superior.

Chapter 6

Austin spent the rest of the night watching more of Darcy's taped reports for Local Four News. As he watched, he tried to make sense of the dilemma he was in. He compiled a list of vampires he had identified in the last few days. There were Darcy's two friends Maggie O'Brian and Vanda Barkowski. They seemed harmless enough. He wrote down Gregori Holstein's name, wondering what kind of relationship the undead guy had with Darcy. A friendly one if he was driving her around in his Lexus, but how friendly? Austin realized he was starting to feel possessive where Darcy Newhart was concerned.

Thank God he didn't have to write her name on the list. That mystery was solved. Darcy had a pulse, so she had to be mortal. But the mystery of her situation still remained. Why did she disappear four years ago on Halloween? And why was she living in the vampire world? And how could she live among them for so long and remain unharmed?

Could Shanna be right? Was there a faction of peaceful vampires who didn't believe in hurting humans? Austin lounged back on the couch, splaying his hands through his hair. Everything had always seemed clear before. There were good guys and bad guys, and the good guys were supposed to win. When he'd worked in Prague, the bad guys had been the ones intent on slaughtering innocent people because of their race or religion. Slaughtering innocents made them bad. Simple and straightforward. No questions and no regrets.

Now, the enemy was the vampire who also slaughtered innocent people for food and pleasure. It should be simple and straightforward. They were demons who deserved to die.

But that was before he knew anything else about them. Roman Draganesti was getting married. How could a demon fall in love? If they were evil, how come some of them were drinking blood from a bottle and taking jobs and watching soap operas on TV? The more he learned about them, the more human they seemed.

With a groan, he trudged off to bed. Maybe it would make more sense after some sleep.

He woke late Friday afternoon and ate a bowl of cereal while he finished watching the last of the videotapes. Darcy did a report on the birthday party of 103-year-old Mabel Brinkley from Brooklyn. Mabel had run a speakeasy in the 1920's and outlived six husbands. Her secret for longevity was a shot of Wild Turkey every day. Then, Darcy covered the cannoli-eating contest in Little Italy, the female impersonator beauty pageant in Queens, and the funeral for poor Mabel when she passed away in the bed of a fifty-two-year-old Cuban dance instructor. Alas, Hector had specialized in the rhumba, but not in emergency resuscitation.

Austin always found himself smiling during Darcy's reports. Without a doubt, her boss had given her the worst stories, but she'd always pulled them off with cleverness and charm. No wonder everyone at the station had loved her.

With a surge of dismay, Austin realized the last videotape contained no reports starring Darcy. These were other reporters doing stories about her disappearance. They showed the vampire club and alley in Greenwich Village where she'd last been seen. They even focused their cameras on the dark splotch of blood on the ground. Darcy's blood.

A police spokesman confirmed that a large knife had been recovered from the scene, and the blood on the knife belonged to Darcy. Interviews with the kids inside the club were all similar. They believed she'd been attacked by a real vampire.

Austin jumped to his feet and paced around his apartment. He needed to get copies of the police reports. He needed to question her cameraman. Of course, the easiest way to get answers would be to ask Darcy herself, but that would blow his cover. How could she stand to live among vampires if she'd been attacked by one? And why would a vampire stab a woman instead of biting her? It didn't make any sense, dammit. And the thought of anyone stabbing Darcy with a knife made his blood boil.

The phone jangled, and he dashed for it, hoping it was Darcy.

"Hello, Austin. Enjoying your days off?" Emma asked.

"I guess." As if he knew how to take a day off.

"Well, I was wondering if you'd care to join me tonight in Central Park?"

She wanted to go hunting? As agitated as Austin was, a little action sounded good. And maybe they could capture a vampire who knew Shanna's whereabouts. "Yeah. I'll be there."

At midnight, he met Emma in Central Park by the entrance of the zoo, close to the gift shop. The revolver in his shoulder holster was loaded with silver bullets. They wouldn't kill a vampire, but they would sure hurt and slow him down. Slow him down enough that Austin could ask him a few questions. And just to be safe, Austin stuffed a few wooden stakes in the inside pocket of his lightweight jacket. Emma's wooden stakes were in the handbag slung over her shoulder.

They strolled north along the brick pathway.

"Garrett turned in his contract to Ms. Stein today," Emma spoke quietly as she scanned the grove of trees on the left. "Ms. Stein was concerned that you hadn't turned yours in yet."

Austin walked on her right, surveying the area to the right. "I turned it in last night at DVN."

"What?" Emma halted. "You went inside DVN at night?"

"Yeah. They hired me to do a show, so I figured I had a legitimate reason to go there. And I'm supposed to be ignorant about vampires, so why would I avoid the place? It seemed like an excellent opportunity to check them out."

"It was, but good heavens, Austin, it could have been dangerous. Did any of the vampires try to jump you?"

"No."

"Well, tell me more. What did the place look like?"

"It looked sorta . . . normal."

"What did you do?"

Austin shrugged. "I turned in my contract to the director of the reality show."

"What's his name? He's a vampire, right?"

"No, she's human. And her name is Darcy Newhart." Austin hesitated, then decided to confess. "She's the mystery woman."

Emma gasped. "The one you took a hundred photos of?" She laughed. "Oh, this is priceless. She's your director?"

"Yes."

"And you're sure she's human?"

"Yes. Definitely."

"How can you be so sure?"

"She had a chocolate drink on her desk. And she has a pulse."

"She let you feel her pulse?" Emma studied him closely. "You're still smitten with her, aren't you?"

More than ever. Austin kept walking. The pathway forked, and he gestured toward the left path that headed uphill. "Let's go this way."

Emma walked beside him. "How does she feel about you?"

He shrugged. He knew she felt desire for him, but she was reluctant to admit it. Or to admit that she was trapped in the vampire world.

"Have you snogged her yet?"

He made a face. "What's that? It sounds kinda nasty."

Emma snickered. "Oh, I'm sure it would be with you."

He shoved her on the shoulder.

With a laugh, she stumbled to the side. "I only asked if you'd kissed her."

"Ah." In that case, he had thoroughly snogged her. And it hadn't been at all nasty.

"Well?" Emma quickened her steps to keep up with him. "Did you kiss her?"

"I plead the Fifth."

"You *did* kiss her!"

"I didn't say that."

She snorted. "Pleading the Fifth is the same as admitting guilt."

"We're innocent until proven guilty here. You Brits have it backwards."

She grinned. "But I'm right, aren't I? You snogged her."

He kept walking.

"You should be careful, Austin. What do you really know about her other than the fact that she consorts with the enemy?"

"I'm doing some research on her. And besides, we have a . . . connection. I can get into her mind very easily, and believe me, there's nothing evil there."

"I hate to rain on your parade, but if she knows you're reading her mind, she could be manipulating what you see."

"She doesn't know I'm there. She's a complete innocent." Austin stopped and looked to the right. In the dim light, he could make out the shapes of trees and a large rock. "Speaking of innocents, did you hear someone cry out?"

"I'm not sure." Emma pivoted, scanning their surroundings.

Austin listened carefully, but could only hear the leaves stirring in the wind and Emma's excited breathing. He closed his eyes and concentrated. An attacker could easily muffle the cries of his victim, but the victim would still be screaming in his mind. One time in Eastern Europe, he had located a group of women and children in an underground torture chamber by tuning in on their silent cries of mental anguish.

Oh God, help me!

"Over there." Austin pointed to the large outcropping of granite. A woman was being attacked on the far side. He removed his revolver and motioned to Emma to go to the right. She took off quietly, pulling a wooden stake from her bag as she went.

He skirted the large boulder, then paused when he heard a feminine whimper. Great. It would be just his luck to pounce on a couple of lovers. He leaped clear of the rock, pointing his gun at them. Holy shit, this was the real thing. Two male vampires had a woman pinned against the rock. One was biting her neck; the other was yanking her pants down her legs. The bastards!

"Release her!" He approached slowly, his gun steady.

The second vampire let go of the woman's trousers and turned to glare at Austin. *Leave us, mortal scum, and forget what you have seen.*

Fortunately, the mental command of one vampire had little effect on Austin. He heard it and swept it aside. "I'm not leaving. *You* are. Permanently."

With a hiss, the vampire strode toward him. "How dare you defy me? You fool, you cannot stop us."

"Oh, yeah?" Austin noted the vampire had a Russian accent as he took aim and fired.

The vampire jerked. He grabbed his shoulder where blood oozed from the wound. His face contorted with pain. "What have you done?"

"I'm using silver bullets. They do sting a bit, don't they?"

The vampire growled and lunged forward.

Austin fired again, and the vampire slipped, falling to his knees.

Meanwhile, the first vampire withdrew his fangs from the woman's neck and turned toward Austin. "You bloody *svoloch.*" He pulled the girl in front of him for protection. "You think a few silver bullets will stop us?"

Austin cursed silently. He couldn't shoot as long as the vampire used the woman as a shield. He moved slowly to the left, searching for a clean shot.

The wounded vampire rose in the air and landed softly on his feet. Blood trickled from his two wounds, and he bared his teeth with a snarl. "I am stronger than you. You cannot stop me."

"Maybe not, but I can take all the fun out of it." Austin shot him again. He howled in pain and crumpled to the ground.

"Svoloch!" The first vampire strode toward Austin, dragging the woman with him. "You will die!"

Suddenly, he jerked to a stop. An expression of shock, then pain crossed his face. He released the woman who collapsed on the ground. He arched his back, letting out a long moan as his body crumbled into dust.

Emma stood there in his place, still holding the wooden stake that she'd stabbed into his back. She looked down at the pile of dust in front of her black athletic shoes. "I did it," she whispered. "I killed a vampire."

The second vampire scrambled to his feet. "You bitch! You killed Vladimir."

"And now, it's your turn." Emma strode toward the wounded vampire with the stake upraised.

"You won't get away with this. Vladimir will be avenged!" The wounded vampire wavered in the air, then vanished.

"No!" Emma hurled the stake at him, but he had teleported to safety, and the stake simply flew through the air. "No, dammit!"

Austin ran toward the injured girl, whipping out his cell phone. He punched 911, then checked the woman's pulse. "I need an ambulance. Quickly. She's dying." The pulse in her neck was very weak. He gave directions to their location while Emma cleaned up the crime scene. She put away her wooden stake and scattered Vladimir's pile of dust.

"We did it!" She punched the air with a closed fist. "Our first kill! Aren't you glad you came?"

"Yes, I am." If they hadn't come along when they did, this poor woman would have been raped and murdered by those damned vampires. They truly were demons. Once again, his job made sense. The vampires were evil and deserved to die.

And he knew what he had to do. He would warn Sean that his daughter was about to marry a demon.

"What time is it?" Maggie whispered. She fidgeted, trying to find a comfortable position in the hard wooden pew.

"I don't know," Darcy whispered back. "About five minutes past the last time you asked me."

Vanda snorted. "And about ten minutes past disaster!" Her booming voice echoed across the high vaulted ceiling.

"Shh! Not so loud." Maggie glanced across the aisle at the other wedding guests.

When they'd entered the church, Darcy had been appalled how all the guests were sitting on the groom's side. Of course, they were all Vamps from Roman's coven, but still, she'd thought someone needed to make Shanna feel welcome. So, she'd taken a seat on the bride's side. Vanda and Maggie had joined her, but the rest of the ex-harem had refused. They were sitting across the aisle, whispering to each other. It was Saturday night, and everyone was waiting for the wedding to start.

And waiting.

Gregori had finally gone to see what was holding things up.

"You look wonderful, Darcy," Maggie whispered.

"Thanks. So do you." Earlier in the evening, Darcy, Vanda, and Maggie had dashed off to Macy's, searching for fancy, new dresses for the wedding. Darcy's dress was a maroon silk sheath with a matching sparkly jacket. Maggie was wearing a hot pink flapper-style dress with rows of spangles. Vanda's dress was slinky, sexy, and purple to match her hair.

Unfortunately, the other ladies had dressed to the hilt in their Old World finery. Cora Lee's ball gown boasted a hoop skirt with row after row of lace-trimmed flounces that looked like they'd been attacked by an army of silk ribbons and flowers. The whole, huge atrocity was bright daffodil yellow, making her look more like a school bus than a delicate flower.

Princess Joanna's head was covered with a veil, then topped with her finest gold circlet. A white wimple was draped under her chin. Her dark green velvet gown had a long train in the back and her matching cloak was trimmed with embroidery. Her jewel-encrusted girdle hung loosely around her hips.

Even Maria Consuela was sporting her favorite hat—a conical headdress set back on her head and covered with a transparent, gauze veil. The flared sleeves on her woolen gown hung down to her knees, the cuffs trimmed with fur.

The vestry door opened, and Gregori appeared with a worried expression. He strode toward them.

Darcy stood and eased into the aisle. "What's going on?"

The ex-harem leaned toward them to listen.

"I don't know," Gregori spoke softly, but Darcy felt sure the Vamps could hear him with their extra-sensitive hearing. "My mom should have been here twenty minutes ago. I hope she's all right."

"Have you tried calling her?" Darcy was concerned, too. Gregori's mom, Radinka, had only been released from the hospital a few days earlier. She'd been injured during the Malcontents' latest attack on Romatech. She'd also befriended Shanna, so Shanna had asked her to be the matron of honor in the wedding.

"Her cell phone is off," Gregori answered. "I tried calling Angus since he was in charge of bringing Shanna and my mom here, but he's not answering. Something's seriously wrong."

The ex-harem began frantically whispering to each other. The news spread across the pews 'til all the guests were quietly discussing the matter. Darcy wondered if the Malcontents were behind this. They were a group of vampires who hated Roman with a passion. Since they believed in a vampire's sacred right to feed off humans, they had rejected Roman's synthetic blood and periodically did nasty things like bomb Romatech Industries.

Gregori sighed. "No one is answering their damned phones. The priest isn't here. I don't know what to make of it."

"I know what has come to pass!" Princess Joanna raised her hands in triumph. Her jeweled rings sparkled in the candlelight. "The wedding has been cancelled. The master has come to his senses and rejected that hideous mortal."

Maria Consuela's cone-shaped headdress bobbed as she nodded enthusiastically. "He has realized how inferior she is. Santa Maria, my prayers have been answered." She lifted her rosary and kissed the jeweled cross.

"Wait a minute." Gregori scowled at them. "I like Shanna."

"Me, too." Darcy came to the bride's defense.

"Ha!" Princess Joanna sneered at them both. "I would expect you to side with her. You modern types always stick together. You whine about being sensitive to other people's needs, yet you do not give a thought to *our* suffering. That mortal wench stole our master and our home!"

"I do declare—" Cora Lee flipped open her lacy yellow fan. "I was never so humiliated in all my life."

Lady Pamela Smythe-Worthing removed a handkerchief from her silk reticule and dabbed at her eyes. "It was simply too horrid to bear. If I wasn't blessed with such a miraculous constitution, I would have withered away in utter despair."

Just go ahead and wither, Darcy thought with a groan. She was so tired of these women's endless complaints. It never occurred to them to actually *do* anything about their fate other than constantly bemoan it.

Maria Consuela clicked through her rosary beads. "The horror was so unexpected. It reminded me of the night I was dragged off to the torture chambers of the Spanish Inquisition."

"Sweet Mary and Joseph." Maggie crossed herself.

Vanda snorted. "No one expects the Spanish Inquisition."

Darcy pulled the wedding invitation from her purse. "This is the right time and place." She showed Gregori the invitation.

He shook his head. "The ceremony should have started ten minutes ago."

"Hallelujah!" Cora Lee jumped to her feet, her hoop skirt billowing to the sides to fill half the pew. Her blond ringlets, gathered in clusters over each ear, bounced in rhythm with her skirt. "The wedding is off! That means we can move back into the master's house."

"Oh, I do hope so." Lady Pamela pressed her handkerchief to her bosom, which was mostly exposed in her Regency-style ball gown of pink watered silk.

"Wait a minute," Gregori warned them. "Hold your horses."

Maria Consuela huffed. "Who would bring a horse into a church? How barbaric."

Gregori rolled his eyes. "Look, I'm sure there's a reasonable explanation for this."

"Reasonable?" Lady Pamela stuffed her handkerchief back into her reticule. "The only reasonable course of action for Roman is to dismiss that foolish mortal and send her packing."

Cora Lee snapped her fan shut. "Then we can have our old rooms back."

"Exactly." Princess Joanna stood. "I propose we move back tonight."

"Wait!" Gregori removed his cell phone from an inside pocket of his tuxedo jacket. "I'll try calling again. We have to find out what's going on first. So, cool it, ladies. Don't get your panties in a bunch."

With a snort, Princess Joanna sat back down. "As if I would wear such a ridiculous undergarment."

"Good grief." Gregori stepped back with a shudder. "I don't even want to think about that." He punched in a number on his phone. "You gotta get them out of my house," he whispered to Darcy. "I can't take it anymore."

"I'm trying. But you can see how stubborn they are." With a gasp, Darcy spotted Connor entering the church. She instantly stiffened. Her lungs squeezed in her chest, making it difficult to breathe. Good God, she hated the way she always reacted when he appeared. It had been four years and she still couldn't put that dreadful night behind her. She opened her mouth to warn Gregori, but the words wouldn't come.

Connor spoke quietly to the guests. Some responded by rushing out the front door. Others used their cell phones to teleport away. So was it true that the wedding was cancelled? Had Shanna had second thoughts about marrying a vampire? Darcy often wondered how such a relationship could possibly work. It just wasn't fair to drag someone into the vampire world. She knew that all too well.

"Hey, Connor!" Gregori motioned for the Scotsman to join them. "What's up?"

Darcy automatically stepped back as Connor

approached. Her heart thundered in her chest so hard, it echoed in her ears.

The Scotsman strode toward them, dressed in formal Highland wear, which included a lacy white jabot shirt, black jacket, and a black muskrat sporran. He bowed slightly to the ex-harem. "My ladies." His gaze lingered on Darcy.

She turned away, unable to meet his sharp blue eyes that always watched her with a tinge of regret.

"We have an emergency situation," Connor announced. "Ian and I brought a limousine to help evacuate the ladies. We must leave immediately."

"What about the wedding?" Gregori asked.

"I'll explain later." Connor gestured toward the front entrance. "Yer lives could be in danger. Please move calmly and quietly toward the exit."

"Eek!" Cora Lee lifted her hoop skirts and skedaddled for the front door. The other ladies rushed after her. Darcy hovered toward the back of the group so she could overhear the men talking. She was uncomfortable being that close to Connor, but her curiosity was stronger. Of course, it was her wretched curiosity that had caused her nightmare to begin in the first place.

"Where are we going?" Gregori asked.

"Romatech," Connor replied. "For the reception."

"And my mother?" Gregori asked. "Is she all right?"

"Radinka is fine. She's with Roman and Shanna. Angus and Jean-Luc are there, so they have plenty of protection."

Protection from what, Darcy wondered. It must be the Malcontents.

Gregori had rented a limousine for the night since there was no way he could cart around ten women in his Lexus. Even so, it had been a tight fit with all the ball gowns. The ex-harem was happy to divide into two groups—half going in Gregori's hired limo and the other half traveling in the limo Connor had brought.

Gregori climbed into Connor's limo. "I want to know what's going on." He sat as close to the driver's seat as possible.

Darcy wanted to know, too, so she scooted down the long side seat to sit next to Gregori.

Connor was in the front driver's seat next to Ian. He twisted to the side, so he could see everyone through the open window. There were six occupants in the back—Gregori, Darcy, Maria Consuela, Princess Joanna, Lady Pamela, and Cora Lee.

"So did the master come to his senses and cancel the wedding?" Princess Joanna asked.

"Nay, milady," Connor answered. "The ceremony is happening as we speak. At a private chapel in White Plains."

"I guess that's why they're not answering their phones." Gregori unbuttoned his tuxedo jacket.

"Oh, fiddlesticks." Cora Lee had taken up the entire back seat with her hoop skirt. "Now we can't move back into the master's house."

Lady Pamela pressed a hand against her bosom. "This is quite beyond the pale. I tell you, that mortal chit is toying with us. She invites us to the ceremony, then sneaks off to get married elsewhere."

"She is evil," Maria Consuela announced. "Roman will rue the day he married that Whelan wench."

"Enough." Connor glowered at the ladies. "Shanna is no' to blame for tonight's problems. 'Tis her father who is wreaking havoc. All day long, he was calling Roman's house, threatening the daytime guards and promising trouble if the wedding wasna cancelled."

"How did he find out about the wedding?" Gregori asked.

"We doona know. Only those who were invited knew about it. Then this evening, Father Andrew called Roman and told him that Sean Whelan was threatening to attack any church in the city if they allowed demonic creatures inside."

"Wait a minute," Darcy interrupted. "Are you saying Shanna's father knows about vampires?"

"Aye." Connor sighed. "I suppose there's no harm in telling ye. Sean Whelan is a CIA operative and head of a team called Stake-Out. Their sole purpose is to terminate all vampires."

Darcy gasped. "This is terrible."

"What is this CIA?" Princess Joanna asked.

"I'll explain later," Gregori told her.

Darcy lowered her gaze to her hands in her lap. So now there were two enemies—the Malcontents and a group of CIA agents called the Stake-Out team. Poor Shanna was marrying into a very dangerous world. No wonder Angus MacKay had offered to walk her down the aisle and play the part of her father. Her real father was a vampire slayer. What a terrible mess.

Beside her, Gregori spoke, "I still don't see how Sean Whelan found out about the wedding. Hardly anyone knew about it. Do you think the priest—"

"Nay." Connor shook his head. "Father Andrew has become good friends with Roman ever since he took Roman's confession. He wouldna tell anyone."

Gregori rubbed his chin. "Well, someone leaked the news."

Darcy thought back. Had she unwittingly told someone? For the last two days, Corky Courrant had been hounding her for information about the wedding. Corky and her crew from *Live with the Undead* had been invited to the reception at Romatech, but Corky was dying to record footage of the actual ceremony. Darcy had refused to divulge any information, for she was certain Shanna and Roman would want to exchange their vows in private.

And then she remembered. Good God, she'd mentioned the wedding to Adam Olaf Cartwright. She'd forgotten about that, or rather, she'd tried her best to forget about that whole encounter. She'd especially tried to shove the memory of his kiss from her mind. But it still sneaked into her thoughts. How could she possibly forget how warm and passionate he had been, how much she had desperately wanted his warmth, and how much she longed to see him again.

So what if she'd mentioned the wedding to him? He didn't know Shanna or Roman. He was a regular person who didn't even know the vampire world existed.

She shivered with a sudden chill. What if she was wrong?

Chapter 7

By the time they arrived at Romatech, the bride and groom were there and already married. This news caused most of the ex-harem to trudge wearily to two round tables in the far corner of the large room. There they sat and sulked, casting sullen glances at the bride. Shanna was across the room with her new husband, chatting happily with Gregori's mother.

With a sly grin, Gregori motioned toward them. "Let's go congratulate Roman for taking five hundred years to find a bride."

"I'm sure he considers her worth the wait." Darcy followed him with Maggie and Vanda.

Gregori glanced at the ex-harem, skulking in their corner. "Life of the party, aren't they? Do they still refuse to be on the reality show?"

"I'm afraid so." Darcy sighed. At least their number was dwindling. Two of the ex-harem had decided to move to Paris and become models. And then another had shocked them all by announcing that she was eloping with her secret lover. With Maggie and Vanda already involved in the show, Darcy needed every remaining woman to participate.

But they all refused.

Gregori greeted Radinka with a peck on the cheek. "Mom, you shouldn't be on your feet. Go sit down."

"I'm fine." Radinka adjusted her son's tie. "Don't worry."

Darcy gave Radinka a hug. "It's so good to see you again."

"Our Darcy, a television director!" Radinka beamed at her. "I'm so proud of you."

Darcy felt the heat of a blush invade her cheeks. "Thank you for calling the casting agency for me."

"I was happy to help. I've always known you would be a blessing to us all. Have I not said so?" Radinka tapped a finger on her temple, which was her way of reminding everyone that she could predict the future, and was therefore, never wrong.

"Yes," Darcy murmured, her cheeks still warm. Honestly, her confinement had always seemed more like a nightmare than a blessing. She turned to the bride, who was wearing an elegant gown of white satin. A series of pleats accented her slim waist, while the veil hung halfway down her back. "Shanna, you look so beautiful. And so happy."

Shanna laughed and glanced at her new husband beside her. "I *am* happy. And thank you for the matching bathrobes. I loved seeing my new initials monogrammed on the pocket. That was so kind of you."

Darcy waved the compliment away. "My pleasure. And I wish you both the very—"

"Fantastic!" Gregori's loud exclamation drew everyone's attention. He'd been deep in conversation with Roman, but now, he grabbed Darcy by the shoulders. "Guess what? Roman signed the lease on that rental property I told you about."

"For the Vamp restaurant?"

"No, the penthouse. For the reality show."

Darcy gasped. "The huge one at Raleigh Place? With the swimming pool and hot tub on the roof?"

"Yep." Gregori grinned. "It covers two floors, plus a third floor for the servants."

"It's perfect!" Darcy turned to Roman. "Oh, thank you!"

"I'm glad to help." Roman's smile faded as he leaned toward Gregori. "I want some concessions from DVN for this—free advertising of my Fusion Cuisine and the new restaurant."

"No problem," Gregori assured him. "I'll get right on it."

Darcy turned to Maggie and Vanda. "Did you hear that? We have the penthouse!"

Maggie squealed and gave her a hug. "I knew it would work out. Everything really does happen just the way it should."

Vanda grinned. "This is going to be so cool!"

After thanking Roman again, Darcy and her friends joined the other ex-harem ladies.

"Did you hear the good news?" Maggie sat next to Princess Joanna.

"Prithee, what good tidings could you possibly bring?" The princess sipped some Bubbly Blood from a champagne flute. "Is the master having the marriage annulled?"

"No." Vanda plunked down in an empty chair. "Roman signed a lease for a giant penthouse. And since I'm going to be on the reality show, I'll be living there. I'll have a bedroom all to myself. And my own bathroom. And a hot tub."

"Land sakes," Cora Lee whispered. She slanted a hopeful glance toward Princess Joanna. "That sure does sound nice."

"We are not humiliating ourselves on television for the peasants," the princess announced. "Besides, with three of the harem leaving, we will soon have more room at Gregori's house."

"Exactly," Lady Pamela Smythe-Worthing agreed. She looked down her nose at Darcy. "I assume you and Maggie will be joining Vanda at that ridiculous penthouse?"

"Probably so." Darcy took the last empty seat at the table.

"Then, there will only be four of us left at Gregori's." Princess Joanna smiled smugly. "We will be quite comfortable."

Darcy heaved a weary sigh. These women were so mule-headed. She was going to be in big trouble with Sly if she didn't deliver the ex-harem. Her dreary thoughts were interrupted by the sound of music. A band had started to play.

"Isn't that the same band that played at the Gala Opening Ball?" Maggie asked.

"Yes. The High Voltage Vamps." Vanda fluffed up her purple hair. "The drummer is kinda cute, don't you think?"

"Hmm." Maggie looked him over. "Not as cute as Don Orlando."

And not nearly as cute as Adam Olaf Cartwright. Darcy silently moaned. That man kept invading her thoughts. She scanned the room, checking out the other guests. There were several handsome men at the reception—Jean-Luc Echarpe, Angus MacKay. Even Gregori was cute in a big brother sort of way. *But they're not Adam.*

Sheesh, she was starting to compare all men, live or dead, to Adam Cartwright. And even worse, none of these men *did* compare. How could they? They were cold creatures of the night. Adam was Apollo, the sun god. He radiated warmth and passion. He was alive.

He was forbidden.

She had suffered too much from being dragged into the vampire world. She refused to do that to another. As much as she wished happiness for Roman and Shanna, she could not foresee such a relationship working. With a sigh, she watched Roman escort his bride onto the dance floor. He took her into his arms, and they gazed at each other with so much love, it was painful to see. Darcy turned away, feeling guilty for the spurt of envy that had snaked into her heart.

A waiter came by their table to refill their glasses with Bubbly Blood, Roman's fusion drink of synthetic blood and champagne. Another waiter circled the table, placing a bowl of food in front of each of them.

Darcy grimaced at the lumpy, dark red mixture in her bowl. "What is this stuff?"

"Oh, Gregori told me about this." Maggie picked up a spoon and poked at the sticky goop in her bowl. "He did the first taste test on it for Roman."

Lady Pamela arched a brow. "Are you suggesting we eat this strange concoction?"

"Yes." Maggie lifted a spoonful to look at it. "Roman invented it just for the reception. It's called Red Velvet Pudding—a mixture of synthetic blood and white wedding cake."

"How disgusting." Princess Joanna shoved her bowl toward the center of the table.

For once, Darcy actually agreed with the bossy old medieval Vamp. With a twinge of nausea, she moved her bowl to the side.

Maggie set down her spoon and watched the bride and groom waltz across the dance floor. "They seem very happy."

Shanna's laughter rang out as she accidentally trampled on Roman's foot.

Lady Pamela sniffed. "Obviously, she's never had the benefits of a proper dance instructor."

"*Si.*" Maria Consuela nodded, her conical hat bobbing. "You can dress her in a lovely gown, but it does not change the truth. She is naught but a lowly serf."

Roman paused in the middle of a sweeping turn to dip his wife to the side and plant a lingering kiss on her mouth.

Maggie sighed dreamily. "That's so romantic. That's exactly the sort of thing Don Orlando would do."

Vanda snorted. "From what I've heard, Don Orlando prefers to waltz in a horizontal position."

Maggie huffed. "Those rumors are false. Don Orlando is waiting for the right woman. Me."

Darcy exchanged a look with Vanda. They both hoped Maggie wasn't going to get her heart broken.

"Oh, look, other people are starting to dance." Cora Lee patted her mouth with a white linen napkin. Darcy shuddered when she realized the southern belle had actually wolfed down her entire bowl of Red Velvet Pudding.

Cora Lee flipped open her yellow fan. "I do declare, I hope someone will ask me to dance."

"Me, too," Lady Pamela said. "I simply adore dancing. Oh, bravo. Connor is coming this way. He does an excellent minuet."

Darcy stiffened. She clenched her hands together and focused on the bare white tablecloth in front of her. It had been hard enough to face him earlier. With any luck, he would ask Lady Pamela or Cora Lee to dance.

"Good evening, miladies." His low voice carried the soft musical lilt that Darcy had once thought was so adorable. But now, it only brought back memories of that terrible night.

"Why, Connor, it's so good of you to stop by." Cora Lee fluttered her fan. And her eyelashes. "Did you try the pudding? It was just the best thing ever."

"I havena tried it yet." An awkward silence ensued.

Lady Pamela fiddled with a button on her pale pink glove. "Lovely weather we're having."

Connor was silent. Darcy glanced up and found him watching her with that tinge of regret in his blue eyes. Memories of that horrid night flashed through her mind. The terror combined with the smell of blood pudding. Her stomach churned.

"Ye're looking lovely, Darcy," Connor said softly.

She swallowed hard at the bile in her throat. Yeah, putrid green had always been a becoming color for her.

"Would ye care to dance?"

She shook her head, avoiding his sad eyes. Maggie nudged her under the table and shot her a disapproving frown.

"I . . . I'm sorry. I can't," Darcy whispered.

Maggie stood. "I'd be delighted to dance with you."

Connor nodded. "Thank you, lass." He raised an arm and escorted Maggie to the dance floor.

Vanda leaned close to Darcy and whispered, "Why are you so mean to Connor? He saved you."

Darcy shook her head, unable to explain. She squeezed her eyes shut to block out the sight of Bubbly Blood and Red Velvet Pudding.

Vanda sighed. "You've got to stop fighting it. Remember what Maggie says—everything happens for a reason. And you are meant to be here."

Here? When her mind screamed with every heartbeat to break free and escape? She still dreamed of the sun. She longed to be with her family. She wanted to run on the beach. She wanted to be with Apollo, the sun god. *Adam.* She wanted to be with Adam.

She took a deep breath and prepared herself for the pain of reality. It flooded over her, washing away her dreams and leaving her feeling cold and empty.

"Oh, no!" Lady Pamela gasped. "Look who just entered the ballroom."

Darcy glanced back. Corky Courrant and her crew from DVN had arrived. Corky surveyed the room, then motioned for her cameraman to follow her. She marched toward the dance floor, obviously intent on first getting footage of the newlyweds.

"That woman is evil," Maria Consuela announced. "I believe she was a torturer during the Spanish Inquisition."

"That is naught but a rumor," the princess assured her. "But she did work at the Tower of London for Henry VIII."

"Oh, mercy." Cora Lee snapped her fan shut. "What if she notices us?"

"I'm sure she already has," Vanda muttered.

"She will come to torture us." Maria Consuela clicked nervously through her rosary beads. "She will tell everyone that the master rejected us for a mortal *bruja.*"

"And she will display our humiliation on television. I simply cannot bear it." Lady Pamela's hand fluttered by her bosom. "Oh, dear, I'm coming down with the vapors!"

"Here." Princess Joanna lifted a bowl of blood pudding to Lady Pamela's nose. "Breathe deeply."

Lady Pamela sniffed and instantly perked up. "Oh, I do say, that smells rather delightful." She leaned over for another whiff.

"Whatever will we do?" Cora Lee tossed her fan onto the table. "I'm so embarrassed. Oh,"—she motioned to Lady Pamela's face—"you have a spot on your nose."

Lady Pamela quickly wiped the drop of blood pudding off the end of her snooty nose. "Perhaps we should leave. We could all run to the powder room and hide."

Darcy had had enough. "Why do you all insist on acting like victims?"

Cora Lee cocked her head, her ringlets bouncing. "Because we are."

"You don't have to be." Darcy leaned forward. "Take charge of your own destiny."

Princess Joanna huffed. "But the master—"

"Forget the master. He cheated on you with another woman, right?" Darcy pinned each woman with a pointed glare and gave them a version of the truth that she hoped would motivate them. "You deserve better than that. You deserve a man who wants you, who will treat you with respect and honor."

Lady Pamela plucked at the button on her glove. "I suppose, but—"

"Listen," Darcy interrupted. "This is what happened. You refused to be mistreated, so you left."

"That is not true," Maria Consuela said. "He threw us out."

"None of the Vamps out there watching television know that."

Princess Joanna narrowed her eyes. "Are you suggesting we lie?"

"I'm suggesting you take charge," Darcy said. "When Corky Courrant comes over, she's going to try her best to humiliate you. But you can stop her. Just say that Roman betrayed you with another woman, so you all decided to leave him."

Cora Lee bit her bottom lip. "Will they believe us?"

"Why not? Take a strong stand on this, and believe me, all the lady Vamps out there will be cheering for you."

The ladies looked at each other, their expressions still doubtful.

Darcy pushed harder. "If you really want everyone to believe that you rejected Roman, you can say that you plan to pick your next master yourselves."

Lady Pamela shook her head. "It simply isn't done."

"There's a first time for everything. Tell Corky you're planning to choose your own master. Then, no one will think you're shameful. They'll think you're strong and brave."

"I've always wanted to be brave," Cora Lee whispered. "But I was too scared."

"She's coming." Vanda motioned toward Corky Courrant who was bearing down on their table with a vicious, smug smile.

"Don't let her humiliate you," Darcy warned them. "It's in your power to stop it."

The ladies shot desperate looks at Princess Joanna.

She squared her shoulders. Her linen wimple wavered as she lifted her chin. "We'll do it. We'll be on your show and choose our next master ourselves."

"Yes!" Vanda tapped the table with her fist. "This is going to be so cool."

Maria Consuela clenched her rosary in her hands. "I can only pray it will not be as painful as the Spanish Inquisition."

"Nothing's as painful as the Spanish Inquisition." Vanda smiled slyly, her eyes twinkling. "But once we find the Sexiest Man on Earth, he's welcome to torture me all he likes."

With a smile, Darcy relaxed in her chair. She'd done it. She had the five ex-harem judges, the huge penthouse with a hot tub, and fifteen male contestants to compete for the title. Everything was falling perfectly into place. "Let the show begin."

Chapter 8

"How's it going?" Gregori asked as they crossed the Brooklyn Bridge on their way home.

"It's great!" Maggie relaxed in the back seat, smiling. "I was going to the break room and passed by the studio where they do *As a Vampire Turns*. I peeked through the window, and I actually saw Don Orlando in person."

"Okay." Gregori smiled at Darcy. "And how is the reality show coming along?"

"Good." Darcy thought about what she'd accomplished that evening. The limousines were rented. She'd hired a vampire-owned business to install aluminum shutters on the bedroom windows at the penthouse, so none of the guests would fry while they slept. Two DVN cameramen were selected. A caterer was hired to provide food for the human contestants. The artist was hard at work, painting two portraits each night. "I only have one problem left. I need to find a host."

"What does the host do?" Gregori asked.

"Well, he's good at breaking bad news. He dresses well and says brilliant things like 'Gentlemen, there is only one rose left,' as if no one in the room knows how to count to one."

Gregori laughed. "And that's it for his job skills?"

"Well, seriously, he needs to be dependable and someone I can totally trust."

Gregori gave her a worried look. "You mean someone who won't run to Sly behind your back to tell him what you're doing, even though Sly is the one signing the checks."

"Exactly."

Gregori was silent as he turned south onto FDR drive. He drove around the southern tip of Manhattan and was zooming north on the West Side Highway when he took a deep breath and announced, "Okay. I'll do it."

"Excuse me?" Darcy asked.

"I'll be your host. You trust me, don't you?"

"Of course. But you already have a job. Don't blow it off—"

"I'm not," he interrupted her. "Look, I haven't taken a vacation in three years. I mean, sheesh, I'm a little limited in where I can go. So, I'll take a few weeks off. The show won't last any longer than that, right?"

"No, a few weeks would do it."

Maggie leaned forward. "This is great! Gregori will be a super host."

"Well, thanks." Gregori grinned. "After all, I am a sharp dresser, and I can even count to one."

Darcy laughed. "You're the best, Gregori. Thank you."

"No, thank *you*. You're actually getting those women out of my house. I'm eternally grateful."

Darcy nodded. "Once they pick the Sexiest Man on Earth and he wins the million dollars, he'll be their new master."

"Poor bugger."

The next night, Darcy took Maggie and the five ex-harem ladies to DVN. She introduced them to Sylvester Bacchus. He ogled Lady Pamela's low neckline on her Regency-style dress. Then, he rushed off to his office to conduct auditions.

"What a dreadful man," Lady Pamela said as they settled around the table in the DVN conference room.

Darcy passed out their contracts. "The good thing about being judges on this reality show is that if any contestant offends you, you can simply boot him off the show."

Cora Lee frowned at the contract in front of her. "I do declare, all these big words don't make any sense to me."

Maria Consuela shifted uncomfortably in her chair. "I . . . I never learned to read."

"Oh." Darcy tried to hide her surprise. "Well, basically, the contract states that you agree to stay on the show until the end, judge the men fairly to the best of your ability, and refrain from . . . biting any of them or attempting any sort of mental communication for the duration of the show."

Princess Joanna frowned. "We cannot read their minds?"

"No. No mind control and no mind reading."

"But we can make out with them, right?" Vanda asked.

Darcy winced. The thought of anyone else touching Adam made her heart twinge. "I suppose you could. If the men are willing."

Vanda grinned and played with the end of the whip she wore around her waist. "Oh, they'll be willing."

Lady Pamela shuddered. "I cannot imagine wanting any man to touch me. I much prefer vampire sex. It's much more civilized."

"*Si*," Maria Consuela agreed. "Mortal lovemaking is too physical and dirty. It reminds me of being tortured."

"Okay. That's settled." Darcy turned to the last page of their contracts. "This is where you sign or make your mark."

While Maggie picked up the signed contracts, Darcy handed a legal pad to Lady Pamela since she was able to write. "Now, I need you all to think about what qualifications a man would need in order to be the sexiest man on earth."

Maria Consuela fingered her rosary. "I do not understand."

"The man who wins the contest will become your new master," Darcy explained. "Right now, I need you to choose what sort of characteristics you want him to have. Then, you'll use those qualifiers to judge the men during the show." The women stared at her blankly. "Look, what kind of master do you want?"

"Oh, I know, I know!" Cora Lee raised her hand like she was in school. "He needs to be extremely handsome and filthy rich."

Darcy nodded. "The rich part will be taken care of when he wins the big cash prize. As for being handsome—that may indeed be one of your qualifications. I'll need you to list a total of ten qualifiers in the order of their importance."

"I agree with Cora Lee," Vanda said. "Number one should be rich. Number two—a handsome face."

"Let me make this clear," Darcy warned them. "The qualifications you pick will determine what sort of master you end up with. So, you might want to consider intelligence, honesty, dependability—"

"Boring," Vanda yawned. "I vote for rich and handsome."

"I agree." Lady Pamela wrote number one and two on the legal pad. "Wealth and good looks are essential."

Darcy sighed. "What about kindness?"

"Fiddlesticks," Cora Lee said. "He could be as kind as a saint, but if he has the face of a mule, I won't be able to abide him."

"That is truly spoken." Princess Joanna motioned toward the pad of paper. "Number one must be wealth. Number two—fair of face."

Darcy groaned inwardly, but refrained from interfering. After all, this was *their* master they were picking out.

"Excellent." Lady Pamela wrote down their decision. "Now, for number three, I propose good manners. Someone who knows how to behave in polite society and address us by the proper title."

"I agree," Princess Joanna announced. "For number four, he should have the voice of a troubadour and be able to charm a lady with fine words."

"Oh, I like that." Cora Lee nodded, her blond ringlets bouncing. "And he must be well-groomed. A sharp dresser."

"Indeed." Lady Pamela added those to her list.

"And he should be a very good dancer," Cora Lee added.

"And a good lover," Vanda said, grinning. "He should know how to please us."

"Posh," Lady Pamela scoffed. "I have no intention of involving myself physically with any man."

"Fine," Vanda muttered. "But we'd better make sure he likes women and does vampire sex well. And he should have a gorgeous body. We'll have to look at him for centuries."

Darcy was ready to scream. Whatever happened to intelligence, honesty, or dependability? "You seem to be doing very well, so I'll leave you to it." She hurried from the room before her frustration could explode. Their ideal man was a fast-talking, well-dressed troubadour who could dance and do vampire sex? Ugh.

She headed toward the break room, which was located by the recording studios in the back. As she rounded a corner, she ran into Gregori. "Hi." She nodded at his companion. "Simone."

"Bonsoir," Simone replied with a smug smile. It was little wonder that Simone had become a famous fashion model for she was stunning. Tall, dangerously thin, with almond-shaped brown eyes and long black hair, she was dressed in her signature outfit—a slinky black catsuit with a rhinestone-studded belt.

"Simone just teleported in from Paris," Gregori explained. "We're starting work tonight on an exercise DVD."

"How interesting," Darcy murmured politely.

"It was Roman's idea," Gregori continued. "Since modern-day Vamps no longer bite, he was worried we could lose our fangs from disuse."

"Ah." Darcy nodded. "Mustn't have those fangs falling out." *But wouldn't that be a good thing?*

"I will be zhe star of zhe DVD," Simone announced. She flipped her hair over her shoulder. "We are waiting for zhe famous director from Milan, Giovanni Bellini. *Naturellement,* I only work wiz zhe best."

"Naturally." Darcy nodded.

Right on cue, a small man in rumpled clothing and a black beret came sauntering around the corner. "Ah, *bellissima!* There you are, as beautiful as ever." He kissed Simone on each cheek.

"Signor Bellini, this is Gregori." Simone hesitated as she looked at Darcy. "And I forget zhis one's name, but it is not important."

"Thanks." She gritted her teeth. "I'm Darcy."

Giovanni nodded at her, then turned back to Simone. "*Bellissima,* this will be the greatest vampire film of all time. I envision doing certain pivotal parts in black and white to signify the bleak despair of the modern age."

Gregori cleared his throat. "Mr. Bellini, it's just an exercise program for our fangs."

Giovanni stepped back, pressing a hand to his chest. "Even exercise can be portrayed as fine art. Imagine the conflict. Man versus his own corrupt, indolent nature. Come, *bellissima.*" He escorted her into the studio.

Gregori winced. "I shouldn't have hired him, but Simone insisted."

"You mean *bellissima?*" Darcy patted him on the shoulder, smiling. "Good luck."

"Yeah, I'll need it." Gregori trudged into the studio and closed the door. The red light came on.

Darcy hurried back to her office. She opened the door and froze.

Adam Olaf Cartwright was sitting at her desk.

Chapter 9

He looked up and smiled. "Hello, Darcy."

Her heart hammered in her chest. Wasn't her world crazy enough without this man turning it topsy-turvy? As she closed the door, she wondered why he was sitting at her desk. Had he looked through her papers? She turned back to face him. He was still smiling. If he had snooped through her things, he didn't look embarrassed about it. Besides, why would Adam be interested in contracts with caterers or limousine rental agencies?

And why did she react this way every time she saw him? Her heart was racing, but everything else seemed to slow down. She noticed every little delicious detail about him. And there was a good ten-second delay in all her responses because her brain was refusing to work properly. At this rate, he would think she was a moron. "Good evening."

He stood and rounded the desk. "Sorry to take your chair, but the others are occupied." He gestured toward the chairs facing her desk. Two packages, wrapped in brown paper and twine, sat in each chair.

"They're portraits," he explained before she could even ask. "I just came from having mine done. Fred is actually very good." Adam grinned, displaying his dimples at their deepest. "You gotta admit, Fred is an unusual name for an artist."

Unusual for a vampire, too, Darcy thought wryly. She tried to ignore her reaction to Adam, but it was hard to do when her heart was dangerously close to exploding in her chest. And all because of a pair of dimples and turquoise eyes. She wondered if Fred had managed to do him justice. "Is one of these yours?"

"No, mine's still a little wet."

Oh yeah, a little wet. She could relate to that.

"Fred said these four were finished," Adam continued. "He was too busy to bring them here, so I offered to do it for him."

"You really didn't need to do that."

"Oh, but I did." A corner of his mouth quirked up. "It gave me the perfect excuse to see you again."

Her heart thumped louder in her chest.

"And then tomorrow, when my portrait is dry, I'll have another reason to drop by and see you. A clever strategy, don't you think?" His left dimple deepened.

She gulped. He was gorgeous. Fair of face with a sexy voice like a troubadour. Sheesh, he was a perfect match for the list the ex-harem ladies were making. Maybe they were on to something after all.

He sat on the edge of her desk. "So, how was your weekend?"

She stiffened, recalling how Shanna's father had almost ruined her wedding. Surely Adam had had nothing to do with it. "I went to a wedding." She watched him closely for a reaction.

He narrowed his eyes as if trying to remember, then nodded. "Right. Your friends, Raoul and Sherry. How'd it go?"

Darcy exhaled in relief. How could he have told anyone when he couldn't even remember the names correctly? "It was fine."

"Good." He glanced away. His jaw shifted slightly, and she wondered if he was grinding his teeth. Suddenly, he gifted her with one of his fabulous dimpled smiles. "So where are they going on their honeymoon? What's the popular place these days?"

Her heart stuttered in her chest. Why was he asking her that? "I—I don't know."

He nodded. "One of my sisters went to the mountains in Canada. Another went to Hawaii." His dimples deepened. "I bet you would choose the beach."

She looked away, her cheeks warming with a blush. He was right about that. But it was not likely to ever happen. She moved toward the door. "I'm very busy . . ."

He plucked a photo off her desk that showed the building where the penthouse was located. "So, this Raleigh Place is where we'll be doing the show?"

"Uh, yes." So he had looked at her stuff. Well, it was normal to be curious, right? After all, it was her own curiosity that had forever changed her life. A shiver skittered down her spine. *Curiosity killed more than the cat.*

He stepped toward her. "Are you all right?"

"I—I'm fine." *Did he really care?*

"You certainly work long hours. It's almost midnight."

Her eye twitched. How could she possibly explain DVN's odd hours to a mortal? "I—I have a lot of work to do." And she needed to get him out of here. If Sly or any of the ex-harem saw him, they would instantly know he was mortal. And then, they would hound her with questions she didn't want to answer.

"I understand." He watched her sadly.

She suddenly suspected he understood more than he was letting on. Her guard went up. "Was there something you wanted, Mr. Cartwright?"

"I want you to be safe." He touched a lock of her hair that rested on her shoulder. "I want you to trust me."

"I hardly know you."

He rubbed the tendril of hair between his thumb and forefinger. "We can change that anytime."

She wanted to sway forward and rest against his strong, broad chest. With effort, she forced herself to step back. "I don't have any time." She opened the door and peeked out. The hallway was clear. "Thank you for bringing the portraits."

"You're welcome." He stepped into the hallway. "When does the show start?"

"We should be ready in two weeks. I'll send all the information to your agent." Darcy headed down the hallway, then froze when she spotted Sly talking to the receptionist. Shoot! Why couldn't he be in his office, molesting Tiffany? Sheesh. When it came to men, even the perverts were undependable. She grabbed Adam's arm and turned him in the opposite direction. "How would you like a tour?"

"Great." He cast her a worried look, but allowed her to escort him past her office. "I thought you were short on time."

"A few minutes won't hurt." She pulled him around a corner and out of view of the receptionist's area. "This is where the recording studios are located." She motioned to the right. "Studio One is where they do the *Nightly News* with Stone . . . Cauffyn." She quickly gestured toward the left. "And this is—"

"Let me guess." He pointed to the number printed on the door. "Could it be Studio Number Two?"

She smiled. "Yes, how clever of you. That's where they do *Live with the . . .*" Her smile froze. "The celebrity talk magazine." Good God, she'd almost said *Undead*.

He didn't seem to notice. He was trying to peek through the window, but the blinds were closed. "It looks dark in there."

"Those shows are done for the night. The last soap for the evening is on right now." She gestured down a side hall to the back of the building. "Studios Four, Five, and Six are the big sound stages where they do the soap operas."

"What about this one, Studio Three?" Adam walked toward it and peered around the closed blinds. "What's going on in there?"

He certainly was a curious one. "That's a small studio where they make commercials and such."

"The red light is on. Are they making a commercial now?"

"No, not exactly." She could hardly explain an exercise program for vampire fangs.

He examined a control panel by the door. "Is this a sound button?"

"No, don't." Darcy reached out to stop him but it was too late. Voices from inside the studio emanated from the small speaker by the door.

"I don't think she can hold that position for very long," Gregori spoke. "It looks kinda awkward."

"She can do it," Giovanni insisted. "She's a professional. And she looks so beautiful. So sexy."

Adam's eyes widened. "What are they doing in there?"

Darcy leaned against the wall. "It's like . . . an exercise."

"R-rated exercise?" Adam asked softly.

"I wouldn't say—" Darcy was interrupted by Giovanni's voice.

"It is time, *bellissima*. Let them out. Show them to me."

Adam gave her a skeptical look. "Would you say X-rated?"

"No!" Darcy huffed. "DVN doesn't do that sort of thing."

"That's it, *bellissima*!" Giovanni exclaimed. "They're so beautiful. So white and perfectly shaped."

Adam arched an eyebrow at her.

She winced. "It's not what you think."

"Now, pull them back in, *bellissima*. All the way in."

Adam leaned close, planting a hand on the wall by her head. "Maybe I have a dirty mind, but it sounds kinda kinky to me."

Embarrassed, she lowered her gaze. Then she realized she was staring at his crotch, so she raised her eyes level to his.

He smiled slightly, only revealing a hint of the dimple in his left cheek. She fought an impulse to poke a finger at it.

He braced a forearm against the wall on the other side of her head, pinning her in. "I've been thinking a lot about that kiss we shared. Have you?"

She opened her mouth to lie, but was interrupted by Giovanni's excited voice.

"That's it, *bellissima*! Now do it in time with the music." The strains of a slow jazz number filtered through the speaker. A saxophone played low and silky. "Do it again, *bellissima*. In and out. In and out."

The music made the wall behind Darcy vibrate. Adam leaned closer, his breath soft against her brow. The heat of his body was so tempting. She'd been cold for so long.

He kissed her brow, then her temple, then her cheekbone. She grabbed at his shirt. Desire pooled between her legs, making her ache with need. He drew her earlobe into his mouth and suckled.

She moaned. What was she doing? She'd sworn not to lose control again. And anyone could come down this hall at any minute. "No." She shoved at his shoulders.

He stepped back, his eyes burning with desire. "Why not?"

She inhaled a shaky breath. "This is a place of business. Someone could see us." She turned the sound button off.

"Then let's go to my place."

"No." Darcy strode down the hall. What a fool she'd been to get carried away. And what about Adam? Had he made a move on her because of the sexy talk and music? *Dammit.* "I didn't realize you were so easily turned on, Mr. Cartwright."

"I'm not." His voice sounded sharp as he followed her. "Look, I'm always turned on when I'm with you. But not with anyone else."

Her eye twitched. Good God, he was acting like they were a couple. She had to stop this before it went any further. "That was nothing more than a response to the most convenient body available."

"Holy shit. You think you were just convenient?"

She turned to look at him. "No, I'm saying you were convenient for me."

He halted with a jerk.

Damn, she felt cold. As cold as that horrible night four years ago. But this had to be done. It was for his own good.

His eyes simmered with anger, and he stalked toward her. "There is nothing remotely convenient about this relationship. It's damned near impossible."

She breathed sharply. Why did she keep getting the feeling he knew too much? There was something dangerous about him, but God help her, it only made her want him more.

He stopped in front of her. The rage in his eyes flickered hot.

Oh God, she wanted that heat. She needed it.

"I still want you," he whispered.

She blinked away tears. He was so damned tempting.

Footsteps and voices echoed in the side hall. The strident voice of Corky Courrant rang out. Dammit. There was no way to get Adam out the back exit without Corky seeing him.

Darcy spun around, looking frantically for an alternative, and spotted a door. "In here." She shoved Adam inside.

"Gee, is this part of the tour?" he asked dryly.

"Yes." She closed the door, then fumbled for the light switch. The lights revealed row after row of clothing racks and shelves.

Adam wandered down an aisle between two long racks.

"This is the wardrobe department," she explained needlessly.

He plucked a hanger off a rack and smiled appreciatively at a skimpy red negligee. "Is modeling for me part of the tour?"

"No." She snatched the nightgown from his hand and jammed the hanger back onto the rack. "Mr. Cartwright, you have to stop flirting with me. This is a purely professional relationship."

His jaw tensed. "Have you kissed any of the other actors? In a purely professional sense, of course."

She folded her arms over her chest. "It's none of your business."

"Have you kissed any of them?" he gritted out. "Did you even want to?"

"No." She glared at him. "But that doesn't mean this flirtation should continue."

He stepped toward her. "This is a lot more than a flirtation, and you know it. What's happening here is special. It's damned frustrating and . . . beautiful."

Somehow, he always managed to say the right thing. Damn him. "There can't be anything between—"

"Hurry!" Corky's voice sounded outside the door. "In here."

With a gasp, Darcy swiveled toward the door. She gasped again when Adam grabbed her from behind and pulled her behind a clothing rack. "What—"

He covered her mouth with his hand. "Quiet," he whispered.

"Hurry!" Corky opened the door. More than one set of footsteps shuffled into the room. "Close the door," she hissed. "And turn off the lights."

"Yes, my darling," a low voice answered.

The male voice was familiar, though Darcy couldn't

quite place it. Then the lights shut off, and she was left hiding in the dark with Adam. He still had one hand clapped lightly over her mouth and an arm around her waist like a band of steel. He was breathing rapidly, his broad chest stirring against her back. His hand released her mouth and skimmed down her neck. He rested his chin against her hair. They remained perfectly still and quiet.

Not so for Corky and her boyfriend. Their lips made loud smacking noises as they kissed. Their bodies crashed into clothing racks as they spun about. The clothes started swinging, knocking into Darcy.

With his hand splayed against her stomach, Adam guided her quietly back behind a second rack of clothes. She was extremely aware of her hips and bottom brushing against him as they moved.

They stopped against a wall of shelves. He pulled her close, her rump pressed against the front of his pants. With a swift intake of air, Darcy realized he had become fully engorged. Or at least ninety-five percent. A guy couldn't get much bigger than that, could he?

"My darling Corkarina, you drive me mad with desire," the male intruder murmured with a Latin accent.

Corky moaned. "Oh, take me, Don Orlando."

Darcy stiffened with a jolt. Oh no! The rumors were true. Poor Maggie. This was awful. Darcy sagged against Adam, and he instantly tightened his hold on her. *Oh, my.* He must have been at only seventy-five percent of his potential. There was definite growth in the last quarter.

She shifted her hips so he was nestled in the crevice of her derriere. Oh yeah, his stock was rising rapidly. And her heart was clanging like the closing bell. He lowered his head and nibbled softly on her ear. Luckily, there was no way they could be heard over the other more boisterous lovers.

Adam stroked the length of her neck with his long fingers. Then, his mouth moved down her neck with soft kisses. She leaned her head back onto his shoulder, allowing him better access. His fingers skimmed down her T-shirt. She shuddered when his palm covered her breast. Gently, he squeezed.

Don Orlando's voice murmured, "Oh, Corkarina, your boobies are like succulent mangoes."

Darcy slapped a hand against her mouth to keep from reacting. She didn't know whether to scream or laugh.

"And I have a hot tamale for you," he added.

Darcy clamped her lips together to keep from howling. This was Don Orlando, the world's greatest lover? Adam's chest vibrated against her as he stifled his own laughter.

Suddenly, the door burst open and a screech rented the air. "Don Orlando, how could you? You said you loved me."

"I do love you, Tiffany."

"What?" Corky screamed.

"I love all the beautiful women," Don Orlando explained calmly. "And they all love me."

"Then feel the love, you bastard." There was a loud smack. "I'll destroy you on my show." Corky stomped from the room.

"Corkarina!" Don Orlando ran after her.

"Slime ball!" Tiffany yelled. She paused, then ventured into the dark room. She fumbled past the racks of clothes until she reached the shelves against the wall.

Fifteen feet from her, Darcy and Adam froze.

She didn't notice them, for she was peering at all

the shoes. "Oh, these look nice." She grabbed a pair and stumbled back to the hallway, closing the door behind her.

"Alone at last," Adam whispered. "I thought they'd never leave."

She turned around in his arms to face him. "I didn't realize it was going to be so lively here tonight."

"Yeah. I kinda expected it to be more . . . dead."

She glanced quickly at his face, but couldn't make out his expression in the dark.

He stuck a hand in his trouser pocket. "I've got something here for us."

"A hot tamale?" Darcy winced. She shouldn't have said that.

He chuckled. "Pardon me while I whip this out." There was a jangling of keys, then he turned on a small flashlight connected to his keychain. He pointed the light at her face.

She squinted and scrunched up her face.

"Lovely as ever." He lowered the light to her right breast, then her left.

"Do you mind?"

"Just making sure I didn't damage the succulent mangoes."

She snorted. "Can you believe that guy?" She took hold of Adam's hand and turned the light down, away from her breasts. Unfortunately, the light was now aimed straight at his groin. Whoa, that had to be one hundred percent. Biggest tamale she'd ever seen, and she'd seen a few in Southern California.

"Wow," she whispered.

"I'm delighted you're impressed." He turned the light to the ceiling. "But if you keep looking at me, I'm going to end up very embarrassed."

"Oh." She stepped back. "We'd better get you out of here."

"Lead the way." He lit the path for her back to the door. "You know, I couldn't help but notice that you don't want anyone to see me."

Darcy shrugged. "I shouldn't get involved with one of the actors." She opened the door and peered outside. "The coast is clear."

He reached across her and shut the door. "Do you find our relationship embarrassing?"

"No." She faced him, her back against the door. *It's just impossible. Impossibly tempting, and impossible to have.*

"Then why are you hiding me?"

Her eye twitched.

"Sweetheart." He touched the corner of her eye and gently caressed the skin with small circles. "You don't need to be afraid anymore. You can trust me."

"I—I'm not afraid."

"Then why are you fighting this?" His fingers outlined her cheekbone and jaw. He leaned forward and kissed her on the lips. "Will you tell me?"

"Hmm?" She couldn't think straight with his mouth nibbling down her neck.

"Why are you afraid for anyone to see me here?"

"Oh." *Because they'll know you're alive?* She couldn't say that. "The judges for the reality show are here, and they mustn't see any of the contestants ahead of time. It would really spoil everything."

"Is that it?" He watched her carefully. "Nothing else?"

"No, I just want to keep you a secret. For right now."

"Any other secrets?"

A rush of heat poured into her, starting at her temples, then sliding down her throat, warming her heart and blazing pure heat into her groin. She sagged against the door. Good God, he wasn't even touching her now, and she was getting all hot? How did he do this to her? She'd never wanted a man so much in all her life.

He stepped back and turned his flashlight off. She couldn't see his expression in the dark, but she knew he was staring at her. She could feel the heat of his gaze.

Slowly, the heat in her body dissipated, leaving her cold and empty once again. "Come." She peeked out the door. No one was in sight, but she could hear screaming from the direction of Sly's office. Corky was giving him an earful.

"This way." She motioned for Adam to follow her.

They moved quickly down the back hallway to the rear exit. Darcy pushed open the heavy door.

Adam paused halfway through. "When can I see you again?"

"In two weeks. Please, promise me you won't come here again."

"Fine." Frowning, he removed a small notepad and pen from an inside pocket of his jacket. He jotted something down. "I want you to call me if you need anything. Or feel free to stop by."

She accepted the piece of paper. He'd given her his address and phone number.

He reached toward her and slid a fingertip down the side of her face. He traced her lips lightly. "Thank you for the tour." He slipped out the door into the darkness.

A cool night breeze swept into the hall, erasing the warmth that had lingered where he'd touched her.

With a sigh, Darcy let the door swing shut. It was going to be a long two weeks.

It took a cold shower to get Austin's mind focused once again on business. He padded into his kitchen, dressed in the SpongeBob briefs his youngest sister had given him for Christmas. Thoughts about his family made him wonder again why Darcy was living among the undead. He knew from his research that she had parents and two younger sisters living in San Diego. Was she completely cut off from her family? Were the vampires holding her prisoner in their world because she knew too much? Had they threatened her family to keep her in line?

That must be it, because otherwise he felt sure she would attempt an escape. He knew from watching her news reports that she was brave and resourceful. Clearly, the vampires had some kind of leverage on her to make her stay with them.

What the hell had happened to her four years ago? Austin had a copy of the police report, but it was inconclusive. She'd gone to a vampire club in Greenwich Village to do a Halloween report on kids who pretended to be vampires. Somehow, she'd ended up in the alley behind the club. The pool of blood and the bloody knife had been traced back to her. The police suspected she was dead, but no one really knew what had transpired in that alley.

The day before, Austin had located her old cameraman, Jack Cooper. Jack was barely scraping by, living in a one-room apartment in a grimy basement with aluminum foil taped to the tiny windows. It was easy to see that Jack had never recovered from that evening. Maybe the aluminum foil cap on his head was a clue. Or his conclusion that vampires were blood-thirsty, mind-controlling aliens who were hunting for him, intending to abduct him like they had Darcy. It was sad that everyone thought Jack was crazy, because he was right about the blood sucking, the mind control, and Darcy's abduction. The vampires had taken her. And they weren't letting her go.

Austin grabbed a can of beer from the fridge. What would it take to get her to trust him? He'd urged her tonight to confide in him, and when she hadn't, he'd invaded her mind, hoping the secrets were there for the taking.

What he saw there had stunned him. No dark secrets. Darcy's innermost thoughts were about how much she wanted him. It had taken every ounce of his resistance not to pull her down on the floor and make love to her right then.

Love on the floor of the wardrobe room? That would have made him as sleazy as Don Orlando. With a snort, Austin set his beer on the coffee table and picked up the legal pad where he'd started a list of vampires. He added Don Orlando's name.

He slid one of Darcy's tapes into the VCR. He'd seen them all now. Some of them more than twice. Sheesh. He was watching her every night instead of sports. He thought about her all the time. And if it was only lust, he'd only think about her gorgeous body, right? But no, he was worried about her. Was he falling in love?

He collapsed on the couch. No, it couldn't be love. It was an intellectual thing. The mystery of her strange lifestyle intrigued him, and he wanted answers. And he was worried about her safety. That was normal.

He'd grown up always protecting his younger sisters. It was natural for him. No big deal.

He grabbed his jacket off the arm of the couch and dug into the inside pocket. He removed the small notepad and flipped through the notes he'd taken in Darcy's office. She'd hired a business called The Shuttered Life to install aluminum shutters in the penthouse. So this meant he and Garrett would be living there with vampires. He'd better pack some wooden stakes in his luggage.

He'd jotted down the name of the caterer Darcy had hired. He'd get Alyssa or Emma an undercover position there. That way, they could come to the penthouse during the day, retrieve information from Garrett or himself, and pass it on to Sean.

He also had the address for Raleigh Place. He'd go there during the day and install hidden cameras and bugs. He removed a computer disk from his jacket pocket. He'd managed to download the DVN employee records from Darcy's old dinosaur computer before he'd heard her approaching the office. He set the disk on the table next to his list of vampires.

He stretched and glanced at the television. Darcy was beginning a report. Oh, this was one of his favorites. He grabbed the remote and turned up the volume.

"I'm here in the South Bronx at the dedication of a new park." Darcy smiled at the camera as she walked down a path. "It's not a park for children. It's not for basketball players, roller skaters, or even chess players. This park is for the dogs."

The cameramen zoomed in on a woman in the distance who was walking her fluffy white poodle. Then, he panned back to Darcy.

"As you can see, the park is divided into sections, depending on the size of your—aagh!" She skidded forward about five feet, her arms windmilling in the air. After a valiant struggle, she regained her balance. She glanced down at her shoes, wrinkled her nose, and gave the camera a wry grin. "Obviously, this section is for the *extremely large* dogs."

Austin chuckled. No matter what happened in her reports, Darcy always made it work. She was brave, funny, clever, and beautiful. Nothing could get her down.

But something had. He tightened his grip on the remote. Something had happened to wrench her out of this sunny, happy life and imprison her in a world of dark demonic creatures. And it was hurting her. He could see it. The sorrow in her eyes. The tense way she clenched her hands together. The fear that caused her right eye to twitch. That nervous twitch never occurred in any of these tapes. It was something new. And most likely, it had started on Halloween four years ago.

Chapter 10

The penthouse at Raleigh Place boasted two floors of opulent décor, including Italian marble floors and columns and Baccarat crystal chandeliers. Darcy figured you could fit a small chamber orchestra into the master bathtub. Or you could feed the entire population of Liechtenstein from the huge pantry in the kitchen.

Even so, she preferred the roof. Maybe it was a result of her forced confinement, but she loved being under the open sky. She loved the evening breeze on her face and the scent of roses that wafted from the glass greenhouse in the corner. She loved how the swimming pool glimmered in the moonlight and cast dancing reflections along the white-painted walls surrounding the roof. A mist hovered over the hot tub, inviting her to indulge in its glorious heat. Huge clay pots sat every five feet along the chest-high walls, each pot containing a green leafy plant that soared high over her head. Some plants were trimmed into huge cones, while others were shaped into fanciful animals. Each topiary was covered with white twinkle lights that glittered like the stars overhead.

In the opposite corner from the greenhouse, there was a tiny pool house. The two rooms contained the bare essentials, in sharp contrast to the grandeur of the penthouse. But Darcy was so enthralled with the roof, she'd decided to make the pool house her office and special retreat.

She paced around the swimming pool, tense with excitement. She was wearing the sparkly maroon dress she'd bought for Shanna's wedding, because tonight, she'd spend some time in front of the camera. Tonight, they would begin filming *The Sexiest Man on Earth*. And after a separation of two long weeks, she would see Adam again.

"Here they come," Gregori announced from the north edge of the roof. Next to him, Bernie aimed his camera at the street twelve floors below.

Darcy rushed to the wall and peered over. A black limousine was slowly coming down the street. Maggie and the ex-harem judges were arriving. The second cameraman, Bart, was in the limo, so he could record their reactions to their new home. Darcy would combine the footage from both cameramen during the editing stage. The limo rolled to a stop at the red-carpeted entrance to Raleigh Place.

Gregori touched the earphones he was wearing. "Audio's coming in. I can hear them talking."

Darcy slipped her earphones on. At once, she could hear the excited voices of the ladies inside the limo.

"Land sakes!" Cora Lee exclaimed. "This place is grand!"

"Look," Lady Pamela said. "A footman is coming to open the door for us."

"That's a doorman," Vanda muttered.

"He's still a servant," Lady Pamela huffed. "Though I must say, it is appalling how servants these days neglect to wear their powdered wigs."

"Or proper livery," Princess Joanna declared. "It is impossible to tell which lord he is serving."

Darcy sighed as she watched from the roof. The ex-harem was so stuck in the past. She'd insisted that they update their wardrobe for the show, but now, she had a dreadful feeling they had completely ignored her. Bart climbed out first with his camera so he could record the ladies exiting the car. Vanda climbed out and strode down the red carpet. She was striking with her purple hair and dress. So far, so good.

Lady Pamela exited next. She adjusted the bodice on her Regency-style gown of pale blue silk. Her matching reticule hung from a ribbon around her wrist. Darcy groaned.

Maria Consuela and Princess Joanna moved onto the red carpet, both wearing long medieval gowns with veils covering their hair.

"I thought you bought them new clothes," Gregori muttered.

Darcy sighed. "You know what they say about old dogs."

Cora Lee struggled to get out of the car, but her hoop skirt jammed in the narrow door opening. Maggie shoved her from behind, and she popped out onto the sidewalk. Then Maggie jumped out and closed the door.

They filed into the building, murmuring their appreciation of the marble floor and gilded ceiling.

"I do declare," Cora Lee exclaimed. "That elevator is so shiny!"

"Yes," Maggie agreed. "That's the elevator for the penthouse. The doors are solid brass."

"How lovely," Lady Pamela's snooty voice could be heard over the others. "Be a dear and push the button for us."

"Ah, actually, I need you to follow me," Maggie said. "This way, please."

"Where are you taking us?" Princess Joanna demanded.

"To another elevator," Maggie explained.

"But this hallway is so plain and dreary," Cora Lee whined.

"Why are we not going to the penthouse?" the princess asked sharply. "Where does this other elevator go?"

"Oh, it goes to the penthouse," Maggie assured them. "It just goes to the . . . kitchen and servants' floor. It's very nice and private."

"Servants' floor?" the princess shrieked.

Darcy and Gregori both winced as her strident voice grated over the headphones.

"Yes," Maggie responded. "We'll have very nice bedrooms all to ourselves on . . . the servants' floor."

"The servants' floor?" Lady Pamela's voice shook. "I'm the daughter of a baron, the widow of a viscount. I cannot live amongst servants!"

"There will only be the six of us," Maggie assured her. "And we'll each have our own bedroom. Here we are. This is the service elevator."

"This is horrid, simply horrid," Lady Pamela sounded shrill. "I—I'm coming down with the vapors!"

"Silly child," Princess Joanna growled. "Where are your smelling salts?"

Darcy rolled her eyes. Lady Pamela's so-called smelling salts consisted of a vial filled with Chocolood.

"I'd better help Maggie." Darcy headed for the stairwell located close to the greenhouse. She glanced back at Gregori and Bernie. "I'll see you in the foyer at ten o'clock."

Gregori nodded. "We'll be there."

Darcy paused at the stairwell door. "Bernie, can you make arrangements for a helicopter? I'd like to get an aerial shot of this roof. It's so lovely."

"No problem." Bernie set down his camera and pulled out a cell phone.

Darcy opened the door to the stairwell. The reception on her earphones was faint now, but she could still hear the sound of screeching voices. Poor Maggie. Darcy rushed down three flights of stairs, then exited on the servants' floor. She could hear the ex-harem in the service elevator.

"Please calm down," Maggie pleaded. "There are six bedrooms on the servants' floor. They're small, but very nice. You'll each have your own room with a lovely view of Central Park."

"The view is of no consequence," Princess Joanna snapped. "It is a floor for peasants. I will not sleep in that hovel."

"It's not a hovel," Maggie insisted.

"This is quite beyond the pale," Lady Pamela declared. "We should be living in the penthouse."

"There are only five bedrooms in the penthouse," Maggie explained. "We need those for all the male contestants. As it is, they're going to have to share rooms."

"They could share the rooms on the servants' floor," Cora Lee offered.

"Those rooms are too small to be shared," Maggie argued.

"Ridiculous," Princess Joanna hissed. "The men should give us their bedchambers. Have they not heard of chivalry?"

The elevator doors opened. The cameraman Bart turned toward Darcy.

She greeted them with a smile. "Good evening. Welcome to your new home."

"This is an outrage!" Princess Joanna glared at her. "You said we would be living in the penthouse."

"The servants' quarters are part of the penthouse, and you'll each have your own room." Darcy led the way to the servants' parlor. "I believe you will find the accommodations quite comfortable." She opened the door.

The ladies trudged inside, grumbling. They stopped in the parlor and looked around. The couches and easy chairs were large and overstuffed; the television was as huge as the one they'd enjoyed at Roman's house. Vanda strolled into the kitchen and checked out the refrigerator. Bottles of synthetic blood, Chocolood, and Bubbly Blood lined the shelves.

"Not bad." Vanda grabbed a bottle Chocolood and popped it into the microwave. "This is really nice."

Princess Joanna sniffed. "Peasants shouldn't live this well. It's ungodly."

Darcy smiled. "Please make yourselves comfortable. And choose which bedroom you prefer."

The doorman arrived with all their luggage. He hauled the trunks to the bedrooms while the women directed him. By the sound of their excited voices, Darcy figured they were adjusting quite nicely.

Once the doorman was gone with a hefty tip, Darcy called all the women back into the parlor. "Before we get started on the show, I'd like to interview each of you. This will be your chance to tell the vampire world about yourself. Each segment will be edited into the show later."

One by one, the women sat for the camera and gave a brief account of their life stories. Afterward, Darcy took them up one floor on the elevator to the kitchen. As she led them to the foyer of the penthouse, she could hear their sighs and gasps of approval. Bart rushed ahead of them so he could catch their reactions.

"It's beautiful," Lady Pamela whispered.

"I just adore a wide staircase," Cora Lee exclaimed. "Why, this one is wide enough for three women in proper ball gowns like mine."

Wide hallways led off the foyer to the east and west wings of the penthouse. The grand staircase swept up to an intermediate landing where it then divided in two. Then, the right and left portions of the staircase curved up to the second floor. An interior balcony ran the length of the second floor and overlooked the foyer. The polished marble floor reflected the lights from the massive chandelier overhead.

"This way." Darcy led them up the stairs to the landing. There, she positioned them in a row.

"Hey, ladies," Gregori called as he and Bernie entered the foyer. "Looks like you're ready to go."

"Yes, we are." Darcy ran down the steps and joined

Maggie behind the cameramen. She signaled Gregori to begin.

"Welcome, ladies, to *The Sexiest Man on Earth*," Gregori announced in a clear voice. "There will be a total of fifteen men competing for the title. As the former harem of coven master Roman Draganesti, you five women hold the honor of being the most prestigious female Vamps in North America. Therefore, you are the most suited to judge this contest."

Darcy watched the women react to the compliment. They lifted their chins and stood a bit taller. It was good to see after the beating their egos had taken with Roman's dismissal.

"Princess Joanna Fortescue." Gregori bowed. "I bid you welcome."

"Thank you, good sir." The princess descended the stairs with her head held high.

"Keep the camera on her," Darcy whispered to Bart. This would be where she'd insert Princess Joanna's bio—with a few careful edits. Darcy had cringed when the medieval woman had claimed all Scotsmen were barbarians. Obviously, the princess had grown up in a time when Scotland had presented a threat to England. But sheesh, that was eight hundred years ago! How long could someone hold a grudge? Apparently, a really long time. Now, it seemed clear that the ex-harem was clinging to more than their old clothes. Their old prejudices had survived the centuries intact.

Princess Joanna stood proudly next to Gregori. In her medieval gown, she looked like a queen surveying her domain.

Gregori bowed once again. "Señora Maria Consuela Montemayor, I bid you welcome." As the second oldest lady Vamp, Maria Consuela was the second to descend the stairs.

"Lady Pamela Smythe-Worthing, I bid you welcome." Gregori bowed to the female Vamp from the Regency period. She lifted the hem of her gown to come down the stairs.

"Miss Cora Lee Primrose, I bid you welcome."

Cora Lee skipped down the stairs, her hoop skirt bouncing.

Gregori bowed to the final and youngest judge. "Vanda Barkowski, I bid you welcome."

"Thanks, dude." Vanda aimed a sly grin at the camera as she came down the stairs.

"This way, ladies." Gregori led them to the west wing and a pair of double doors. They filed in and sat on two leather couches facing him.

"This is the portrait room." Gregori motioned to the wall behind him.

Darcy flipped on the lights and all fifteen portraits were illuminated by track lighting on the ceiling. She'd hung the portraits herself, seven on the top row and eight on the bottom. Her eyes automatically sought out her favorite portrait.

The artist had done a decent job, though she thought Adam's eyes were a deeper blue. For some reason, he hadn't smiled so his dimples weren't showing. But even with a serious expression, his portrait made her breath catch and her heart flutter. For the last two weeks, she'd fallen asleep remembering the feel of his mouth, the taste of his lips, and the heat of his body. She would have to be strong and keep her distance. Otherwise, he presented a temptation that was too hard to resist.

"The Sexiest Man on Earth will be selected

according to your own list of criteria," Gregori explained. "The most important qualification was that he be rich. By the end of this show, the winner will be rich. The second qualification was that he be fair of face. So tonight, using these portraits, you will judge these men by their looks. Maggie will give each of you five black orchids. Below each portrait is a narrow shelf. You will place an orchid by the portrait of each man you wish to eliminate. Five men must be eliminated tonight."

Cora Lee frowned at the black orchids that Maggie dropped in her lap. "We have to make a decision tonight? *Five* decisions?"

"Yes," Gregori replied. "Who would like to go first?"

The ladies glanced at each other.

Princess Joanna stood slowly, gathering her five black orchids in her hands. "As the eldest, I will go first."

Darcy had never seen the princess look so flustered. The medieval Vamp wandered down the double row of portraits. She clenched her hands together, crushing the flowers. She glanced toward the other ladies for guidance.

"Well," Cora Lee ventured. "It seems fairly obvious that we should eliminate the African. I couldn't possibly have a black master. My dear papa would roll over in his grave."

"And we must be rid of any Moors," Maria Consuela added.

"Cut!" Darcy strode over to the women. "Ladies, I will not allow racial bias on this show. Please set aside your old prejudices. For Pete's sake, this is the twenty-first century!"

"It is?" Cora Lee tilted her head. "It seems like

only yesterday I turned a hundred. Where does all the time go?"

"Your numbers are meaningless to us." Princess Joanna looked down her nose at Darcy. "Only a mortal would count time because he has so little of it."

"I cannot do as you say," Maria Consuela told Darcy. "You do not understand how much we Spaniards suffered to rid our country of those dreadful Moors."

"I sympathize with the hardships you must have endured in the past, but that was a long time ago," Darcy insisted. "And frankly, it's time to get over it. I will not have you selecting these men by race or religion. You are to make your decision tonight based solely on good looks. Any remarks I don't like will be edited from the show. Do you understand?"

Cora Lee snorted. "And I thought we had freedom of speech."

Darcy sighed. "Just be careful what you say."

Maria Consuela glared at her. "That's what they told us during the Spanish Inquisition."

Darcy shook her head in frustration as she walked back behind the camera. "Roll 'em."

Bart turned the camera back on. Princess Joanna glanced back at Darcy with a defiant look, then placed her five black orchids in front of five portrait frames. Darcy groaned.

Maggie leaned close. "You can't expect to wipe out centuries of hatred in one night."

"I guess not." Darcy watched in dismay as each of the judges used their black orchids to reject five men. Vanda was the only one who didn't take race into account, but she was outnumbered four to one.

Darcy studied the five women as they returned to their seats. They were smiling and evidently, quite proud of themselves. The more she thought about it, the more Darcy decided this was a good thing. These were women who had existed for centuries, never having to make an important decision for themselves. Tonight, they had managed to do it. True, they did it in defiance of her instructions, but still, it was a big step toward independence. They had every right to be proud.

Their moment of glory would have to be short-lived, though. It was time for the big surprise of the evening. Darcy motioned for Gregori to approach.

"Ready for all hell to break loose?" She passed him the flashlight containing a black light bulb.

"Yep. Just tell me which guy to do last."

Darcy told him, then he strode back in front of the camera.

"It's time to take a closer look at the five men you rejected this evening." Gregori aimed his flashlight at a portrait and switched it on. "With a total of five black orchids, Tadayoshi of Tokyo is eliminated from the competition."

Darcy turned off the track lighting. Gregori's black light illuminated some previously invisible paint on Tadayoshi's portrait. Suddenly, he acquired long, white fangs.

"Oh, those are nice," Cora Lee whispered. "But I was afraid he'd be one of those frightful *ninja* masters."

Darcy winced. That would be a good line to edit.

"With four orchids beneath his portrait, Derek of Philadelphia will also be eliminated from the competition." Gregori pointed the black light at Derek's picture. His long fangs glowed in the dark.

Vanda sighed. "What a shame we had to lose Blackula. He was so handsome."

Darcy agreed, though the other ladies looked doubtful.

"Also with four black orchids, Harsha of New Delhi will be eliminated from the competition." Harsha's white fangs appeared like magic when the black light hit his face.

"An interesting trick," Princess Joanna admitted, "but I do not see a purpose for it."

"With three black orchids, we'll be saying goodbye to Ferdinand of Salzburg." Gregori shone his light on Ferdinand's face, and the Austrian's fangs gleamed.

Lady Pamela sighed. "It is rather silly, isn't it? We already know the men are vampires."

Maria Consuela fiddled with her rosary. "And if you've seen one fang, you've seen them all."

"I'm not so sure about that," Vanda said with a grin.

"Come to think of it, I have seen a few with a ghastly yellowish tint." Lady Pamela shuddered. "There's simply nothing worse than a vampire with poor dental hygiene."

Princess Joanna frowned. "And some of them are crooked."

"But some are longer than others," Vanda said. "You know, size *is* important."

Cora Lee heaved a huge sigh. "My poor Beauregard, God rest his soul. He had the longest fangs I've ever seen."

Gregori frowned at them, clearly uncomfortable. "Ladies, if you don't mind, we still have one more contestant to eliminate. Seth from New Jersey received three black orchids." Gregori aimed his flashlight at Seth.

The ladies waited.

Vanda exchanged a look with Darcy.

"Where are his fangs?" Lady Pamela asked.

"I didn't like him," Cora Lee said. "His hairline is receding."

"His bloody fangs are receding," Princess Joanna grumbled.

"There must be something wrong with that painting." Maria Consuela squinted at it.

"No," Gregori said quietly. "There's nothing wrong with the painting."

The room fell silent. The ladies exchanged confused glances.

Vanda rolled her eyes, obviously impatient with how slowly the women were thinking. "Gee, I wonder why he doesn't have any fangs."

The four women gasped. Even Bart flinched and nearly dropped the camera.

Princess Joanna jumped to her feet. "Are you saying there was a mortal in the contest?"

Gregori shrugged. "Looks that way, doesn't it?"

Maria Consuela stood, clutching her rosary to her chest. "I demand a straight answer. Is that man a mortal?"

"Yes," Greg admitted. "He's one of several mortal men in the contest."

The women gasped again.

"Oh, my! This is horrid, simply horrid!" Lady Pamela fumbled in her reticule for her smelling salts.

"This is an outrage!" Princess Joanna turned to Darcy, her eyes seething in anger. "How dare you sully our contest with mortals?"

Vanda shrugged. "They might be cute."

Lady Pamela scoffed. "A mortal could never be the sexiest man on earth. The very notion is ludicrous." She unscrewed the top off her vial of Chocolood. "I'm quite up in the boughs over this."

Princess Joanna strode toward Darcy. "How could you! We trusted you, and you have betrayed us."

"Indeed." Lady Pamela sniffed at her vial. "First you put us in those dreadful servants' quarters."

"And now," Princess Joanna continued, "you insult us by forcing us to endure the company of mortals."

Cora Lee bounced to her feet. "We can't have a mortal master!"

"Then don't pick a mortal," Darcy told them. "Look, you're still in control here. You're the ones who decide which men are eliminated."

The women looked at each other.

"Then tell us which ones are mortal," the princess demanded.

Darcy shook her head. "I can't do that. You'll have to figure it out yourselves."

"We can do that." Maria Consuela clicked through her rosary. "We can smell them."

"Actually, you won't be able to do that." Darcy gave them all an apologetic look. "They'll be wearing a vampire repellent anklet that will make them impossible to detect by smell."

Princess Joanna huffed. "Then we will read their minds."

"No, you signed a contract stating you wouldn't."

"This is horrid, simply horrid." Lady Pamela drank her entire vial of Chocolood.

"Whatever will we do?" Cora Lee whimpered. "We can't have a mortal master."

"We won't." Princess Joanna lifted her chin. "Darcy thinks to play this evil game with us, but she will see. The mortal men will not compare to the vampire men. We will detect them as easily as a terrier seeks out vermin."

Maria Consuela nodded. "*Si*, it is true. The vampire men will be naturally superior."

"Of course!" Lady Pamela pressed a hand to her bosom. "The mortal men will fail miserably at each of our tests."

"Yes." Princess Joanna faced her co-judges with a fierce expression. "Hearken to me, ladies. We must be vigilant and eliminate this mortal threat."

The ladies huddled together, making their plans.

"Sweet Mary and Joseph." Maggie looked at Darcy. "I knew there was a reason for you to be here. Do you realize what you've done?"

"Yeah. I made them hate me more than ever."

"No. Look at them. I've never seen them so excited, so impassioned. You've given them a purpose for their existence."

A chill inched down Darcy's spine. Surely Maggie was exaggerating. She tended to be a bit overdramatic.

A buzzing sound came from Darcy's headphones and she slipped them on to listen.

"May I have your attention, please?" Darcy waited for Bart to focus his camera on her. "The gentlemen are arriving."

Chapter 11

Austin rode in the back of a Hummer limousine
with six other men. Four of them were human for
sure. He remembered George, Nicholas, and Seth
from the auditions. And then, there was Garrett aka
Garth. The humans had been instructed to come to the
Rising Stars of Tomorrow Agency at nine P.M. with
their luggage.

A man from Romatech Industries had been there, a
short chemist by the name of Laszlo Veszto. He'd
given each of them a plastic anklet to wear underneath
their socks. It had to be in contact with their skin. And
they had to wear it for the entire duration of the show.
When the men questioned why, the chemist replied
with a convoluted explanation of pheromones.

At nine-thirty, two Hummer limousines arrived at
the agency with ten men. Austin figured they were the
undead competition, but found it odd that the small
chemist gave them anklets, too. The fifteen men
climbed into the limousines for the short ride to

Raleigh Place. Austin noted the vampires didn't react like they normally did around humans. No sniffing, no hungry glances.

Conversation was sparse on the short trip. No one wanted to reveal a weakness to another competitor. When they stopped in front of Raleigh Place, the vampire named Maggie greeted them and escorted them up to the penthouse. The huge foyer was empty. Maggie arranged the men in three rows on the staircase, the top row standing on the landing. She told them to wait, then headed down a hallway. The men exchanged nervous glances, though none of them spoke or acknowledged they were nervous.

Soon, a cameraman came rushing down the hallway. He ran up the stairs and shot close-ups of each man. Austin couldn't see Darcy anywhere. Then, he heard footsteps and feminine voices. The women were coming. Another cameraman was ahead of them, walking backwards. The male vampire, Gregori, was leading a group of five women. The judges, most likely. One of the ladies was the purple-haired Vanda, but the other four females were unknown. And strangely dressed. They had to be really old.

Austin leaned forward to see further down the hallway. Yes, there she was. Way behind the others. Darcy was coming with the vampire Maggie. He leaned forward some more and nearly lost his balance. Thank God he was standing next to the railing, or he would have tumbled down the stairs. Damn, she looked good. She looked more than good.

When she entered the foyer, her gaze wandered over all the contestants, then rested on him. He nodded his head slightly and smiled. She looked away. Austin kept his gaze on her, hoping she would glance his way again. But the longer he watched her, the more he realized she was looking everywhere but at him.

"Gentlemen, welcome to *The Sexiest Man on Earth.*"

Austin switched his gaze to the speaker.

"My name is Gregori, and I'll be your host." He motioned toward a female vampire. "Maggie will be your hostess."

Austin glanced back at Darcy, wondering what kind of relationship she had with this Gregori. Was he hosting the show as a favor to her?

"The five judges for this contest are standing before you," Gregori continued. "May I introduce Princess Joanna, Maria Consuela, Lady Pamela, Cora Lee, and Vanda."

Vanda waved. The other ladies curtsied. Austin glanced back at Darcy, wondering how long she was going to ignore him.

"Fifteen of you have arrived," Gregori announced, "but only ten of you will remain. Our lady judges have already voted five of you off the show. But first, a word from our sponsor."

There was a silent pause. The male competitors exchanged glances. Austin figured this was a commercial break for Vampire Fusion Cuisine.

"Welcome back." Gregori smiled at a nearby camera. "It's time to learn which five men will be going home tonight. They are," he paused for dramatic effect, "Tadayoshi, Derek, Harsha, Ferdinand, and Seth. Gentlemen, you must take your leave. The limousines are waiting for you. As for the rest of you—your luggage will arrive shortly. Maggie and I will see you to your rooms. Congratulations and welcome."

As Austin shook hands with Seth, he felt relief that there would be one less human in the penthouse to protect. He glanced down at the foyer and saw that the five vampire judges had left. So had Darcy and the cameramen. Shoot, that was it? Apparently, they were done for the night.

The limo drivers brought all the luggage into the foyer, and the men descended the stairs to collect their bags. The five losers for the night left with the limo drivers.

Maggie escorted Austin and five other contestants to the east wing of the penthouse. She pointed out the kitchen, fitness room, and sauna. "There are three bedrooms on this side. You'll need to share rooms." She looked at a clipboard she was carrying. "I have Reginald and Pierre in one room, Garth and George together, and Nicholas and Adam together."

Austin exchanged a relieved look with Garrett. Thank God they didn't have to share rooms with a vampire.

"Where is the director's office?" Austin asked.

"Darcy's in the pool house." Maggie gave him a curious look. "Why? Is there a problem?"

"No, not at all." He silently cursed as he lugged his bag up the back stairs to the second floor. The pool house? Who the hell used a pool house for an office? He'd put a camera in the penthouse library, expecting that to be her office. He hadn't put any cameras in the damned pool house.

Maggie showed Reginald and Pierre to their room first. Then, she led the four humans to their rooms. Austin's bedroom was next door to Garrett's.

"The kitchen is fully stocked with drinks and snacks," Maggie explained. "A caterer will bring you

hot meals each day. For security reasons, please do
not go into any other bedrooms. You may leave the
building as long as you're back in time for the show
each evening. Since we will be recording at night, we
are encouraging all contestants to sleep during the
day."

Austin suppressed a laugh. Right, some of the contestants were dead during the day.

"We'll begin recording tomorrow night at eight P.M.
in the library. Good night." With a final smile, Maggie
left.

The men rolled their luggage into their bedrooms.
Austin hefted his suitcase onto his bed and removed
his laptop. He glanced at Nicholas. "I hope you don't
mind if I use the desk."

"No, not at all." Nicholas dropped his bag on his
bed. "I'm starving. Want to check out the kitchen?"

"Sorry, I've got some work to do. But don't let me
stop you." Austin set his laptop on the desk.

"See ya later." Nicholas headed out the door.

Whew. Alone at last. Austin punched in the code for
the hidden cameras he'd installed. He spotted a group
of men on the west end of the penthouse. Gregori was
showing contestants to their rooms. They were probably all vampires. Gregori made his leave and headed
for the main staircase. Where was he going? To see
Darcy?

Austin felt a nasty twinge that he recognized as
jealousy. And it didn't help that Darcy had set up her
headquarters in the damned pool house where he
didn't have a camera. Was she going to sleep there,
too?

He switched his view to the camera in the foyer.
Gregori had reached the bottom of the stairs and was

headed for the portrait room. Austin switched to the portrait room. Shoot. Darcy was there. That creepy Gregori was meeting her alone.

Darcy was removing a portrait from the wall, probably one of the rejects for the night. She carried the portrait to the far corner of the room and set it on the floor, propped against the wall. She straightened suddenly, pivoting toward the door.

"Gregori!" She ran across the room. She gave him a hug and a peck on the cheek. "You were great!"

He was scum. Austin watched to see where the vampire placed his hands on Darcy. A brief touch on her shoulders. Austin decided to leave his wooden stakes in the suitcase for now.

"Thanks. It was fun." Gregori glanced at the portraits on the wall. "So you're removing the losers?"

"Yes." Darcy plucked a second portrait off the wall. "Can you get Derek's?"

"Sure." Gregori removed the painting and followed Darcy to the corner where she was stashing them. "I thought it was really embarrassing how racist the ladies are."

"It's awful! I'll have to do some very careful editing."

"Yeah. They're really stuck in the past." Gregori set down his painting. "But I think you handled them really well."

"Thank you." Darcy located the fifth painting that needed to be removed.

Gregori wandered toward her, studying the portraits. He stopped in front of one and leaned close to read the nameplate. "Adam Olaf Cartwright. Who's he?"

Austin tensed and held his breath.

Darcy froze for a few seconds, then grabbed the fifth painting off the wall. She strode toward the corner. "He's a contestant, of course."

"Mortal or vampire?"

Darcy deposited the painting, then straightened. "We agreed that you wouldn't know ahead of time."

"I know, but—" Gregori glared at Austin's painting. "This guy was staring at you all evening."

Darcy clenched her hands together. "I wouldn't call it *all* evening. It was more like ten minutes."

"Ten minutes that he couldn't take his eyes off of you."

Austin narrowed his eyes. *You got a problem with that, scumbag?*

Darcy's laugh was short and forced. "Don't be silly. He was probably looking at the camera, not me. I'll have to remind the guys to ignore the camera and act naturally."

Gregori crossed his arms. "Have you been seeing him?"

She shrugged. "A few times, but it was work related."

Austin snorted. *More pleasure than work, sweetheart.*

Gregori frowned. "I don't want you to get hurt."

Darcy scoffed. "Don't worry. Nothing's going on."

Austin ground his teeth. *Nothing?* For the last two weeks, he'd been haunted with the memories of kissing her mouth, touching her breasts, and feeling her sweet rump pressed against his groin. Was that what she called nothing?

"What's up?" Garrett peeked into his room.

Austin jumped in his chair, then quickly turned off

the volume on his laptop. "Dammit, Garrett. Give me a warning, will you? I don't want my roommate to see what I'm doing."

"What are you doing?"

"Making sure all the cameras are working."

"Cool." Garrett shut the door and paced toward the computer. "Anything interesting? Who's that—the host and director?"

"Yeah, but it's really boring."

"Turn it up," Garrett urged. "I want to hear."

With an inward wince, Austin turned on the volume.

"I thought those ladies were going to tear this room apart when they found out about the mortals," Gregori said.

Darcy sighed. "Yeah, it wasn't pretty."

Austin relaxed. He was no longer the topic of conversation.

"I just hope your boss will understand," Gregori said.

"Yeah." Darcy headed for the door and turned off the lights.

Austin switched to the camera in the hallway. The sound was faint, so he turned the volume on high.

"I thought for sure I'd be able to tell the mortals from the Vamps." Gregori strolled toward the foyer.

"No one can smell them because of the anklets," Darcy said as she walked beside him. "They work like a charm. Even the vampires are wearing placebo ones. That way, when they're all wearing swimsuits, no one will be able to tell who's who."

"Holy anklet." Austin rolled down his sock and examined the anklet. "I thought it might have some kind of homing device, but it looks like it's just a chemical thing to block our smell."

Garret nodded. "I thought those vampires in the limo seemed too . . . indifferent."

Austin pulled his anklet off. "I'll give this to Emma tomorrow when she comes with the caterer. She can have it analyzed." Of course, without the anklet, he'd smell like a tasty morsel to the vampires.

"Are you sure you want to take that off?" Garrett asked.

"I'll get another one. I'll tell the director I lost mine."

"You mean Miss Darcy? You still think she's human?"

"Yes. I don't know why she's involved with these vampires, but she'll do her best to protect us from getting bit."

Garrett snorted. "You trust her more than I do. You know what the contract said—DVN isn't liable for puncture wounds."

Austin laughed. "I have no intention of getting bit." But he did have a good reason now for seeking out Darcy. And he knew exactly where to find her. The pool house.

As Darcy wandered about the greenhouse, she let the warm humid air caress her face and melt away all the tension that had built over the course of the evening. Shelves like stair steps lined each side of the path, each shelf filled with pots of brightly colored flowers—impatiens, lilies, peonies, and more exotic flowers she didn't recognize.

One side of the greenhouse was devoted to roses. A few climbing roses had been trained to cover an archway that began the path down the rose garden. In the middle, against the wall, a small fountain trickled water into a pool.

Toward the back of the greenhouse, a small tropical area thrived with lemon and banana trees. A stone bench sat under a willowy palm. Darcy sat and eased off her shoes. This would be the ideal setting for testing the next two qualifications—good manners and charming speech.

"Darcy!"

She spotted Maggie coming toward her. "Hi. Did you get the men settled in their rooms?"

"Yes. And I kept the mortals together like you asked."

"Thanks. I don't know how I'd manage without you." As long as she had Maggie's help, Darcy could avoid spending any time with the mortals. Or rather, one mortal in particular.

Maggie stopped next to her. "Actually, that's what I needed to talk to you about. Tomorrow night, I'm supposed to go back to DVN for another audition."

"Oh, that's right." Darcy gave her an encouraging smile. "Don't worry. You'll be great."

Maggie winced. "I'm awfully nervous. I'm going to read opposite Don Orlando. I hope he likes me."

"I—I'm sure he will." Darcy stifled a groan. She hadn't told her friend about Don Orlando's affair with Corky and Tiffany and God knows how many other women. She couldn't stand the thought of destroying Maggie's dream. Maggie was always the optimist who claimed everything happened just as it should. Even though Darcy couldn't agree with that, she hadn't realized until now how much she needed Maggie to believe it. As long as Maggie believed in happy endings, it still seemed possible.

"I think we should film in here tomorrow night." Darcy stood and picked up her shoes.

Maggie walked alongside her. "You want to test the men's good manners here?"

"Yes, I thought—aagh!" Darcy slipped in a puddle of water.

"Are you all right?" Maggie reached out to steady her. "You shouldn't walk in your hose. It's too slippery."

"Yeah, and I'll tear them up, too. Just a minute." Darcy wiggled out of her pantyhose, then stuck them into her shoes. "You know, this is exactly what we need. We'll make a big, muddy puddle in the middle of a path tomorrow night and see how the guys manage to keep the women from muddying their shoes."

"Oh, I like that! It's like that story about Sir Francis Drake putting down a cloak so the queen could walk over it."

"Exactly." Darcy carried her shoes as she walked barefoot. "We can do a whole obstacle course here in the greenhouse. And I think we'll have Lady Pamela conduct the tests. She seems to be the expert on propriety."

Maggie snorted. "That's true."

They exited the greenhouse and stopped by the stairwell. Maggie opened the door. "I'm going to the servants' floor. You want to join us in the parlor?"

"No, I'm tired. Good luck with your audition tomorrow."

"Thanks." Maggie slipped into the stairwell. The heavy door banged shut. Darcy closed her eyes and felt the cool breeze against her face. The first night was over. Time to relax. With a sigh, she headed across the roof to the pool house.

A splash of water drew her attention. There was a man in the pool doing laps, his long, lean body zooming neatly through the water. He exuded the perfect combination of strength and grace. She stepped closer. His back was bare and tanned, his shoulders broad. The muscles in his back and shoulders rippled with each stroke. His legs were long and powerful.

He had to be mortal. Vampires were never that tanned. And nothing this beautiful could last an eternity. Even the most spectacular of sunsets could only last a few moments. For this mortal, this was his moment, the culmination of youth, strength, and grace—all the more beautiful because his zenith was short-lived, and this moment in time was rare.

Darcy's eyes filled with tears. The vampires had it all wrong. They thought they were the beautiful ones because they managed to stay young forever. They didn't realize that an eternity of youth and beauty became cheap when it was stolen, and meaningless when it was the norm.

The man reached the end of the pool and shoved his thick, wet hair back from his face. Darcy caught her breath. Oh God, she should have known it was him. Her shoes slipped from her hand and clattered onto the cement.

He turned toward the noise and smiled at her.

Her knees turned rubbery. He pushed off the edge and swam toward her. She glanced toward the pool house. It would look cowardly if she ran away. But darn it, she'd been so determined to stay away from him.

He stopped and rested a tanned forearm on the tiled edge of the pool. "Hi, Darcy."

Just the sound of Adam saying her name made her feel warm and light, like she could fly to the sun and never be cold again. "Hi."

"The water's great. Want to join me?"

She scoffed. "In case you haven't noticed, I'm wearing a dress."

"Oh, I noticed. I can't take my eyes off of you."

Her face grew warm. "Actually, I need to talk to you about that. You shouldn't look at me, because I'm usually very close to the camera."

He tilted his head, still watching her. "There's no camera now. Just you and me."

"And I have some work to do. Good night." She leaned over to pick up her shoes.

"How does that dress come off? Is there a zipper in the back?"

She jerked straight, forgetting the shoes. "Excuse me?"

"You need to take off the dress to swim."

"I'm not swimming with you. The water's far too cold."

"Oh. In that case . . ." He planted his palms on the tiled edge. The muscles in his arms and shoulders bunched as he hauled himself out of the water.

Darcy stepped back. Her mouth fell open.

He slowly straightened. Water glistened on his tanned skin. Rivulets sluiced down his body, seeking the easiest path around well-defined pectoral and abdominal muscles. His chest hair lay flat and wet against his chest. It appeared dark brown like the hair on his head. Moisture and darkness had combined to hide the blond highlights that normally made him appear golden as a sun god. Tonight, he looked darker and even more dangerous to her peace of mind.

"We'll find something warmer." He padded to the hot tub.

Speechless, Darcy watched him walk by. His cotton boxer-style swimsuit would never be classified as sexy, but the wet material had glued itself to his body. As he passed by, she became very aware of how low the swimsuit rested on his narrow hips. The material clung to his rump, clearly outlining each buttock and the muscles that flexed with each step he took.

The waistband was so low, she could see two dimples on his lower back. Oh God, that brought his total dimple count up to four. And made her want to examine every inch of him for more.

He stepped into the hot tub and punched a button on the control panel. With a whirring sound, the water began to swirl about. He smiled at her as he settled on a seat. "Feels great."

Steam rose from the water, promising her warmth and comfort, an end to the chill that had tormented her for four long years.

"Come on, Darcy," he spoke quietly.

Oh, God, he was the devil. He knew just how to tempt her and torture her at the same time. She walked slowly toward him. "If I was judging the contest, you would definitely be the winner. But I'm not, so you're wasting your time."

"I don't give a damn about the contest. And time with you is never wasted. Come in, and I'll show you."

She snorted. "Oh, you're good. But there's no purpose for this." Only heartache for wanting something she couldn't have.

"No purpose?" He frowned at her. "What about friendship?"

She laughed. "You just want to be friends? I've heard that one before."

He grinned. "So have I. But I mean it, Darcy. Don't you need someone to talk to?"

How could she confide in a mortal that she lived among vampires? "I'm sorry." She turned to go.

"Wait." He lunged across the spa, causing a wave of hot water to spill over the edge and warm her bare feet. "I need to tell you something. It's about the anklet I'm supposed to wear."

She turned back to him. "What about it?"

"I—I lost it, somehow. Is it important?"

She swallowed. More than important. It was essential for keeping him safe. "I'll make sure you get another one."

"What exactly is it?" His eyes looked wide with innocence.

"Didn't Laszlo tell you?"

Adam shrugged. "Something about pheromones and how we're attracted to each other by our nose."

"That's true." And Adam always smelled wonderful—warm, healthy, and sexy.

"Come and sit a while." He patted the tile edge of the hot tub. "Soak your feet and relax. It's been a long night."

She found herself smiling. "You don't give up, do you?"

"Not with you." He smiled back. "Look, I'll keep my distance." He floated back to the far side of the tub.

Darcy removed her sparkly jacket and dropped it on a patio chair. "Just for a little while." She sat carefully on the edge making sure she didn't snag the silk sheath on the rough cement. She dangled her feet over the side, but the hot, bubbly water felt so wonderful, she immersed her legs to just below the knees. Her narrow dress rode up to the middle of her thighs.

"Feels good?" he asked softly.

"Yes."

"Did everything go well tonight for the show?"

"Yes."

"Are you sleeping in the pool house?"

What a rascal. "Yes."

"Alone?"

"Yes."

He grinned. "You're very agreeable tonight."

She suppressed a laugh. "Yes." And now, he'd ask to spend the night with her, thinking she would continue to say *yes*.

"Have you ever been in love?"

She blinked. That had surprised her. "Yes. I suppose." She sighed. "I'm not sure. Maybe I just wanted to be in love."

"Did he love you?"

"He said he did. We were together about a year in college. I thought we were engaged, but—" She shrugged. "Obviously, we disagreed on that."

"He was stupid to let you go."

"I think he was a little too young to commit himself."

Adam snorted. "The guy was stupid."

"That's a bit harsh, don't you think?"

"No. Any man who would let you go has got to be stupid."

"He was just immature."

"That's a nice word for stupid."

Darcy laughed. "Okay, he was stupid." Surprisingly enough, the declaration made her feel great. "So, I guess the big question now is how intelligent are you?"

He smiled slowly, his dimples deepening. "I'm smart enough."

And living in a different world than her, too. She really shouldn't flirt with the poor guy. Unfortunately, he was damned near irresistible. Somehow, she would have to resist.

He moved toward her. His hand curled around the instep of her left foot. "Can I give you a foot massage?"

"N—" The word died in her throat as his strong fingers pressed into the sole of her foot. Oh, boy, was he good. "Yes."

He massaged slow circles down her foot. "Feels good?"

She sighed and closed her eyes. "Yes."

He tugged gently on her toes. "You're doing a great job with the show."

His compliment spread through her like a ray of sunshine. "Thank you."

He switched to her right foot. "Can I tell you a secret?"

She opened her eyes. "Don't tell me you're an axe murderer."

He smiled as he continued to massage her foot. "No, I'm not. Believe it or not, I'm kinda . . . sensitive for a guy."

She snorted. "You can't be gay. Not the way you kiss."

His eyes twinkled. "Are you sure? You might need another sample for verification."

She laughed. "You are definitely a lady's man."

"That's true. About my secret . . ." His hands skimmed up the back of her legs to her calves. He massaged the muscles there.

She lifted her eyebrows. "If you're making a move on me, that's hardly a secret."

He rested a cheek against her knee. "The secret is I can sorta tune in on whatever people are feeling."

"You mean you're good at reading body language?"

"No." He gave her a worried look. "I can just sense it."

She leaned back. "You mean you're empathic?"

"Yeah." He scooted closer 'til his chest was pressed against her legs. "Do you know what I sense from you?"

"Could it be doubt?" She gave him a skeptical look. "Or let me guess. You have this sudden sensation that I want to sleep with you."

He grinned. "You think this is part of a pickup routine?"

She nodded. "But you get points for originality."

He kissed her left knee. "Thanks. But seriously, I get the impression that you're trapped somewhere you don't want to be."

She stiffened. Good God, maybe he was empathic.

He watched her carefully. "Is that true, Darcy? Do you need some help?"

She swallowed hard. "I—no. I'm fine."

"There's nothing you want to tell me?"

Her eyes filled with tears. Now, the knight in shining armor comes along? What a damned cruel world. Why couldn't she have met him four years ago? He was everything she wanted. Everything she needed.

He stood in front of her. Hot water dripped off him onto her thighs. She wanted to melt with him.

He touched her shoulders. "Let me help you."

She stood. She was a foot or so taller since she was standing on the ledge for sitting. She looked down at him and ran her fingers into his hair. "Adam, you're everything I ever wanted, but it's too late."

"No." He grabbed her around the waist and pulled her off the ledge. "It's never too late." He sank into the hot, bubbly water, taking her with him.

And the last of her resistance melted away.

Chapter 12

Austin pulled Darcy onto his lap and covered her face with kisses. He aimed his kisses closer and closer to her mouth. She turned her head to meet him, and the heat flared between them. Their tongues entwined. Their arms wrapped around each other in a tight embrace.

And still, they weren't close enough. He lifted her slightly and pushed up her dress so she could straddle his lap. They held each other tight, her breasts pressed against his chest. He could feel her erratic breathing as she trembled in his arms.

"Sweetheart." He nuzzled her neck. He'd wanted so badly for her to trust him, but somehow, along the way, that desire had grown into something more powerful. He needed her to love him. He needed to protect her. He needed to keep her forever.

She skimmed her hands across his shoulders, then down his back. "You're so beautiful."

Smiling, he rubbed his chin against her soft hair. "Shame on you. That was my line."

She leaned back on his lap. "Shame on you for dragging me in here while I'm wearing my best dress."

"We can take care of that." He sought the zipper in the back. As his hand ran down her spine, her back arched.

She gave him a teasing smile. "You realize this dress is not supposed to be in hot water."

"Then we'll move it to the cold water cycle." He tugged the dress over her head and tossed it into the swimming pool.

Darcy laughed. "Great. Chlorine. That's a big help."

He studied the wet bra that clung to her skin. "I'm happy with the results." He brushed a thumb over a nipple, and it puckered. He circled the pebbled skin 'til the tip hardened into a tight nub. With a moan, Darcy closed her eyes.

He nibbled up her neck to her ear, then whispered, "I want to taste you."

She answered by feathering kisses along his cheek and jaw. That had to be a yes. He kissed her deeply. His heart pounded in his ears. His groin swelled, demanding attention. He unhooked her bra, slid it off, and tossed it onto the cement. A sudden breeze swirled the mist from the hot tub around her, making her look almost unreal. A magical vision of beauty, too perfect for any man to hold on to.

Her eyes flickered open. "Is something wrong?"

For a second, he thought there was a red glint to her eyes, but it had to be some kind of weird reflection.

His own photos were always coming out with red eyes.

"You're perfect." He cupped her breasts, then leaned forward to press a kiss onto the upper swell of her left breast. He could feel the pounding of her heart. His own heart was thundering in his ears. It seemed to grow louder and louder.

He grabbed her waist and lifted her 'til her breasts were even with his mouth. He drew a nipple into his mouth and suckled. Groaning, she arched her back. His hands moved lower, pressing her hips against his stomach. He slid his hands into her underwear and cupped her derriere. She reacted by rocking against him, rubbing herself against his stomach.

His erection nearly exploded. With gritted teeth, he rested his cheek against her breasts and fought for control. That was when he realized that the night was much lighter than it had been before. And the roar in his ears wasn't coming from him. He looked up and winced. That whirring sound was unmistakable. Suddenly, a beam of light shot down and illuminated the hot tub.

"What?" Darcy stiffened. She looked up, but Austin blocked her with his hand.

"Don't." He squinted up through the light. "It's a chopper."

"What?" She gave him a frantic look. "A helicopter?"

"Yes." Austin cursed. "I should have heard it coming."

"Oh my gosh!" Darcy covered her mouth with a trembling hand. "I told Bernie to rent a helicopter, but I didn't think he could do it tonight. This is terrible!"

More terrible than she realized. As far as Austin could tell, he and Darcy were being filmed. He lowered them both into the water up to their chins. "I'll take care of this. Whatever you do, don't look up."

She moaned. "I'll be ruined. I'll never work again."

"Trust me. I'll get you out of here."

"How? I'm practically naked."

"I brought a big towel with me from my room. Wait here. Stay low, and don't look up."

"Okay." She hugged herself and kept her chin down.

Austin climbed from the hot tub and strode toward the patio chair where he'd left a towel. He kept his face turned away from the helicopter and hurried back to the hot tub. He stretched out the towel to conceal Darcy. She climbed from the tub, and he wrapped the towel around her. The helicopter was close enough now to cause a strong wind that whipped at the towel and made her shiver. She hunched her shoulders and ducked her head down.

"Hold on." He grabbed her jacket off the patio chair and draped it over her head. He located her bra and shoes and handed them to her. Then, he fished her dress out of the swimming pool.

And still the helicopter hovered overhead. A beam of light followed Austin's every movement. He handed Darcy her soggy dress and saw the panic on her face.

"Don't let it get to you," he yelled over the roar of the whirring blades. "They don't know who you are. Where are the other ladies staying?"

"On the servants' floor, three flights down."

He glanced toward the east stairwell. "Fine. We'll go there. Everyone will think you're one of the judges. You can return to the pool house later."

"Okay."

Austin led her toward the stairs. The spotlight from the helicopter picked them up. Austin glanced down. With the light behind him, his body cast a long shadow on the cement.

He halted with a jerk.

Darcy stopped. "What's wrong?"

He stood there, unable to answer. All the air had been sucked out of his lungs. All the blood leached from his head. The ground swayed, and he stumbled to the side.

"Are you all right?" She reached out to touch his arm.

He lurched back. No, this couldn't be true. He glanced down at the ground once more. His shadow was there, alone, mocking him for being so blind. Such a stupid fool.

"Adam?" She looked so worried. Hell, why was she worried about him? She was the one with the problem. Darcy Newhart had no shadow. She was fucking dead.

"Are you all right?" she yelled over the noise.

He swallowed hard. "Go on without me. I—I'll make sure we didn't leave any clues behind." Or proof that he'd been there, consorting with the enemy.

"Okay." She ran to the stairwell and went inside.

The door banged shut and he stood there, staring at it while the damned helicopter whirred overhead. His stomach churned. Holy necrophilia. He'd made out with a dead woman.

Slowly, he realized the helicopter was moving away. He scanned the pool area and noticed his flip-flops by a patio chair. He grabbed them and paced across the roof. The half-moon shone down on him, taunting him with the evil truth. Darcy was a creature of the night.

"No!" He hurled a flip-flop at the moon. It flew over the wall and disappeared. He ran toward the wall, throwing the other flip-flop. "Dammit, no!"

He ran down the stairs, then realized he couldn't bear to spend the night in the penthouse. Not with all those vampires. Not when his own Darcy—

He took the elevator to the ground floor, then ran outside onto the sidewalk. He ignored the grit of cement against his bare feet. He kept running 'til he reached Central Park. And still he ran. He ran until he was sweating and gasping for air.

He slowed and collapsed onto a bench. Dammit to hell. There was no running from the awful truth.

Darcy was a vampire.

"I think I made a terrible mistake." Darcy stood in Vanda's bedroom, shivering in wet underwear and a towel.

"Here." Vanda tossed her another towel. "Dry off while I find you something to wear." She rummaged through a dresser drawer. "These should suit you." She picked out a pair of white cotton panties. "What kind of mistake?"

"I got overly friendly with Adam in the hot tub."

Vanda's eyes widened. "Oh. In that case—" She dropped the white panties and picked up a red silken thong. "This is more like it."

With a snort, Darcy grabbed the white panties and pulled them on. "I shouldn't have done it. I had to be out of my mind."

"It's called lust, dear." Vanda tossed her a T-shirt and some pajama bottoms. "Nothing wrong with it."

"It's very wrong!" Darcy pulled on the T-shirt.

"He's a mortal. It could never work." She slumped on Vanda's bed.

Vanda sat beside her. "You have feelings for him?"

Darcy's eyes filled with tears. "I tried to fight it. I know any kind of lasting relationship with him is impossible."

"With love, anything's possible."

Darcy shook her head. "Not this."

Vanda stood and paced across the room. "Did I ever tell you what happened to me?"

"No." Darcy wiped her face. Vanda was always supportive, but she rarely confided anything personal.

"I came from a small village just south of Krakow. We were a large family. Very poor. When my mother died in 1935, I became a mother to my younger brothers and sisters."

"That must have been difficult," Darcy murmured.

Vanda shrugged. "The worst was yet to come. When the German tanks moved toward our village, the men prepared a resistance. My father begged me to escape with my two younger sisters. I packed some food, and we fled south to the Carpathian Mountains. I . . . never saw my father or brothers again."

Darcy blinked to keep from crying. "I'm so sorry."

"The trip was very hard on my thirteen-year-old sister," Vanda continued. "By the time I found a shallow cave, Frieda could barely walk. I gave her the last of our food and water. My fifteen-year-old sister, Marta, left to get water and didn't return. I wanted to search for her, but I was afraid if I left Frieda, she would die. Finally, though, I had to go. I found a stream and filled our water bags. I was headed back to our cave when night fell. When Marta stepped from the shadows, I was so happy to see her. But she just stood there, so pale, with an odd look on her face.

"She swooshed toward me so fast, I didn't realize what was happening. She knocked me down and sank her fangs into my neck. I was barely conscious when she carried me—she was suddenly very strong—to a deep cave and introduced me to the vampire who had transformed her. Sigismund. He transformed me that night."

Darcy shuddered. "I'm so sorry."

Vanda sat on the bed. "The next evening, I rushed back to my little sister to see how she was. She had died. All alone."

"Oh, no. How awful." Darcy touched Vanda's shoulder.

Vanda's eyes glimmered with unshed tears. "I found a good purpose for the hunger that plagued me every night. I fed off Nazis and left many of them to die in southern Poland."

Darcy swallowed. "I'm sorry you've suffered so much."

Vanda snorted. "You think I told you all that for pity? What I want to say is I would go through all the pain and horror a million times over if it could only bring my sister back. If you love this Adam, you should embrace the feeling, no matter what. There is nothing more sacred than love."

At noon the next day, Austin wandered into the penthouse kitchen and found Emma heating up some Chinese food. He passed her the anklet. "We need to get this analyzed."

"No problem." She dropped it into her tote bag and looked him over. "You look like shit."

"I feel like shit." He sat at the table.

She spooned some sweet and sour shrimp and fried rice onto a plate and set it before him. "Feel like talking?"

"No." He motioned to a black and green bruise along her forearm. "What happened to you?"

"A bit of a tussle. Nothing I couldn't handle."

He narrowed his eyes. "You went hunting again, didn't you?"

"Eat your food before it gets cold."

"I told you not to go hunting alone."

She rested a hand on her hip. "And who would go with me when you and Garrett are on assignment here? Alyssa isn't up to it."

"Wait until we're done here. It'll only be a week or two."

Her mouth thinned. "I don't like to wait. Besides, I managed just fine on my own."

"You killed one?"

"Killed what?" George wandered into the kitchen.

Emma smiled. "I killed a roach in the laundry room. But don't worry. When I come back, I'll bring some insecticide."

"Good." George heaped his plate full. "I hate roaches."

"I cannot abide any sort of pest." Emma gave Austin a pointed look.

Pest. She would add Darcy to her list of pests. Holy shit. What was he going to do? How could he add Darcy to his list of vampires? It would make her a target for termination. Wasn't getting murdered once in her life enough? He recalled all the tapes he'd enjoyed watching. She'd been so clever, so happy, so full of life.

"You're not eating," Emma reminded him.

"I lost my appetite." *I've lost my heart.* Holy shit. Reality had become a nightmare. Did it feel this awful for Darcy, too?

With help from her cameramen, Darcy set up the obstacle course in the greenhouse.

Bernie added some potting soil to the puddle to make it muddier. "Guess what, Miss Newhart? I got that aerial footage you wanted." He exchanged a grin with the other cameraman.

Bart snickered as he moved potted plants away from the puddle.

Darcy watched them both carefully. They didn't glance her way at all. "You managed to get a helicopter that fast?"

Bernie snorted. "The guy told me he was booked solid for three months. But after a little mind control, he was much more helpful."

Bart laughed. "Yeah, he even forgot to charge us."

Darcy winced. She hated the way vampires invaded people's minds. "So, everything went well?"

"Oh, yeah. Just great." Bernie shot Bart a knowing look.

"Okay." Darcy exhaled in relief. They weren't smirking at her. They must not realize she was the woman in the hot tub.

"Hello?" Lady Pamela called from the greenhouse entrance. "I was told to come here."

"Yes." Darcy took Lady Pamela through the greenhouse, explaining how the obstacle course worked. "Don't worry. I'll be close by with the cameramen."

She twisted her silk reticule in her hands. "Where will the other ladies be?"

"They'll be watching the whole thing on the servants' floor. We rigged up a direct feed to the television in the parlor. They'll see and hear everything."

"And when it's over, we decide which men to eliminate?"

"Yes, two men." Darcy led Lady Pamela to the stairwell. The cameramen followed. "You're the judge tonight. The other ladies will most likely follow your suggestions on who should leave."

Lady Pamela nodded thoughtfully. "I shall do my best to discover which ones are mortal, so we can rid ourselves of their horrid presence."

Darcy led her down one flight of stairs. "Your actual goal is to test them on good manners and speech."

"I understand. But obviously, it will be the mortals who possess bad manners and speech."

Darcy sighed. "Right." She exited onto the top floor of the penthouse. "Gregori brought the men upstairs to the billiards room. They're right here." She motioned to the room next door.

Bart and Bernie rushed in with their cameras.

Lady Pamela glided in and curtsied to the ten contestants. "How do you do?"

Darcy hovered by the door, watching. Some of the men bowed in return. She scanned the room 'til she spotted Adam. He stood quietly in a corner, next to Garth, regarding the other men with an intense look in his eyes. Anger? Had something upset him?

"Good evening," Gregori began. "Tonight, each of you will take a stroll through the greenhouse with Lady Pamela. You each drew a number from a hat. That number will determine the order for tonight's proceedings. Who has number one?"

One of the male Vamps stepped forward. "I do."

Gregori checked the Vamp's number. "Lady Pamela, your first escort is Roberto from Buenos Aires."

Lady Pamela curtsied. "Charmed."

Roberto escorted her toward the stairwell and opened the door for her. Bernie ran ahead to record the couple from the front. Darcy followed with the cameraman Bart. As they ascended the stairs, Lady Pamela dropped her handkerchief. Roberto picked it up and presented it to her with a bow. He made it through all the obstacles in the greenhouse without incident.

They returned to the billiards room for contestant number two. Otto of Düsseldorf was huge with the neck and shoulders of a professional linebacker. Darcy secretly thought of him as the Vamp on steroids. Obviously, he planned to spend eternity exercising his muscles. He successfully returned Lady Pamela's hanky when she dropped it. They proceeded into the greenhouse.

"Oh, my!" Lady Pamela stopped in front of the manmade mud puddle. "Whatever will we do?"

"Ya, dat is one big mud puddle." Otto had apparently forgotten to exercise the muscle in his head.

"Oh, dear. I would hate to soil my slippers." Lady Pamela looked helpless, which in her case didn't require any acting.

"Do not fret, *fraulein*. De Otto is here." He hefted her high into the air so suddenly that she squealed. "Ya, you like my big, bulging muscles, don't you?"

Darcy rolled her eyes.

Lady Pamela giggled.

Otto strode through the mud and continued down the path.

"Begging your pardon." Lady Pamela smiled coyly at him. "You can put me down now."

"Oh, you are light like de feather. De Otto forgot he was carrying you." He set her down. "De Otto is very strong." He flexed his biceps.

"Oh, my." Lady Pamela touched the tip of her finger on his bulging muscle. "That is impressive."

"All de ladies like de bulges." He winked at her. "Just vait till I get you into de Otto Zone."

Darcy covered her mouth to muffle any gagging noises. Otto successfully maneuvered all his bulges through the rest of the obstacle course and returned Lady Pamela to the billiards room.

Contestants four and five were Ahmed from Cairo and Pierre from Brussels. They both made it successfully through the course. Number six was Nicholas from Chicago, one of the mortals. He picked up Lady Pamela's hanky on cue. Then they approached the mud puddle. Nicholas whipped off his jacket and laid it over the puddle.

"Oh, how chivalrous." Lady Pamela watched approvingly.

"May I?" He lifted her in his arms, stepped onto his jacket, and skidded forward in the mud. His arms flailed. Lady Pamela flew into the air, screeching, then landed in the mud puddle with a great splat.

"Aagh!" She scrambled to her feet. "Look at me!" Her face and arms were speckled with mud. Globs of mud drooled down her gown. "You clumsy oaf! This is horrid, simply horrid!"

Inwardly wincing, Darcy let Lady Pamela vent her rage for a good five minutes. After all, a little drama was good for the ratings. "Okay." She finally stepped in. "Pamela, why don't you go downstairs and change gowns so we can continue with the show?"

She sniffed. "That's Lady Pamela to you." She stalked off toward the stairwell.

"Nicholas, you might as well get changed, too." She handed him his muddy jacket.

His shoulders slumped. Mud dripped off his slacks and white dress shirt. "I'm not gonna win the million dollars, am I?"

"That will be decided by the judges." Darcy watched him trudge toward the stairs. As she waited for Lady Pamela to return, Darcy realized this would be the ideal time during the editing stage to insert Pamela's bio.

After thirty minutes, Lady Pamela returned to the billiards room, wearing a new gown. Contestant number seven was asked to step forward.

It was Adam.

Austin had a good idea what was expected of him. Whether or not he wanted to do it was another question. He was tempted to act like a complete ass and get booted off the show. That would certainly alleviate the agony of being near Darcy. He could see her standing next to the cameraman. He could hear her sweet voice. But he could never have her. She was dead.

He bowed his head to Lady Pamela. "Good evening."

She motioned toward the stairwell. "Will you take a turn with me?"

"Delighted," he grumbled. He lifted his arm so she could hook her cold, dead hand around his elbow.

They climbed the stairs. One cameraman stayed in front of them, while Darcy and the second cameraman trailed behind.

"Lovely weather we're having," Lady Pamela said in her snooty voice. "I simply adore a warm summer evening."

"Yes." Frustration swelled inside him. He was sick of this pretense. "But in the summer, the nights are too short."

"True. Winter nights do give us more time."

They had reached the landing on the stairs. Austin glanced back. Darcy was giving him a puzzled look. Too bad.

"Maybe you should travel to the southern hemisphere for the summer." He continued up the stairs. "They're having their winter season now."

"Really?" Lady Pamela looked intrigued as she followed him. "You mean they're having longer nights down there?"

"Sure. Or you could go to Antarctica. The nights there are six months long. They say the penguins are very well dressed."

Lady Pamela giggled. "You silly man! No one lives in Antarctica." She dropped her hankie on the top landing. "Oh, dear."

Austin handed it to her and opened the stairwell door.

"Why, thank you." She glided out onto the roof. "Have you ever been to the southern hemisphere?"

"No, I've spent most of my time in America and Eastern Europe." He escorted her into the greenhouse.

"Ah. Were you born in Europe?"

"No. I was working there."

"Indeed. In what capacity, may I ask?"

What the heck. He smiled at the lady vampire. "I was an international spy."

She burst into giggles and slapped his arm. "My word, you say the silliest things."

He glanced back. Darcy was giving him a skeptical look.

"Oh, dear." Lady Pamela stopped in front of a mud puddle. "Whatever will we do?"

"Allow me." Austin stepped onto the wooden bench between two potted plants. Lady Pamela remained where she was, looking helpless. He gritted his teeth. He'd had to touch her old dead carcass. "Excuse me." He grabbed her around the waist, lifted her over the puddle, and then set her down on dry cement.

"Why, thank you. That was very clever of you."

He stifled a groan. It sure wasn't rocket science. Obviously, the purpose of this test was to see which man could best take care of a bunch of ditzy, dead females.

The next problem arose when they arrived at a stone bench under a dwarf palm tree. Lady Pamela announced she wanted to sit for a spell. While she hesitated, Austin noticed the bench was covered with dead leaves. He scooped off the leaves and covered the bench with his jacket. Lady Pamela smiled at him as she sat.

Austin sat beside her. Darcy and her damned cameraman moved closer. The whole situation irked him. Here he was, forced to flirt with a lady vampire while his beautiful, dead Darcy eavesdropped. "I must confess, Lady Pamela, that your gowns are the most exquisite I have ever seen."

"Oh, my!" She beamed at him. "How wonderfully kind of you."

"My pleasure. I think it's so pathetic when women try to dress like men." Darcy stood there in her khaki slacks and T-shirt. She crossed her arms and glared at him.

"Oh, I couldn't agree more." Lady Pamela stood. "Shall we continue? The roses smell heavenly."

Austin grabbed his jacket off the bench. He shook it out as he followed the lady vampire to the rose garden.

"I would dearly love a rose," she murmured.

Of course she would. "Which color would you like?"

She smiled at him. "A pink one, if you would be so kind."

"No problem." He eased around the big clay pots until he located a budding pink rose. He snapped the stem and carried the rose back to Lady Pamela.

She sighed. "I do hope it doesn't have too many thorns."

He took the hint and started pinching off the thorns. The last one proved a tough one. He managed to rip it off but ended up with a tiny hole in his index finger.

"Oh, my." Lady Pamela's eyes grew wide. "Is that . . . *blood?*"

"It's nothing. Just a flesh wound," he said dryly as he handed her the rose.

She dropped the rose on the ground and moved closer to him. "Let me see your bleeding finger." She licked her lips.

Austin stepped back. "I'm okay. It was just a little nick."

Her eyes gleamed. "Let me kiss it and make it better." She reached for his hand.

He jumped back.

She bared her teeth. "Just a little taste."

"Cut!" Darcy leaped between them. "Pamela, go to the servants' parlor and have a . . . snack. You'll feel much better."

She glared at Darcy a moment, then sniffed. "That's Lady Pamela to you." She turned on her heel and marched off.

Darcy heaved a sigh of relief. "Adam, why don't you come with me? I have a first-aid kit in the pool house."

He glowered at her. "I don't need first aid."

She glanced at the cameramen. "Guys, go back to the billiard room. Lady Pamela will be ready to continue after her snack."

The cameramen strode toward the stairwell.

"Come on." Darcy reached for Austin's arm.

He stepped back.

She frowned at him. "Will you come with me, please?"

He looked away. The sight of her was so painful. How could he mourn her death when she kept appearing in front of him? "It's nothing. You're not liable for puncture wounds, remember?"

She snorted. "True, but I'd rather you didn't get hurt."

Too late. He was already nursing the worst heartache he'd ever had the misery of encountering.

"This way." She motioned toward the pool house.

Reluctantly, he followed her. They passed the swimming pool. He glanced at the hot tub. Dammit.

She gave him a worried look. "You were having an odd conversation with Lady Pamela."

About the length of nights? Was Darcy concerned that he knew about vampires? Or that he knew about her? Well, wasn't that too bad. She'd let him kiss her several times. Just when in the course of their relationship had she planned on telling him that she was dead? "I was bull-shitting her."

Darcy's eyebrows rose. "Why? Are you suddenly interested in winning the contest and the money?"

"I don't give a damn about the money. In fact, I'm beginning to wonder why I'm here at all."

She opened the door to the pool house. "I thought . . ." She closed her eyes briefly. "Maybe I was mistaken."

She'd thought he was interested in her? He had been, dammit, until he'd found out the truth. He wandered into the pool house. The main room was a combination den and kitchen. White wicker furniture was strewn about, covered with cushions in a tropical print. Darcy's papers were on the kitchen table. The night before, on the way to the swimming pool, he had snuck into the pool house and hidden a camera over the front door. He hadn't used it yet. The last thing he wanted was to watch Darcy drinking blood or falling into her death sleep.

"Over here." She wandered into the tiny kitchen. The only appliances consisted of a small refrigerator and microwave. She turned on the water over the single sink. "Come and rinse off your finger."

He stuck his hand in the cold water.

She handed him a towel. "Something's wrong. I can tell. You won't even look at me."

He shrugged and dried his hand.

"Do you really not approve of women wearing pants?"

"No. I just told Lady Pamela what she wanted to hear."

Darcy stiffened and frowned at him. "Is that what you do? Tell women what they want to hear?"

He dropped the towel on the counter. "I need to go."

"You need a Band-Aid." She opened the first-aid box.

"I don't need anything! It's just a little prick."

Anger flared in her eyes. "Your finger or you?" She ripped open a Band-Aid package.

He seethed with frustration. Dammit, he hadn't known she was dead when he pursued her. But she had known. She should have stopped him.

"Give me your finger." She reached for his hand.

He stepped back. "Give me the Band-Aid."

She tossed it on the counter. "Fine. Bandage yourself."

"I will." He struggled to put it on with his left hand.

She glared at him. "I don't understand you. You keep asking me questions and saying things like you know too much . . . stuff."

"You're imagining that."

"Am I? All I ever hear from you is how I should trust you and confide in you, and when I finally feel like I can trust you, you turn away."

He gritted his teeth. "I haven't gone away. I'm still here."

"You won't even look at me or touch me. What happened?"

He finished attaching the bandage. "Nothing. I . . . decided this wasn't going to work."

"*You* decided? I don't have any say in the matter?"

No, you're dead. "Good-bye." He strode toward the door.

"Adam! Why did you do this to me?"

He paused at the door and looked back. His heart squeezed in his chest. Holy crap. Her eyes were full of tears. He was making her cry. *Dead women don't cry.*

She stalked toward him. "Since you're so sensitive and empathic, tell me what I'm feeling now." A tear ran down her cheek, and it struck him like an ice pick ripping at his heart.

He looked away. "I can't."

"You can't feel it? Or you can't admit that you're the one causing me so much pain?"

He flinched. "I'm sorry." He ran toward the stairwell, but realized he couldn't face those other vampires yet. He slipped into the greenhouse so he could be alone. He sat on the bench and dropped his head into his hands. How could he admit he was causing Darcy pain? Dead people didn't feel pain. They didn't cry. They didn't look at you like you were breaking their heart.

Holy shit. How could he deal with this? If he admitted she was in pain, he would have to admit she was still alive. He'd have to deal with the fact that she was a vampire. And his job at the CIA was to terminate vampires.

What an unholy mess. If only he had known ahead of time. He could have hardened his heart, avoided seeing her. Ah, sheesh. What a load of crap. Everyone had warned him she was a vampire. She'd even tried to push him away, but he had refused to listen. This wasn't her fault. He had stubbornly ignored all the clues because his heart was already lost. Now, he had no choice but to face reality.

He was in love with a vampire.

Darcy closed the door to the pool house and leaned against it, trembling. She struggled to breathe. Her knees wobbled, and she slid down the door to sit on the green all-weather carpet.

He'd hurt her. She must have actually fallen for him and his fast talk. Telling women what they wanted to hear. The bastard.

She'd been so pathetically easy. She'd been so cold,

so lonesome, so miserable for the last four years that she'd latched on to the first man who had offered her warmth and love. Tears spilled over, and she brushed them away with growing anger. How dare he turn a one-eighty on her? Wasn't it just last night he had said any man would be stupid to let her go? Well, by his own standards, Adam was stupid. Good riddance.

She stood on shaky legs. She needed to get back to the show. It was her job, and she couldn't afford to lose it. But damn, her heart was under attack by a double-edged sword. How could she see him again, and how could she stand *not* to see him? He'd made her so-called life bearable again. For the last four years, she'd been forced to dwell in darkness. Only three slender rays of light—Gregori, Maggie, and Vanda—had kept her sane. Then, Adam had burst into her dark existence like a brilliant sun. He'd been the sun god, promising her warmth and life.

But it had only been a false echo that taunted her. She could never experience life again. She could never be with Adam. She'd known it all along. But still, she'd fallen for him. She'd wanted to believe that love could conquer all, that love was as sacred as Vanda claimed. Tears rolled down Darcy's face. She couldn't handle seeing him again so soon, so she went down the west end stairwell to the servants' floor.

The ladies were in the parlor, chatting. Lady Pamela was sipping hot Chocolood from a tea cup. On the TV, Darcy could see Gregori and the contestants in the billiard room. The cameramen were there, recording the men as they talked about the show.

"Are you all right?" Vanda watched Darcy with narrowed eyes.

"I'm fine," she lied, hoping it wasn't noticeable that she'd been crying. There was no way to check her appearance in a mirror, one of the minor drawbacks to being a vampire. Major drawbacks included losing her family, her savings, and her career in journalism. Hell, she'd lost her entire life because of this stupid, secret world. If Connor hadn't been so concerned about keeping their damned secret, he could have teleported her to a hospital instead of Roman Draganesti's house. She might have lived. But now, she would never know. It was too late.

"Are you ready to finish the obstacle course?" she asked Lady Pamela. "There are still three men who need to be tested."

"Must I?" Lady Pamela made a face. "I'm so dreadfully tired. And besides, I already know which men must be eliminated."

"So do we," Cora Lee piped in. "We have to get rid of that buffoon that dropped Lady Pamela in the mud."

The ladies all murmured in agreement.

"And we must be rid of the Moor," Maria Consuela announced.

"You mean Ahmed?" Lady Pamela asked. "He was perfectly well-mannered. And his speech was flawless."

"Not to mention he's very handsome," Vanda added.

"Indeed." Lady Pamela set down her tea cup. "The second man to go must be Antonio of Madrid. He had the most dreadful lisp."

"Of course he does!" Maria Consuela exclaimed. "He speaks perfect Castilian Spanish."

"Well, it sounds rather silly in English," Lady Pamela insisted. "The man told me I thmelled like a thweet red rothe."

Princess Joanna shuddered. "God forbid we should have a master who speaks like that."

Maria Consuela huffed. "Then when do I have a say in who is removed from the contest?"

"You'll get your turn," Darcy assured the Spanish vampire. "I have you down for judging qualifier number nine—strength." With a small jolt of surprise, Darcy realized that the same women who had felt uncomfortable making a decision the night before were now eager to have their say.

"Oh, look." Cora Lee pointed at the TV. "Who is that?"

When Darcy glanced at the television, her breath caught. One of the cameramen had gone to the roof and was aiming his camera through the glass panes of the greenhouse. Adam was sitting on the bench, hunched over, his head resting in his hands.

"I think it's Adam." Vanda gave Darcy a curious look.

Cora Lee sighed. "The poor man. He looks so sad."

Darcy swallowed. He looked absolutely miserable. That should have made her sad, but a small kernel of satisfaction curled in her heart. Yes! He was hurting, too. He really did care.

"You should have let me taste his blood," Lady Pamela grumbled. "I would have known in an instant if he was mortal or Vamp."

"He *is* one of us," Princess Joanna announced. "He must be. He was too knowledgeable about our nights."

"That was odd." Vanda exchanged a worried look with Darcy.

Darcy's throat went dry. She glanced again at the television. Adam was rubbing his forehead with his hand. Had he discovered their secret? Was that why he couldn't look at her or touch her all of a sudden?

"I agree." Maria Consuela said. "Adam must be a Vamp."

Darcy sighed. "Since you know which men to eliminate, let's go ahead with the orchid ceremony. Take two orchids from the fridge and meet us in the foyer in five minutes."

They agreed. Darcy took the elevator to the second floor of the penthouse and asked all the men to come to the foyer. She sent Gregori to fetch Adam and the second cameraman. She arranged the men in two lines on the grand staircase. Then, she quickly moved across the foyer so she could be far away when Adam arrived.

The five lady judges marched into the foyer, their heads held high. They formed a line under the huge chandelier.

"Gentlemen," Gregori announced, "two of you will be going home tonight. The limo is waiting downstairs. You'll know you're leaving when you receive a black orchid. Are you ready?"

As the men nodded, Bernie panned the camera over their faces.

"One more announcement before we begin," Gregori continued. "The amount of the prize money has just gone up. Now, the winner of *The Sexiest Man on Earth* will receive *two* million dollars."

The women gasped. Bart caught their reactions on his camera, while Bernie recorded the men's.

"Lady Pamela, you may begin." Gregori motioned for her to step forward.

She moved forward, holding two black orchids. "We look forward to furthering our acquaintance with those of you who will remain. Now, for the orchids." She took a deep breath. "Nicholas of Chicago."

Nicholas, dressed in a clean set of clothes, trudged down the stairs to accept the orchid. "Sorry I dropped you." He went back up the stairs and accepted condolences from the other men.

"Antonio of Madrid," Lady Pamela announced.

With a crestfallen expression, Antonio accepted the orchid. "I am tho thorry."

Darcy glanced at Adam. Of all the remaining men, he alone looked sad. He wandered off to his room without looking back. The judges, host, and cameramen went to the portrait room for the final revelation of the evening. Darcy joined them.

"Two million dollars!" Cora Lee grinned. "Land sakes, our new master will be filthy rich!"

"Yes, but we must make sure he is a vampire," Princess Joanna warned.

"Oh, Darcy, do tell us that after tonight, we will be rid of all the pesky mortals," Lady Pamela begged.

"I can't say." Darcy retrieved the special flashlight from the wall safe. She handed it to Gregori and whispered in which order to reveal the men. Then, she dimmed the lights.

The women settled on the couches, their faces bright with excitement.

Gregori approached the portraits. "Tonight, you eliminated Antonio of Madrid." He flipped on the flashlight. Instantly, Antonio's white fangs appeared.

"Oh, dear." Lady Pamela winced. "I was so sure a vampire would never have a speech impediment."

"And you eliminated Nicholas from Chicago."

Gregori shone the light on Nicholas's portrait. For a tense moment, the women stared at his picture. Nothing happened.

"Yes!" Cora Lee bounced to her feet. "He's a mortal!"

"I did it!" Lady Pamela jumped up, grinning. "I discovered one of the mortals."

The women hugged each other, laughing.

Gregori popped open a bottle of Bubbly Blood. "This calls for a celebration." He poured seven glasses full. Darcy helped him serve the judges. Then, Gregori handed her one and kept one for himself.

"Congratulations, ladies!" He raised his glass. "You are one step closer to choosing your new master. And your master is one step closer to becoming a very wealthy man."

The women laughed and clinked their glasses together. The cameramen focused on their happy faces.

"You're not drinking." Gregory looked at Darcy. "You really should, you know. The show is turning out great."

Darcy looked down at the mixture of champagne and blood in her glass, Yeah, great. She was helping the ex-harem find a new master. And she was helping them learn to make their own decisions and stand up for themselves. But it all seemed empty without Adam.

In his bedroom, Austin observed the ladies' celebration on his laptop. With his roommate Nicholas gone, his spying had become much easier.

Garrett stood behind him, watching the scene. "So, that's the game they're playing. They're trying to figure out which of us is human, so they can get rid of us."

"It sure explains why the anklet is so important."

Austin tugged at his pants leg to look at his new anklet. Maggie had brought it to him right after sunset with a warning that he had to put it on immediately.

"Yeah." Garrett rested a hand on the back of Austin's chair as he leaned forward. "What's that they're drinking?"

"Something with synthetic blood in it." Austin watched Darcy lift the glass to her mouth. She took a sip, then licked her lips. Lips he had kissed. A mouth he had explored. Shit.

He jumped to his feet so fast, the chair tipped backwards and Garrett caught it. He strode toward the window and looked out. He couldn't see much of anything in the dark, only his reflection in the glass. Darcy wouldn't even make a reflection.

Holy crap. Did everything have to remind him that he was alive and she was dead? Or worse, she was undead. Dead during the day, but walking and talking and crying real tears during the night. She was alive just enough to torture him.

And tempt him. She was still so damned beautiful. Still so smart. Still so *Darcy.*

"Something wrong?" Garrett asked.

"Everything's wrong." Austin paced across the room. "This is a waste of time. We're not learning anything useful."

"I know the names of a bunch of vampires. That's more than I knew a few days ago."

"We were supposed to get friendly with them and learn about Shanna. It isn't happening." Although Austin had to admit he had certainly been friendly with one of them. Unfortunately, he'd forgotten all about Shanna when Darcy was in his arms.

"Well, it's hard to be friendly with a pack of murderous creatures," Garrett muttered.

"Oh, come on. Those women are harmless. They just want to wear pretty clothes and have someone take care of them. Sheesh, they get bent out of shape if your manners aren't impeccable."

Garrett snorted. "You're getting soft. Do you think the men are harmless, too?"

"I talked to a few of them tonight. Roberto owns an aluminum shutter company in Argentina. Otto runs a health club in Germany." Though Austin couldn't quite see a correlation between being healthy and undead.

Garrett frowned. "They probably commit crimes all the time. I bet they use mind control to steal money from people."

"Then why would they want the prize money so bad?"

"I don't know," Garrett mumbled. "But if they ran out of synthetic blood, they'd bite you in a minute."

Maybe so. Austin shook his head. But wouldn't he do the same if it was the only way to survive? "The point is they *do* drink synthetic blood. So, their intent is not to harm humans. Meanwhile, the really vicious vampires are trolling Central Park for victims as we speak. And here we are, picking up hankies."

"It's our assignment."

"It's stupid! We should go to Central Park and stop innocent people from getting attacked."

"We can't leave. George is still here. We can't leave him unprotected. And you know you can't go against Sean's orders."

Austin paced back to the window. He knew Garrett was right. But he wasn't finding out anything about

Shanna. All he had was a list of vampires that Sean would want to terminate. How could he put Darcy's name on it? No wonder he wanted to run away from this assignment.

"They're leaving the portrait room." Garrett switched to the camera in the foyer. "The women are going toward the kitchen. *Whoa!*"

"What?" Austin strode back to the desk.

"The host guy just vanished."

"He must have teleported. Probably back to his apartment."

Garrett pointed at the one figure in the foyer. "Isn't that the director?"

"Yes." Austin moved closer. Darcy was standing alone in the foyer, her hands clenched together. She walked to the base of the staircase, then stopped. She looked at the front door, then back at the stairs.

"What's she doing?" Garrett asked.

"Trying to make up her mind." Austin's heart began to pound as Darcy mounted the stairs. What was she doing? At the landing, the staircase divided in two— one section going east, the other west. Was she coming to the east wing to see him?

She reached the landing and hesitated once again. Holy indecision. It would be better if she went to one of the male vampires. They were her own kind.

"She's coming our way," Garrett said.

Austin's heart raced. *Please, come to me.* What the hell was he doing? He couldn't have a relationship with a vampire.

Garrett headed for the door. "I'd better get back to my room." He let himself out.

Austin switched the view on the monitor to the surveillance camera in the upstairs east wing hallway. He saw Garrett slip into his room. And a few minutes later, Darcy entered the hallway, headed his way.

He turned off the surveillance equipment and closed the laptop. What did she want? He'd been ugly to her in the pool house. He should dread this meeting. He should refuse to see her. But knowing she was seeking him out made him want to jump with joy.

Chapter 14

Darcy questioned herself with every step. Why put herself through more torture? But she'd seen Adam, sitting on the bench. In what he had thought was a private moment, he'd let his true feelings show. He was suffering as much as she.

She'd been the one to decide who would sleep where, so she knew exactly where he was. She raised her hand to knock on his door. Another twinge of self-doubt made her hesitate. He was a mortal. *Let the poor man go!* She had no right to involve him in the vampire world. He would learn the truth eventually, if he didn't know it already. And he would resent her for it. Just like she resented Connor. She stepped back. If she loved this man, she should let him go.

Love? Did she love him?

The door opened. Her breath hitched. He stood in the doorway, looking at her. His hair was tousled. His jacket was off. His dress shirt was unbuttoned, revealing that wonderfully muscled chest and stomach. And his eyes, there was so much pain and longing there. She knew in an instant—*Yes, I do love him.*

He leaned a forearm against the doorjamb. "I thought I heard someone out here."

She nodded. Now that she was here, all the words she'd planned to say vanished from her brain.

He frowned. Apparently, he was having similar difficulties.

"How's your finger?" She winced. What a dumb thing to ask.

"I think I'll live."

Which was more than she could ever do. Sheesh. How could she word this? *Oh, by the way, have you noticed I'm a vampire?*

"I said some rude things to you earlier tonight." He watched her sadly. "I'm really sorry. I never wanted to hurt you."

Tears gathered in her eyes and she blinked them away. "I'm sorry, too. I said some things I shouldn't have."

"I don't recall you doing anything wrong."

"I called you a prick."

The corner of his mouth quirked up. "It was more of an insinuation, but I deserved it."

He deserved more than she could give. She stepped back.

"What's up with the judges?" he asked.

She blinked. "Excuse me?"

"They dress so strange. One looks like a blond Scarlett O'Hara, and some of the others look like escapees from a Renaissance festival."

"Oh." Darcy clenched her hands together. "I admit they have rather odd tastes, but that's their idea of evening wear. Speaking of which, tomorrow night, all the men will be judged on how well you're dressed." She hoped he didn't notice how abruptly she'd changed the subject. Luckily, she wasn't breaking any rules. All the men were being warned to dress their best and be prepared to dance.

Adam shrugged. "I don't have a tuxedo."

"That's all right. The suit you wore tonight will be fine. You looked . . . wonderful." Good God, she was acting like a gushing teenager. "I—I should go."

He was frowning again. "About the dancing competition . . ."

"Yes? Cora Lee will be judging that."

"The Scarlett O'Hara knockoff?"

"Yes." Darcy attempted a smile. "Most likely, she'll expect you to do a waltz or a polka. Those are her favorite dances."

"Not into hip-hop, is she?"

Darcy let out a nervous laugh. "No. I believe most of the men are brushing up on the waltz tonight."

"I won't be."

"You waltz really well?"

He snorted. "I don't waltz at all."

"Oh." Her heart sank. Then, tomorrow would be his last night on the show. Unless . . . "I could—" No, she couldn't.

"You could what? Teach me how to waltz?"

"No, I can't. I'm sorry."

"I know." He smiled sadly. "It wouldn't be fair to the other contestants, would it?"

She sighed. "No."

"You're basically very honest, aren't you?" he asked softly.

She swallowed hard. The one thing she really needed to be honest with him about, she couldn't manage to do. "Sometimes the truth is too difficult to say."

"I know." He watched her, his eyes growing more intense.

A sudden wave of heat washed over her. It filled her, enveloping her cold, dead heart with soothing warmth. The heat rose to her face, flaming her cheeks and rushing through her head like a fever. She closed her eyes briefly, basking in the glorious heat. How did he do this to her? Make her so hot just by looking at her? No man had ever had such an effect on her. But then, she'd never loved a man as much as she did Adam.

"Oh, God." Adam pushed away from the doorjamb and dragged a hand through his hair.

"Is something wrong?"

He shook his head. "No. Yes. I—I don't know." He grimaced. "I'll probably be eliminated tomorrow night."

"Do you want to be eliminated?"

"I don't know what I want anymore. It's all screwed up."

He looked so agitated, Darcy was tempted to read his mind to find out what was wrong. She'd never read a mind before. She'd always spurned all the nasty little vampire tricks—mind control, teleportation, levitation. She didn't want any part of it. Especially mind reading. It was such a terrible invasion of privacy. "I—I'll be sorry to see you go."

He nodded. "It's what I need to do. It's for the best."

She took a deep breath. He was right. It was for the best. "Then, you'll be gone tomorrow night." *And I may never see you again.* The last remnant of heat drained from her, leaving her cold and empty once again.

"I'll have to go as soon as the orchid ceremony is over. So, I'll say . . . goodbye, now."

She swallowed. "Goodbye." She extended her hand.

He frowned at her hand, so she stepped back, letting her arm fall to her side. He couldn't even touch her. How could her heart ache so badly when it was dead?

"Darcy." He reached out and held her by the shoulders. He touched his lips briefly to her brow. "Goodbye." Then, he turned and shut the door.

The next evening, Austin dressed in his dark gray suit with a silver and blue striped tie. Tonight, he'd be kicked off the show for sure. His bags were already packed. He'd ride off in the limo and never see Darcy again. It hurt like hell, but it was for the best.

He headed for the library with Garrett and George. There were five male vampires left in the game—Otto from Düsseldorf, Ahmed from Cairo, Roberto from Buenos Aires, Pierre from Brussels, and Reginald from Manchester. Gregori explained what was planned for the evening as he walked them to the staircase. One of the vampire judges arrived with the two cameramen, Darcy, and Maggie. Darcy looked beautiful, as usual, even though she was only dressed in pants and a T-shirt. Her eyes met his and lingered a moment before she looked away.

The judge was the one they called Princess Joanna. She was certainly dressed like a medieval princess, though Austin figured her domain had disappeared hundreds of years ago.

She was going to judge them on their presence—

how well they were dressed and how well they carried themselves. She called them one by one with her regal voice. As instructed, each man descended the stairs and walked halfway across the foyer. There, they were supposed to pose for a moment under the chandelier. Then, they were to pivot and walk to the library.

"I feel like I'm in a fashion show," Austin growled.

"Or a beauty pageant," Garrett grumbled.

"God, no." Austin grimaced. "Please don't tell me there's going to be a swimsuit competition."

"Garth from Denver," Princess Joanna called.

Garrett responded to his false name by straightening his shoulders and pasting a small smile on his face. He began his descent of the stairs. Austin debated whether or not he should slide down the banister. But when his name was called, he behaved himself. He didn't want to upset Darcy. He marched down the stairs, then strode across the foyer to the mid-point.

Darcy was by the front door, watching him. Her eyes glistened in the light from the chandelier. Were those tears in her eyes? She looked both sad and happy. A sad resignation in her eyes, but a sweet loving curve to her smile. Oh, he knew it was love. He'd read it in her mind the night before. And now, her expression seemed to be telling him she would still love him no matter how sad it made her.

He smiled slightly, then turned toward the library.

When all the men were in the library, Gregori explained that the next phase, the dancing competition, would take place on the roof. They went up the west end stairwell and found all the ladies waiting on the roof. A quartet of musicians were setting up by the greenhouse. They tuned up their string instruments. No electric guitars. It was definitely going to be an old-fashioned dance. All the patio furniture had been moved aside to leave a wide terrace between the pool and the outer wall.

Gregori wandered around the terrace, lighting tiki torches. When he was done, he turned to the men. "Gentlemen, you may ask any of the judges to dance. However, all of you must dance at least once with Cora Lee." He motioned to the Scarlett O'Hara knockoff. "She will be judging this part of the competition."

Cora Lee smiled at the men. "I do declare, this will be such a delightful evening."

The quartet began the strains of a waltz. Pierre asked Cora Lee to dance. She accepted and off they went, swirling around the terrace. Roberto asked Lady Pamela to dance. Maria Consuela and Princess Joanna declined to dance with anyone.

"I never do the waltz," the princess declared. "It is much too vulgar."

"It is evil." Maria Consuela stood next to a tiki torch and fiddled with her rosary.

Vanda laughed and took off dancing with Ahmed. When the first waltz was over, Garrett made his move. He asked Cora Lee to dance, then spun her expertly around the terrace. Afterward, he returned to where Austin was standing.

Austin shut his mouth, which had been hanging open. "Where the hell did you learn to do that?"

Garrett smiled. "I took a course in ballroom dancing. I figured in our line of work, you gotta be able to function at a fancy party."

"Oh." Austin grimaced. He should have thought of that.

Cora Lee squealed, drawing their attention. Otto was dancing with her, or rather, he was swinging her around like a rag doll.

"Ya, you are light like de feather," Otto declared in his booming voice.

Cora Lee giggled. Her feet touched ground and she skipped along, keeping up with Otto's large strides. "Oh, Otto, you are so big, I can hardly keep up with you."

"Ya, de Otto is big and strong." He lifted Cora Lee once again and whirled about. Lady Pamela and her partner jumped out of the way of Cora Lee's swooping hoop skirt.

Cora Lee burst into laughter. Otto whooshed her into the air again as he spun about. Her foot knocked against a tiki torch. Austin watched as suddenly everything seemed to happen in slow motion. With a shout, he ran toward the torch as it tipped over. Maria Consuela screamed. The torch landed against the hem of her medieval gown and the flames spread. All the women started screaming. The music screeched to a halt. Austin kicked the torch aside, but the flames were already shooting up Maria Consuela's dress. He grabbed her from behind and tossed her into the deep end of the pool.

She landed with a great splash and a hiss as the fire extinguished. She sank to the bottom while steam rose off the surface of the water.

Austin stopped by the side of the pool. The others gathered around him. The cameramen pushed their way into good recording positions. Maria Consuela looked like a black lump at the bottom of the pool. Could a vampire drown? Austin didn't know. He glanced at the other vampires. Maybe not. They sure didn't look very concerned. But then again, maybe they were just a bunch of cold, heartless bastards.

"Can she swim?" he asked.

Vanda peered into the water. "Apparently not."

Austin exchanged a look with Garrett. He shrugged his shoulders with a look that said let her drown. After all, she was a vampire.

Austin looked at Darcy. She gave him a beseeching, frantic look. The Spanish vampire was probably her friend. "Sheesh." He kicked off his shoes and glared at the male vampires. "Don't any of you swim?"

They shook their heads.

Austin took off his jacket, handed it to Garrett, and dove into the cold water. He pulled Maria Consuela off the bottom of the pool. She immediately started kicking and flailing her arms. Dammit. He was supposed to be killing vampires, not saving their ass. He grabbed her arms and crossed them in front of her to subdue her. Then, he held her against his chest and pushed off the bottom of the pool. They broke the surface.

Maria Consuela wheezed and sputtered. She gulped down air, then started screaming in Spanish. As far as Austin could tell, she was cursing Otto with some kind of plague. He gripped her tightly and stroked toward the ladder. Her dress was too tangled around her legs for her to negotiate the ladder, so he heaved her over his shoulder and carried her out of the pool. He set her down on a chaise lounge.

"Madre de Dios!" Maria Consuela collapsed dramatically. "You have saved my life."

"Indeed. You are a hero!" Lady Pamela exclaimed.

"I do declare." Cora Lee pressed a hand against her bosom. "I have never seen a man act so bravely."

"If you'll excuse me." Austin retrieved his jacket from Garrett. "I need to change into dry clothes. I won't be able to dance, so I understand if you need to reject me—"

"Fiddlesticks," Cora Lee interrupted him. "I'll just wait until you get back. It's the least I can do."

Austin retrieved his shoes. "You don't understand. I can't dance with you because I don't know how."

Cora Lee gasped. She exchanged a desperate look with the other women.

"He should be forgiven for his ignorance." Maria Consuela fumbled for her rosary and kissed it. "We have all fallen short in the eyes of the Lord."

A religious vampire? Austin shook his head. The more he learned about the vampire world, the more it confused him.

"He's a hero," Lady Pamela declared. "I would be honored to teach him how to waltz."

Vanda grinned. "I'd like to teach him a few moves myself."

"We mustn't punish him," Cora Lee insisted. "He's a hero."

"Indeed." Princess Joanna studied Austin. "He is a man who knows how to protect his own."

Austin groaned inwardly. He had a terrible feeling he wasn't going home tonight after all.

Darcy declared a thirty-minute break to give those in wet clothes time to change.

"Thank you," she murmured to Adam as she passed by him on the way to Maria Consuela. He gave her a frustrated look, then tramped off in his soggy clothes.

With Maggie on one side and Darcy on the other, they helped support Maria Consuela on the trek back to the servants' floor. The other ladies trailed along, gossiping about Adam.

"He must be a vampire to be so wonderfully brave," Lady Pamela declared.

Maggie shot Darcy a look of alarm. Darcy realized her friend was worried that a mortal might actually win the contest. Not only would the show end up insulting the entire vampire world, but the ladies would end up with a mortal master. A disaster, to be sure, but luckily, Darcy knew it could never happen.

"Don't worry," Darcy spoke over Maria Consuela's

head to Maggie. "One of the qualifiers is strength. There's no way any mortal is going to be stronger than a vampire."

Maggie exhaled in relief. "Good."

They reached the servants' parlor, and Maggie took Maria Consuela to her room to change.

"Land sakes, all that dancing has left me positively famished." Cora Lee sauntered into the kitchen and grabbed a bottle of Chocolood from the refrigerator. "Would anyone like to share this with me?" She popped it into the microwave.

"I will." Lady Pamela retrieved two tea cups and saucers from the cabinet.

Darcy filled a glass with ice, then took another bottle of Chocolood from the fridge. "Have you decided who should be eliminated tonight?" She poured the chocolate and blood mixture into her glass.

Lady Pamela shuddered. "How *ghastly*. I cannot fathom how you can drink that stuff cold."

Darcy shrugged. She usually added some chocolate syrup, too. "The colder it is, the less I can taste the blood."

Vanda snorted. "But that's the best part."

"I know who needs to go." Cora Lee removed the Chocolood from the microwave and poured the warm liquid into the tea cups. "That clumsy George trampled my feet three times. And he never apologized for it, even when I yelped in pain."

Lady Pamela gasped. "What appalling behavior."

"I agree." Princess Joanna put a bottle of Type O synthetic blood in the microwave. She liked her meals simple. "As for the best-dressed contest, I wish to eliminate Ahmed of Cairo."

Darcy frowned. "You're not doing that just to

please Maria Consuela? I realize she had quite a scare this evening."

"Nay, though I can certainly sympathize with her. I was frightened out of my wits a fortnight ago when I was badly burned." The princess cast a disparaging glance toward Cora Lee.

Cora Lee winced and rushed into the parlor with her tea cup.

"My reasoning is sound." Princess Joanna withdrew her bottle from the microwave and poured the contents into a glass. "The man was wearing scruffy brown loafers with a black suit."

Lady Pamela gasped. "Horrid, simply horrid."

"Ghastly!" Vanda added sarcastically as she popped a bottle of blood into the microwave.

Princess Joanna stiffened. "Prithee, you should take this more seriously. This is our new master we are choosing."

Vanda shrugged. "Aren't we doing fine without a master? I mean, we haven't killed each other." She grinned at the princess. "Though we did come close."

Princess Joanna huffed and stomped into the parlor. She sat in an easy chair. The ladies gave each other worried looks.

"If we didn't have a master, who would make decisions for us?" Cora Lee asked.

Darcy sat next to her. "You made a decision tonight to eliminate George."

"Oh." Cora Lee sipped from her tea cup. "I suppose I did."

"But who would pay the bills?" Lady Pamela asked.

Vanda removed her dinner from the microwave. She sauntered into the parlor, drinking straight from the bottle.

Princess Joanna frowned at her. "Such manners are a disgrace. We need a master to keep us in line."

Vanda swallowed. "Seems to me, all we need is money."

Lady Pamela set down her tea cup with a clink. "A master would take care of us."

Vanda sprawled on the couch beside her. "I think an occasional dose of vampire sex is all we need. And we wouldn't have any trouble finding lots of Vamp men for that."

Princess Joanna's frown deepened. "Are you suggesting we consort in a promiscuous manner? I assure you, I am far too dignified for such behavior."

Vanda rolled her eyes. "I'm just wondering what a master is really good for, other than sex and money."

The ladies sat there, silently. Vanda's question seemed to have them all stumped. Darcy watched, fascinated. The women were starting to question things they never would have before.

"I wouldn't mind a master if he was brave and heroic," Cora Lee whispered.

"Like Adam," Lady Pamela said.

Darcy winced.

"Did you see his face during the fashion contest?" Cora Lee asked. While the princess was judging, the other ladies had watched the competition in the parlor on the television.

"You mean when he stopped under the chandelier?" Lady Pamela asked. "He had the saddest look on his face. I thought I was going to cry."

"I wonder what made him so sad." Vanda gave Darcy a questioning look.

Darcy felt a blush creep into her cheeks.

Luckily, at that moment Maggie strode into the

parlor. "Good news. Maria Consuela wasn't injured. She's just a little shaken by it all."

The women murmured their relief.

"Tell us what happened last night at DVN," Vanda demanded.

"Oh, yes! Do tell." Cora Lee exclaimed. "Did you see Don Orlando?"

Maggie grinned. "I did a screen test with him."

The ladies all sighed. Except for Vanda. She was frowning.

"How did it go?" Darcy asked.

Maggie leaned against the wall and hugged herself. "He looked deep into my eyes and asked for my phone number."

The ladies sighed again.

"Did you hear what Corky Courrant's been saying about him on *Live with the Undead?*" Vanda asked.

Maggie scoffed. "I don't listen to such vicious gossip."

"What did Corky say?" Cora Lee sipped from her tea cup.

"She said he goes through women like Kleenex," Vanda said.

"That's not true!" Maggie cried. "He's just looking for the right lady Vamp."

"Then he must be looking in every coffin in America," Vanda grumbled.

"What is Kleenex?" Princess Joanna demanded.

Vanda gritted her teeth. "It's a disposable handkerchief."

The princess sniffed. "I don't believe in disposable things. They are evil."

Vanda snorted. "Right. They're garbage. And Don Orlando treats women like garbage."

"Stop it!" Maggie shouted. "I won't let you talk that way about him."

Darcy was waging an internal battle, debating whether or not to tell Maggie the truth. But poor Maggie looked so hurt. Darcy decided she would wait until later. Maggie needed to know about Don Orlando's affairs with Corky and Tiffany, but she deserved privacy for the dismal news. "Did you pass the screen test?"

"Yes, I did," Maggie announced defensively. "And I'll be a star with Don Orlando, too. Just wait and see."

"What happens next?" Darcy asked.

"I have one more interview before they make their final decision. I have to talk to your boss."

"Sly?" Darcy stifled a groan. She'd have to warn Maggie about him, too.

"I am ready." Maria Consuela entered the parlor.

"Okay." Darcy went to the refrigerator to retrieve two more black orchids. "Let's go."

As they took the elevator to the first floor of the penthouse, Darcy explained the upcoming schedule. "After tonight, we're taking a break for three nights. You can all stay here if you like."

"Where will you go?" Maggie asked.

"I'm going back to Gregori's," Darcy answered. "Tomorrow night, I have to go to DVN to edit the first show. It'll make its debut the next night on Saturday."

"How exciting!" Cora Lee clasped her hand together. "We can watch ourselves on television."

"Yes." The elevator opened onto the kitchen. Darcy led the ladies to the foyer. "The show is scheduled for midnight Wednesdays and Saturdays. I'll be editing the second show this Sunday. You guys will have the day off. Then, we'll start shooting again Monday."

They filed into the foyer. Gregori had the men ready on the staircase in two lines of four. As usual, Darcy looked for Adam first. He was now wearing dry clothes. He didn't look up as the ladies arranged themselves in a line. Was he upset with how things had turned out?

The cameramen got into position. Bernie focused on the women, and Bart on the men.

Gregori began, "Tonight, two men will receive black orchids. If you receive one, you will be expected to leave immediately. The limo is waiting for you outside."

The eight men nodded. Bart panned slowly over their faces.

"One more announcement before we begin," Gregori continued. "The prize money for the winner has risen once again. The Sexiest Man on Earth will now receive *three* million dollars."

The men looked excited, all except Adam. The lady judges gasped, then smiled at each other.

"Princess Joanna, if you will step forward," Gregori said.

She strode forward and stopped beneath the chandelier. "This orchid is for Ahmed of Cairo."

Ahmed slumped with disappointment and moved down the stairs.

"Santa Maria be praised." Maria Consuela crossed herself.

Darcy winced. She'd have to edit that out.

Ahmed accepted the orchid, then trudged back up the stairs.

Cora Lee joined the princess under the chandelier. She held up her black orchid. "This one is for George from . . . some place." She giggled. "I forgot."

George Martinez from Houston cursed under his breath as he descended the stairs. After he accepted the orchid, the men dispersed to their rooms.

Darcy and the others went to the portrait room. She removed the flashlight from the wall safe and passed it to Gregori with whispered instructions. The ladies settled on the couches.

"Tonight, you eliminated Ahmed from Cairo." Gregori clicked on the flashlight and aimed it at the Egyptian's portrait. The black light made his fangs magically appear.

"Oh, what a shame," Cora Lee whimpered. "He was a vampire."

Maria Consuela frowned. "He was a Moor."

"And you eliminated George from Houston." Gregori illuminated George's portrait. There was no change.

Cora Lee jumped up. "I did it! I found another one of those rascally mortals."

The women stood and cheered. While Gregori poured glasses of Bubbly Blood, Darcy removed two more portraits from the wall. Now, there were only six men left—two mortals and four Vamps. By a strange turn of events, Adam had survived another round. Even though he hadn't wanted to.

"Congratulations." Gregori raised a glass to toast the judges. "You are one step closer to finding your new master. And your master is one step closer to being a very wealthy man."

"Three million dollars!" Vanda shouted.

The ladies burst into laughter and clinked their glasses together. Darcy set down her glass, unable to drink. When the ladies found their new master, they would all move away. She would lose all of them, just like she had Adam. She slipped out of the room and wandered across the foyer. An endless eternity stretched out before her with no family and very few friends. It was going to be very lonely.

It was four-thirty in the morning when Austin arrived back at his apartment in Greenwich Village. He would have to return to the penthouse in three days, but after he'd learned about their mini-vacation, he'd decided to leave immediately. He needed to get out and clear his head.

He'd watched the celebration in the portrait room via his surveillance camera. Seeing the vampires cheer the removal of another *rascally* mortal had irked him. Those damned vampires thought they were so superior. And if that wasn't bad enough, he'd seen Darcy's reaction. She hadn't celebrated at all. She'd put down her glass with a forlorn look and wandered off. Dammit, she didn't belong with those vampires. But she couldn't belong with him, either.

He was so pissed off by then, he'd grabbed his bags and hauled ass. Garrett had decided to leave, too, since the other human, George, had been eliminated from the show.

Austin flipped the three deadbolt locks on his door, turned on the alarm system, then collapsed on the couch. Videotapes littered his coffee table. All the videos of Darcy's newscasts. He'd enjoyed them so much when he'd thought she was alive. He slid in the last tape, the one that reported her disappearance. It showed the alley in Greenwich Village, the blood stain on the ground. The reporter explained that the police had discovered a knife with Darcy's blood on it. She was presumed dead.

Dammit, he should have known she was dead. But how could he believe it when he was falling in love with her?

Austin switched the television off. He leaned back and closed his eyes. He'd gone to that alley several times to look it over. The blood stain was gone, washed away by four years of rain and snow. But that must have been where she had died. His beautiful Darcy. Gone.

What was he supposed to do now? He trudged to the kitchen, grabbed a beer from the refrigerator, and wandered back to the couch. The computer disk was still on the coffee table. He inserted it into his laptop. DVN was a joint corporation with several major investors. The president in charge of production was Sylvester Bacchus, Darcy's boss.

Austin's gaze drifted to the legal pad where he was writing his list of vampires. Darcy's friends were on it. Gregori, Maggie, and Vanda. Holy crap, she would hate him forever for turning in her friends. And she could literally hate forever.

With a sigh, he listed the male contestants from the reality show, along with all the information he'd learned about them. Then, he began to list the female vampires. With each name, he felt a twinge in his gut. Dammit. They were vampires. The enemy. Why did he feel like he was betraying them? *Because they're Darcy's friends.*

He collapsed against the back sofa cushion. How could he do this? Hadn't Darcy suffered enough? She might be one of the undead, but she was also an innocent. He knew that deep down in his bones. Darcy could never hurt anyone.

And her friends? They did believe they were

superior to humans, but he couldn't imagine them hurting anyone. They weren't anything like the vampires he and Emma had seen in the park. And they didn't seem to constitute a threat to humanity like Sean insisted. They actually cared about each other. They were capable of love. He'd heard it in Darcy's thoughts. She was in love with Adam. In love with him.

Could Shanna and Roman Draganesti actually be in love?

Dammit, how could such a relationship work? It was impossible. And even if these modern vampires were harmless, they couldn't have always been that way. Darcy's friends were obviously a great deal older than she. They could have been around for hundreds of years before the invention of synthetic blood. They had to have been feeding off humans.

And it was his job to protect humans. The vampires had to go. They were already dead, so why should he care? He was letting his emotions get in the way of his job. Refusing to do his duty was tantamount to treason. He couldn't betray his country or all the innocent people who were relying on him to do the right thing. With a growl, he seized a pen and scrawled Darcy Newhart on the bottom of the list. On the top, he wrote *Vampires Must Die.*

His heart cringed in his chest. The pen dropped from his hand. *Oh, God.*

He jumped up and paced across the room. How could he do this to Darcy? *Darcy is dead,* he repeated over and over as he paced the floor. *Darcy is dead.*

And he was cursed. For he was still alive and didn't know how he could live with himself.

* * *

The next evening, Darcy rushed to DVN to begin the editing process. Sly had arranged for an experienced technician to train her. She needed five segments, each lasting ten minutes. The remaining ten minutes of the hour-long show was reserved for commercial breaks. As part of the rental agreement on the penthouse, Roman Draganesti was expecting free commercial time on each show to advertise his Vampire Fusion Cuisine.

Gregori was going to be busy the next three nights in Studio Three making new commercials for Chocolood, Bubbly Blood, and Blood Lite. This had worked out perfectly for Darcy, allowing her to catch a ride with Gregori to DVN. Maggie was also excited about it, because Gregori had offered to let her star in one of the commercials.

By eight-thirty, Darcy was satisfied with the opening segment of the show—a tour of the penthouse and the arrival of the female judges. She looked up, startled, when Sylvester Bacchus barged into the workroom.

"You gotta see this!" He switched the television on to DVN's live broadcast. "I told Corky to do some promotion for the new show." He turned up the volume as Corky came on the screen.

"Welcome to *Live with the Undead*! I'm Corky Courrant with the hottest celebrity news in the vampire world. Tomorrow night is the night we've all been waiting for! The debut of DVN's first and only reality show, *The Sexiest Man on Earth*. But first, let's see what's going on with the sexiest man on the soaps."

"Oh, shit," Sly muttered. "Not this again."

A picture of Don Orlando flashed on the right half of the screen. It had been digitally embellished with a pair of goat horns.

"Is Don Orlando really the greatest lover in the vampire world?" Corky asked. "Or does he change partners every two hours because he's unable to satisfy a woman for longer than that?"

Sly shook his head. "He should have never cheated on her. She's going to crucify him."

Corky smiled sweetly. "I'm a fair person, so I'm going to let you, the viewers, decide. Email me at the address on the screen, Corky at DVN.com, and vote for which answer is correct. Is Don Orlando a stinking fraud or merely an odious pig?"

Darcy sighed. She still needed to talk to Maggie.

"And now for the main story," Corky continued with a wide grin. "Everyone is eagerly awaiting the first show of a hot new series that will debut tomorrow night, then air every Wednesday and Saturday. It's the vampire world's first reality show, *The Sexiest Man on Earth*. It stars the famous former harem of coven master Roman Draganesti and some of the hunkiest, sexiest men in the vampire world!"

An aerial shot of the penthouse roof came on screen. Darcy sat up. Her nerves tensed.

Sly waved a dismissive hand. "Don't worry. I asked Bernie to give her a little advance footage. It's just teaser stuff, great for promotion."

"Here at *Live with the Undead,* we're going to treat you to an exclusive preview of DVN's hottest new show," Corky continued. "And just how hot is this show going to be?" She laughed. "Hot enough to smoke up your screen, and we'll show you what I mean. Believe me, this guy gets my vote for *The Sexiest Man on Earth.*"

A scene wavered on the screen as if a cameraman

was struggling to focus on something in the distance. Slowly, the image grew sharper.

Darcy gasped.

"Yes!" Sly slapped a hand against his thigh.

The picture was a bit hazy since it was recorded at a distance in the dark without sufficient lighting. But it was certainly clear enough to make Darcy want to scream.

"I knew that hot tub was a great idea." Sly grinned. "Look at this. Off comes the dress. Then the guy throws it into the pool."

Darcy sank in her chair. "You've seen this before?"

"Sure. Bernie showed it to me last night. We watched it about ten times. Now here's my favorite part." Sly pointed at the television. "Off comes the bra."

Darcy covered her mouth to keep from groaning out loud.

"Wow, that's cool," the technician said, his eyes riveted to the screen.

Sly turned to Darcy, smiling. "Great work, Newhart. I just wish it had come out a bit clearer. So, was that one of Draganesti's ex-harem ladies?"

Darcy winced. "You could say that." Oh, God, this was terrible. The only thing keeping her from running from the building, screaming and ripping out her hair, was the fact that the recording had been fuzzy. It was just clear enough to tell there were two nearly naked bodies making out in the hot tub, but the faces weren't clear. Thank God. She was safe for now.

"Man, is she hot. I need to get to know her a little better, if you know what I mean." Sly winked. "So tell me, Newhart, who is she?"

Chapter 16

Darcy swallowed hard. If the truth got out, Sly would probably fire her as a director and offer her a job as DVN's first porn star. "I believe the woman in question was unaware that she was being recorded."

"So?" Sly scratched at his goatee. "She was in a hot tub. It's not like she had any expectation of privacy."

"A good point." And one she would be sure to remember in the future. Although she doubted she'd ever experience such a sexy scene again in her long, miserable life. "I don't believe I should divulge the woman's name without her permission."

"Well, you should. I could make her a star." Sly handed her his card. "Just give her this and tell her I want to meet her."

"Will do." Darcy dropped the card into her purse. "I need to work now, or we won't have the show ready for tomorrow night."

"Fine. Make it great." Sly sauntered out the door.

With a sigh, Darcy switched off Corky's show. "Let's get back to work."

The technician finished scribbling a note, then handed it to her. "Could you, uh, give this to the lady in the hot tub?"

Darcy noticed his name and phone number on the note. Rick was one of the few mortals who worked at DVN. "You realize the lady in question is a vampire?"

"Yeah." He sipped from his coffee. "So?"

"You don't think it could be dangerous to date a vampire?"

He reached into his paper bag and removed a doughnut. "I work with you all. You seem safe enough to me." He crammed half the doughnut into his mouth.

The hot, yeasty smell was heavenly. Darcy was so tempted, but the last time she'd tried real food, it hadn't stayed down.

"I just want some fun, and that lady is hot." Rick stuffed the rest of the doughnut in his mouth. "Besides, it's not like I'm looking for a commitment, you know."

"I see. You don't think there could be a lasting relationship between a mortal and a Vamp."

"Not really." He licked the sugar off his fingers. "Can I ask you something?"

Darcy nodded. She'd known a relationship with Adam couldn't work. She just hadn't expected the truth to hurt this much.

"Is it hard giving up real food?"

She turned away. "Yes." She dropped Rick's note into her purse. "Let's get back to work."

They'd been working about ten minutes when the door cracked open and DVN's receptionist peeked in.

Darcy glanced up. "Can I help you?"

"Yes." She slipped inside. "Corky asked me to give this to you, so you could pass it on to the sexy guy in the hot tub." She handed Darcy a business card. Corky had written on the back *Call me.* She'd included her private phone number and a drawing in red ink of two entwined hearts.

"How sweet," Darcy ground out, tempted to rip the card in two. "Anything else? I have work to do."

The receptionist blushed almost as red as the dyed streaks in her hair. "Could you, uh, give him this, too? But don't tell Corky. She'd kill me."

"What is it?" Darcy accepted the note.

"It's *my* phone number." The receptionist rushed from the room.

Darcy tossed the card and note into her purse. So, it was Adam's lucky day. He was rapidly acquiring a fan club. And all because he knew how to remove a lady's bra in record time.

She took a deep breath and shoved her frustrated emotions to the side. She could scream later. Right now, she needed to work. Five minutes later, the door opened. She glanced up. Well, speak of the devil.

"Good evening." Don Orlando swaggered into the room. He was wearing black leather pants low on his hips, and a black silk cape, which looked a bit odd without a shirt underneath. He took a wide stance in his black leather boots. His hair was so black, Darcy suspected it must be dyed. Did that mean his mound of chest hair was dyed, too? Just how much of Don Orlando was fiction? No one seemed to know his real name.

He raked his dark eyes over her and smiled slowly. "You know who I am, of course."

Either a stinky fraud or an odious pig, according to Corky. "Yes, I do."

"I wish to know the name of the sexy woman in the hot tub."

Darcy stifled a groan. "I can't divulge her name."

He smirked. "Just tell her Don Orlando de Corazon, the greatest lover in the vampire world, wishes to woo her. She will comply."

"Right." *Over my dead body, which was unfortunately, too close to the truth.* Darcy stood and headed to the door. "I have a lot of work to do. So, if you could move your little booties somewhere else, I'd appreciate it."

He turned with a flourish of his cape and left. Darcy shut the door and locked it.

Austin rose before dawn and went to the office. Since it was a Saturday, Sean wasn't there, and he was grateful for that. He didn't want to answer questions. He borrowed a white surveillance van from Homeland Security and visited a local cable company where flashing his badge got him a clipboard full of invoices and a work shirt with the company logo. He drove to DVN and arrived by eight o'clock in the morning.

"We got a complaint about four in the morning from Sylvester Bacchus," he explained to the mortal security guard. "The internet connection was going on and off."

"Really?" The guard took the clipboard and regarded the invoice with a suspicious eye. "I wasn't notified about this."

"They probably forgot to tell you." *You will believe me,* Austin projected his thoughts into the guard's head.

The guard handed the clipboard back. "Come on in."

"Thanks. This won't take long." Austin headed for the offices with his tool box. Sylvester Bacchus's office was easy to find since he had a big brass nameplate on his door. Austin closed the door and went to work. The computers at DVN were basically dinosaurs, so he had to download everything onto disks. When he was done, he made sure everything looked the way it had before.

As he crossed the lobby, he waved at the security guard. "Everything's fixed."

Back in his apartment, Austin made labels for each of the disks and downloaded all the data onto his laptop. He now had all the information anyone would ever want to know about DVN. All he had to do was email it to Sean. But if he sent the information, Darcy would be targeted with all the other vampires.

He shut the laptop and looked at the stuff on his coffee table. Videos of Darcy, disks from DVN, and the damned list that said *Vampires Must Die*. He couldn't take it anymore. The more he tried to do the right thing, the worse he felt.

Sometimes, being the good guy really sucked.

It was Saturday night and time for the debut. Gregori drove Darcy and Maggie to the penthouse. There, they found the lady judges in their parlor, waiting excitedly for the show to begin. The Bubbly Blood was chilling in an ice bucket.

Midnight arrived, and the ladies were glued to the screen. All televisions had been removed from the rooms upstairs. The male Vamps needed to remain ignorant about the mortal competitors, so they weren't allowed to watch the show until it was finished. And of course, the mortals had to be kept completely in the dark. That was easy to do, since the two mortals had left the penthouse entirely.

As the show came to a close, Darcy grew tense with worry. The last scene was the one in the portrait room when the ladies discovered for the first time that some of the contestants were mortal. Soon, the ladies' outrage would explode on the screen. How on earth would Sly react? He'd wanted a big twist, but this might be a bigger one than he could handle.

When the closing credits began, the ladies poured Bubbly Blood and toasted each other. Darcy accepted a glass with a growing sense of doom. Any minute now . . .

The phone rang. She set down her glass with a sigh.

Gregori answered the phone. "Sure, she's here." He handed the receiver to Darcy. "It's Shanna Draganesti."

Darcy blinked. Shanna? Why would she be calling? "Hello?"

"Darcy, I need to talk to you. It's important."

"Okay." Darcy waited for Shanna to talk.

"I mean in person. I'm at our new house in White Plains. Can you teleport here?"

Darcy's grip on the phone tightened. "Actually, no. Maybe Gregori can drive me—?" She gave him a questioning look.

"No, that'll take too long." Shanna's voice faded. It sounded like she had covered the receiver to talk to someone else. "Connor wants you here now."

Darcy's heart lurched in her chest. "I—I'd rather not—"

"It's urgent, Darcy. You need to teleport here now."

"I don't . . . know how. I've never done it before." Her face flooded with heat as she realized Shanna was sharing her inadequacy with Connor. Her eye twitched. "Look, Gregori can drive me. We'll leave right away."

"Keep talking," Shanna said. "Connor's coming to get you."

"No!" Darcy gasped for air. "I don't want to teleport, and I sure don't want to go anywhere with—" A figure materialized beside her. A man in a red and green kilt. "Connor." The phone slipped from her hand and clattered on the floor.

"I'm sorry, lass, but ye need to come with me." The Scotsman wrapped a strong arm around her, and everything went black.

Terror whipped through Darcy. She was trapped and helpless, just like she'd been four years ago. She couldn't feel her body. The only thing keeping her from floating away like vapor into a black void was the steel-like grip of Connor. Once again, he was abducting her against her will. She hated him for it, and she hated herself for being so damned afraid. Good God, if she had any courage in her at all, she'd push herself away and fade into oblivion, never to materialize again.

As soon as her feet touched ground, a room wavered before her eyes and came into view. A living room with two wingback chairs, a television, and a sofa. Shanna was sitting in a chair, watching them. Darcy broke free from Connor and stumbled.

"Careful." He reached out to steady her.

"Don't—" The words *touch me* stuck in her throat when she saw his face. Regret had etched lines on his brow and dulled the blue of his eyes. The truth scraped at her like overlong fingernails, and she looked away. God have mercy. His decision that night haunted him as much as it did her.

Shanna set her phone down on the coffee table next to her drink. "Thank you for coming, Darcy."

Like she'd been given any choice. Darcy pivoted, surveying the comfortable room decorated in blue toile with yellow accents. "Is this your new house?"

"Yes. Roman wants to keep the location a secret. The Highlanders know, of course, since they do our security." Shanna motioned to the blue velvet couch. "Please have a seat."

Darcy circled the coffee table and sat close to Shanna. "What's wrong? Are the Malcontents causing trouble again?"

"Not so much, now that Petrovsky is dead. I'm afraid our latest security problems are caused more by my father."

Darcy glanced briefly at Connor who was standing still, his arms crossed over his broad chest. "I heard a little about your father the night of your wedding."

Shanna sighed. "At least we were still able to have the wedding. Would you like something to drink?"

"No, thank you."

"I need to go to Roman's townhouse to fetch the file," Connor announced quietly. "I'll return soon." He faded away.

Darcy breathed easier once he'd teleported away.

Shanna smiled. "I saw your show. You did a fabulous job."

"Thank you."

"I know the ex-harem probably hates me, but I really do wish them well." Shanna's smile widened. "I just wish them well far away from my husband."

"I understand." Darcy wondered what on earth could be so urgent that she was here. "If it helps, I can assure you that none of the harem ladies ever harbored romantic feelings for Roman. It was simply a matter of convenience."

"Thanks. That's good to know." Shanna sipped from her drink as an awkward silence fell between them.

"Why am I here?" Darcy finally asked.

Shanna shifted uneasily in her chair. "I think we should wait until Connor returns."

Darcy sighed. She really didn't want to discuss anything with Connor around. It was so hard to concentrate when she kept imagining what he had done four years ago. "It doesn't bother you to be surrounded by vampires?" Darcy blurted out. "I mean you're not frightened or . . . repulsed by us?"

Shanna smiled. "I was a bit freaked at first, but once I got to know Roman and his friends, I knew they'd never hurt me."

"But Roman—I mean—" Darcy was curious how a relationship could work between a Vamp and a mortal. If somehow, Adam could accept her as a vampire, perhaps . . .

"You're wondering how I could marry a vampire?" Darcy nodded.

"I was already falling in love with Roman when I found out the truth." Shanna's eyes filled with tears. "And he loves me so much. He's willing to do anything to give me the normal life I want. He's even trying to become mortal for me."

"What?" Darcy sat up. She dug her fingers into the sofa cushion. "Is such a thing possible?" *Oh, please, say it is.*

"Roman believes it's possible. But even so, the first experiment failed."

Darcy's heart plummeted to her stomach. She slumped back on the couch.

"Oh." Shanna winced. "I should have realized— I'm sorry."

Darcy shook her head. Her throat had contracted too tight to say anything.

"I am sorry." Shanna leaned over to touch Darcy's knee. "Connor told me how unhappy you are."

Darcy swallowed. "He should know."

"I know." Shanna watched her sadly. "But I know Connor very well. He wouldn't knowingly hurt anyone. He's a good man."

Darcy gritted her teeth. "I've heard it before." And yet, here she was, a vampire against her will. He hadn't asked for permission. He'd just assumed she would be grateful to spend eternity as a blood-sucking creature. No matter what the price. She squeezed her eyes shut.

The price had been too high, dammit. She'd lost everything. Her family, friends, career. And she was still losing. She would lose Adam once he knew the truth. But if she could become mortal again . . . "Tell me about the experiment."

Shanna sighed. "Well, it's basically the reversal of the process that transforms a person into a vampire. During the transformation, a mortal is drained completely of blood. Roman believes a chemical is released from the attacking vampire, and it's this chemical that induces the coma. When the chemical wears off, the person dies a natural death. But if a vampire feeds his own blood to that person, he will become a vampire."

Images flitted through Darcy's mind of Connor feeding his own blood back to her. She swallowed hard. "Go on."

"To reverse the process, a vampire would be

completely drained by another vampire, so the bite will release the chemical that induces the vampire coma. Then, if the subject is infused with human blood, he should awaken as a human."

Darcy took a deep breath. "And you say it failed?"

"The first attempt did." Shanna grimaced. "That poor little pig. I objected, but Roman said it was the only way."

Darcy stiffened. "They made a vampire *pig*?"

Shanna made a sour face. "Yeah. It sounds terrible, I know, but I'm grateful Roman didn't go ahead with his original plan and do the experiment on himself." She shuddered. "Thank God we talked him out of that."

Roman was willing to risk his life in order to be a mortal with his wife. "He loves you very much."

Shanna nodded. "He's at Romatech now, trying to figure out what went wrong. Laszlo has a theory, but if he's right, then the experiment will never work."

"Oh." Darcy's heart sank lower.

"Laszlo believes it's like turning back time, that the vampire in question must be returned completely to his former human self. In other words, the human blood infused into him must contain his own specific human DNA."

"They can't insert Roman's DNA into some synthetic blood?"

"That's what Roman planned to do, but last night they discovered his DNA was mutated. And since Roman is over five hundred years old, there's no way to know what his original human DNA was like."

"Oh." It was impossible. She was still trapped. Forever.

Shanna leaned back in her chair, frowning. "That

last discovery has really screwed up everything. We were so sure we could have children, but now . . ."

"You wanted to have children with Roman?"

"Yes, very much." Shanna gazed off into space. "It seemed so simple. Roman just erased the DNA from live human sperm and inserted his own. We tried artificial insemination a few times." She splayed her hand across her belly. "I could be pregnant now. I hope so."

Darcy sat up, alarmed. "But you just said his DNA isn't human. It's mutated."

"Roman only figured that out last night. Now, he wants to stop the attempts to get me pregnant."

"But you don't?"

Shanna shrugged. "I love him just the way he is. And I would love our child, no matter what."

Darcy's gaze lowered to Shanna's abdomen. "The baby's DNA would be half vampire."

"I know." Shanna smiled. "Don't worry. We only attempted insemination three times. Chances are nothing happened." Her smile turned sad. "I wanted children so bad."

"I'm sorry." Darcy reached over to touch her hand.

Shanna squeezed her hand back. "I'll keep praying. And I'll pray everything works out for you, too."

Darcy sat back, releasing Shanna's hand. "I'm afraid it's hopeless for me."

"There's always hope." Shanna's eyes twinkled. "I believe I told Roman that once."

Connor's image wavered before them, then became solid. Darcy's nerves tensed. He placed a plastic DVD case and a manila folder on the coffee table. On the folder, written in bold letters, she read the words STAKE-OUT TEAM.

"Sorry it took me so long." Connor took a seat in the blue toile chair opposite Shanna. "While I was at the townhouse, we received another call from Katya."

"Oh, dear." Shanna frowned.

"Who is she?" Darcy asked.

"Katya and Galina are joint coven masters for the Russians," Connor explained.

"Female coven masters?" Darcy asked. "I didn't know such a thing was possible."

"It is revolutionary," Connor admitted. "They took over after Petrovsky died."

Shanna snorted. "You mean after they both killed him."

"Aye, those are two ladies I wouldna want to anger." Connor grimaced. "But they are verra angry now. Another one of their coven was murdered tonight in Central Park."

"How many is that now?" Shanna asked. "Three?"

"Aye. Three Malcontents killed in the last few weeks. Katya accused us of doing it. I denied it, but she's certain we know more than we're saying."

"Do you?" Darcy's journalistic instincts kicked in. "Do you know who's doing it?"

"I can make a bloody good guess." Connor gestured toward the folder. "Our wee friends from the CIA. The Stake-Out team."

Shanna groaned.

Darcy thought back. "Didn't you mention them before? The night of Shanna's wedding?"

Shanna nodded wearily. "My father's in charge of the Stake-Out team. He tried his best to stop my wedding."

Connor frowned. "They're up to other mischief as well."

Darcy glanced at the folder with a sense of foreboding. "How can a mortal manage to kill a vampire? Wouldn't a Vamp use mind control to stop him? Or simply teleport away?"

"Each member of the team has a certain amount of psychic power," Connor explained.

"My father has quite a bit," Shanna added. "I inherited my abilities from him."

"I see. So, these mortals are vampire slayers with psychic power. It sounds frightening."

"It is." Shanna sighed. "I tried to tell my father there were two kinds of vampires—the good, bottle-guzzling, modern Vamp and the nasty Malcontents. But he wouldn't listen. He hates all vampires with a passion. Roman's afraid he would even hurt me now that he considers me a traitor."

"I'm so sorry. It must be very difficult for you."

Shanna gave her a sad look. "My father's making it difficult for everyone. Even you, I'm afraid."

"Me? But I've never met any of them."

"My father held me prisoner for a while until Connor was able to rescue me," Shanna continued. "I met most of the team, so I recognize them when I see them."

Connor moved to the couch, next to Darcy. She immediately stiffened. "I am sorry, lass, but ye must know about this." He turned the folder to face them and opened it.

The first sheet of paper was titled Sean Whelan and contained information on him.

Connor pointed to a box with the number 10 inside. "This is how the CIA ranks psychic power. A ten is the highest." He turned the page to reveal Sean Whelan's photo.

Connor turned to the next profile. It was on Alyssa Barnett. Psychic power: 5. Connor turned the page to her photo, then continued to the next profile. Emma Wallace. Psychic power: 7.

"She's British," Connor commented. "Transferred over from MI6, most likely because of her psychic abilities. It is a bit rare amongst the mortals." He turned to her photo.

The women were young and pretty, Darcy noticed. "I've never seen any of these people."

"Just wait." Connor turned to the next profile.

The page was titled Garrett Manning. Psychic power: 3. Connor turned to his photo.

Darcy gasped. She was looking at Garth Manly. "No. This must be some kind of mistake."

"No mistake." Shanna frowned at Garrett's photo. "When I saw him climb out of that limo on your show—I couldn't believe it."

Darcy jumped up and skirted the coffee table. A CIA operative on her show? She paced across the room. "I don't understand. He auditioned for the show. I picked him myself."

"Well, he is rather handsome," Shanna conceded. "I can see why you would choose him."

Darcy paced back toward the sofa. "He was easily one of the best. You should have seen the others. They were so—" She halted suddenly. The others had been so bad. Unbelievably bad. Her shoulders slumped. "I was set up. From the beginning."

"Probably so," Connor agreed. "But you shouldna flay yerself over it. The question now is why is he there? What is he planning to do?"

"I—I don't know." Darcy paced across the floor again. "He's been behaving himself. As far as I know."

"No one on yer set has been harmed in any way?"

"No."

"Still, you should double yer security, especially during the day. I'll gladly take care of that. I doona like the thought of a vampire slayer living in the same house as yer Vamps."

"Oh, my God." Darcy halted, breathing heavily. All her friends could be in danger. All the male contestants, too. And all because she had allowed a CIA man on her show. "This is terrible."

"I'm afraid it gets worse." Connor rotated the folder so it would be facing her. He turned Garrett's photo over. "There's another one."

A chill ran up Darcy's spine. "No," she whispered. "No." *Please, don't let it be him.*

She stepped closer to the coffee table and read the name of the last profile. Austin Olaf Erickson.

Olaf. Psychic power: 10. The room swirled around her head.

Connor turned the page to reveal the last photo.

Adam.

Chapter 17

Darcy's legs gave out. She plopped onto her rear, still staring at the photo on the coffee table.

"Are ye all right, lass?" Connor stood.

She shook her head, still staring at the photo. *Adam.*

Shanna leaned forward. "Are you involved with him?"

"I—I don't even know his real name." Darcy lowered her head into her hands.

"You *are* involved with him," Shanna whispered.

Why bother to deny it? One look at his picture, and she'd collapsed on the floor. Darcy raised her head and gazed at Adam's photo. No, not Adam. Her chest contracted, squeezing the air from her lungs and crushing her heart. She'd spent so much time thinking about Adam when he wasn't Adam. Longing for Adam when he wasn't Adam. He'd been the first thought in her mind when she awoke, her last thought when she fell into her death sleep. And her thoughts had always centered on the futile hope that somehow, in spite of all her fears and doubts, he could still love her and they could be together.

It was all a lie. A useless, hopeless dream that turned to dust in the light of the truth, just like she would in the sun. Adam was gone. No, Adam had never existed. But her dream had been real. And it nearly killed her to lose it. The loss tore at her heart, then slowly twisted into something more sinister.

Betrayal.

He'd lied to her. Hell, he probably didn't care about her at all. He was simply working undercover. Now his conversation with Lady Pamela made sense. He'd talked about the different lengths of nighttime because he knew he was talking to a vampire. He'd wanted the judges to think he was a vampire. He was fooling them, fooling her. And his remark about being an international spy? Lady Pamela had laughed at his silliness, but he was the one laughing at them all.

"Oh my God," Darcy gasped. She looked at Shanna in horror. "I told him about your wedding. It was my fault. Oh, no." She covered her mouth. "I'm so sorry."

Shanna's eyes widened. "What did you say?"

"He asked me to go out that Saturday, and I said I had a wedding to go to. I mentioned your names, but that was all."

Connor nodded. "That's how Sean Whelan knew the date of the wedding."

"I didn't say where," Darcy assured them. But now, she remembered how Adam had pressed her for more information. He'd wanted to know where Shanna was taking her honeymoon.

"It's all right." Shanna smiled. "We still had our wedding."

Darcy gritted her teeth. "It's not all right." Anger flared inside her, but it wasn't hot. She'd thought she was cold the last four years, but it was nothing compared to the icy rage that shuddered through her now. Adam had used her, and she'd been so desperate for warmth and attention, she'd fallen for him. She'd come close to destroying Shanna's wedding because of him. Damn him for treating her like a pathetic, lonely woman.

She motioned toward the plastic DVD case. "What is that?"

"Surveillance on Austin Erickson." Connor opened the case and removed the disk. "We've been studying the Stake-Out team. We plan to visit them all on the same night and erase their memories."

Connor inserted the DVD into Shanna's recorder and turned on the TV. "I did surveillance on Erickson to get an idea of his schedule. We doona want to miss him on the appointed night."

Darcy slowly stood. On the TV screen, she saw a dimly-lit garage. Someone parked a dark sedan and climbed out. Adam. No, make that Austin. No, make that *Lying Scumbag*. He walked toward an elevator. The screen went black momentarily, then showed the living room of an apartment. Austin was inside, moving about.

"I levitated to the fourth floor and shot this through the window," Connor said.

"I hope no one noticed you hanging around in mid-air," Shanna commented dryly.

The corner of the Scotsman's mouth quirked. "I wasna seen." His smile faded as he regarded Darcy. "This Erickson is a dangerous one. We've never seen a mortal with that much psychic power."

Shanna's eyes widened. "More than me?"

"Ye're strong," Connor conceded. "But ye havena been trained for it." He motioned to Austin on the screen. "This man has."

Darcy clenched her hands. They felt brittle and cold enough to crack like a sheet of ice. "What kind of psychic power? Does he control people?" Had he manipulated her mind to make her fall for him? No, that couldn't be right. Her feelings involved more than her brain. And he couldn't have manipulated her heart.

"I'm no' certain how much he can do," Connor replied. "But surely ye would have noticed if he tried to read yer mind."

"Right." Darcy exhaled with relief. She could always tell when someone tried to enter her mind. "I would have felt cold."

Shanna winced. "It doesn't work that way for a mortal. When my father tried to read my mind, it was very warm."

"Aye. 'Tis cold as death from a Vamp, but hot from a mortal," Connor agreed.

Hot? Darcy sank into a wingback chair. Good God. All those times she'd flushed with heat, she'd attributed it to attraction, even lust. And all along, it had been him, invading her mind. Without her knowledge and against her will.

Connor's eyes narrowed. "He has read yer mind, hasn't he?"

That manipulating bastard. Her eye twitched. "I—I don't think he learned anything valuable from me."

"Probably not." Connor crossed his arms. "They never knew where the wedding was to take place."

Darcy nodded. All Austin could have learned from her was her most private fears and desires. And that was bad enough. He might even know she'd fallen in love with him. Empathic, ha! She'd thought he was exaggerating, but no, it was a gross understatement. Another lie.

She snatched his profile from the folder. "Can I keep this?"

"Aye. We have it all on computer." Connor turned off the television. "What are ye planning to do?"

"Get even." Darcy noted Austin's address on the profile.

"I doona think it's a good idea for ye to see him right now. Ye're too upset. Let me talk to him."

"He's *my* problem. I'll deal with it."

Connor hesitated, frowning.

"You made decisions for me in the past," Darcy added quietly. "Don't do it again."

A hint of pain crossed his face. "Verra well. I will leave this to you. But be careful. We doona know how he will react."

"I only spent a short time with him," Shanna said as she stood. "But he seemed like a nice guy."

"He seemed like a lot of things," Darcy muttered as she folded his profile and slipped it into her trouser pocket.

"I thought he had a more open mind than the others," Shanna continued. "This could be a good thing, you know. If you can convince him that some vampires are good, he could tell the others on the team."

Darcy balled her hands into fists. She didn't feel like being a diplomat tonight. "I want to go now."

"All right." Connor gathered together the DVD and folder. "I'll take ye to Roman's townhouse. Then, Ian can drive ye to the apartment."

This time, Darcy didn't object when Connor draped

an arm around her shoulders and teleported away.
Thirty minutes later, Ian double-parked on a narrow
side street in Greenwich Village. It was only a few
blocks from the alley where her life had changed forever.

"I'll find a place to park," Ian said. "How much
time do ye need?"

Darcy glanced at the clock on the dashboard. "I
think thirty minutes should be enough." She'd known
Ian for four years now, yet it still rattled her that he
looked like a teenager but was over four hundred years
old.

"I'll be waiting for you outside his apartment at
two-forty-five." Ian left the lights flashing on Roman's
BMW and dashed around to open Darcy's door.
"Come." He led her to the front door of the apartment
building.

"The mortal is verra strong, both physically and
psychically, so be careful." Ian removed some tools
from his sporran. In less than a minute, he had the
door unlocked.

"Thank you." Darcy walked into the building and
went up the elevator to the fourth floor. The hallway
was long and dimly lit. Austin's apartment was
halfway down, facing the street.

A sudden reluctance swept through her. What was
she doing? Sure she was pissed, but this confrontation
was going to hurt her as much as it would him. Because, dammit, she still cared. For the past few weeks,
she'd felt attraction, desire, worry, even love for this
man. The emotions had poured into a deep, hungry
well, and it couldn't drain empty in just a few minutes.

She tried the doorknob. Locked, of course. Would
he hear her if she knocked? Would he even let her in?

She considered finding Ian to let him fiddle with the locks. Or there was another possibility. She'd never tried it before. She'd never wanted to admit she was capable of it. It was a vampire thing.

But she was a vampire. Time to stop pretending she was merely a human with an eating disorder who kept odd hours. She was a creature of the night, and that was the reason Austin Olaf Erickson had come into her life.

She rested a palm against the door and concentrated. She only had to teleport to the other side—only move a few inches through space. She closed her eyes and focused her thoughts. Slowly, the floor beneath her feet disappeared. The door beneath her hand vanished. She quelled a sudden burst of panic and willed herself forward a few feet. Now, she concentrated on regaining her form. The room came into view, the same room she'd seen on Connor's surveillance disk. A quick look around assured her the room was empty.

She'd done it! She glanced back, noting the three deadbolt locks and alarm system control panel by the door. With a surge of pride, she realized even a macho, international spy couldn't keep her out. Now, where was that lying scumbag?

She moved quietly across the room. Austin obviously spent a lot of time on the leather couch that sat opposite the television. The coffee table was littered with videotapes, a laptop, and old computer disks. Not very modern for an international spy. And not very sober, either. A dozen empty beer bottles decorated the end table.

In one corner of the room, a workout bench was surrounded by an assortment of weights. To the left, the living area opened into a small kitchen. To the right, she spotted a closed door.

She opened it and wandered inside. Moonlight from the window illuminated several pieces of furniture—a dresser, a bedside table, and a queen-sized bed. Her eyesight and hearing had grown keener since becoming a vampire. She could hear his soft and regular breathing, see each fold and twist of the bed sheet around his legs and hips. Apparently, he moved a lot in his sleep. He'd pushed the sheet down to his hips. She could see the waistband on his boxer shorts.

He was a beautiful man. Moonlight caressed the breadth of his back across the shoulders, the golden tint of his skin, the indentation of his spine as it came down his lower back. Darcy circled the bed, looking at him. The curve of his biceps, the soft, curly hair on his chest, the thick, tousled hair on his head, the little crease on his cheek where his dimple was. His skin looked bronzed and warm. How she had loved that warmth. But she had confused his body warmth with a warm, loving character.

Her eyes brimmed with tears. She'd fallen for him so fast. His jaw was shaded with whiskers, darker than the sun-bleached hair on his head. It gave him an aura of danger, as if a pirate lurked beneath the golden surfer-boy. But the skin along his cheekbones was soft and smooth. His thick eyelashes rested against the soft skin, lending him a look of sweet innocence.

She had believed in that innocence when all along there'd been a pirate underneath. *How could you?* Her thoughts screamed in her head. *How could you lie to me?*

He moaned and turned onto his back.

She stepped back. Had he heard her thoughts?

He shook his head slowly, his face contorting with a grimace. "No," he mumbled. He kicked at the sheet. "No." His hands fisted. His eyes moved rapidly beneath his closed eyelids.

A bad dream, that was all. Well, he deserved bad dreams.

"No." He curled into a fetal position. "Darcy."

She inhaled sharply. He was dreaming about her. And his voice had sounded wrenched with pain. A guilty conscience? Or had he fallen for her, too? She backed out of the room. She recalled the way he had looked that night in the greenhouse when he'd thought no one was watching. He'd looked miserable.

She approached the couch. Were all these empty beer bottles his way of drowning the pain? The labels on the videotapes caught her eye. *Local Four/Darcy Newhart*. What on earth? She grabbed one and inserted it into the VCR. She located the remote control on the couch, then turned on the television. The volume was fairly low, but she punched the mute button just in case.

The tape started. Her knees gave out, and she plopped onto the couch. Oh, God, she remembered this. It was the opening of the dog park in the Bronx. She was there, alive, walking in the sunlight. She pressed a hand against her mouth. Her eyes stung with tears. Dammit. She wasn't going to cry. That life was over.

She turned off the television and examined the videos. A dozen in all, they covered her entire career and beyond. The last one's label read *Darcy's Disappearance/Death?* With a gasp, she dropped it on the table. Good God. She squeezed her eyes shut and concentrated on taking deep breaths.

A calmness settled over her when she realized Austin Erickson had been watching those tapes. He'd studied her like a test subject in order to manipulate her. The lying scumbag.

She picked up a computer disk and read the label. *DVN/employee records*. That bastard. She picked up two more. *DVN/subscribers*. *DVN/advertisers*. Good God, he must have downloaded everything from DVN. Is this what he'd done in her office? He'd come pretending that he wanted to see her, but all along he'd been seeking a way to destroy her workplace, her acquaintances, her entire world.

She glimpsed something yellow beneath the disks and pushed them to the side. She lifted the yellow legal pad to make out the writing in the dim light. Her name was scrawled on the bottom of a list. And in the top margin, he'd written *Vampires Must Die*.

With a strangled cry, she dropped the pad on the table. A shudder coursed through her body. *Die?* He meant to kill her? She clenched her hands together and looked at the list once more. Gregori, Vanda, Maggie, the list went on naming all the people she cared about. Panic flooded her, threatening to drown her with the full extent of Adam's betrayal.

She leapt to her feet. She would not be victimized like this. Her life had been stolen from her before, but never again. That bastard, she should march in there and knock his head off. But first, she needed to protect her vampire friends. No more pretending she wasn't one of them. She was, and this was war.

She ripped the first few pages off the legal pad and tore them up into tiny pieces. She eyed his laptop. It was probably full of information. She'd take it with her when she left. As for the disks, they needed to go.

She gathered them up and strode into the kitchen. She opened the microwave and tossed them inside. Three minutes should be enough. She pushed the start button and stood back, smiling grimly as the sparks began to sizzle inside. Maybe the whole damned thing would blow up.

"Hold it right there," a deep voice spoke quietly. "Put your hands up where I can see them."

Darcy turned slowly and saw Austin move from the doorway of his bedroom. Moonlight glinted off the metal revolver in his hand.

As he advanced, he pivoted from side to side, aiming his gun at the shadows. "Did you come alone?"

He couldn't see well, Darcy realized. "I'm alone."

He froze at the sound of her voice. "Darcy?"

She flipped on the kitchen light and enjoyed the shocked look on his face. "Surprised to see me, *Austin?*" She motioned to his revolver. "If you're planning to kill me now, you'll have to do better than that."

Chapter 18

She knew who he was.

In a moment of crisis, Austin's training usually kicked in, allowing him to shove all emotion into storage and react with cool logic and precision. That was how it was supposed to work. But one look at Darcy's face, and his emotions were screaming to be let out. She knew who he was. Crap.

He scanned the room to make sure she was alone. The locks on his door were secure. The control panel was still blinking, so the alarm was still on. She must have teleported in.

A videotape was partially ejected from the VCR. She must have watched some of the tape. The computer disks were missing from the coffee table. Bits of yellow paper littered the table and floor. The list he'd made with the title *Vampires Must Die*. She'd seen it. With her name on it. The emotional door cracked open. "Shit."

"If you're referring to yourself, I agree." Darcy

stood in the kitchen, her arms crossed, her expression harsh with anger.

A blade of emotion stabbed at his heart. *Not now.* He pushed the pain aside and strode toward her. "I can explain."

"Don't bother. I already know everything, *Austin.*" She wielded his name like a weapon, and each time she said it, it slashed at him, marking him as a liar.

A series of loud pops erupted from the microwave.

"What are you doing?" He ran to the kitchen and punched the button to open the microwave door. All the computer disks lay in a melted heap of plastic. Thank God he'd already downloaded everything onto his laptop and a memory stick. Still, it looked like the carousel plate in his microwave was ruined.

He gave her an irritated look. "Cute."

She glanced at his boxers. "I could say the same thing."

Sheesh. Of all the nights to be wearing these stupid SpongeBob briefs. Splashed across his groin was SpongeBob proudly claiming to be boss of his pine-apple. "My little sister gave these to me for Christmas."

Darcy arched her eyebrows. "You have a family? I thought something like you slithered out from under a rock. Or maybe, you were hatched in a green, slimy pond."

"I know you're angry."

"Oh, wow. You really do have psychic powers."

"Not psychic enough." He wasn't thrilled with how things had turned out, either. He'd found the perfect woman only to lose her. "I actually thought you were human until a few days ago."

She stiffened. "I *am* human."

"I meant *alive*." He set his gun down on the counter within his reach. "I thought you were an innocent mortal trapped in the vampire world. I wanted to save you."

She tilted her head, studying him. "You thought I was a mortal? You couldn't tell the difference?"

"No! You had a pulse, dammit. How can a vampire have a pulse? And you were drinking cold chocolate. And whenever I read your mind, you were thinking about beaches and the sun and your family. What kind of vampire longs for the sun?"

She gritted her teeth. "I do."

"You had me completely fooled. I thought you were in terrible danger. I thought you needed rescuing."

"And you were going to be the hero and save me?" She stepped closer, her eyes glimmering with pain. *"You're too late."*

He flinched. He was too late. She could never be his.

"I saw the title on your handy little list. 'Vampires Must Die.' So now, instead of saving me, you want to kill me?"

The pang dug deeper at his heart. "I could never hurt you."

"You're lying again! You have hurt me."

"I didn't mean to. I thought you were alive when I—but when I discovered you were dead—"

"Do I look *dead* to you?" She jabbed a finger at his chest. "Did I feel *dead* when you were touching me? Did I taste *dead* to you in the hot tub?"

"I thought you were alive, dammit!" He shoved her poking finger aside. "But when we got out of the hot tub, I could see my shadow. And you didn't have one. That's when I realized the truth."

Her eyes narrowed. "And that's when you dumped me."

"What did you expect me to do? Make love to a dead woman?"

She gasped, then drew back her hand and slapped him hard. "Can a dead woman do that?"

He tasted blood on his lip. Sheesh, he should have known not to insult a female vampire. Darcy was incredibly fast and strong. He wiped his mouth and saw the red streak on his hand.

She stiffened, staring at his hand.

"What's wrong, Darcy? Did you forget to eat before coming?"

Her eyes blazed with anger. "I've never bitten anyone. If you knew me at all, you would know I could never do that."

"But you have the urge, don't you?" He stepped toward her. "You can't help it. It's what you are."

"Stop it!" She shoved him back and strode from the kitchen. "I'm not like that. I'm not evil. And neither are my friends."

He followed her into the living room. "I've seen your kind in action. They attack people, rape and murder innocent women."

"Those are the Malcontents." She paced across the room. "The rest of us aren't like that."

"You have the same urges, the same thirst for human blood."

"Aagh!" She lifted both hands in frustration. "How can you be so blind? You've seen my friends on the show. You have to know there's nothing evil about them."

He was so damned frustrated, he had to lash out. "Your dear *friends* predate the invention of synthetic blood. So, they must have preyed on the innocent. That makes them evil."

"What gives you the right to judge what is evil?"

"I represent the innocent. The victims."

"You don't believe I was a victim?"

His heart stuttered. Of course she was a victim. And an innocent. Dammit, he wanted this to be simple. Either right or wrong. Not this murky mess that didn't make any sense.

She paced toward him. "I never lied to you about my name or my profession." She pointed at the videotapes. "I never investigated you behind your back. I never invaded your workplace, pretending I wanted to kiss you when all I wanted was information. I never invaded your head. I never put your best friends on a hit list. I never betrayed you or planned to stab you in the back. So tell me, Austin, which one of us is *evil?*"

He fell back onto the couch. Holy shit. He'd tried so hard to convince himself he was on the right side— the human side. But was he the one being inhuman?

He looked at the stack of videotapes. He'd fallen in love with the human Darcy. When he'd found out the truth about her, he'd thought he could simply turn off those feelings. Announce her dead, bury the feelings, and go on with the assignment. But he couldn't. Holy crap.

He was compromised.

And he was still in love. Even though he knew who she was.

"I have to go." She trudged toward the door. The last few steps, she closed her eyes and frowned with concentration.

She bumped into the door. "Damn," she muttered, then leaned her forehead against the door.

His sweet Darcy. "Not much of a vampire, are you?"

She shot an angry look at him over her shoulder. "I'm having trouble focusing." She flipped the first deadbolt lock.

She was leaving him. Leaving, feeling betrayed. He couldn't let her go like that. He watched her turn the second and third deadbolt lock. "You were all I ever wanted in a woman."

Her hand stilled. "Don't lie to me."

"The way I felt was never a lie. It was real."

She turned to face him. Her eyes glistened with tears.

He gestured toward the tapes. "At first, I was curious. I wanted to know what had happened to you. But the more I got to know you, the more intrigued I became. The more fascinated and attracted. The more I realized I was in love with you."

Her face crumbled. "And now, you can't bear to touch me. You think I'm repulsive."

He winced. God, he wished that was true. It would be easier if he couldn't stand to touch her. But now, even knowing who she was, he still wanted her. "Darcy." He stood. "You were the most beautiful woman I've ever known."

"Past tense." She closed her eyes and looked away. "You don't believe this can work, do you?"

"No. I don't."

"I told myself that so many times. I tried to resist you. But I wanted you so much."

Austin sighed. They were both suffering. Somehow, that knowledge didn't help much. "If you want Garrett and me off the show, I understand."

She drew in a shaky breath. "It would be hard to explain this mess to my boss. Sly's going to be mad enough that I let mortals on the show, but hiring two vampire slayers—"

"We never planned to hurt anyone. We were only gathering information."

"Which you planned to use against us."

He groaned inwardly. He couldn't deny that. "My boss is desperate to find his daughter."

"And murder his son-in-law?" Darcy shook her head. "Roman and Shanna are very happy. You should leave them alone."

"You don't think she's in any danger, married to a vampire?"

Darcy scoffed. "You don't understand how much they love each other. But then, I don't suppose you know much about love."

Ouch. He knew it hurt like hell.

Darcy sighed. "If you and Garrett can get yourselves eliminated in the next round, that would help. Then, you'd both be gone, and I'd still have a job."

"Fine. We'll just keep all the spy stuff a secret."

She nodded. "That would be the best for both of us."

"How did you find out?"

With another sigh, she leaned against the door. "The show made its debut on DVN tonight. Shanna saw it and recognized you. She called Connor, and they told me who you are."

He winced. "We thought you'd finish recording everything before the first show aired."

A knock on the door startled her. "That's my ride. I—I'll see you at the penthouse Monday night?"

"Yes. Wait a minute." He strode toward the door and switched off the alarm system. "You can go now. Good night."

She looked at him, her face pale. "Good night."

She was only a few inches away, but it felt like a chasm stretched between them. Two different worlds.

"Such a shame," he whispered. How would he ever get over her?

She grimaced. "Yes, it is." She opened the door.

Austin tensed when he saw the kilted Scotsman in the hallway. The youthful-looking vampire shot Austin an irritated look, then took Darcy's arm and led her away.

Out of his life. Back to the world of vampires. Austin slowly closed the door.

What the hell was he going to do? Betray Darcy and her friends? Or betray his job at the CIA? Either way, he couldn't escape the outcome. He would be a traitor.

Ian escorted her around the block to where he'd parked the car. "Connor just called. Gregori's been trying to find ye. He says yer boss wants to see you right away."

Darcy groaned. "Of course he does." Sly wanted to pitch a fit because of the mortals on the reality show. This was the conversation she'd dreaded. Great. Wasn't it enough that her heart was in shreds? She didn't want to lose her job, too. Besides, she still thought including mortals had been a great twist. How was she to know those mortals would be undercover spies? That little fact she would never admit to Sly. She was stuck in a weird position. She'd have to protect Austin and Garrett in order to protect herself.

Ian opened the car door for her. "I'll drive ye to

DVN. Gregori's headed that way. He'll take ye home when ye're done."

"Thank you." Darcy climbed into the front passenger seat.

Ian zipped around to the driver's side and got in. "I have a cell phone if ye'd rather teleport. It would be faster."

Darcy fastened her seat belt. "I'd rather you drive, if you don't mind."

"All right." Ian started the engine and they drove off.

Darcy didn't want to try teleporting again. She was still too upset to concentrate properly. Her last attempt had been so embarrassing. Bouncing off the door? Sheesh. It had reminded her of a sci-fi show where the doors failed to swoosh open and the actors crashed into the door.

She realized she was trying not to think about Austin. Or his confession of love. Or his belief that they had no future. Dammit, future was the one thing she did have. In abundance. Why couldn't she spend it with the man she loved? Shanna was happily married to Roman. Why couldn't Austin be happy with her?

Do you expect me to make love to a dead woman? His words rushed back, flooding her with pain and frustration. They couldn't have a future. His mission in life was to battle her own kind. He would have to give up his job to be with her. He'd have to give up his whole way of life to dwell in the darkness with her. It'd been so hard for her to adjust. How could she expect him to do it? He was right. It was impossible.

Ian dropped her off at DVN. She wandered across the lobby, aware of the furious glares being cast her way by the other vampires. Great. She was enemy number one in the vampire world.

The receptionist frowned at her. "Mr. Bacchus is expecting you. I'll tell him you've arrived." She punched a button on her phone. "She's here."

She's doomed, Darcy thought as she walked down the hall. She knocked on Sly's door.

"Come in."

As Darcy entered, Tiffany rushed past her into the hall. Great. Hopefully, Tiffany had left him in a good mood. Darcy shut the door. Sylvester Bacchus stood behind his desk, his arms crossed, his brow creased with a ferocious scowl.

Tiffany must be overrated. Darcy squared her shoulders and lifted her chin. "You wanted to see me?"

Sly narrowed his beady eyes. "I watched the debut tonight. The whole freaking vampire world watched it."

Darcy swallowed. "That was what we'd hoped for."

He skirted the desk. "The show finished two hours ago. In that time, we have received fifteen hundred phone calls and emails. Do you know what they're saying, Newhart?"

"They . . . like the show?"

With a snort, he stopped in front of her. "They hate you."

She gripped her hands together. "I can explain—"

"I thought I told you that the Sexiest Man on Earth had to be a vampire."

"He will be. The mortals will never pass all the tests."

"Did I say you could include mortal scum on a vampire show?"

"No, but you wanted a big twist, one that would shock everyone. I believe I have accomplished that."

He raised a hand to hush her. "Let me tell you what you've accomplished. You've pissed off the entire vampire world."

"I—" She stopped when he pointed a finger at her.

He stepped closer 'til the tip of his pointing finger was an inch from her face. "I have two words to say to you."

She braced herself for it. *You're fired.*

The corner of Sly's mouth lifted. "You're brilliant."

Her eye twitched.

"You have single-handedly caused an uproar! This is the most exciting event since the introduction of synthetic blood."

"Excuse me?"

Sly paced across the room. "We're averaging over seven hundred calls and emails an hour. Vamps all over the world are royally pissed. At *us*! It's fantastic."

"Huh?"

"When Wednesday night comes, the entire vampire world will come to a screeching halt while everyone watches our show. Tell me, do they kick off another mortal in the next show?"

Darcy thought back. Yes, Nicholas was booted off when he dropped Lady Pamela in the mud. "Yes, they do."

"Great!" Sly slapped his thigh. "You're a genius, Newhart. It's like you've created a war on television. Vamps will be glued to the screen to make sure the mortals are defeated."

"I see."

"They will be defeated, won't they?" Sly paused in mid-stride. "I'm warning you, Newhart, a Vamp has got to win."

"Yes, sir."

"Have you finished recording yet?"

"No. We have three nights left."

"And the last night—when are you shooting that?"

"This Friday."

Sly nodded. "I want to be there to personally hand over the harem and the check to the winner. It'll be great!"

"Yes, sir."

Sly grinned. "That's it, Newhart. Good work."

"Thank you." She headed for the door.

"Just remember, a Vamp has to win."

"No problem." Darcy exhaled in relief as she strode to her office. She still had a job. And Austin had agreed that he and Garrett would get eliminated in the next round. In her office, she worked on the second show that would air on Wednesday.

After a few minutes, the receptionist came in with a stack of phone messages and emails. "Sly wanted you to see these."

Darcy thumbed through the messages. Oh, no. Vamps from around the world were complaining about the ex-harem's old clothes and hairstyles. Some were even poking fun at them.

Darcy had tried so hard to get the ladies to modernize. These messages might do the trick.

She worked until Gregori and Maggie arrived. They were relieved she still had a job and that the show would continue.

Maggie studied the messages that blasted the ex-harem's taste. "You know what this means?"

"That Lady Pamela will have the vapors?" Gregori muttered.

Maggie smiled. "Yes. But then, we'll be doing makeovers."

Chapter 19

"This is just wrong," Gregori muttered. "You can't pay me enough for this kind of humiliation."

Darcy winced. "Actually, I'm not paying you at all." It was Monday night, and she was in the hot tub with Gregori and Vanda, getting ready to record the fourth episode of *The Sexiest Man on Earth*. "You agreed to help me out of the goodness of your heart, remember?"

Gregori sank deeper into the hot bubbly water. "That's my problem. I'm too damned nice. Nice guys never get the girl."

Vanda laughed. "Come on, Gregori. You have two women all to yourself right now."

He snorted. "I haven't noticed either of you being very friendly. I'm sitting here all alone in my little corner—"

"Pouting." Darcy finished his sentence for him.

He splashed water at her face. "You said I would be well dressed for the show. That means tuxedos, not this—this spandex underwear I'm wearing. It barely covers the goods."

"Stop worrying." Darcy splashed water back. "You look great in a Speedo."

"Yeah." Vanda winked at him. "You look as sexy as those male dancers last night."

"Don't remind me." Gregori scowled at them. "I never should have taken you ladies to that raunchy club."

"But we had fun," Vanda protested. "And we needed to celebrate the successful makeovers."

"You cost me four hundred dollars!"

"We did?" Darcy asked. "But we only ordered one drink apiece and that was just for looks."

"You forget that Vanda stuffed some money into the leopard guy's furry underwear," Gregori grumbled. "Money she got from me."

Darcy shrugged. "It was only a buck."

"It was a twenty," Gregori growled. "And then all the ladies had to try it. Over and over."

Darcy winced. No wonder the male dancers had practically climbed all over the ex-harem ladies. "I'm sorry. I didn't realize they were spending so much money."

"Why didn't you stuff some money?" Vanda asked.

Darcy shrugged. "I wasn't in the mood." And they weren't Austin. Even with male dancers gyrating in front of her face, she'd only wanted to think about Austin. She should have been angrier with him. He'd lied to her. Spied on her and her friends. But he'd also confessed to being in love with her. How could she stay angry when he loved her?

"Not in the mood?" Vanda looked aghast. "But

leopard guy was so hot. And I loved that cowboy with the sexy pants."

"Those were chaps," Darcy clarified. And they were indeed sexy when the cowboy forgot to wear his trousers underneath. At some point, while she was getting whiplashed with the flying fringe of Cowboy's chaps, she'd realized how easily she had forgiven Austin. The only explanation she could come up with was that she still loved him very much. Too much to just give up.

"Well, I was definitely in the mood." Vanda fanned herself. "Cowboy was packing quite a six-shooter."

"Yeah." Darcy grimaced. "I was afraid he'd have an accidental discharge."

Vanda laughed. "And that firefighter guy—wow! I've never seen such a long hose."

"Enough!" Gregori growled. "I really don't want these mental images. It's bad enough that . . ."

"What?" Darcy asked.

"Nothing. I'm glad the ladies enjoyed themselves."

"Me, too." Darcy nodded. After their makeover, the ladies had looked young and beautiful. It had been wonderful at the club, watching them realize how attractive they still were. And how much power they could still wield over men.

Gregori crossed his arms, frowning. "If you ever want to go there again, I'll drop you off and come back later."

"You didn't enjoy it?" Vanda asked.

He snorted. "The cowboy asked me for my phone number."

Darcy choked, trying not to laugh. "Poor Gregori. Too sexy for your own good."

He glowered at her. "And now you want to use me as man bait? This was not part of my job description."

"But it's the only way to test the next qualifier," Darcy insisted. "Qualification number seven states that the Sexiest Man on Earth has to like women."

"That was my idea." Vanda smoothed back her wet purple hair. "That's why I get to do the judging tonight."

"And qualification number eight says he must know how to please a woman," Darcy continued. "Vanda will verify that, too."

"Yes." She sighed. "It's a tough job, but somebody has to do it."

Gregori looked appalled. "You're going to make out with all six guys? In front of the cameras?"

"Don't worry." Vanda adjusted her bikini top so her purple bat tattoo could be seen. "I won't do anything too shocking."

"No nudity," Darcy warned her. Sheesh, Sly was going to love this episode. She only hoped Austin would refuse to get in the hot tub with Vanda. The thought of Vanda making a move on him was too awful to contemplate. But surely, Austin would refuse to cooperate. After all, he was supposed to get eliminated tonight.

Maggie walked across the lit pool area until she reached them. "The men are ready and waiting in the greenhouse."

"They're all wearing swimsuits?" Darcy asked. "And their anklets?"

"Yes. And they drew numbers to see who would go first."

"Who is first?" Vanda asked.

"Otto." Maggie grimaced. "He's wearing an itsy-bitsy bikini. And he's oiled his skin up. He said he wanted his bulges to glisten in the moonlight."

Darcy groaned.

Vanda grinned. "I'm ready."

"I'm not." Gregori sank in the water up to his chin.

"Let's get started." Darcy cued the cameramen.

Maggie walked back to the greenhouse where she'd release the men one at a time. The pool lay between the greenhouse and the hot tub. A patio chair had been positioned on each side of the pool. Maggie opened the glass French doors to the greenhouse. Otto appeared in the opening, his massive body swallowing up the entire space.

"That's our cue." Darcy climbed out of the hot tub. With a groan, Gregori did the same. Darcy sauntered to the patio chair on the south side of the pool. Gregori headed to the chair on the north side. The cameras followed their progress.

It *was* a bit embarrassing, she had to admit. Here she was in a revealing bikini, dripping water as she walked, just to see if she could catch a man's attention. And all of this would be seen on international vampire television.

Poor Gregori. This could be really embarrassing for him.

Otto strode across the terrace. As soon as he realized the cameras had turned to him, he paused to strike a pose.

"Ya, I am pumped up for tonight." He turned his back to the cameras to show off more bulges. Then he pivoted to the side to show off his biceps.

Darcy grew tired of watching and sat in the patio chair. She waved at Gregori on the other side of the pool. He sat and scowled at her. The purpose of this exercise was to test each man's sexual preference. When the contestant left the greenhouse, he would either look in Darcy's direction or Gregori's. Unfortunately, Otto was too in love with himself to notice either of them.

Finally, Otto ran out of poses and strode around the pool. He stopped in front of Darcy. "You vant de Otto, ya?"

"Oh, yeah." Darcy pointed at Vanda. "But she wants you first."

"Ya, de ladies have to vait deir turn." Otto chuckled as he strolled toward the hot tub. He jumped in, sloshing water over the side. "De Otto has arrived to pump you up."

It wasn't long before Vanda was personally checking out Otto's bulges. Darcy turned her chair to the side to keep from seeing more than she wanted. Gregori drew her attention when he pretended to be choking himself and gagging.

"My bulges are growing, ya?" Otto announced with his booming voice. "It is time to play in de Otto zone."

"Cut!" Darcy jumped to her feet. "That's enough, Otto."

"Bye, Otto." Vanda retreated to the far side of the hot tub.

Otto climbed out and passed by Darcy on his way back to the greenhouse. She gazed at the sky to avoid seeing any bulges that had recently occurred. Then, she lowered herself into the hot tub to warm up.

Vanda grinned. "I believe Otto passed the test."

Darcy nodded. And the other ladies, who were watching this on the television in their parlor, would most likely agree.

Gregori sat on the edge of the hot tub and dangled his feet in the water. "How can you stand that guy? He's so full of himself."

Vanda shrugged. "I've seen worse."

"But I thought you ladies were only interested in vampire sex," Gregori said.

"True." Vanda smoothed back her hair. "But I'm working on the theory that a Vamp would have to be good at sex in order to project good sex in his mind."

Darcy had never engaged in vampire sex, but she wondered if it was possible with Austin. After all, he did have psychic powers.

Gregori motioned toward the greenhouse. The next contestant was standing in the doorway. "It's show-time again." He stood and strode back to his chair on the north side of the pool.

Darcy strolled toward her chair. Her steps slowed when she realized Pierre from Brussels wasn't looking at her. She cast a warning glance at Gregori. He was lounging in his patio chair, gazing at the stars, completely oblivious to the fact that he'd acquired a new admirer.

Pierre crossed the terrace, then headed north around the pool. Gregori sat up with a jerk and gave Darcy a murderous look.

She winced and mouthed the word, "Sorry."

Pierre stopped next to Gregori and murmured something. Even across the pool, Darcy could see how red Gregori's face was. Pierre completed his walk toward the hot tub and stepped in. Vanda talked to him for a while. Then, she shook hands with him. He headed back to the greenhouse, circling the pool to the north.

Gregori saw him coming and dove into the pool. His teeth were chattering by the time he joined Darcy and Vanda in the hot tub. "That pool is freezing." He sank into the hot water up to his chin and closed his eyes.

"Looks like I'll have to eliminate Pierre," Vanda said. "What a shame. He was so cute."

Darcy cursed silently. Only two men could be eliminated tonight, and she had hoped it would be both the CIA men. "What did he say to you, Gregori?"

Gregori opened one eye to glare at her. "The incident will never be spoken of again."

"Poor Gregori." Vanda grinned. "I told you you looked sexy."

Austin waited in the greenhouse, growing increasingly annoyed. It looked like the reality show was having a swimsuit competition after all. The other men were wearing skimpy little briefs, but he refused to play the role of male sex object. His tropical print swim trunks were long enough to reach midthigh.

Reginald from Manchester was the third contestant to depart for the pool. When he returned to the greenhouse, dripping wet, Maggie handed him a towel and asked him to go downstairs and put on dry clothes for the orchid ceremony. Austin noticed the British vampire was surprisingly scrawny. The guy must have been wearing a lot of padding under his clothes.

"Number four?" Maggie asked.

"That's me." Austin joined her at the French doors.

"You'll go around the pool to the hot tub," Maggie instructed. "After you talk to Vanda for a while, you'll come back here. Understand?"

"Yes." *And I get myself eliminated, too.*

"Okay, they're ready." Maggie opened the door.

As Austin walked across the terrace, he took in the scene. The host was headed toward a chair on one side of the pool, and Darcy was on the other side. His mouth dropped open. Holy hot mama. Her little red bikini was wet and molded to her body. Her nipples had puckered from the cool night air. The bikini bottom was tied on each hip, the strings dangling and begging to be unraveled. Her skin was pale under the moonlight. She looked too fragile to touch, yet so alluring, he knew he'd never keep his hands off her.

Her eyes met his. There was such a sad longing in her eyes, it tore at his heart. Her gaze dipped over his body, then returned to his face. The longing in her eyes turned more intense, more desperate. She wanted him, too. If he didn't get off this show soon, he'd lose all resistance. Even now, his body was succumbing. His groin was swelling. His heart was pulling him toward her.

He had to stop this. Now. He dove into the pool and let the icy water douse his desire. He crossed the pool and climbed out. He shivered, his skin pebbling with goose flesh.

Vanda watched him from the spa. "Come in. You look cold."

He rubbed his hands over his arms. He ought to refuse. Wouldn't that get him eliminated? "No thanks."

"Don't you want to warm up?" Vanda floated across the tub and paused next to his feet. She plucked her tiny microphone off her bikini top and tossed it into the swimming pool. "Oops. How clumsy of me. Now, no one will hear me talking about the night you and Darcy heated up the hot tub."

Austin tensed. "I don't know what you're talking about."

Vanda smiled. "It was recorded on camera. They played it the other night on DVN."

Austin's mouth fell open. His make-out session with Darcy had been aired on vampire television? He glanced back at Darcy. She was standing by the pool, her expression wary.

"Don't worry," Vanda continued. "No one knows it was Darcy. Besides you and me, that is. Most people think it was Lady Pamela or Cora Lee since they both have long blond hair. But I recognized Darcy's dress when you tossed it into the pool."

"Did you tell anyone?"

"No." She scooted back across the tub. "At least, not yet. Why don't you sit down for a while?"

Was she threatening to expose Darcy? Austin wasn't sure, but he didn't want to take any chances. So, he stepped into the hot tub and settled on the seat across from Vanda.

She smiled. "Isn't that better?" She glanced past him and winced. "Oh, dear. Darcy's glaring at you now." Vanda swooshed across the water to sit next to him. "Shall we make her jealous?"

"I'd rather not."

"Right. No need to, actually. She was lost the minute she saw you at auditions. She called you Apollo, the sun god." Vanda ran a finger along his jaw.

Austin slid down the seat. "I don't want to upset her."

Vanda glanced over her shoulder. "Too late. She looks really pissed."

Austin crossed his arms over his chest. "What do you want from me?"

Vanda rested an elbow on the edge of the spa and studied him. "I want to know if you really care about her."

After a pause, he decided there was no harm in confessing the truth. "I'm in love with her."

"Ah." Vanda propped her chin on her hand. "On the recording, it looked more like lust. Are you sure you're feeling love?"

"I'm sure." Unfortunately. He'd tried to bury his feelings, but they continued to grow and deepen in spite of everything.

"Darcy has suffered too much. She deserves to be happy."

Austin arched a brow. "Are you claiming to care about her?"

"Yes. Does that surprise you?"

He took a deep breath. A week ago, he wouldn't have believed vampires could feel compassion or loyalty for each other, but they clearly did. They seemed to feel everything just as deeply as when they were alive. *I am human*—Darcy's words came back to him. "I've been having to readjust my thinking."

"She deserves the best. She has the soul of an angel." A corner of Vanda's mouth lifted. "Unlike me."

"Are you admitting that you're evil?"

Her smile widened. "Some would say I am."

"What have you done? Committed murder?" He said it nonchalantly, but he was dead serious.

Her smile faded. "I prefer to call it administering justice."

He narrowed his eyes. "Would you ever harm an innocent?"

"No," she replied easily. "Would you?"

"No."

She moved closer. "Then don't ever hurt Darcy."

Austin caught the implied threat in her voice. "I don't want to, but it's not that simple."

"You claim to love her. She loves you. Sounds simple to me."

"No, it's . . . complicated. My job is important—"

"More important than Darcy?"

"No. But I shouldn't allow myself to be in a position where I have to choose." Sheesh, and he shouldn't be in a position where he was discussing matters of the heart with a vampire.

"If you love her, there's only one choice."

"It's not that easy. I would have to give up everything. My life—my beliefs would all change."

"And you're not ready to do that?"

Could he do it? Turn his back on the Stake-Out team and the CIA? Join Darcy and live among the vampires? He'd be considered a traitor by his country. He'd have a tough time even getting a decent job.

"I've had a difficult life." Vanda gazed at the stars. "I've seen terrible things. Concentration camps, torture, death. Unbelievable human cruelty. There were times when I begged God for the courage to end it all. I couldn't bear to see more horror."

"I'm sorry." And he wasn't just saying it. He was actually feeling compassion for these vampires.

Vanda sat up and looked at him. "I would endure it all again a thousand times over if it would bring my little sister back to life." Tears glimmered in her eyes. "She was so clever and full of life. She would have been like Darcy if she'd survived."

Austin nodded, his own eyes tearing up.

Vanda floated toward him. "There is nothing more sacred than love. Don't let it slip away from you."

It felt like a tear had ripped through the darkness to reveal a light, and Austin could finally see. "You're not at all evil, are you?" None of these modern-day Vamps were truly evil.

"We all do the best we can with the lot given us."

Austin stood. "I wish you well, then." He strode back toward Darcy. She gave him a furious look, then turned her back.

"We need to talk," he said quietly, aware that the cameras were on them. He continued on to the greenhouse.

Maggie gave him a towel. "Please get dressed for the orchid ceremony in the foyer."

He trudged toward the stairwell. No wonder Darcy was mad. He had a sinking feeling he would not get eliminated tonight.

Chapter 20

Darcy accompanied Vanda back to the servants' parlor to see what the other ladies thought about the night's competition. Unfortunately, they all agreed with Vanda, so it looked like her hope of eliminating both CIA agents was dashed. Vanda changed into dry clothes, gathered two black orchids from the fridge, and then, the ladies strolled to the foyer for the ceremony.

Princess Joanna stumbled when one of her stiletto heels snagged on the thick hallway carpet. "God's wounds, a lady could break her neck in these slippers."

"You'll get better with practice." Darcy reached out to steady her. "You all look wonderful."

"Thank you." The princess looked elegant in her expensive black dress adorned at the neck with a strand of pearls.

"At first, I felt completely naked without my corset," Cora Lee announced. "But now, I just love it. For the first time in over a hundred years, I can actually breathe."

Cora Lee and Lady Pamela had both opted for a youthful style—satin hip-hugger pants and cropped, sparkly halter tops.

Princess Joanna frowned at them. "You two should be ashamed. You are showing too much flesh."

"It is evil." Maria Consuela's dress reached her ankles.

Lady Pamela shrugged. "My old gowns displayed most of my bosom, and no one objected to that."

"But to reveal one's navel—it is ungodly." Maria Consuela twisted her rosary in her hands. "I have never seen my navel."

"What?" Darcy asked. "But when you take a bath—"

"I bathe in a shift as any proper lady should."

"Oh." Darcy realized she might have the ladies wearing modern clothes, but some of their ideas still remained archaic.

The ladies entered the foyer. The men had all changed into suits. Gregori strode forward to welcome the ladies, while the six contestants remained on the landing of the staircase.

Darcy glanced briefly at Austin. His broad shoulders looked so good in a suit. Unlike Reginald, he needed no padding in his clothes. Light from the chandelier picked up the golden highlights in his hair. It looked like he'd toweled it dry quickly, but the disheveled result only made him look sexier.

His eyes met hers, and she looked away. She was not going to forgive him so easily this time. He'd told her he would get eliminated tonight, but then, he'd climbed into the hot tub with Vanda. And since Vanda had thrown away her mike, Darcy had no idea what they'd talked about. She'd had to stop filming afterward to get Vanda a new mike.

"Good evening," Gregori began. "Tonight, two more men will be eliminated. But first, an important announcement. The winner will now receive *four* million dollars."

The cameramen caught everyone's reactions. Even Darcy was surprised. Sly had never mentioned he was willing to go over three million.

Vanda moved to the center of the foyer. "My first orchid goes to Pierre of Brussels."

Pierre trudged forward to accept the flower. Then, he went upstairs to retrieve his luggage.

"And the second orchid goes to Reginald of Manchester." Vanda handed him the orchid.

The remaining contestants congratulated each other and dispersed to their rooms. Gregori and the women strolled to the portrait room, the cameramen trailing.

"Tonight, you eliminated Pierre." Gregori shone the special flashlight on the Belgian's portrait. His fangs appeared.

"Oh, fiddlesticks," Cora Lee mumbled. "He was a Vamp."

"And you eliminated Reginald." Gregori moved in front of the Englishman's portrait.

"Surely he's a mortal," Lady Pamela insisted. "He has such bad teeth."

"And he's so scrawny," Cora Lee added. "I do declare I've seen more meat on a starvin' possum."

Gregori aimed his flashlight at the portrait. Reginald's crooked fangs glowed with a yellowish tint.

"*Santa Maria,* may the saints preserve us." Maria Consuela reached for her rosary.

Princess Joanna stood, wobbling slightly in her stiletto heels. "This is terrible! Two vampires cast out.

Prithee, Darcy, you must assure us there are no mortals left to plague us."

Darcy winced. "I can't say. But remember, tomorrow night, we're testing the men on their strength."

The princess sat with a sigh of relief. "Good. No mortal man could ever be stronger than a Vamp."

"I will be the judge tomorrow night." Maria Consuela kissed the cross of her rosary. "And with the Lord's blessing, I shall discover the inferior beings and banish them from our presence."

Darcy doubted the Lord was into detecting inferior beings, but still, she hoped the ladies would eliminate Austin and Garrett. She'd be in big trouble if either of the mortal men made it to the last round. She had no doubt that Austin *was* the sexiest man on earth, but still, she couldn't allow him to win.

The more important question was could there be a future for her and Austin? She had no doubt she was in love with him. Even his rejection and lies hadn't managed to squelch her feelings for him. Vanda's words kept coming back to haunt her. *There is nothing more sacred than love.* How could she throw this love away without giving it a chance? Roman and Shanna were giving it a chance. Why couldn't she?

If only she could bridge the gap between their two worlds. But there was no middle ground for her. She could never share the sun with Austin, never live a normal life with him. She was trapped in her world, and he would have to be willing to join her there. Was it fair to expect so much from him?

Maybe she shouldn't ask for too much. Maybe she should take it one small step at a time. The way it was now, he could barely stand to touch her. He thought she was dead. She'd have to get him over that. She needed to prove how alive and touchable she was. She needed to show him how much she loved him.

It seemed suddenly clear. Austin was in the penthouse for one more night. Tonight would be perfect.

She just needed the courage to seduce him.

Garrett ripped open a bag of potato chips. "Four million dollars? I'm tempted to win the damned contest."

"No way are they giving that money to a mortal." Austin sat at the kitchen table and popped open his can of cola. "I think our time is almost up here. Did you collect much information?"

"A little. Just the names of the vampires."

Austin nodded, relieved that Garrett hadn't acquired much. "Emma and I killed a vampire the other night in Central Park."

"No shit?"

"He was attacking a woman. We saved her life."

"Cool." Garrett crammed some chips into his mouth.

"None of the vampires here would attack someone."

Garrett snorted. "They would if they got hungry enough."

"I think Shanna Whelan was right about there being two kinds of vampires. She called them the law-abiding modern Vamps and the Malcontents."

"She was brainwashed," Garrett mumbled with his mouth full.

"Think about it. There are obviously two different groups, cause we saw them ready to fight each other in Central Park. And I heard them when we tapped their phones. They hate each other."

"It's a damned shame they don't kill each other off. It would make our job easier."

Austin took a sip from his cola. "I think we should learn more about these two different factions."

Garrett shook his head. "Getting into their politics would be a waste of time. We just need to kill them."

Austin finished his drink in silence. He needed to contact Shanna Whelan. Or Draganesti, as her name was now. She'd be able to tell him more about vampires. And what it was like to be married to one of them.

He was a goner, he could feel it. He could no longer believe that all vampires were evil demons. Everything he'd learned in the past few weeks pointed to a world that was curiously parallel to the mortal world. Just like humans, vampires could be good or evil. They could love or hate. And since he was in love with one of them, he was trying to make peace with their world so he could accept it. Still, turning his back on the CIA and his old life would be tough. Too tough.

He tossed the can into the trash. What was he thinking, that he could marry Darcy and live happily ever after? Well, she could live forever, but he'd grow old and die. How long would it take before she was tired of his old ass? And a hundred years from now, he'd be long gone and forgotten.

So was it worth it to throw away his life's work for some flimsy dream? If he was sensible, he'd get himself eliminated tomorrow night. And never see Darcy again. But for the first time in his life, being sensible sounded stupid.

He said good night to Garrett and trudged up to his room. He turned on the computer and checked the surveillance cameras. The last two vampires, Otto and Roberto, were in the billiards room, playing pool. The foyer and portrait room were empty. He switched to the pool house and instantly regretted it.

Darcy looked fresh from the shower, her hair damp and her body scantily clothed in skimpy pajamas. His feelings of longing and despair came hurtling back. How could he give her up? Vanda's talk in the hot tub had reminded him how rare and special love could be. Darcy was clever, brave, everything he'd always wanted. She was also nervous and agitated. She was pacing back and forth across the room. From her facial expressions and mumbled words, he gathered she was arguing with herself.

She strode to the kitchen and removed a bottle from the fridge. She shook it, unscrewed the top, and poured dark red liquid into a glass. Austin winced. She took something else from the fridge. Chocolate syrup? She squeezed some into the glass, then stirred the concoction with a spoon. Then, she added some ice cubes.

She left the kitchen, sipping from the glass. Austin sat back in his chair, his heart sinking. She might try to disguise the taste, but the result was the same. She was drinking blood.

He strode to the bathroom and took a hot shower. He stuck his head under the nozzle, but the stinging spray couldn't wash away the memory of Darcy drinking blood. How could he join her world?

There is nothing more sacred than love. Vanda's words drifted around him and clung to him like hot steam. How could he give her up? He loved her. But could he commit to a vampire?

He dried off, then padded back to the bedroom with the towel wrapped around his waist. He glanced at the computer screen. Darcy was no longer in the main room of the pool house. She'd probably gone to the bedroom where he didn't have a camera.

He checked the foyer and staircase. Empty. The east wing hallway.

His breath hitched, and the towel tumbled to the floor. Darcy was headed his way. She'd put on a white bathrobe to cover her skimpy shorts and tank top.

He strode to his suitcase and pulled out a pair of clean boxer shorts. Red silk. Well, it was better than Sponge-Bob. There was a light tap on the door. Holy moley. He tugged on the shorts and closed the laptop. He shoved wet hair out of his face and cracked open the door.

Her face was pale and tense. Her gaze drifted over his body, then back to his face.

He tried to keep his expression blank. "This is not a good idea."

She pressed a hand against the door to keep him from closing it. "You said we should talk."

"I changed my mind."

She frowned. "This is your last night here."

Our last chance to be together, the words hovered over them, unspoken. "I'm not sure it can work."

Anger flickered in her eyes. "Are you giving up without a fight? That doesn't sound like a macho super-spy." She shoved the door open with a surprising spurt of strength.

Vampire strength. Could she actually overpower him? Austin stepped back. "Are you angry?"

"You think?" She shut the door, then paced across his room. "You agreed to get yourself kicked off the show tonight. And yet, you're still here."

"I wasn't trying to stay on. It just happened."

"Right. You just can't help being the sexiest guy on earth. It must be an awful trial for you."

He propped a shoulder against the wall and folded his arms across his chest.

"Are you trying to get me fired?" She continued to pace. "Don't you realize this is the only network where I can work?" She stopped to glare at him. "Are you totally insensitive to what I'm going through?"

He gritted his teeth. "Are you done?"

"No!" She strode toward him. "You should have never climbed into the hot tub with Vanda."

"We only talked. You know that. You were watching." He gave her an irritated look. "Like a hawk."

She snorted. "Well, you've certainly recovered from your repulsion. Or maybe it's just me who repulses you."

"You never repulsed me!" He pushed away from the wall. "You just confused the hell out of me. Thinking about the sun and the beach. Drinking ice cold chocolate. Having a damned pulse. How can you be dead and have a pulse?"

She planted her hands on her hips. Her breasts heaved with each angry breath. "I am not *dead.*"

"Undead, then, if it makes you feel more *alive.*" He lurched toward her and yanked the bathrobe off one shoulder. He ignored her gasp and pressed two fingers against her carotid artery. Her pulse throbbed against his fingertips.

"Well? Am I dead yet?"

"No." *Dammit.* How could he walk away from her when she was alive? "Your heart rate is actually a little fast."

"Could be that I'm a little miffed." She lifted her eyebrows. "Or a little excited."

He lowered his hand and stepped back. "How?"

"How could I be excited?" She tilted her head and examined his body. "Well, I'm all alone with the sexiest man on earth, and it's been five years since I've—"

"I meant how can you have a freakin' heartbeat?"

"How can I not? I'm walking and talking. I'm thinking about you naked. Now, how could I do that if my heart wasn't pumping blood to the various parts of my body?"

Blood was certainly getting pumped to certain parts of *his* body. And it didn't help that she kept glancing at his shorts. Five years? "What happens to you during the day?"

She sighed. "When the sun rises, my heart stops. Then, when the sun sets, it's like being struck with a divine defibrillator. Everything jerks back into motion."

"It sounds painful."

She smiled slowly as she untied the sash to her bathrobe. "Oh, but it hurts so good."

Holy seduction. He watched her robe slide to the floor in a heap next to his discarded towel. As he lifted his gaze to her face, his attention snagged on her tank top. It was stretched across her breasts, the thin white cotton almost transparent. Her nipples were plump and pink. All it would take was a touch of his fingers and they would pucker. No, correction. All it took was a look. They pebbled before his eyes, the tips hardening into pink nubs. His groin responded in similar fashion—growing hard, but hardly a nub.

She stepped toward him. "You said you were in love with me. Is that true?"

He closed his eyes briefly. His groin was swelling, his heart aching. "Darcy, you should have someone of your own kind. Someone who can love you and live with you forever. I can't give you what you need."

"But I want you."

"Dammit." He marched toward the door. "You

know I work for the CIA. If I go around killing vampires, it's going to cause a strain on our relationship, don't you think?"

"You could quit."

And be sucked into the vampire world, living only at night, constantly surrounded by creatures who considered him a snack. "You're asking me to give up everything."

"Then forget it." She leaned against the door to keep him from opening it. "Forget the happily ever after. It's a crock. It hardly ever happens, even in the mortal world."

"Don't say that, Darcy. You deserve to be loved."

Her eyes glimmered with moisture. "We don't always get what we deserve, do we? I learned that the hard way. So now, I'll just take whatever I can get. Even if it's just one night."

His body screamed *yes,* but still he fought it. Because, damn it all, one night would never be enough.

She locked the door. "One night."

He leaned his back against the wall. He would give in, he knew it. How could he resist when he wanted her so much? But if she thought they could simply shake hands afterward and go their merry way—then she didn't know how deeply he felt.

Her eyes wavered with a hint of insecurity. "Are you repulsed by me?"

"God, no." Not when he was considering giving up everything for her. Holy irony. How many times in the past had he been the one satisfied with a one-night stand? Was this some sort of divine payback? The thought that she could settle for one damned night was slowly twisting his guts. It trivialized their feelings, their connection to each other. It pissed him off.

"Are you afraid of me?" She lifted her chin. "I've never bitten anyone, and I never will. I'd rather die."

"You don't bite?" he ground out the words.

"No, I don't."

"What a shame. I do."

She stepped back, her eyes wide. "You . . . want to bite me?"

"Sure." He crossed his arms, acting nonchalant in spite of his growing anger. "I like to bite."

She gave him a wary look. "You mean hard?"

"Not enough to hurt. It's more like a series of nibbles, a scraping of teeth over the more sensitive parts of your body. Then, there's the swirling of the tongue. And let's not forget the joys of suction."

Her mouth fell open. Then, she recovered and licked her lips. "Where exactly would you want to bite me?"

He looked her over slowly. "The base of your neck where it meets your shoulder. And the soft place a few inches below your belly button."

"Here?" She slipped her hand under the elastic waistband of her pale blue shorts.

"Yes." His voice sounded hoarse, so he cleared his throat. He motioned to her sequined flip-flops. "And your toes."

"Oh." She kicked off her slides and wiggled her toes into the thick carpet. "Anywhere else?"

"Your calves. Inner thighs. The back of your thighs where they curve into your delicious little bottom."

She turned sideways and lifted the hem of her shorts to reveal the curve of her derriere. "Here?" She stroked the skin. Her eyelids lowered slightly. "Anywhere else?"

His erection strained against the flimsy silk of his boxer shorts. "Hip, below the waist where it widens."

She shimmied her shorts down her hips a few inches, then skimmed her hands over the bare skin. "Anywhere else?"

"Underside of your breasts, where it's full and heavy."

"Ah." She rolled up her tank top 'til the plump curves were revealed. She stopped just before she reached the nipples. She cupped her hands beneath her breasts and lifted. When she looked at him, her eyes darkened and began to shimmer.

Holy crap. He tensed. "Your eyes are glowing red."

"It means I'm hot. And I'm ready."

"It's an automatic thing?" Damn. If she had no control over her vampish behavior, what else would she do? Would her fangs spring out? What if she was actually stronger than him?

She strolled toward him. "Tell me where else you want to bite me."

He wasn't going to let her overpower him. He had other strengths at his disposal. He gathered his mental power and zeroed in on her brain. She halted with a gasp. Her eyes closed as a pink blush colored her face then crept down her neck.

Take off your shirt.

Her eyes opened. She smiled slightly. "As you wish." She pulled the tank top over her head and dropped it on the floor.

He was admiring her breasts when an icy wisp of psychic power drifted toward him and hovered around his head. He automatically swatted it away, and the cloud dissipated.

"You're very strong," she whispered.

"You're not."

She shrugged. "I've never tried it before. I don't believe in invading people's privacy."

"Then you don't like me getting in your head."

"I don't like vampires doing it. They're so terribly cold. But you, you're so wonderfully hot." She blushed. "I don't have anything to hide from you, and it feels so good to be warm inside. I've been cold for so long."

Cold because she was literally dead half the time. What was he getting into? Every morning he would wake next to a dead woman. But he couldn't ignore the pain and longing in her eyes. Her pain had become his own. Her world would become his own.

She stood before him, naked except for a pair of shorts. Her eyes had turned sky blue again, filled with a mixture of desire and fear. She was afraid he would reject her.

"You were telling me where you'd like to bite me," she reminded him quietly.

"Yeah, there's one more place. But I wouldn't bite you there. I'd make love." He leaned forward and breathed in the scent of her shampoo. Gently, he moved her hair back. There, on her neck, were two little scars from a vampire's fangs. Poor Darcy. No wonder she always wore her hair down. He caressed the scars with his fingertips.

She shuddered. "Where would you love me?"

He whispered in her ear, "Your clit." He lifted her in his arms, strode toward the bed, and dropped her on the comforter.

"Austin?"

"Yes." He was taking her, and damn the consequences.

Chapter 21

Darcy's heart was thundering in her ears as she reached for him. *Yes!* If all else failed, she would at least have this one glorious night. Austin fell onto the bed and pulled her into his arms. *Yes,* her mind repeated the same word since she was too excited to think of anything else. She scattered kisses over his face and raked her hands into his hair. It was thick, damp, and oh, so soft, a wonderful contrast to the darker whiskers lining his jaw.

He was planting kisses all over her face, too, and she didn't mind that he seemed rushed. Even frantic. So what if this quickly careened out of control and exploded? She loved the aura of desperation, and it would be one hell of an explosion.

Their mouths found each other, instantly opening and melding together. He invaded her with his tongue at the same time that he entered her mind.

I'm here, Darcy. You'll never feel cold again.

She opened for him, both mentally and physically,

reveling in the heat from his mind and body. A wave of awe swept through her as she realized just how open she was. He was in her mind and would soon enter her body. He would know every inch of her, inside and out. And the wonder of it was she wasn't afraid. She trusted him. She'd never trusted anyone so much before.

He pulled back and looked at her. "Darcy." He brushed back her hair. "You honor me."

He'd heard her thoughts. She felt as if her heart would burst with an overabundance of love. She wanted to show him how much. She had to. With a lightning-quick move, she shoved him onto his back and pinned his arms down.

"Whoa!" His shocked expression turned wary. "You're, uh, really strong."

Stronger than she'd realized. Cool. She examined Austin's muscular arms and chest. Why, she was as strong as a macho super spy. He clenched a fist and strained against her grip on his wrist. He couldn't budge her. Very cool.

Frowning, he studied her. "I guess this turns you on. Your eyes are red again."

She smiled. "Don't worry. I'll be gentle." She released his wrists, letting her fingers glide up his arms, over his biceps and shoulders, and onto his chest. She splayed her hands into his curly chest hair, then followed the trail of dark brown hair to his navel. What a gorgeous man. She could eat him alive.

He propped himself up on his elbows, watching her with a worried look. "I'd rather you didn't."

Oh, the rascal had heard her. "I meant it metaphorically. Relax." She shoved him back down. "I said I'd be gentle." She grabbed the waistband of his sexy red underwear and pulled.

Rip. She winced as the flimsy silk tore in two. "Oops."

He lifted his head to look at his ripped shorts.

"Sorry." She gave him an apologetic smile. "I'm a little overly eager." She glanced down at him. "I'm not the only one."

With a groan, he let his head drop back on the bed. "If you don't know your own strength, you should st—" He gasped when she curled her hand around him.

"I should what?" She gently stroked the shaft.

He gritted his teeth. "Continue."

She drew little circles around the tip. "I thought you could be persuaded."

"Yeah, I'm easy." His eyes flickered shut. His chest heaved with rapid breaths.

He was such a beautiful man. And so large. She traced a vein on his shaft, then snuggled close to him so she could retrace it with her tongue. A moan rumbled deep in his throat. She trailed kisses up to the tip, then took him into her mouth.

Do you like this, she asked him in her thoughts.

God, yes. You're so good. You're— "Wait!" He struggled to sit up.

She released him with a smack of her lips. "Hmm. Tastes like chicken."

"It's not funny. You've never made love as a vampire, right? Do you even know what to expect?"

She nuzzled her cheek against his shaft, then kissed him. "I expect to have a good time. I'm being gentle."

"But you can't control your eyes. Or your strength. What if you can't control your fangs and they pop out?"

She paused with her mouth on his cock.

"Holy body piercing." He pushed her away from him and pinned her on her back.

She bit her lip to keep from laughing.

He glowered at her. "It's not funny."

"But I wouldn't have bitten you." Typical male, so worried about the preservation of the family jewels.

"I heard that." He raked his gaze over her while he kept a tight grip on her wrists.

She figured she was strong enough to throw him off. If she wanted to.

He arched a brow at her. "But you don't want to."

She smiled slowly. "Oh, dear. I'm totally at your mercy. Whatever will you do?"

He smiled back. "I'll be doing all the nibbling from now on."

She sighed. "I suppose I can live with that." Especially if he nibbled in all those places he'd mentioned before.

Not a problem. He nuzzled her neck and nipped at the spot where her neck curved into her shoulder.

She wiggled since the spot was ticklish. He nibbled a path to her breasts. He released her wrists to cup one of her breasts with his hand. He flicked his thumb over the nipple. When it hardened, he took it into his mouth.

She arched her back as her mind exploded with pleasure. When the sensation mellowed, she realized he'd retreated mentally to the fringes of her mind. She gripped his head tighter. "Don't leave me."

I'm still with you. He lifted his head from her breast. "Your reactions are too exciting. If I don't back off a bit, I'll explode."

"Oh, Austin." She kissed his brow. "I love you so much."

"I love you, too." He kissed the underside of her breasts, then the curve of her hip. He pulled down the waistband of her shorts to nibble on her belly.

She wiggled against him. This was all well and good, but she was anxious to get on with it.

"Good." He yanked off her shorts.

She gasped. Hmm, telepathy could certainly come in handy.

He knelt at her feet and looked her over. "You're so beautiful, Darcy."

He lifted a foot and nipped at her toes. She bent her knee to let the leg fall open. His gaze zeroed in on her most private flesh. Excitement surged through her, causing her groin to tingle and ache. He worked his way up her leg, nibbling at her calf. She bent her other leg to spread her legs wider apart. He paused, his eyes riveted on her.

Hot moisture seeped from her, and she groaned with need.

He glanced at her with the hint of a smile. "You sexy strumpet."

Take me, please.

I'm getting there. Be patient. He kissed the inside of her thigh.

Now!

Bossy, aren't you? He released her leg and settled between her legs. When he touched her, she bucked. *Whoa. This isn't the rodeo, darlin'.*

"Sorry." She pressed a hand against her chest, gasping for air. "I'm just so excited. I've wanted you for so long."

Shh. Relax and enjoy. He gave her a long, slow lick.

She screamed.

He glanced toward the door, wincing. "There's a CIA operative next door. Let's try to keep it down."

"Right." She gripped the comforter in her fists and planted her feet firmly on the bed. "Okay. I'm ready. Do your worst. I mean your best."

His mouth twitched. "Sure."

Darcy gasped at the feel of his mouth on her again. She clutched at the comforter and closed her eyes. Good God. He was so sweet, so loving, so thorough, so *damned slow*! He quickened the pace, and she realized through the sensual fog that he'd heard her. *Oh, sorry.* But she was so impatient. She lifted her hips, wanting more pressure. He instantly responded by grabbing her hips. Good God, this telepathy stuff was good!

A little to the right. No, the other right. Faster. Fast— She spun out of control, unable to give directions any longer. But he didn't seem to need any. She was climbing, soaring, reeling, teetering on the edge, and he kept pushing 'til—

She screamed. Her body convulsed. Her legs clamped together.

"Aah." He wrenched his body out from between her legs. "Holy moley, you're strong."

With a moan, she rolled onto her side. Her body continued to rack with the sweetest spasms.

He collapsed beside her and pulled her into his arms. "Are you all right, sweetheart?"

"Yes," she gasped.

They both stiffened when a loud banging shook the door.

"Hey, Austin!" Garrett shouted. "What's going on? Do you need backup?"

He yelled, "I invited a girlfriend over. Go away."

There was a pause. "You sure you don't need backup?"

Darcy rolled her eyes when she heard snickering on the other side of the door.

"Get lost, you creep," Austin shouted. When all was quiet, he rolled her onto her back. "Now, where were we?"

She laced her hands around his neck. "I had just experienced the biggest, most colossal orgasm of my life."

"Ah. Well, it's a tall order, but we'll see if we can top it." He lowered his head to her breasts.

Darcy's breath caught as all the sensations came rushing back. It wasn't long before her legs were spread and his fingers were drenched with more moisture.

"Do I need a condom?" he whispered.

"No." She shook her head, her eyes closed. He was teasing her with such sweet little circles. "No diseases."

His hand paused. "And children?"

Her eyes opened. Her heart stuttered at the concerned look on his face. "I can't have any."

A flicker of pain crossed his face. "I thought not. I'm sorry."

She swallowed and mentally forbade the tears that threatened to come. Austin would be such a good father. It was just one more reason why she shouldn't allow him to stay with her.

"No. I love you." He moved between her legs and positioned himself against her. "No matter what."

She cried out when he plunged inside her. She wrapped her arms and legs around him and held tight.

I love you. He repeated the words in her head as he thrust into her body. They clung to each other mentally as their sensations melted together and drove them higher and higher.

His body jerked, then pumped into her. His groan reverberated in her ears and inside her head. Her own body responded with a sensual shattering. She didn't know if it was bigger than the first one, but it was definitely sweeter, for they experienced it together.

He collapsed beside her and pulled her into his arms. "Are you all right, sweetheart?"

She shivered as her body heat quickly dwindled. "I'm getting cold again."

"Here. Get under the covers." He scooted off the bed and folded back the comforter. She slipped underneath as he turned off the lights. Moonlight filtered through the window, glinting off his hair with a silvery tint.

He settled beside her with a smile. "I'll heat you up again as soon as I recover from round one."

"Is this a boxing match?" She snuggled close to him.

He winced. "Don't expect nine rounds."

Smiling, she fondled the curls on his chest. "You're no longer in my head."

The corner of his mouth quirked. "I'm conserving my energy."

"Have you always had telepathic powers?"

He closed his eyes. His breathing slowed, and she wondered if he'd fallen asleep. He looked so harmless and handsome.

He opened his eyes and stared at the ceiling. "It runs in my family, but skips every other generation. My grandfather was telepathic. My mother's father."

"The one you're named after?"

He nodded slightly. "Papa Olaf. When I was very young, I would hear people say something, but their lips weren't moving. And when I answered them, they looked at me like I'd grown two heads. I was afraid something was wrong with me."

"That must have been very confusing."

"Yeah. Papa Olaf understood, though, and he told me what was happening. At first, I was scared, but he made it fun, like we were in a special, secret club just for us." Austin smiled. "We would spend hours fishing on his favorite lake in Minnesota, having long conversations without either of us saying a word."

Darcy suppressed a twinge of sorrow. She still missed having long talks with her sisters. "You were lucky to have him."

"Yes. He warned me to be careful with the gift, but as I grew older, I became bolder and . . . conceited, I guess. I considered myself the grand protector of my three younger sisters. When their friends came over, I would read their minds and chase them off if I didn't like what I heard."

Darcy snorted. "I bet your sisters loved that."

He grinned. "I wondered at the time why they weren't properly appreciative. Now, I realize I was acting like a know-it-all bully." His smile faded. "My powers took a big leap forward when I was about fifteen, and I started bragging about what I could do. It upset my father. He'd always been envious of the close relationship I had with my grandfather. He became convinced that Papa Olaf was an evil influence in my life. He even thought my grandfather was training me in the occult."

"Oh, no." Darcy propped her head up on her hand. "What did your father do?"

"He forbade me to ever see my grandfather again. I reacted angrily, claiming he could never stop us from talking to each other because we could enter each other's minds at will. That freaked him out enough that he packed up the family and moved us to Wisconsin. He told me my powers were evil, and I should never use them again."

"Oh, I'm so sorry." Darcy stroked Austin's brow. "It must have been terrible for you."

He shrugged. "That's when I realized I wasn't nearly as powerful as I'd thought. I couldn't reach my grandfather over a long distance. I was in a new high school, and I didn't want to be seen as a freak. My sisters were mad at me because the move had separated them from their friends. I . . . I gave in. I wanted everyone to be happy with me, so I tried to be normal. I tried to make my father proud. I was on the football and swim teams. The perfect student all through high school and college."

Darcy sighed. She knew too well what it was like to feel trapped in a world where you couldn't be yourself. "What happened to your grandfather?"

"I was in college when he called and asked me to come see him." Austin closed his eyes briefly. His lips thinned as a pained expression pinched his face. "I hardly recognized him, his health had deteriorated so badly. I hadn't realized how much he needed me. He begged me to stop denying who I really was, to embrace my gifts and use them for the power of good. He told me to never be ashamed, that there was a reason God had made me the way I was, and that it was up to me to discover that reason."

"He was a good man," Darcy whispered. His philosophy reminded her of Maggie's, though she would never understand what good could come from being a vampire.

Austin sighed. "I felt like I had betrayed him. And betrayed myself. So, I promised him on his death bed that I would do as he asked. I joined the CIA and developed my skills so I could fight evil."

"Like me?" she asked dryly.

He gave her an irritated look. "Don't insult the woman I love."

With a smile, she rested her head on his shoulder. Now she understood why Austin was driven to use his powers to protect the innocent and defeat evil. She couldn't expect him to give it up. His gift was too rare and special to be squandered away. "I bet you used to dress up like a superhero for Halloween."

He chuckled. "Yes. I especially liked the capes."

"And you had Superman underwear?"

He nodded. "And Spiderman pajamas. My lunchbox was the Incredible Hulk."

She smoothed a hand over his muscular chest and defined abs. "Oh, yeah. You're incredible, all right."

He rolled onto his side, smiling. "I bet you had a Malibu beach Barbie."

Darcy laughed. "And the beach house, too."

"An all-American sweetheart." He rubbed a hand up and down her back. "Tell me what happened to you."

Her smile faded. "I'd rather not."

"I want to know."

"I died. End of story."

"You were a television reporter. I've seen the tapes. You were entertaining and clever." He brushed her hair back. "I've been trying to figure out what happened. I went to see your old cameraman, Jack."

Darcy's breath hitched. "How is he?"

"Not good. Something scared the hell out of him. He thinks you were abducted by blood-sucking aliens."

She winced. "Poor Jack."

"Tell me what happened. It was four years ago on Halloween."

"I was doing a story on kids who pretend to be vampires." She gave him a doubtful look. "Do you really want to hear this?"

"Yes. Tell me."

Darcy shuddered as she allowed the memories to escape from the mental file where she kept them locked away. "We went to a club in Greenwich Village, not far from Washington Square. It was called Fangs of Fortune. Jack had his old video camera. We were going to interview a few kids and leave."

She closed her eyes briefly. "A couple from NYU came to our table. Draco and Taylor. Draco had dental implants that looked like fangs. Taylor was a sweet girl, just wanting to be noticed. They posed for the camera, then left. Then, I spotted a pair of odd-looking men, and I went to their table."

"Who were they?" Austin asked.

"Gregori, dressed in a tuxedo, as usual. The other was a Scotsman dressed in a red and green kilt."

Austin stiffened. "He sounds like the vampire who kidnapped Shanna when I was guarding her. Tall, red hair pulled back into a ponytail, and he talks like a cross between Shrek and Billy Connolly?"

Darcy smiled sadly. "Yes. That would be Connor." She'd thought his accent was so cute at first. "I thought they might be police officers. They did admit they were there because they'd heard bad things were happening at the club. I just thought they meant drugs."

She sighed. "I told them they looked too old to be playing pretend like the kids. Connor said they had no need to pretend. And that I had no idea how old he really was."

Austin frowned. "It sounds like he was toying with you."

"I thought they were joking. Especially when Connor claimed he was actually a vampire."

Austin sat up. "He admitted it to you?"

"He and Gregori were joking back and forth. I didn't believe a word of it, and they knew it. I even asked Connor if the Loch Ness monster had been the one to transform him. And he said I shouldn't make fun of his dear Nessie. We were laughing and having a good time until I asked Jack to come over and record them. Then, they got very nervous."

"Jack's camera wasn't digital?"

"No. All of a sudden, I felt this icy cold in my head that said I would not record them. The voice told Jack and me to leave. The next thing I knew, Gregori and Connor were no longer at the table. They were at the bar, drinking something red that looked like blood. I was so disgusted and confused, I grabbed my purse and headed for the nearest exit."

"To the back alley?" Austin whispered.

Darcy covered her face, but the horrid memories flooded her mind. "It was too awful."

Austin wrapped his arms around her. "Not if you share it with me. Tell me."

She lowered her hands. "I'll try."

Chapter 22

"I slipped into the alley with Jack," Darcy began.
"My nerves were on edge, and I remember jumping
when the metal door banged shut. A nearby Dumpster
stank. When I heard scuffling noises, I was afraid it
might be rats." She snorted. "I wish."

"What happened?" Austin asked.

"I heard a woman scream, so I ran around the
Dumpster. It was Taylor, the girl I'd met in the club.
A man had shoved her against the wall, and his face
was pressed against her neck. I thought it was her
boyfriend Draco. His clothing looked similar. But the
embrace wasn't consensual. Taylor was clearly terrified. I grabbed the guy's shoulder and yelled at him to
stop."

"But he didn't," Austin guessed.

Darcy grimaced. "He made this awful, animal-like
growl deep in his throat. It scared me, but he was hurting Taylor, so I tried to pull him back. That's when
Jack turned on his camera lights, and I realized the

attacker wasn't Draco. And he was biting Taylor on the neck. I was so furious then. I pounded on his back. Jack yelled at me to stop, but it was too late."

"He attacked you?"

"He shoved me back with so much force, I was airborne. I crashed into Jack, and we fell onto the cement. I was okay, but Jack was just laying there with this shocked look on his face. I grabbed the cell phone from my purse and called 911. I told them a woman was being murdered in the back alley." Darcy covered her face. "A woman *was* murdered. I didn't know it would be me."

"Shh, sweetheart." Austin held her close. "You're all right now."

She lowered her hands and took a shaky breath. "I looked around for some kind of weapon. And then, Jack whispered, 'Vampire.' I thought he was in shock, but he shoved the camera at me and told me to look for myself. While I was getting to my feet, Jack jumped up and ran away."

"You're kidding." Austin's eyes glittered with anger. "That bastard. I should go back and kick his ass."

"No." Darcy touched Austin's face. "He was terrified. He already knew the truth. I picked up the camera and looked through it. I couldn't see the assailant, and Taylor was dangling against the wall like a rag doll with two punctures on the side of her neck. I was so stunned. He was right in front of me—a real vampire."

"What did you do?"

Darcy snorted. "I reacted like a journalist. I pressed the record button. And then, he turned and looked at me. Blood was dripping from his fangs. I knew I had to do something, or he would kill Taylor and me both."

Darcy's eyes filled with tears. "I told him I had proof of his existence, and I would broadcast it all over the news. He would be hunted down like an animal. He dropped Taylor, and she collapsed onto the ground. I asked her if she could move. I told her to run. But she just sat there and cried."

Austin kissed Darcy's brow. "My brave sweetheart."

"I threw the camera at him, but he knocked it aside. And then, he moved so fast, all I saw was a blur. He caught me from behind and pulled me back against him. He stank of blood. I could feel his breath on my neck and the scrape of his teeth."

Austin tightened his hold on her. "The monster bit you?"

"No. The back door banged shut, and Connor came toward us, yelling at the vampire to let me go. He called the vampire a Malcontent and demanded that they stop preying on the innocent. The vampire replied that he liked his meals fresh."

"Then, it's true," Austin said. "There are two factions—the Vamps and the Malcontents."

"Yes. The Malcontents enjoy terrorizing mortals, and they hate the Vamps for trying to stop them." Darcy sighed. "Gregori said he would take Taylor home and erase her memory. He took the tape from the camera with him."

"And what happened to you?" Austin asked.

Darcy shivered. "The Malcontent backed away from Connor, dragging me with him. Connor told him I was going to slow him down, that he should let me go. Connor kept moving toward us, and the Malcontent was scared. I could feel him breathing hard on my neck. And then he said he needed a distraction."

She touched Austin's face and looked into his eyes. "In that tiny moment of time, I knew real terror. Everything seemed to slow down. I opened my mouth to scream, but the vampire was faster. He pulled out a knife and thrust it into my chest."

Austin gathered her into his lap. "I'll kill him. I'll track him down and kill him."

"It's all a blur after that," Darcy whispered. "I remember Connor shouting with rage. I remember so much pain. And shock. I realized I was going to die. The Malcontent disappeared. And Connor knelt beside me. He kept saying he was sorry, that he should have stopped it. I remember his eyes were blue. I was staring at him. I didn't want to die alone. Then, Connor said I was not to worry. He would take care of me."

Darcy slipped out of Austin's lap and curled up on the bed. Shivers coursed through her body.

"Darcy." Austin lay beside her and wrapped his arms around her. Still, the shaking wouldn't stop.

Darcy. He flooded her mind with his strong, warm presence. *You're safe. You're with me, now.*

She exhaled a long breath. She'd made it through the story. She could shove the horrid memories back into a dark corner of her brain. "I didn't want to become a vampire."

"Of course not."

"I was barely conscious when they transformed me."

"Who did it?" Austin whispered. "Who bit you?"

She swallowed hard. "Connor."

Austin's breath hissed between clenched teeth.

"That bastard. I should hate him, but he saved your life."

She snorted. "He could have teleported me to Romatech or to a hospital, but he was more worried about keeping the big secret than keeping me alive. I lost my family, my home, my job, my savings, my ability to have children. I lost the daylight and any hope of a normal life."

"But you're here now. That's a hell of a lot better than being dead."

"I'm dead during the day," she whispered.

"But alive at night. Let's say the cup is half full instead of half empty. And I'm willing to share that cup with you."

She turned toward him with sad eyes. "You'll lose your job if they find out you're involved with a vampire."

He shrugged. "Maybe. We'll just take it one day— rather, one night at a time. We'll make it work."

"I hope so." She took a deep breath and closed her eyes. A scent tickled her nose. It smelled rich and delicious. *Austin.*

"If Shanna and Roman can make it work, so can we."

"Yes, but they still have problems." Darcy felt an odd throbbing as if her heartbeat was amplified throughout her body. She struggled to concentrate on the conversation. "Shanna wants to have children, but it may never be possible."

"No, I wouldn't think that could work."

The throbbing grew louder. Darcy wondered if there was something wrong with her heart. "Roman wanted to become mortal again, but that didn't work either."

"What?" Austin propped himself up on an elbow.

Darcy gasped when she noticed the vein in Austin's neck. It wasn't her heartbeat she was hearing. It was his. It was his blood, pounding through his arteries, calling to her.

"Darcy." He touched her shoulder.

She jumped. "Yes?"

"I asked you a question. Are you all right?"

"Yes, I'm fine." *God help me, I'm hungry.*

"Is there a way to turn a vampire back into a mortal?"

"Roman thought there was, but they experimented on a pig and it died. There's no way Shanna's going to let Roman try it on himself." Darcy's gaze wandered back to the vein in Austin's neck. Good God, she could actually see it pulsing. She could smell the blood. This was terrible. This had never happened to her before. But then, she'd not been around any mortals for the last four years. And now, she was acting just like a . . . a vampire.

"How does the experiment work?" Austin asked.

"It *doesn't* work." Darcy gritted her teeth with frustration. A curious ache pinched at her gums.

"Why not?"

"Aren't you wearing your anklet?" She glanced down, but the comforter was covering his legs.

"I took it off when I showered. Darcy, why doesn't the experiment work?"

"Something about our DNA. It's mutated. Roman thinks it will only work with the original human DNA." The smell of Austin's blood flooded her brain. His heartbeat thrummed through her body. Good God, what if Austin was right? She had no control over her eyes or her strength. What if her fangs sprang out?

She jumped from the bed and scrambled for her clothes on the floor. She couldn't find her underwear, so just grabbed her shorts and pulled them on.

Austin sat up. "What's wrong?"

"Nothing." She located her top and pulled it on. The tingling in her gums was growing stronger. Oh, God, what if she bit him? What if she *killed* him?

He climbed out of bed. "Don't go. We still have round two."

She donned her bathrobe. "I don't want to fall asleep here. The sun will shine through your windows." She stuffed her feet into her slides. "I'll be more comfortable in the pool house."

He grabbed a pair of underwear from his suitcase and started putting them on. "I'm coming with you."

"No!"

He glanced sharply at her. "Don't push me off. You made the decision to come here tonight, and it was beautiful. You can't back out of this now."

A sharp pain lanced her gums. "I have to go." She wrenched open the door.

"Dammit, Darcy!" He strode toward her. "You will tell me what's wrong!"

"It *was* beautiful." Her eyes blurred with tears. "But it can't happen again. I'm sorry." She rushed down the hallway.

"We have to talk," he yelled. "I'll be at your place in five minutes!"

"Hey!" Garrett's voice rang out. "What's going on?"

Darcy speeded up so the second CIA man wouldn't see that Austin's girlfriend was a vampire. It was bad enough that she was breaking Austin's heart. She didn't want him to lose his job, too. With her supersensitive hearing, she could still detect their voices.

"Problem with the girlfriend?" Garrett asked.

"I'll fix it," Austin grumbled. "This is only temporary."

Tears welled in Darcy's eyes as she climbed the stairs to the roof. The problem wasn't temporary. She was stuck being a vampire forever.

Five minutes later, Austin knocked on the pool house door. No answer. "I know you're in there, Darcy." He'd watched her on the surveillance camera while he'd thrown on his clothes. She'd grabbed a bottle of Chocolood and a box of tissues and gone straight to her bedroom.

He knocked louder. "We need to talk."

The door cracked open. Her eyes were red from crying. Damn, he hated to see her suffering. He hated even worse not knowing why. "What the hell happened?"

"I'm really sorry," she whispered.

"We were talking about that experiment, then all of a sudden—wait, is that it? You're upset because the experiment failed?" He tried to pry the door open, but she was holding it steady with her super strength. "Don't shut me out, Darcy. You know I love you."

A tear rolled down her cheek. "I can't ask you to give up everything for me."

"You don't have to ask. It's my choice."

She shook her head. "No. I won't have anyone sacrificing themselves for me. I won't allow it."

"Why not? Don't you know you're worth it?"

She sniffed as another tear tumbled down. "I don't believe in sacrificing oneself."

"Of course you do. You did it yourself when you saved Taylor."

Her face crumbled. "And look what happened. I lost everything. I won't let that happen to you. You would grow to hate me. After you lost your job and your friends and your family, you would hate me."

"No!" He rested a hand on each side of the door and leaned forward. "Darcy, you were Taylor's hero. Let me be yours."

Her breath caught in a sob. "I'm sorry." She shoved the door shut.

He stared at it in disbelief. God damn it. He was willing to give up everything for her, and she'd slammed the door in his face? He curled his hands into fists. "No!" He punched a fist against the door, then stalked back to his room.

Damn, damn, damn! Each step increased his rage. How could she do this? He'd come such a long way, all the way from being a vampire hater to her lover. She couldn't just toss him aside.

She wouldn't, dammit. He'd show her. He wasn't that easy to dismiss.

Thirty minutes later, Darcy jerked to a sitting position at the sound of loud banging on her door. "Oh, go away," she moaned, falling back onto her tear-soaked pillow.

There was a silent pause, and she imagined Austin pacing outside with indignation. Or maybe he had left and accepted the inevitable. Fresh tears ran down her face. She was doing the right thing. She was probably saving his life, but there was still a secret hope deep in her heart that he would burst through the door and re-fuse to ever give her up.

The banging started again. *Oh, please. Don't make me have to reject you again.* She rolled over and pulled a pillow over her ears to muffle the noise. The banging continued. She tossed the pillow aside since the damp pillowslip chilled her ears.

"Darcy, if you don't come here, I'm breaking the door down!"

Vanda? Darcy stumbled from the bedroom to the front door of the pool house. "I'm coming." She didn't have to yell too loud since Vanda's hearing was as good as her own.

"Well, thank God. I was beginning to think you were sick or something," Vanda muttered.

Darcy opened the door. "I'm fine."

Vanda's eyes widened. "The hell you are. You look awful."

"Thanks." Darcy peered through her swollen eyes at the figure huddled behind Vanda. "Oh, no. Maggie, what happened?"

"Yeah, she looks awful, too." Vanda dragged Maggie into the pool house. "I thought you'd be able to cheer her up, but—"

Darcy took one look at Maggie's red-rimmed eyes and tear-stained face and burst into tears.

"Great," Vanda muttered. "This is going to be fun."

"Oh, Darcy. It was terrible," Maggie wailed with a fresh supply of tears.

Darcy wrapped her arms around her. "Poor Maggie."

With a sigh, Vanda shut the door. "Looks like I brought the right stuff." She lifted an unlabeled bottle. "Now, we can all get hammered."

Darcy sniffled. "What is it?"

Vanda strode into the kitchen. "Gregori gave it to me. It's Roman's latest venture into Vampire Fusion Cuisine. Still in the experimental stage, though. Not for sale yet."

Darcy and Maggie wandered toward the kitchen, their arms still looped around each other.

Vanda shook her head. "You two look pathetic." She slammed three glasses onto the counter and opened the bottle. "Wow!" Her eyes watered as the fumes from the bottle engulfed her face.

"What is that stuff?" Darcy asked.

"Blissky. Half synthetic blood, half pure Scots whisky." Vanda poured some into the three glasses. "Here you go."

Darcy added some ice to hers, then joined her friends in the sitting area. She settled into a wicker rocking chair.

"Bottoms up." Vanda raised her glass in salute.

After they'd finished gasping and coughing, Vanda refilled their glasses. She set the bottle down on the glass-topped wicker coffee table. "Okay. Who's first?"

Maggie tossed back her glass, then croaked, "Me." She leaned back against the floral printed cushions of the loveseat. "I went to DVN for my interview with Mr. Bacchus."

"Oh, no," Darcy groaned. "That was tonight?"

"Yes." Maggie wiped the moisture off her face.

"I'm so sorry, Maggie. I meant to warn you about him." But she'd gotten too immersed in her own problems with Austin.

Maggie's lips trembled. "You knew he was a lecherous creep?"

"What happened?" Vanda demanded. "Did he make a move on you?"

Maggie shuddered. "It was more like he wanted me to make moves on him. I was so shocked, I just stood there, gaping at him. Then he said, as long as my mouth was open, I might as well put it to good use."

"That Sly," Darcy muttered. "Always a smooth talker."

Vanda snorted. "I hope you told him to go to hell."

Maggie winced. "I should have. But I was so horrified, I just ran from the room." She slumped against the cushions. "Now, I'll never get an acting job. I'll never be with Don Orlando."

Darcy drank her shot of Blissky to bolster her courage. "About Don Orlando, you should know the rumors are true."

"No." Maggie's face crumbled. Vanda refilled her glass.

"He's had an affair with Corky Courrant and Tiffany," Darcy said. "And there could be others."

"Scumbag," Vanda growled.

New tears tumbled down Maggie's face. "I was so sure he was perfect for me." She grabbed her glass and drank.

Darcy sniffed. "I'm really sorry."

"Men." Vanda gulped down some Blissky. "Even dead, you can't live with them." She refilled their glasses. "Your turn, Darcy. Why are you upset?"

She sighed. "A man."

"Of course." Vanda lifted her glass and announced, "Men suck."

"Especially vampire men," Maggie grumbled, then looked stunned by the truth of her statement. The women burst into laughter and downed another shot of Blissky.

"Oh, my God." Maggie wiped her eyes. "I can't believe it. I'm actually getting drunk."

"You've never been drunk before?" Vanda asked.

"No, I was raised in a very strict Catholic family. Drinking was evil. Sweet Mary, everything was evil."

Maggie lounged back with a dreamy look. "I thought with enough love and religion, I could change the world. So, in 1884, I joined the Salvation Army. I had the smartest little uniform, and we marched around Manhattan with our brass band, preaching about the evils of rumdom, slumdom, and bumdom."

"Really?" Darcy asked. "You never told me this."

Maggie shrugged. "I didn't last for very long. I was only nineteen and so naïve. After a few weeks, I joined the slum brigade, and we went into this seedy area close to the docks. We had baskets of fresh bread, and we were going to feed the poor. But then I got separated from the others and by the time the sun set, I was hopelessly lost." Frowning, she touched the scars on her neck. "I ended up feeding the poor, all right."

Darcy blinked. "You mean literally?"

The ladies looked at each other, then burst into giggles.

"To Maggie and feeding the poor." Vanda raised a full glass.

They clinked their glasses together and drank.

Vanda turned to Darcy. "So, who's the bastard in your life?"

"Austin, but he's not a bastard."

Maggie frowned. "I don't think we know him."

"Oh." Darcy propped her feet against the edge of the coffee table to make her rocking chair move. "You know him as Adam."

"Adam's giving you trouble?" Vanda asked, her expression confused. "But he told me in the hot tub that he's in love with you."

"You were talking about me in the hot tub?"

"Sure." Vanda frowned. "I warned him never to hurt you."

"He's not hurting me. I'm hurting him."

"Hurray!" Maggie slouched on the loveseat, grinning. "Kick his ass."

Vanda gave her an annoyed look. "Darcy isn't enjoying this."

"Oh, sorry." Maggie leaned forward and plummeted onto the floor.

"What did you say his name was?" Vanda asked. "Austin?"

Maggie rolled onto her back and hiccoughed. "I thought his name was Adam. Or Apollo, the sun god."

"Adam is his stage name," Darcy clarified.

"Adam, Austin, Apollo." Vanda shrugged. "A dick by any other name would smell as sweet."

A burst of giggles came from the floor where Maggie was sprawled.

With a snort of laughter, Darcy pushed too hard against the coffee table. Her chair rocked back, then teetered on the edge. "Aagh!" She crashed onto the floor.

Vanda lurched to her feet and stood swaying over her. "Are you all right?"

"I'm fine." Darcy giggled as she rolled onto the floor. "I'm in love." She burst into tears.

"Oh, great." Vanda helped her up. "We'd better get to a safe place before the sun rises."

"The bedroom." Darcy lurched toward the room, followed by Vanda and Maggie. They collapsed onto the king-sized bed.

The sun must be breaking the horizon, Darcy thought. She could feel the heavy pull of the death sleep.

"You know, there's one good thing about being a vampire," Vanda whispered on Darcy's right.

"What's that?" Maggie asked from Darcy's left.

"No matter how screwed up we are, we'll never lose a minute's sleep over it."

"True." Darcy reached for their hands. "Thank you for being here." With good friends, maybe she could survive this. She slipped into oblivion.

Chapter 23

Darcy woke with a monstrous headache. Vanda and Maggie looked equally as miserable as they stumbled back to their rooms on the servants' floor. As Darcy showered and dressed, she realized she couldn't face Austin. If she saw him, she might beg him to take her back. So she stopped by the cameramen's room and asked them to proceed without her.

Maria Consuela was judging the contest tonight. Gregori escorted her to the penthouse library. The rest of the ex-harem, including Darcy, watched from the servants' parlor.

Cora Lee squealed, pointing at the television where the library could now be seen. "There they are!"

"Not so loud," Vanda muttered.

Maggie groaned. Darcy rubbed her throbbing temples.

Gregori smiled at a camera. "Welcome to *The Sexiest Man on Earth*. There are only four contestants left, and two will be eliminated tonight as we test each man's strength. Our judge tonight is the lovely Maria Consuela of Spain."

Maria Consuela inclined her head toward the camera in a calm, regal manner. Only her tight grip on her rosary hinted at her nervousness.

"Our first contestant tonight is Roberto from Buenos Aires." Gregori opened the library door, and Roberto entered the room.

He looked suave, his black hair slicked back from a high forehead. He bowed to Maria Consuela. "At your service, *señora*."

"*Gracias*." Maria Consuela stood by the fireplace and motioned to a nearby wingback chair. "I believe this chair would look much better in front of the desk."

"*Claro*." Roberto lifted the chair high over his head. He walked to the desk and set the chair down. "Is this better?"

"Why, yes." Maria Consuela's dark eyes gleamed with approval. "And that little settee in the corner, I believe it should be here by the fireplace."

"Of course." Roberto easily lifted the antique love seat and placed it by the hearth. He straightened, adjusting his cufflinks. He hadn't even wrinkled his suit.

Maria Consuela beamed. "*Gracias, señor.* You may go now."

Roberto bowed. "My pleasure, *señora*." He left the room.

Lady Pamela sighed. "He's most definitely a Vamp."

"Aye," Princess Joanna agreed. "We should keep him."

The ladies turned back to the television when Gregori brought in the next contestant.

Garth of Colorado smiled. "Good evening."

Darcy held her breath. Garth Manly, aka Garrett the CIA man, needed to be eliminated tonight.

Maria Consuela inclined her head to him. "If you would be so kind, would you please move this settee to the corner?"

"No problem." Garrett tried to lift the settee, but it proved too long and unwieldy for him. Finally, he lifted one end and pushed it. The legs scraped across the wooden floor.

Maria Consuela huffed. "You are scratching the floor."

"Sorry." Garrett gave the settee one final shove.

Maria Consuela narrowed her eyes. "Can you lift the desk?"

Garrett frowned at the huge mahogany desk. "Not by myself. You need at least two people. Maybe more."

Maria Consuela pursed her lips. "I see. You may go."

Darcy sighed with relief. Garrett had been found out.

Maria Consuela leaned toward a camera. "I suspect that man is a mortal."

"Hurray!" Cora Lee clapped. "We found another mortal!"

"Quiet," Vanda grumbled, rubbing her forehead.

Lady Pamela sniffed. "You are certainly in a foul mood."

"Shh," Darcy hushed them when the next contestant entered the room. Austin.

"Oh, look, it's Adam!" Cora Lee exclaimed. "I like him."

Darcy wanted to growl, but it would hurt her head too much.

"Hi, how are you?" Austin looked tired. Drawn and tense.

Maria Consuela tapped her chin with her finger. "I believe that chair should go here by the fireplace."

"Okay." Austin strode to the desk, lifted the wing-back chair, and set it down close to Maria Consuela.

Darcy sat up, her heart stammering. He'd made it look so easy. But then, it was only a chair. Mortal men could probably move chairs all day without straining themselves.

Maria Consuela's brows lifted. "And the settee in the corner? Could you put it in front of the desk?"

"Sure." Austin circled behind the settee. He glanced at the camera, his expression harsh with emotion.

Darcy felt alarm bells clanging in her aching head.

Austin leaned over, then straightened with the settee balanced on one hand in the air.

The ladies gasped.

Darcy's jaw dropped. Vanda and Maggie shot her confused looks. They knew as well as she did that he was mortal.

"It must be some kind of trick," Darcy whispered as she watched him walk across the room with the settee in the air.

"I knew it." Princess Joanna nodded with satisfaction. "That man is a vampire."

Darcy sank into her chair. What was Austin doing? He was supposed to get eliminated. He had told her he would. The truth dawned on her with a startled gasp. He intended to stay. He wanted another night. With her.

Austin lowered the settee to the floor. "Anything else?"

"No." Maria Consuela smiled. "That was marvelous. *Gracias.*"

Austin left the room. Dammit. Darcy gritted her teeth. How on earth had he managed such a trick?

"The last contestant," Gregori announced. "Otto of Düsseldorf."

Thank God. Darcy sat up, hoping He-Man Otto would twirl the desk on his finger like a basketball. If anyone could beat Austin, it would be him.

"Ya, de Otto is here." He marched in and posed for one of the cameras. The material on his jacket strained over his back muscles. "Ah, de Otto must take off his coat before it is ripped into tiny pieces by his big bulges."

He made googly eyes at the camera while he removed his jacket. "Ya, all de ladies love de big bulges."

"Oh, my." Maria Consuela collapsed into the wing-back chair. "You're so strong."

"Ya, you vant to see how strong?" He circled to the back of her chair. "De Otto vill lift you high in de air."

"Santa Maria." Maria Consuela clutched the arms of the chair. "Are you sure?"

"Ya. Do not fear. You are light as de feather." Otto grasped the chair under its arms. He straightened suddenly, causing Maria Consuela to squeal as she rose in the air.

"You see. It is easy." Otto started to lower the chair when he yelped. "Aagh!" The chair tipped, spilling Maria Consuela onto the floor with a splat. Her scream was cut off when the chair landed on her head.

"Aagh!" Otto doubled over. "I broke a nail. De fingernail bent backvard."

Gregori rushed forward and pulled the chair off Maria Consuela. "Are you all right?"

"No!" She scrambled to her feet, glaring at Otto. "You clumsy fool! I haven't been so abused since the Spanish Inquisition!"

"But de Otto is hurt." Otto stuck his sore finger into his mouth and sucked.

Darcy's eye twitched. The unbelievable had happened.

Otto of Düsseldorf had failed the strength test.

Coward. She was avoiding him. Austin stood on the staircase landing, watching the ladies file into the foyer. Darcy was nowhere in sight.

Gregori strode toward the center of the foyer. "Welcome to another orchid ceremony on *The Sexiest Man on Earth.* Tonight, two men will leave, and two will remain. Those last two men will compete for the title and a whopping *five* million dollars."

The cameramen scurried to catch all the excited reactions. Maria Consuela joined Gregori under the chandelier with two black orchids in her hands.

"Are you ready?" Gregori asked. When she nodded, he continued, "Who will be eliminated? We'll know real soon, but first, a word from our sponsor—Romatech's Fusion Cuisine." He paused, then started again with a smile. "We're back. And Maria Consuela is ready to give out her orchids."

She nodded. "The first one goes to Garth from Colorado."

"That figures," Garrett mumbled. He descended the stairs to receive his orchid. Then, he climbed back to the landing to stand near Austin. "I guess you're next," he whispered.

Austin held his breath.

"The second orchid goes to Otto of Düsseldorf."
Maria Consuela glared at the German vampire as he
lumbered down the stairs.

Otto trudged back up the stairs. He examined
Roberto and Austin, and his massive shoulders
slumped. "Dis is terrible. De Otto has been crushed
by two girly-men."

"Let's go." Austin walked back to the east wing
with Garrett. While Garrett retrieved his bags, Austin
went to his room to watch the surveillance camera in
the portrait room.

The ladies sighed when the black light revealed
Otto as a vampire. Then they cheered when they
learned Garrett was mortal.

"We've done it!" one of the ladies exclaimed.
"We've rid ourselves of the last mortal!"

Austin winced. Darcy was probably furious. He'd
have to convince her that no harm was done. He could
still lose to Roberto in the final round.

He accompanied Garrett downstairs and helped
him load his luggage into the Hummer limo. Otto was
already inside, grumbling to himself. The limo drove
away, and Austin went straight to the roof and the pool
house. He knocked. No answer. He tried the door. It
wasn't locked, so he let himself in.

"Darcy? Are you here?" The main room was empty.
Bedroom, too. He headed back to the kitchen and filled
a glass with ice water. Then, he wandered to the sitting
area and set his glass on the coffee table. There were
three empty glasses there and an almost empty bottle.
He lifted the bottle and sniffed. Whoa! He eyed the
rocking chair knocked over on its back. So, Darcy had
gotten soused after rejecting him. He slowly smiled.

The front door creaked open, and he turned.

Darcy's mouth fell open.

"Hi, sweetheart." He lifted the bottle in his hand. "Did you want to get drunk again?"

Her gaze flicked to the bottle. "I had enough last night."

"Strange." He clunked the bottle down. "I didn't."

She winced, then quietly shut the door.

He sat on the wicker love seat. "Did it work?"

She approached him warily. "Did what work?"

"Did getting soused make you forget that you love me?"

Her eyes reflected pain as she sat on the end of the wicker chaise lounge. "Nothing could make me forget that." Her expression hardened. "I also remember that you agreed to get yourself eliminated from the show."

"I couldn't leave. Not without talking to you."

"Then send me a telegram." Her eyes flashed with anger. "Are you trying to get me fired? That's what'll happen if you win."

"I won't win. I'll be obnoxious and rude tomorrow night."

"There's no taping for the next two days. The second show airs tomorrow night. You won't see me again 'til Friday. That's the final night of taping. And you had better lose."

"I will. Trust me."

"Trust? Don't make me laugh, *Adam*."

"I have never lied to you about how I feel."

Her eyes narrowed. "How did you do it? How did you lift a settee with one hand?"

He focused on the overturned rocker. Slowly it rose in the air, then landed in an upright position.

Darcy gaped at it, then at Austin, then back at the chair. "How?"

"Telekinesis."

"Good God, how powerful are you?"

He shrugged. "I feel pretty damned helpless where you're concerned. I want to spend the rest of my life with you, and you're brushing me off like it's nothing."

"You think it's *easy* for me?" She rubbed her forehead. "I have a monster headache."

"Looks like you have two choices. You can either marry me or spend eternity in a drunken stupor."

She glared at him as she massaged her temples. "Oh, thanks. That's about the loveliest proposal a girl could hope for."

He perched on the end of the chaise beside her. "Allow me." He pressed his fingers into her scalp and rubbed small circles.

She closed her eyes. "I shouldn't let you touch me."

"Why not?"

"Because my resistance melts away."

"Good." He moved his hands to her neck and massaged her there. "You hate being cold, sweetheart. Stop fighting this, and melt with me."

She moaned, her eyes still closed. "I want you to be happy, Austin. How can you be happy with me?"

"I love you. Of course, I'll be happy with you." He focused on his glass of water. It slid across the table to within his reach. He fished out an ice cube, then drew a line with it down Darcy's neck.

She stiffened, her eyes flying open. "That's so cold."

"Yes, but I'm here to heat you up." He nuzzled her neck, licking away the cold trail of water left behind by the ice.

She shuddered. "Do you realize what you're doing?"

"Seducing you?" He skimmed the ice cube along her collarbone, then down between her breasts.

Her skin pebbled with goosebumps. "I can't leave the vampire world. I'm stuck here. You would be forced to share it with me."

"I know." With the ice, he drew two circles on her T-shirt, outlining her breasts. "I just have one question for you."

She shivered. "What is it?"

He rubbed the ice over her nipples, soaking her T-shirt and bra. "Will you still love me when I'm old and gray? Or bald?"

"Of course."

"Then it's settled." He tossed the ice cube onto the table.

"You make it sound so easy." She shuddered. "Shame on you. You know how I hate the cold."

"But you love it when I warm you up." He pulled her shirt over her head. Then, he reached behind her to unhook her bra.

"God help me, I love you." She wrapped her arms around his neck.

Yes! A surge of victory swept through him as he pushed her down onto the chaise lounge. She *did* love him. She *did* want him. He made love to her breasts, then unzipped her jeans and tugged them down her legs. They snagged on her sneakers, so he jerked off her shoes and jeans all at once. She lounged on the floral cushions, wearing nothing but red lace underwear.

"You look incredible." He perched on the lounge next to her.

"Thank you." She reached for him.

"Just a minute." He plucked another piece of ice from his glass and studied her panties. "Hmm."

Her eyes widened. "Don't you dare."

"But I promise to warm you up."

She scrambled off the chaise, but he caught the waistband and popped the ice cube onto her bottom. "Aagh!" She wiggled out of the underwear.

"Wow." He rose to his feet, grinning. "I've never seen a lady drop her pants so fast."

"You rascal." She planted her hands on her hips and looked him over. "We have a serious problem."

"What?"

Her eyes twinkled with mischief. "I'm completely naked, but here you are, still in a suit and tie."

"Oh. No problem." He started to take off his coat, but she stopped him.

"I think I like this." She circled him slowly, skimming a hand across his chest, over his arm, and across his back. "It makes me feel . . . wild and wanton."

He inhaled sharply when her breasts brushed against his arm. His groin tightened. "I have to admit I like the view."

"So do I." She lifted the end of his tie and ran the tip down her neck and between her breasts.

He grabbed her hips and pulled her against his erection. "Are you ready to be warmed up?"

"Is that a heating iron or are you just happy to see me?" She wiggled out of his arms. "Come." She tugged on his tie, leading him like a dog on a leash.

And he went. Gladly. Hell, he felt like howling. After all, the woman he loved was leading him to the bedroom. And watching her swaying rump from behind was an added bonus.

She stopped when she reached the bed. She turned slowly. "Let me undress you." But he already had his coat and shoes off. Her eyes widened. "You're certainly in a hurry."

"Sweetheart, I'm about to explode."

"Really?" She hooked a leg around him and rubbed her inner thigh against his pants. "Are you suffering?"

"Vixen," he muttered as he loosened his tie and pulled it over his head.

She began to unbutton his shirt with irritatingly slow patience. With a growl, he unhooked his belt, unzipped his pants, dropped them, and kicked them aside. His underwear followed suit, and she was still unbuttoning his shirt.

"Enough." He yanked his shirt and undershirt over his head at the same time. He focused on the door, and it swung shut.

"Wow," she breathed.

With his mind, he pulled the comforter down the bed. Clean white sheets and pillows were revealed. "Climb in, sweetheart."

She snorted. "Well, that's a neat trick, but if you really want to impress me, you'll know how to make the bed, too."

He grabbed her around the waist and plopped her on the mattress.

"And do the laundry. Not to mention the dirty dishes."

"I just love it when you talk dirty." He pushed her down and gave his full attention to her breasts.

With a moan, she splayed her hands into his hair. "I tried to stay away from you. I knew I couldn't resist you."

He shoved her knees apart and settled between her thighs. "I'm here to stay."

She jolted when he tickled her between the legs. She was hot and wet. He spread the moisture around while she trembled and gasped. The scent of her desire lured him in closer. He planted his mouth on her and quickly convinced her that they could indeed find domestic bliss together.

She cried out. He nuzzled close to feel the throbbing spasms. Holy moley. He needed to be inside her fast.

"I love you," she gasped.

He glanced up and saw her red glowing eyes. He hesitated only a few seconds, but she used that time to push him down and roll on top of him.

"I love you," she repeated as she trailed kisses down his chest. She teased his nipples with her tongue.

His erection wedged against her bottom, and he almost lost it. "Darcy, I can't wait."

She straddled his hips and lowered herself onto him. Each time she wiggled to accommodate his size, he groaned.

"Now." He grabbed her hips and forced her down. *Faster,* he told her with his mind. *I can't wait much longer.*

She sat up and tossed her hair behind her shoulders. She began to rock slowly, her eyes closed, her mouth slightly open. He'd never seen her so beautiful, so sexy. He cupped her breasts and gently squeezed. With a moan, she fell forward onto his chest. He grabbed her hips to increase the pace. Her breathing grew ragged, her fingers dug into him.

He was pushing up, grinding their hips together. Not much longer. He gritted his teeth, fighting for more time. He'd make her come with him, somehow. He reached between them and tweaked at her slick, hot nubbin. She cried out. He wrapped his arms around her, and they shattered together.

Suddenly, she stiffened and jerked free from his embrace. She sat up, her whole body shaking.

"Darcy, what's wrong?"

"No!" She slapped both hands over her mouth. Her blue eyes filled with horror.

"Darcy?"

She scrambled off of him. Her eyes turned red, and she doubled over, crying out in pain.

He couldn't leave her like this. "What can I do?"

"Go! Run away!"

He jumped back when he saw the white flash of fangs. Holy crap. Her fangs had come out. He tumbled out of bed.

A cry ripped from her throat, a cry so replete with pain and terror, he hesitated. She needed help. But what could he do?

"Run!" She grabbed a pillow and sank her fangs into it.

He shuddered at the sound of ripping fabric. That could have been his neck. Feathers floated around her head.

He ran to the kitchen, grabbed a bottle of Chocolood, and dashed back to the bedroom. He unscrewed the top. "Here."

She remained curled in a ball, crying.

"Darcy!" He nudged her arm with the cold bottle.

She sat up with an angry hiss. He jumped back. With her eyes bright red and her fangs distended, she crawled across the bed toward him.

Holy shit. He felt like he was trying to feed a wild animal. He gingerly offered her the bottle.

She seized it and upended it. She guzzled it down so fast, drops of blood escaped and ran down her neck and chest.

Austin gulped. How could he live with this? He turned away to get dressed. He could hear the gulping sounds behind him. Finally, when he was buttoning his shirt, it became quiet.

He turned. She set the empty bottle down on the bedside table. Then, she used the sheet to wipe the blood off her chest.

"Are you all right?"

She shook her head, unable to look at him.

"Have your fangs ever come out before?"

"Only once. After I was transformed. It's an automatic reaction, then. But that was four years ago. I—I've never wanted to bite anyone. I thought I was safe."

"You were just hungry. We'll make sure—"

"No!" She looked at him, her eyes glistening with tears. "I've already eaten tonight. I'm not that hungry. It was—I don't know. I lost control."

"From the sex?"

A tear rolled down her face. "We can't do this again. I could have killed you."

"But you didn't. You attacked a pillow." The slashed pillow made him wince.

"I had to bite something." More tears slid down her cheeks. "I can't let you live with me. I'm too dangerous."

His heart plummeted. "We'll figure out something." This couldn't be happening. He couldn't lose her now.

"*No.*" She turned her head away. "I want you to leave. Now."

It felt like his heart had fallen into a vat of acid, and he was left with nothing but shriveling, gnawing pain. He considered arguing with her, begging her, anything to keep her. But she wouldn't even look at him.

One last feather floated down onto the bed, landing next to the blood-stained sheet. He glanced at the slashed pillow. She was right. She could have killed him. He stumbled toward the door and left.

Chapter 24

Austin couldn't stay at the penthouse. His bedroom there reminded him too much of Darcy. The scent of her shampoo lingered on the pillows, making it impossible to sleep. He took the subway back to his apartment in Greenwich Village. Even then, he couldn't escape the pain or the memories.

The next day, he went to the office. He wasn't there five minutes before he realized how difficult it would be to continue working for the CIA. He could no longer fight every vampire with the conviction they were all evil. He needed to convince Sean that it was only the Malcontents who were attacking people. If he could steer the Stake-Out team's focus toward the Malcontents and away from law-abiding Vamps, then it would be worth keeping his job.

Emma stopped by his desk and looked him over. "You look tired. It must be hard being the sexiest man on earth."

"Exhausting."

She snorted. "Well, wake yourself up, Lover-boy. Sean wants you and Garrett in the conference room in five minutes."

Austin groaned. Sean probably wanted a report on the reality show and DVN. None of those vampires were a threat to humanity. Even humongous Otto was all bark and no bite.

He wandered over to Garrett's desk. "How's it going?"

Garrett glanced up. "I'm going over my list of vampire contestants. Where was Reginald from?"

Austin frowned. "Reginald? Was he a vampire?"

"Yeah, I think so."

Austin sighed. "I'm having trouble remembering. I think the vampires must have messed with my memory."

"Really?" Garrett's eyes widened. "When did that happen?"

"I don't know. If they erased my memory, how can I remember it?"

"Oh." Garrett shifted his gaze back to his paper. "I remembered these names."

"Can I see your list? Maybe it'll help jog my memory."

"Sure." Garrett handed him the paper.

Austin scanned the list of names. Garrett hadn't been very industrious if this was all he had discovered while working undercover. "You don't have their last names. It'll be hard to track them down."

Garrett shrugged. "We never knew their last names."

"Are you sure?" Austin lifted an eyebrow. "Or did they erase your memory, too?"

Garrett looked confused. "I don't know."

"Did you find out where Shanna is?"

"No." Garrett stood slowly. "Or maybe I did, and they erased it."

"Damn." Austin crushed the paper in his fist. "Sean expects us to give detailed reports, but we can't remember much."

"But I do remember. I remember the penthouse and the five lady judges and—"

Austin listened while Garrett rambled on and on, then slipped into his head without the guy noticing it. Austin couldn't erase memories like a vampire, but he could certainly muddle someone's memory by projecting contradictory images. Garrett stopped talking and closed his eyes as his mind overflowed with the mental pictures Austin sent.

"Hey, are you all right?"

Garrett rubbed his forehead. "It's hot in here."

"Maybe you're coming down with something. Or maybe it's just an aftereffect from those vampires messing with our heads."

"Yeah." Garrett nodded. "That could be it." He wandered toward the conference room.

"I'll be right there." Austin's heart raced as he headed for the shredding machine. Garrett had been pathetically easy to confuse, but still, messing with a fellow agent's head was too much like treason. But what could Austin do? He couldn't let Sean terminate the good Vamps.

Austin fed Garrett's list into the shredder and punched the button. Damn it to hell. He'd just become a double agent.

He rushed to the men's restroom and splashed cold water on his face. He breathed deeply until he was calm. Then, he marched toward the conference room.

Garrett had been easy to manipulate. Sean Whelan would not.

He entered the conference room and gave Garrett and Sean a nod. "Good morning." He shut the door.

"You're late." Sean sat at the head of the table. Garrett sat on the right, his shoulders slumped.

Sean tapped the end of his pen on the table. "We have a problem."

"Yes?" Austin approached the table.

"I want your reports, but Garrett doesn't have one. He says you don't either. He says the vampires messed with your heads."

Austin took a seat. "Yes, I believe they did."

"How could you let that happen?" Sean glared at him. "I can understand Garrett having trouble repelling their mind control, but you—Austin, your power is rated off the charts! You should have been able to stop them."

Austin narrowed his eyes as if in deep concentration. "I do remember some things. But nothing of any value. We don't know where your daughter is. I'm sorry."

Sean's jaw clenched. "What do you remember?"

Austin shrugged. "I can't recall their names, but there were several vampires there. They were harmless."

Sean snorted. "Now, that's an oxymoron, a harmless vampire."

"They would have never harmed us."

Sean slammed his pen onto the table. "They've been messing with your head. That *is* harming you."

"I remember some names," Garrett offered. "Roberto. No, maybe it was Alberto. And there was a beach house."

Austin shook his head. "No, it was penthouse."

"Oh yeah, that's right." Garrett grimaced. "Why am I remembering a beach house?"

Austin slipped into Garrett's mind and fed him more pictures. "I remember the contest, and there were five judges."

"Poodles," Garrett said.

"What?" Sean shot him a confused look.

"The judges were fluffy pink poodles." Garrett frowned and rubbed his glistening forehead. "That can't be right."

"Those bastards." Sean banged a fist on the table. "They're toying with us." He stood and paced about the room. "This has been a waste of time. We're no closer to finding my daughter."

Austin took a deep breath. "I think we should concentrate our efforts on the vampires who are actually attacking people. The Vamps at DVN just want to entertain each other with dorky soap operas and sell a few bottles of Chocolood. They may be guilty of bad taste, but they're basically harmless."

Sean stopped his pacing to stare at Austin. "If the vampires messed with your head, everything you say is suspect. There is no such thing as a harmless vampire."

"I remember enough from the reality show to know that those vampires would never harm humans."

Sean scoffed. "Is that what you remember, Garrett? A bunch of sweet, harmless vampires?"

Garrett's face flushed with heat. "There was never any biting. The poodles were nice." Sweat beaded on his brow. "I mean, the ladies."

Sean frowned at him. "You look ill. Have you checked your neck for tooth marks?"

Garrett paled. "Oh, my God." He unbuttoned his collar and ran his fingers over his neck. "I'm all right."

"No, you're not." Sean ground his teeth. "You've been brainwashed. Get an appointment with the Company shrink."

"Yes, sir." Garrett wiped his moist forehead. "I do feel strange, like I'm running a fever."

Sean narrowed his eyes. "You may go," he ordered quietly.

"Thank you, sir." Garrett weaved toward the door and left.

Austin stood to make his leave.

"Sit."

He sat back down. A swoosh of hot air surrounded his mind, powerful and suffocating. Austin knew who it was, and he also knew his mind was full of memories he couldn't allow anyone to see. Memories he had claimed were forgotten. And memories about Darcy. Sean's mental forces tightened like a vise. Austin instantly erected a firewall and began gathering his power.

"Not bad," Sean whispered. "You do realize, don't you, that when a human invades your mind, you feel heat? How interesting that Garrett was feeling hot."

Austin's power had reached critical mass. He dropped the firewall and unleashed his power, shattering the vice that had surrounded him.

Sean stiffened with a gasp.

Austin stood. "Don't try that again."

"And you expect me to believe the vampires messed with your mind?" Sean's face was pinched with anger. "As strong as you are, they couldn't do anything to you. Unless you wanted it."

Austin gritted his teeth. He had hoped to steer Sean's focus onto the Malcontents and away from Darcy and her friends. But it would never work. Sean no longer trusted him.

Sean gave him a scathing look. "What happened to you, Austin? Did you let one of those vampire bitches seduce you?"

He balled his hands into fists. "I assure you, I am in complete control of myself."

"Then prove it. Go back to the penthouse and stake them all while they sleep."

Austin swallowed hard. "No."

Sean planted his palms on the table and leaned forward. "Think twice before you answer, Erickson. Are you disobeying a direct order?"

His heart raced, causing a thundering sound in his ears. "Yes. I am. I'll turn in my resignation today."

"You stupid fool."

Austin shook his head. "You are the one who refuses to learn the truth. There are two kinds of vampires. You should leave the harmless Vamps alone and concentrate your efforts on the Malcontents. They are the dangerous ones."

"They're all dangerous!"

"No, they're not! For God's sake, Sean, talk to your daughter. Shanna will tell you the truth."

"Don't talk to me about her! She turned against me. And now, you've betrayed me, too. Get out of here!"

Austin strode to the door. "I'm going to continue the fight against evil. We will still be on the same side."

"*You* are evil, you traitor! Get out of here," Sean yelled.

Austin closed the door behind him. Alyssa and Emma were hovering outside, their faces worried. He removed his ID card and handed it to Emma.

"You mustn't leave," she whispered. "You're the strongest one amongst us."

"I'll still be fighting the bad guys." Austin smiled sadly. "Be careful out there." He walked out and took the elevator to the ground floor.

He'd screwed up everything. Sean knew where the reality show was being filmed, and he was furious enough to wreak revenge on the Vamps who were there. Austin would have to go back to the penthouse to make sure Darcy and her friends were protected. There was only one night of recording left. Once it was over, Darcy and her friends would be safe.

And what would he do then? He'd lost his job. He'd lost the girl. He'd tried to do everything right, but it had all fallen apart.

You can either marry me or spend eternity in a drunken stupor. Austin's unfortunate choice of words continued to haunt Darcy. She couldn't marry him. How could she subject him to a life of darkness and a wife who could turn into a monster at any given moment? She still shuddered every time she remembered the pain of her fangs elongating, the powerful urge to use them, and the overwhelming lust for blood.

Fortunately, her reaction of horror and disgust had been just as strong as her need for blood. That alone had helped her maintain enough control to keep from biting Austin. But what if it happened again and again? What if she slowly grew accustomed to it, and the horror faded away? Then, there would be nothing to keep her from biting Austin or transforming him against his will. And then, he would hate her. Just like she hated Connor.

Tears blurred her eyes. As far as she knew, she and Gregori were the only Vamps in the world who were completely bottle-fed. She knew the rest of her friends must have bitten people in the past, but she'd always had trouble imagining it. Sweet little Maggie sinking fangs into someone?

But now, she knew how it could happen. When her fangs had shot out, she'd desperately craved blood. And if it happened night after night, it would eventually lose its aura of terror. It would become normal. In time, it would even become pleasurable.

She couldn't drag Austin into that trap. And spending eternity in a drunken stupor was pathetic. The only recourse she could think of was over-work. She could at least be productive. And it would keep her mind from dwelling on Austin.

Wednesday, she arrived at DVN soon after dusk and went straight to work editing the third show which would air that Saturday. After a few hours, Sly peeked in her office. Darcy was tempted to throw a stapler at him for being so creepy to Maggie.

"Well, Newhart, did you find out who the babe was in the hot tub?"

"No." She concentrated harder on her work so he'd know he was interrupting her. "I'm afraid it will always be a mystery."

"Hmm." He scratched his beard, oblivious to her hints that he was bothering her. "Most of the phone calls and emails indicate that people think it was Cora Lee or Lady Pamela."

Darcy sighed and kept working.

"We're still getting emails about how dowdy the ladies are dressed," Sly continued. "Did you get that taken care of?"

"Yes. They're all thoroughly modernized. It won't show up for a few episodes, but I think you'll be very pleased."

"Good." Sly propped himself against the doorjamb like he intended to stay another five minutes. Darcy stifled a groan.

"Are you still on schedule?" he asked. "You're recording the last show this Friday?"

"Yes, sir. We'll have the winner Friday night." And it had better be Roberto, or her goose was cooked.

"Great! I'm planning to be there for the final ceremony, so I can give away the check. I'm having a great big one made up."

"Sounds good."

"And I told Corky Courrant to be there, so she can do some post-ceremony interviews."

"Sounds exciting," Darcy mumbled.

"It is exciting!" Sly turned his head, his attention drawn by something in the hallway. "Hey, Tiffany! You're late." He glanced back at Darcy. "I've got a meeting to go to. See you later." He closed the door.

Darcy shuddered. Right. He and Tiffany had something important to discuss. Darcy worked until midnight, then took a break to watch *The Sexiest Man on Earth* as it aired its second show on international vampire television. It was the one where Lady Pamela took the contestants for a walk through the greenhouse. Watching Austin made her heart twist with pain. When he poked his finger on a rose thorn, the cameramen did an excellent job of showing Pamela's desire to taste his blood.

Darcy's eye twitched. She massaged the jumpy nerve at her temple. She'd made the right decision. Austin could never be safe living with her in the vampire world. It was like dangling a bottle of wine in front of a group of recovering alcoholics. When the show ended, her phone rang.

"Darcy!" Maggie sounded happy. "We all loved the show."

"That's good." She could hear excited voices in the background. "What's going on?"

"We're partying! Bart, Bernie, and Gregori came down to the servants' parlor to watch the show with us. We're all having Bubbly Blood to celebrate. Oh, and Roberto wanted to come. He said he was lonely all by himself in the penthouse, but Gregori told him he couldn't, that it wasn't fair for the contest."

"I see."

"Vanda's trying to talk Gregori into taking us to another male dancer club. Bart says there's a really hot one close by, though I don't know how he knows."

Darcy raised her eyebrows. Bart liked male dancers? "I see."

"Can you come with us? Gregori could teleport you here in a second."

"No, thanks. I've got a lot of work to do."

"Oh, okay." Maggie sighed. "I just don't want you to be sad because—oh, that reminds me. I guess I should tell you."

Darcy frowned at the hesitancy in her friend's voice. "What's wrong?"

"Gregori heard something outside in the hall, and he went to check it out. It was Adam. Or Austin. Whatever."

Darcy's heart skipped. "What was he doing?"

"Gregori said he was walking around the penthouse, worried about security. He said we needed more guards night and day."

Darcy caught her breath. Did Austin know something? He was, after all, a CIA operative. He might have good reason to be concerned for their safety. "Maggie, let me talk to Gregori."

"Okay." There was a pause.

"What's up, sweetcakes?" Gregori spoke.

"I think you should take the ladies out. Keep Bart and Bernie with you. And call . . . Connor. Ask him if he can spare a few guards for the penthouse."

"What's going on? You sound as worried as that guy, Adam."

"I'll explain later. But believe me, if Adam is worried, then there's a good reason for it. Be careful." Darcy hung up and went back to work.

She worked long hours again on Thursday night and had two more shows ready to air. When Friday arrived, the ladies dressed in their finest new evening gowns. This would be the night they finally acquired their new master. And it would be the last night Darcy would ever see Austin.

Chapter 25

Darcy met Maggie and the five judges in the portrait room. "Tonight, you'll be judging the men according to the last qualification on your list—intelligence. I've prepared a question for you." She handed the paper to Lady Pamela.

The ladies sat on the couches that faced the two remaining portraits on the wall. Austin and Roberto.

Loud voices reverberated in the foyer. The door swung open.

"I'm here!" Sly announced. He strode inside, carrying a four-foot-long posterboard check. He propped it against the wall, then turned to greet the ladies. "Wowza, you look hot!"

Princess Joanna and Maria Consuela blushed and lowered their gazes to their hands in their lap. Lady Pamela and Cora Lee giggled. Vanda raised an eyebrow and glared back at Sly. Maggie slipped behind Darcy, her face pale.

Darcy realized how uncomfortable Maggie was in Sly's presence. "Could you see if the men are ready?"

"Sure." She rushed from the room.

Sly watched her leave. "She looks familiar." He turned back to the ladies and focused on the two blondes. "So, I hear one of you is fond of the hot tub."

Darcy cleared her throat. "Has Corky Courrant arrived yet?"

"No, she's finishing up her show at DVN," Sly answered. "She'll be here soon."

The door opened. The cameramen swooshed in. Maggie and Gregori walked in, followed by the last two contestants. Darcy eased over to a dark corner of the room. It was going to be miserably hard to be in the same room with Austin, but tonight would be the last time. Maggie joined her in the corner with a sheepish smile. They were both hiding out and knew it.

The cameramen turned on their lights and began doing closeups. Darcy blinked when she noticed how Austin was dressed. Roberto looked slick as usual in an expensive suit, but Austin was wearing faded jeans and a wrinkled T-shirt. His shaggy hair stood up in spikes. Whiskers lined his jaw.

Darcy realized he was trying to look messy and disrespectful, but his strategy was backfiring. He looked sexier than ever. With a sinking heart, she also realized there was no need for her to hide in the corner. Austin wasn't looking at her. He was glowering at his scruffy brown boots. Meanwhile, Roberto was casting languorous looks toward the female judges.

"Welcome to the final episode of *The Sexiest Man on Earth*," Gregori began. "Tonight, the ladies will make their final choice. Either Roberto of Buenos

Aires or Adam of Wisconsin will win the title and become the Sexiest Man on Earth."

Bart zeroed in on the two men. Roberto flashed a dazzling smile. Austin ignored the camera and scowled at his boots.

"Tonight, all five ladies will be judging." Gregori introduced them while Bernie focused his camera on them.

"We also have a special guest," Gregori continued. "Sylvester Bacchus, the producer of this show, will present the winner with a check for five million dollars."

Sly smiled for the camera. "This is the night we've all been waiting for. Since the show's debut, we've received over five thousand phone calls and emails. I'm sure you're as eager as I to see who will win."

"Indeed," Gregori agreed. "Tonight's winner not only receives the title of the Sexiest Man on Earth, but a check worth five million dollars."

"And that's not all!" Sly raised his hands dramatically. "The winner will be receiving even more!"

"But first," Gregori interrupted, "a word from our sponsor. How do you celebrate those special vampire occasions? With Bubbly Blood, of course. Romatech's fusion of synthetic blood and champagne." Gregori's smile froze until the cameraman stopped recording.

Darcy's eye twitched. Obviously, everyone assumed both the male contestants were vampires.

Gregori cued the cameraman to start again. "And we're back, just in time for Sylvester Bacchus's important announcement."

"Yes." Sly smiled when the camera switched to him. "As you know our five beautiful judges were once part of Roman Draganesti's harem. It would be a crime to leave these women without a master to take care of them. So, tonight's winner not only wins the title and the money, but he also becomes a master with all these lovely women in his brand-new harem!"

Austin's head snapped up. His mouth fell open.

Roberto's eyes gleamed. Licking his lips, he looked the ladies over.

Darcy glanced at the women. A few weeks ago, this was what they wanted more than anything. A new, wealthy master who would take care of their every need. But somehow, they didn't seem very excited or relieved. Instead, they looked uncomfortable, even embarrassed. Darcy suspected they'd developed enough pride that they didn't enjoy being labeled as a contest prize.

She glanced at Austin. He was looking at her now. No, glaring. No doubt, he was a bit peeved at the thought of winning a harem. But it served him right. She'd warned him over and over to get himself eliminated.

"Tonight's winner will be judged on how well he answers one question." Gregori turned to the two male contestants. "Who would like to go first?"

"Me," Austin grumbled. "I want to get this over with."

Gregori's brows lifted at Austin's surly tone. "Very well." He turned to Roberto. "If you would excuse us a moment?"

Maggie rushed forward to escort Roberto outside. Austin stood in front of the judges, waiting.

Gregori nodded at the ladies. "You may ask your question."

Lady Pamela read the question out loud. "If you were our master, and we were your harem, and we were embroiled in a terrible disagreement, how would you resolve our conflict?"

Darcy inched forward, curious how Austin would answer. So far, he was simply glowering at his boots.

He lifted his chin and gave the judges an irritated look. "I would do nothing." He turned to leave.

Shock and dismay flitted across the women's faces.

"Prithee," Princess Joanna said. "Could you explain your refusal to be of assistance?"

Austin hesitated. "Look, you're intelligent women. You can solve your own problems." He strode toward the door and left.

Vanda cast a furtive glance toward Darcy. "He's a jerk."

Darcy held her breath. With Vanda's help and Austin's abrupt behavior, this prickly situation might work out all right.

Princess Joanna sniffed. "He has no sense of chivalry."

"And that sour expression." Maria Consuela frowned. "I knew torturers from the Inquisition with friendlier faces than that."

Cora Lee crossed her arms, pouting. "He practically snarled at us like a rabid dog."

"And his manner of dress was most disrespectful," Lady Pamela added. "We cannot have such a man for a master."

Vanda smiled. "Then it's all settled. Adam is out."

Darcy heaved a huge sigh of relief. She mouthed the words *thank you* to Vanda. Now, Austin wouldn't find himself stuck with a harem. And she could keep her job.

Maggie came in with Roberto. He strode toward the ladies and bowed. Lady Pamela repeated the question.

Roberto's smile was as oily as his slicked back hair. "Allow me to say it would be a great honor to be your master."

"We thank you, good sir," Princess Joanna answered. "But how would you resolve a disagreement amongst us?"

Roberto shrugged. "The question is moot. There would be no disagreement."

"I beg your pardon?" Lady Pamela asked.

"As the master, only my opinion will matter. Therefore, you will always agree with me, and we will live in peace and harmony."

There was a moment of silence. Roberto smiled, apparently believing the era of peace and harmony had begun.

Vanda's eyes narrowed. "What if we don't agree with you?"

"I am the master. You will do as I say, and believe as I tell you to believe."

More silence. The women exchanged looks.

"If you will step out for a moment?" Gregori motioned to the door. "The ladies must make their final decision."

Roberto bowed, then strode from the room.

"Well." Cora Lee sighed. "At least he was well dressed."

"He's handsome," Lady Pamela murmured. "And he . . . bows well."

"And yet," Princess Joanna said, "there is something about him that makes me want *to rip his head off.*"

Maria Consuela nodded. "He is evil."

"He's an arrogant bastard," Vanda muttered.

"Aren't those good qualities for a master?" Cora Lee asked.

Vanda snorted. "If that's true, I don't want a master."

"But we must have one!" Lady Pamela insisted. "We cannot fend for ourselves."

"We've been doing fine," Vanda replied. "We don't need a man to take care of us."

The princess frowned. "But we need money to survive. We must have a master in order to have money."

Cora Lee tilted her head. "Can someone remind me what was wrong with Adam?"

Darcy gulped.

"No." Vanda stood. "We all agreed. Adam is out."

"He wasn't well dressed," Lady Pamela answered.

"Fiddlesticks." Cora Lee huffed. "We'll just teach the man how to dress."

Maria Consuela stood to face them. "He was discourteous. He refused to help us resolve our dispute."

"True." Princess Joanna rose slowly. "But he refused because he believed we could resolve it ourselves. He said we were intelligent."

Cora Lee jumped to her feet. "You mean he wouldn't try to tell us what to think? Or say?"

The princess nodded. "I fear we have misjudged Adam."

Darcy's jaw dropped. She shot Vanda a look of desperation.

"Listen!" Vanda raised her hands. "We don't need either of them. We're doing fine on our own."

"I vote for Adam," Princess Joanna announced.

"Me too," Cora Lee and Lady Pamela piped in.

"I will also," Maria Consuela said. "We must have Adam."

Darcy groaned inwardly. She could kiss her career goodbye.

"I vote *no* to both of them," Vanda insisted. "Look how far we've come. Don't throw it all away now."

"The vote has been cast, and the majority wins." Gregori motioned for the ladies to sit. He retrieved the special flashlight from the wall safe. Maggie opened the door and invited both men to return. Austin looked nervous, but Roberto's smile oozed with confidence.

Sly stepped forward. "It will be my honor to announce the winner who will bear the title of Sexiest Man on Earth."

"If for any reason," Gregori interrupted, "the winner is unable to fulfill his duties as the Sexiest Man on Earth, the runner-up will be given the title and reward in his stead."

Sly held the four-foot-long check in front of his chest. His eyes twinkled with excitement. "Roberto of Buenos Aires?"

"Yes?" Roberto stepped forward. His eyes gleamed as he reached for the check.

"You lose." Sly chuckled at his cruel joke.

Roberto's smile froze. "What?"

Austin's face paled. He stepped back.

"The Sexiest Man on Earth is Adam from Wisconsin!" Sly announced.

Gregori pushed a stunned Austin forward.

"Congratulations!" Sly grabbed Austin's hand and pumped it. "Here's your check for five million dollars." He shoved the giant posterboard into Austin's arms.

The ladies, except for Vanda, clapped politely.

Sly motioned to the women. "And here is your brand-new harem!"

Austin's gulp was audible. "I—I don't deserve this." He tried to hand the check back to Sly.

Sly laughed. "Now, don't be shy. The ladies picked you."

"Then they are fools!" Roberto shouted. "How could they choose this . . . this ruffian over me?"

"Hush," Maggie told him

"Look," Austin said. "I don't want a harem."

The ladies gasped.

"You don't want us?" Cora Lee whimpered.

"I'm sure you're very nice ladies, and I've actually grown fond of you all, but you don't want me. I—I'm not your type."

Princess Joanna frowned. "You prefer men?"

Bart's eyes lit up. Literally.

"No!" Austin gritted his teeth. "I only want one woman. The one I love. Darcy." He shot her a beseeching look for help.

Everyone stared at Darcy. Bart stuck his camera in her face. She winced at the bright lights in her eyes.

"Well, isn't that sweet," Cora Lee murmured.

"Yes," Lady Pamela agreed. "We'll just keep Darcy in the harem, too. Then, we can all be happy."

"Wait a minute," Austin interrupted. "That's not gonna happen." He gave Darcy an apologetic look. "I know this will cause trouble, but everyone should know that I'm mortal."

A series of gasps crossed the room. Vanda and Maggie exchanged worried looks with Darcy.

She sighed. Now it would really get ugly. "It's true." She walked forward and took the flashlight from Gregori.

"It cannot be true," Princess Joanna insisted. "We saw him lift the settee with one hand."

Darcy pointed the flashlight at Roberto's portrait,

and his fangs appeared. She lit up Austin's picture. Nothing.

More gasps.

"He's a *mortal*?" Sly demanded. "I just gave five million dollars to a damned *mortal*?"

"I didn't intend to win." Austin held out the check. "You can have it back."

"No." Darcy shoved the check back at Austin. "You earned it. You're the Sexiest Man on Earth."

His eyes flashed. "I don't want a harem! Why didn't you tell me about that?"

"You weren't supposed to get this far," Darcy shot back.

"This is your fault!" Sly pointed a finger at Darcy. "You let a mortal win. I warned you what would happen."

Darcy's eye twitched. "He won fair and square."

"No!" Sly shouted. "No mortal could defeat a vampire. You've betrayed us all." He leaned forward and hissed, "You're fired."

Darcy flinched. She tried to turn away, but Bart had the camera in her face. Great. Fired on international television and labeled a traitor in front of the vampire world. She'd never find employment again.

"You can't fire her." Austin glared at Sly. "It was *my* fault. She begged me over and over to get myself eliminated."

"But that would have been fixing the contest," Gregori observed. "By attempting to stay in, you kept it fair."

"Who gives a shit about being fair?" Sly yelled. His eyes narrowed on Gregori. "You're fired."

Gregori shrugged. "You should have that phrase patented. You do it so well."

Lady Pamela raised a hand to attract everyone's attention. "We still have a problem here. We cannot have a mortal master. How would he protect us?"

"Aye," Princess Joanna agreed. "Our master must be a vampire."

"Well, he's not," Sly growled. His eyes widened suddenly as if an idea had just popped into his head. He cast a sly look in Austin's direction. "Though his condition could be changed."

Darcy gasped. "No."

Austin dropped the check on the floor. His face paled.

The ladies exchanged looks.

"Are you suggesting we transform him?" Princess Joanna asked.

Sly shrugged. "If you want him, take him."

"Whoa!" Austin raised his hands. "I'm not agreeing to this."

"You can't transform someone against their will," Darcy insisted.

"Why not?" Sly sneered. "Did anyone ask you for your permission?"

Her eye twitched.

"Come on, ladies." Sly gave them an encouraging smile. "You'll get the man you wanted and five million dollars. Which one of you has the guts to do the deed?"

Austin grabbed the check off the floor. "Look, ladies. I'll give you the check if you leave me alone."

Their eyes widened.

"You'd give us the money?" Vanda asked.

"No!" Roberto cried. "He is disqualified. That money is mine!"

"Hush," Gregori muttered. "Look, Sly. Darcy's right. You can't transform this guy against his will."

Sly glared at him. "Who's listening to you? You're fired, too." He turned to the camera. "Ladies and gentlemen, this will be the most exciting moment in vampire history! A live transformation performed right before your very eyes."

"You can't do it." Darcy clenched her fists. "You can't transform someone without killing him first."

"Your point?"

She gave an exasperated huff. "It's murder. Don't you think that's a bit . . . unethical, even for television?"

Sly shrugged. "But imagine the ratings."

Austin stepped in front of a camera. "I'd like to state for the record that I'm thoroughly opposed to murder. Especially my own."

Princess Joanna waved a hand in dismissal. "Relax, young man. We're not going to kill you."

"No." Maria Consuela clutched her rosary. "It is evil."

Lady Pamela shook her head. "We don't need a master that badly."

"Yes, you do!" Roberto jumped forward. "You need me."

"Hush," Vanda muttered.

"You don't need a master at all," Austin stated. "You just need a little financial assistance to help get you on your feet." He laid the check across the ladies' laps.

"Oh, my!" Cora Lee gasped. "All this money. Whatever will we do with it all?"

"I—I suppose we could go into trade?" Lady Pamela suggested.

Vanda grinned. "Let's open our own male dancer club. With vampire men."

The ladies jumped to their feet, all jabbering at the same time. Laughing, they scurried toward the door with their giant check.

"Wait!" Roberto called after them. "Come back with my money."

"Adios, Roberto." Vanda shut the door.

"Come back!" Roberto stomped a foot on the floor. "You must do as I say. I am your master!"

The ladies' laughter could be heard from the foyer. Maggie grabbed Austin and escorted him from the room. Darcy sighed with relief that he was safe.

Sly turned to her. "You crazy bitch."

She gulped. Her nightmare wasn't over.

"Hey." Gregori grasped Sly by the arm. "Don't talk to her like that."

Sly pulled his arm free. "Look at what she's done. We don't have a winner. The women have run off with the money. The whole thing is a freaking disaster."

"I disagree." Darcy lifted her chin. "It's more like a miraculous transformation. Those ladies once believed they couldn't survive without a master. They were trapped in the past and frozen with fear and self-doubt. But they blossomed before our eyes. Now, they're strong, independent, intelligent women who know the truth. They don't need a master."

Sly snorted. "And you think that's good? Every male vampire in the world is going to hate you."

"I don't hate her," Gregori said.

"You're an idiot," Sly snarled. "How can we have a Sexiest Man on Earth contest without a winner?"

"Adam was the winner," Darcy insisted.

"He's a mortal!" Sly hissed. "You've insulted the entire vampire world."

Darcy squared her shoulders. "That's a chance I'm

willing to take. When the ladies wanted to follow their dream, Adam encouraged them. That makes him the Sexiest Man on Earth."

"You're an idiot, too. You're both fired."

"Then, let's get outta here." Gregori held out a hand to Darcy. She lifted her chin to make a dignified exit.

"You were great," Gregori whispered as they walked down the hallway.

"I'm doomed." She stopped as her whole body started to shake. "I've lost Austin. I've lost my career. And vampires all over the world will hate me."

"Not your friends." Gregori patted her on the back. "And I think you'd be surprised by how many friends you have."

She took a deep breath. "I hope you're right."

"Thank you for not . . . attacking me," Austin told the ladies in the foyer.

Cora Lee giggled. "Thank you for all this money."

"Are you really opening a male stripper club?" Austin asked. "For vampires?"

"Yes." Vanda laughed. "I think we should call it Horny Devils." She looked him over. "Do you need a job, cutie?"

"I'm not that desperate." But he might get there fast, especially if Sean Whelan blacklisted him. The front door burst open, and Corky Courrant entered with her crew. "Time for me to go." Austin nodded to the ladies. "Good luck to you."

He ran up the stairs to fetch his luggage from his room.

"Wait up." Maggie zoomed to catch up with him. "I'm not sure you should just leave. You know all about our world."

"I won't tell anyone."

"I could try erasing your memory," she suggested. "But I'm not sure you want to forget Darcy."

One vampire wouldn't have enough power to erase his memory. More the pity. It would be such a relief. No memory and no pain. But the memories were too priceless to give up, no matter the cost of the pain. "I want to remember her."

"I understand." Maggie frowned as she walked beside him. "I'm sorry it didn't work out for you."

"So am I." He opened the door to his room. "I'm sorry I made her lose her job. Would you tell her that for me? And tell her I wish her a long and happy . . . life."

Maggie nodded. "I'm sure she wishes the same for you."

A few minutes later, Austin took his bags down the back stairs. When he reached the first floor, he could see the foyer. It was bright with lights and cameras. Corky was busy interviewing the ladies.

He spotted Darcy standing to the side. She turned to look at him. He raised a hand in farewell. She did the same.

So that was it. No final kiss or embrace. With a sigh, he headed toward the service elevator in the kitchen. No final proclamations of undying love. No final rush into each other's arms. No tears spilled over a love that could never be. Just this savage pain in his chest as he slipped away into the dark night.

Chapter 26

A day later, Austin realized he was going to live.
And still have bills to pay. He considered other jobs in
law enforcement, but human criminals had somehow
lost their appeal. He was only interested in the undead
variety.

To keep his mind off Darcy, he took a temporary
job in construction. The labor wore him out so he was
able to sleep at night. He worked until the next Saturday, then took a day off.

He sat on the couch, drinking a beer and wondering
what to do with his life. He'd reached some of his old
contacts from his days in Eastern Europe. He was
considering going back. He knew the languages. He
knew there were bad vampires there. Still, he was reluctant to leave New York. Darcy was here. He wanted
to be here in case she needed him.

Who was he kidding? She had plenty of friends.
She didn't need him. He eyed the box that now held

the videotapes of her old newscasts. He should return the tapes. He should let go.

He clunked the beer bottle down on the coffee table. First, he'd watch all the tapes one more time. One last tribute to Darcy. He stacked the tapes in chronological order, then inserted the first one into the VCR. For the first hour, he smiled. Into the second hour, he felt like crying. By that evening, he had reached the last tape. He was sprawled on the couch, thoroughly depressed, with the last slices of a take-out pizza congealing on the coffee table.

A news anchor described Darcy's disappearance, his face plastered with false concern. No one knew where she was.

"She's dying in an alley, you bastard," Austin growled. If only that damned experiment had worked. If Darcy could change back into a mortal, she'd stop rejecting him. What had gone wrong with the experiment? Something about mutated vampire DNA and the need for the person's original DNA.

The next newscast started. The reporter was standing in the alley behind the vampire club. Though Darcy's body had never been found, the police had recovered a knife stained with her blood. Poor Darcy. Knifed in the chest.

Austin sat up with a jerk. Holy crap! The bloody knife. Her original human DNA. He slapped a hand against his forehead. Was that what Roman needed to make the experiment work?

Austin threw on a suit so he would look like he was still with the CIA. He looked up Gregori's address and phone number on the computer and scribbled down the information. He made some calls and discovered the evidence on Darcy's case had been moved to a central lockup facility in Midtown.

He drove there. It was nine P.M. on a Saturday night, so the place was dead. Only one officer on duty.

Austin approached the officer and planted an image of a CIA ID card in the officer's head. "I'm with the CIA." He flashed an ID card from a video rental store.

The officer nodded. "How can I help you?"

"I need to check the evidence for the Darcy Newhart case. It's four years old."

The officer pushed a clipboard toward him. "I'll need you to sign in."

Austin wrote the name Adam Cartwright.

The officer thumbed through an index file, then removed a card. "Here it is. Bin number 3216."

"Thanks." Austin waited for the officer to buzz him in. He strode down the narrow aisles till he located the box labeled 3216/Newhart. He pulled it off the shelf. Inside, he found a broken video camera, Darcy's old purse, and in a plastic bag, the bloody knife. He stuffed the plastic bag inside his coat and returned the box to the shelf.

Back in his car, he examined the knife through the plastic covering. This could be it. Darcy's one chance to become human again. And their one chance to be together. He set the bag on the passenger seat. His hands shook as he dialed Gregori's number on his cell phone.

"Hello?" Gregori answered.

"I need to speak to Darcy."

There was a pause. "This is Austin, right?"

"Yes. I have something important to tell Darcy."

"Haven't you done enough? She lost her job because of you."

"I wouldn't bother her if this wasn't extremely important."

"I have a better idea. Don't bother her at all." Gregori hung up.

Great. Her friends were protecting her. Austin drove to Gregori's address and parked. He buzzed the apartment.

"Yes?" A female voice came over the intercom.

"Vanda, is that you? I need to talk to Darcy."

"Austin?"

"Yes. I have something vital to show Darcy."

"She's already seen it," Vanda replied dryly. "Look, she's cried enough over you. Leave her alone."

Austin released the intercom button with a sigh. He could break into their apartment, but then he'd have a bunch of angry vampires screaming at him. Darcy would be too upset to listen. He needed an ally. Someone who could present Darcy's options to her without breaking and entering. Shanna Whelan? He wasn't sure where she was. She and Roman had moved out of the townhouse to get away from Sean's threats. But the townhouse was still there. And the kilted Scottish guards.

Connor. He was the perfect choice. He was the one who had transformed Darcy. He should be the one to tell her the news.

Austin drove to Draganesti's townhouse on the Upper East Side. The steps leading to the front door were dark, lit only by a blinking red light on a surveillance camera equipped with a night lens. He rang the doorbell and glanced up at the camera to allow the guards inside a good look at his face.

A deep voice, laced with a Scottish accent, spoke

over the intercom. "Push the button and state yer purpose."

He pressed the button on the intercom. "I want to speak to Connor."

No answer. Austin waited. He pivoted, surveying the quiet street. And waited. He had pushed the button on the intercom to remind them he was waiting, when the door slowly opened.

An unwanted shiver crept down his spine.

"Come in," Connor said. He smiled slightly. "Ye're just in time for dinner."

They're all bottle-fed, Austin reminded himself as he stepped into the dimly lit foyer. Connor was just trying to scare him. Or maybe, the bastard enjoyed playing with his food.

There were three kilted Scotsmen in the foyer. Connor was in the middle with the youthful-looking vampire on the right. A black-haired Scotsman was on the left. Behind them, there was a large staircase and a reserve troop of six more kilted vampires.

Connor crossed his arms and regarded him curiously. "Well, laddie. Ye have some bollocks coming here."

"I need to talk to you. In private."

Connor tilted his head toward the black-haired Scotsman. "Dougal, search the perimeter. Make sure our wee friend from the CIA has come alone."

"Aye, sir." Dougal and two of the reserve guards went out the front, closing the door behind them. Two more reserve guards zoomed out the back door.

"I'm alone," Austin said. "And I'm no longer with the CIA."

Connor arched a dubious brow. "Raise yer arms, please, so Ian can check you for weapons."

Austin lifted his arms as the youthful vampire circled behind him. "I have a knife in my jacket." In less than a second, the last two reserve guards were flanking him with swords pointed at his chest.

Austin blinked. That was fast. Ian removed the plastic bag containing the bloody knife and handed it to Connor.

"I wasn't going to use it," Austin muttered.

"You wouldna have had the chance." Connor turned the bag over, examining the knife. "This blood is old."

"Four years old. It's Darcy's." Austin noted the automatic flinch in Connor's hands.

A hint of remorse flitted over the Scotsman's face before he resumed his usual blank expression. "Any other weapons?"

Ian finished patting down Austin's legs. "Nay. He's clean."

"This way." Connor marched toward a door behind the staircase.

Austin followed, still flanked by the two armed guards and trailed by Ian. He went through a swinging door to find himself in a kitchen.

"Sit." Connor motioned toward the table. He glanced at Ian and the guards. "You may go."

Austin approached the table, but didn't sit.

Connor set the bloody knife on the table. "So, this is the knife that killed Darcy?"

"No, it wounded her. You're the one who killed her, you bastard." He rammed a fist into Connor's jaw. Austin smiled grimly when the Scotsman stumbled back. The vampire's jaw had been hard as stone, but the pain had been worth it, just to see the shocked expression on Connor's face.

"Why the hell did ye do that?"

Austin flexed his sore hand. "You deserved it."

Connor sat at the table and motioned to the chair across from him.

Austin sat. Apparently, he didn't need to worry about a counterattack. Connor must have agreed he deserved the hit.

"So ye've left the CIA?" Connor asked.

"I resigned a week ago after a major disagreement with Sean Whelan. I wanted to concentrate only on the Malcontents, but he still believes all vampires are evil."

"And ye no longer believe that?"

"No. I got to know some Vamps while I was doing the reality show. They're harmless." Austin sighed. "Sean ordered me to stake them during the day while they're helpless. I refused."

"Sporting of you."

Austin was surprised by the twinkle of amusement in the Scotsman's eyes. "I thought so."

Connor lounged back in his chair. "Rumor has it that ye actually won that contest and all the money, but ye gave the check to the ladies."

Austin shrugged. "They needed it."

"Aye. But so do you if ye're unemployed."

"I intend to find another job."

"Ye worked in Eastern Europe for a while."

Austin swallowed. "How do you know about that?"

"Ian has grown quiet adept at breaking into Langley. Ye're fluent in Hungarian and Czech?"

"Yes." Austin suddenly felt like he was on a job interview. "I'd like to continue the fight against the Malcontents if you know of an organization that—"

"Later," Connor interrupted him. "Several Malcontents have been murdered lately in Central Park. What do ye know of that?"

Austin took a deep breath, but remained silent.

"The Russians have accused us of doing it, but I think it's yer bloody Stake-Out team. Since ye're no longer with the CIA, you wouldna mind telling me if I'm right?"

Austin hesitated. "The Malcontents deserve to die. They attack the innocent."

"Aye." Connor crossed his arms. "Since you and Garrett were involved in the reality show, I'm betting the assassin is either Sean Whelan or one of the females on the team."

Damn. He needed to call Emma and tell her to stop.

"'Tis one of the ladies, then," Connor said softly. "You wouldna feel the need to protect Sean."

Austin shifted in his chair. This vampire was too sharp.

Connor gestured toward the knife. "And why have ye brought this here? Are ye hoping to torment my guilty conscience?"

"So you admit to your guilt? Why didn't you take her to a hospital? Or to Romatech? They have tons of synthetic blood there. You could have saved her."

Connor's eyes clouded with pain. "She was such a brave lass. She dinna deserve to die."

"But you killed her."

He shook his head sadly. "A vampire can smell how much blood a mortal is carrying. We can hear the beating of their hearts. The knife had nicked a major artery. She was bleeding internally. Only a few more beats and she would have been gone."

"You don't think there was enough time?"

"I know there was not." Connor heaved a sigh. "I know she hates me. But believe me, there was no other way to save her."

"I believe you." The pain in the vampire's eyes was real.

Connor touched the plastic bag. "How did ye get this?"

"I stole it from the police."

The Scotsman's eyebrows rose. "I'm impressed."

"Darcy told me about Roman's experiment to transform a vampire back into a human. She said it didn't work because they needed the human's original DNA."

"Aye." Connor lifted the knife, his eyes widening. "And this is Darcy's human blood."

"With her human DNA." Austin leaned forward. "I think it's possible the experiment could work on her."

"Have ye told her?"

"No. Her friends are protecting her from me."

"Why?" Connor frowned. "What did ye do to her?"

"I made her lose her job. And I fell in love with her."

"Ah. And ye would prefer to love a mortal than a vampire?"

"I'd be happy with her any way I could get her, but it's not about me. It's about Darcy and her happiness. This needs to be her decision."

Connor set the knife back on the table. "I'll have to check with Roman to see if he believes it could work."

"Then will you tell her? I think it should come from you."

Connor sighed. "I couldna give her a choice before."

Austin handed him the knife. "This time, you can."

At midnight, Vanda and Maggie dragged Darcy into the living room to watch another episode of *The Sexiest*

Man on Earth. Sly was still airing the show on Wednesdays and Saturdays. The vampire public demanded it. According to Corky Courrant, it was the most popular show since the formation of DVN.

In the week since she'd been fired, Darcy had kept busy helping the ladies start their business and find a townhouse of their own. For now, they were all staying in Gregori's cramped apartment. The ladies were too happy to be bothered about the close quarters. They even invited Darcy to participate in their male dancer club, but she declined.

Now she sat, scrunched on a couch between Vanda and Maggie. The ladies loved seeing themselves on TV, but watching the show and seeing Austin was torture for Darcy. Knowing she couldn't have him didn't lessen her love for him. It only increased the poignancy of her longing. By the end of the show, she was thoroughly depressed. The jubilant ladies filled glasses with Bubbly Blood.

"Cheer up." Maggie handed her a glass. "At least Sly agreed to let us keep all the money."

Gregori snorted. "He had no choice. Roman was the one who put up the funds, and he insisted you all keep it."

"The master did care about us after all." Cora Lee grinned. "You should be happy, Darcy. Your show is the biggest hit ever."

"Indeed," Princess Joanna agreed. "Sly would be a fool not to beg you to do another one."

Unfortunately, Sly *was* a fool. "He'll just hire someone else," Darcy muttered.

"I don't think so," Vanda countered. "Corky Courrant's been playing your interview over and over. She's making you famous. Sly will have to ask you back."

"Vanda's right." Gregori sipped from his glass. "Corky's taken up the cause of female Vamp liberation, and she's named you the hero of the movement. Sly will look like a complete scumbag if he doesn't take you back."

Unfortunately, Sly *was* a complete scumbag. Darcy wasn't going to hold her breath waiting for him to call.

"The founder of the female Vamp liberation movement." Maggie gazed at Darcy with admiring eyes. "I knew it. I knew there was a reason for you to be with us. This was all meant to be."

Darcy's heart swelled with emotion. She was meant to be here. Meant to be a vampire. Her eyes misted as she regarded all her friends. At last, she was making peace with her world.

"Being the marketing genius that I am," Gregori continued, his eyes twinkling, "I've decided to take full advantage of your celebrity status. I convinced Roman to start a new line of female Vamp products, and we want you to be our spokesperson."

Darcy's mouth fell open. "You mean, I would have a job?"

"Yes." Gregori smiled. "You would make commercials, go on tours. Be an inspiration to Vamp women all around the world."

The ladies squealed and gathered around Darcy to congratulate her. She was too stunned to do anything but babble incoherently. In the midst of all the noise, the phone rang.

Gregori answered it. "Sure, come on over." He glanced at the women. "Step back, please. We have a visitor coming."

The women crowded against the far wall as a figure materialized before them. Shoulder-length auburn hair. A red and green plaid kilt. *Connor.* Darcy stiffened.

He immediately focused on her. "We need to talk. Alone."

Her heart pounded in her ears. What doom was he bringing tonight? And why? Her life was finally looking hopeful again.

"Come, ladies." Gregori motioned toward the door. "Let's give them some privacy."

Darcy perched on the edge of an easy chair as her friends filed from the room. Connor paced about, his kilt swishing around his knees. He was nervous, she realized, and that only served to make her pulse race faster.

He cleared his throat. "I've been enjoying yer show."

"Thank you."

"I gather ye dinna tell yer boss about Austin working for the CIA?"

"No. Sly was furious enough just to find out he's mortal."

Connor folded his arms across his wide chest. "He came to see me a few hours ago."

"Austin?"

"Aye. He had something important to tell you. And yer friends here weren't letting him get through to you."

Darcy's heart stuttered. Austin had tried to reach her? While she remained speechless, she heard muffled whispers behind the door. Her friends were listening in. Her nosy, overprotective friends. "Austin's been trying to reach me?"

"Aye." Connor glanced at the door where the whispers had grown in volume. "I suppose they were trying to protect you."

Darcy raised her voice. "How silly of them. They should know I can take care of myself."

The whispers cut off.

Connor's mouth twitched. "Well done, lass," he said softly.

Darcy motioned to the chair next to her. "What did Austin say?"

"He claimed he was no longer with the CIA." Connor took the offered seat. "We checked on it, and it's true. In fact, Sean Whelan has blacklisted him from any government employment."

"I see." Poor Austin. He was in worse shape than her.

"Ye told him about the experiment to transform a vampire back into a mortal."

"Yes." Darcy frowned. "I told him it didn't work."

"Because the vampire's original human DNA is needed."

"Yes." Darcy wondered where this was going.

"Austin brought me the knife from yer attack four years ago. It was covered with yer blood. Yer human blood."

Darcy fell back against the chair. "You mean . . . ?"

"Aye. I took the knife to Roman. He isolated yer human DNA. He thinks ye're the best candidate we'll ever find."

She pressed a hand against her chest. Her heart was thundering in her ears. "I—I could become mortal again?"

The whispers resumed outside the door.

Connor leaned forward, bracing his forearms on his knees. "I have to tell ye, lass, there's a possibility ye could perish during the procedure."

"How—how big a possibility?"

"Roman estimates a seventy-five-percent chance of success."

And a twenty-five-percent chance she could die.

The door burst open, making her jump in her chair.

"Don't do it!" Maggie rushed into the room.

"I agree." Gregori marched in. "You shouldn't risk your life, Darcy. You have a perfectly good life here."

The other ladies murmured in agreement.

Darcy's eyes filled with tears. She did have a promising future in the vampire world. But she didn't have Austin. And he still wanted her. That was why he'd brought Connor the knife. "Austin wants me to do it?"

Connor shook his head. "He dinna say. He only said ye deserved to be happy. And ye deserved to have a choice."

He wants me to choose. She could have a bright future as a celebrity in the vampire world. She had wonderful friends who cared about her and a female liberation movement she'd managed to start. On the other hand, she could have Austin. And her family. And sunshine. And a one in four chance of dying.

"Don't do it." Maggie knelt beside her chair. "We need you."

"I'm not sure we're enough." Vanda's eyes glimmered with tears. "There's nothing more sacred than love."

"But *we* love her!" Maggie exclaimed.

A tear tumbled down Darcy's cheek.

"Enough of yer blethering," Connor stood. "This is Darcy's decision. I couldna give her a choice before, but now, I can."

Darcy wiped her cheeks. "I need to talk to Connor alone for a moment."

Her friends trudged slowly from the room and shut the door.

Darcy drew a shaky breath. "If I go through with this, I might not survive, so I want you to know how I feel."

Connor sat heavily in the chair next to her. "I know ye hate me. I doona blame ye for that."

"I've been telling myself I should hate you, but I realize now I was angry with myself. I was . . . ashamed." More tears slipped down her cheeks, and she brushed them away.

"Why, lass? Ye were verra brave to rescue that young girl."

Darcy shook her head. "I was a coward. I blamed you for transforming me, for not giving me a choice. But the truth was I had a choice. When you poured your blood down my throat, I could have refused. I could have turned my head and died with dignity. But I didn't. I was afraid. I didn't want to die."

"No one wants to die, lass."

"I drank your blood." Tears streamed down her face. "I was so appalled with myself."

Connor grabbed her hand. "You did what ye had to do to survive. And ye made the right choice. Look at all the good ye've done. Our world is a better place because ye're here."

"I made the right choice," she repeated to herself. A sense of peace filled her heart. Maggie was right. Her life as a vampire had been meant to be. And if she hadn't survived, she would have never met Austin. She squeezed Connor's hand. "Thank you."

His blue eyes glistened with tears. "Have ye decided, lass?"

"Yes. I took the cowardly choice before. This time, I choose to be brave."

Chapter 27

Monday night, the phone rang, jolting Austin
from a deep sleep. The clock read only eleven-thirty.
He'd gone to bed early after an exhausting day on a
new construction site. His nerves clenched as he fumbled for the receiver. A call this late usually meant bad
news. "Hello?"

"The procedure is scheduled to begin in twenty
minutes."

Procedure? "Who is this?" he asked, although the
caller's Scottish accent made it fairly obvious.

"Connor. I thought ye might want to be here for
Darcy."

"She—she's doing it?" Austin's heart lurched in his
chest. "She's going to be changed back—"

"Aye," Connor interrupted him. "They're prepping
her now. All her friends are here, so—"

"Where?" Austin jumped out of bed.

"Romatech. Ye know where it is?"

"Yeah. White Plains. I'll be there. Tell Darcy I'm

coming." Twenty minutes? Damn, he'd never make it in time.

"Ye should know there's a possibility she'll no' survive."

His heart plummeted into his stomach. He could have sworn both lungs had collapsed cause he couldn't breathe. He heard a clicking sound. "Wait!" Too late. Connor had hung up.

He dropped the receiver back into its cradle. Holy crap. He should have never given them the knife. Darcy could die.

He threw on some clothes, grabbed his wallet and keys, and charged out the door. *Try to think positive.* The elevator took an eternity to reach the ground floor. *Think positive. She'll be mortal.* He sprinted to the parking garage. His hands shook as he fumbled to unlock the car. He climbed in and started the engine.

She could die.

He sped out of the garage and zoomed north on the West Side Highway. His gaze darted to the dashboard clock every few seconds. Was she afraid? Dammit, of course she was afraid.

She could die.

His heart hammered when twenty minutes had passed. They were starting the procedure. And he wasn't there. He sped past a police car in the Bronx. Holy shit. He glanced in the rearview mirror. No flashing lights. Thank God. He turned north onto the Bronx River Parkway.

She could die.

Finally, he reached the outskirts of White Plains. He swerved into the entrance of Romatech, ignoring the guard station and the kilted Scotsman who shouted at him. He screeched to a halt by the front door and ran inside. Two Scottish guards grabbed him.

"Where's Darcy?" He struggled. "I have to see her."

"Ye're Austin Erickson?" The first guard restrained him while the second one removed Austin's wallet and checked his ID.

"Yes." Austin yanked his arm free from the vampire's grasp. "I'm here to see Darcy Newhart."

The second guard returned his wallet. "Connor told us ye were coming. This way."

Austin followed the guards down a hallway, around a corner, and down another hallway. Finally, they opened a pair of swinging doors.

Austin rushed inside and halted when he saw Gregori and all the ladies from the reality show. Gregori was leaning against a wall, his arms crossed. He shot Austin a hostile look. Vanda was pacing about the room. Maria Consuela and Princess Joanna were kneeling together with a priest, all of them praying in Latin. Maggie took one look at him and started crying. Lady Pamela and Cora Lee sat on each side of Maggie, whispering assurances. Then they looked at Austin with accusation in their eyes.

He should have never recovered that knife. It would be his fault if Darcy died. He cleared his throat. "How is she?"

"How do you think she is?" Gregori growled. "They're draining every drop of blood out of her."

Vanda slowed to a stop in front of him. "Connor comes out about every five minutes to tell us what's happening."

Austin strode toward Gregori. "Tell them to stop. It's not too late to keep her a vampire, right?"

Gregori snorted. "Why would you want to stop it? She wasn't good enough for you as a vampire, was she?"

Austin clenched his fists. "I love her just the way she is. Now go in there and tell them to stop!"

Gregori hesitated, so Austin strode toward the door. "Darcy! Don't do it!" The door was locked. He pounded on the door. "Don't risk your life for me, dammit!"

The door opened suddenly as Connor exited. Austin tried to go in, but the Scotsman shoved him back and held him against the wall with one hand. Austin strained against Connor's grip, but the Scotsman was incredibly strong.

"Ye're making too much noise out here," Connor growled.

"You have to stop the procedure," Austin whispered.

"She's entered the vampire coma," Connor announced softly. " 'Tis too late."

Maggie burst into tears. Cora Lee and Lady Pamela joined her. Vanda stumbled to a chair and collapsed. Gregori slumped against the wall, his eyes closed.

Austin's eyes filled with tears. What the hell had he done? He had no right to take Darcy away from these people who loved her. "You can still let her stay a vampire."

Connor shook his head. "It was her choice. She deserved to have a choice, and ye know it."

"Listen! If things go badly, if she's dying, I want you to make her a vampire. She'll be safe that way."

Connor dropped his hand, releasing Austin. "I asked her about that, and she said no. If she dies, we have to let her go."

"No!" Austin paced away, refusing to accept this. He marched back to Connor. "I won't let her go. You'll change her back into a vampire." He leaned closer. "And then, you'll change me."

Connor's eyes widened. "Are ye serious?"

Austin pulled down the collar of his shirt. "What are you waiting for? Go for it, you bastard!"

Gregori strode toward them. "You're willing to become a vampire to save Darcy?"

"Yes. I'll do whatever it takes."

Connor exchanged a look with Gregori. "I wasna certain she'd made the right choice. Or that this man was worthy of her. But now, I see that he is."

Austin's vision blurred with tears. "Don't let her die."

"We'll do our best." Connor slipped back inside the operating room.

Austin leaned forward, pressing his forehead against the door. *Live, Darcy. You have to live.*

"I misjudged you," Gregori spoke behind him. Austin turned. The young vampire extended a hand, and Austin shook it. They waited by the door in silence.

After a few minutes, Gregori perked up. He pressed an ear against the door.

"What is it?" Austin asked.

"They're getting excited," Gregori whispered. "I can hear them. She . . . she's responding. She's breathing on her own."

"I'm going in." Austin wrenched open the door and marched inside. Darcy was lying on an operating table with bright lights illuminating her pale face. Roman Draganesti and the short chemist named Laszlo were hovering over her.

"Ye shouldna be here," Connor muttered.

"Buzz off," Austin growled.

"Is that any way to talk to yer new boss?"

"I don't care—what?" Austin glanced at the Scotsman before returning his gaze to Darcy.

"She's coming around," Roman announced.

Austin stepped forward. "Is she all right?"

Roman glanced up. "You must be Austin."

"Yes, sir." He stopped beside the operating table. "Is she all right? Did it work?"

Roman checked her life signs on a nearby machine. "She's doing great."

"We did it!" Laszlo twisted a button on his lab coat. "This is a momentous achievement, sir."

Darcy moved her head and moaned.

Austin touched her face. "Darcy?"

Her eyes flickered open. "Austin?"

"Yes." He took her hand. "I'm here, sweetheart."

Her gaze flitted around the room. "I—I'm alive."

"How do you feel?" Roman examined her eyes with a small flashlight.

"Tired. Weak. Thirsty."

"Thirsty for what?" Roman clicked off the flashlight.

Darcy licked her lips. "Water. Juice." She slowly smiled. "A vanilla milkshake."

Roman smiled. "That's a good sign."

The short chemist removed his latex gloves. "I could go to the cafeteria and bring her back something."

Roman nodded. "Just some juice for now. Thank you, Laszlo."

"My pleasure." Laszlo plucked at the button on his lab coat. "It's been an honor to participate in such a miraculous event." He scurried from the room.

Loud cheers erupted from the waiting room. Laszlo had obviously spread the good news.

Austin brushed Darcy's hair back from her brow. "Do you hear that, sweetheart? All your friends are happy for you."

She gazed at him, her eyes shimmering with tears. "I was so afraid."

"I'm sure you were. I was terrified."

"Aye, that he was." Connor stepped forward. "The lad even offered to become a vampire if we would stop the procedure."

Darcy's eyes widened. "Oh, no, Austin. I would have been so angry with you."

"I know, but I figured you'd get over it in a century or two. And we would have been together."

She smiled.

And he was undone. "Marry me. I know this isn't the most romantic setting for a proposal, but I can't wait. Please say you'll marry me."

A tear trailed down her cheek. "I will marry you."

Austin grinned. He leaned close to wipe her tear away. "Now, don't cry. I'm not much of a catch right now. I don't even have a job, and—"

"Wait a minute, lad," Connor interrupted. "I told Angus MacKay about you, and he wants to hire you. We need your help in locating Casimir. He's somewhere in Eastern Europe."

Austin straightened. "Who is Angus MacKay? And who is Casimir?"

"Casimir is the leader of the Malcontents," Roman explained. "He's the cruelest, most vicious vampire in the world."

"As a mortal, ye have the advantage of snooping

about during the day," Connor continued. "And with yer psychic abilities and CIA training, ye're the best man for the job."

Austin swallowed. It was just the sort of mission he'd always wanted. He glanced at Darcy.

"You should do it," she whispered.

"I won't leave you."

"I'll come with you. I was always good at research and investigation. I can help."

"It could be dangerous." Austin corrected himself. "It *will* be dangerous."

Darcy smiled. "I always wanted to do more serious stuff."

Austin turned to Connor. "Darcy and I are a team. You'll need to hire us both."

The Scotsman's mouth twitched. "Aye, we can do that."

"I have a villa in Tuscany you can use as your base," Roman offered.

"Thank you," Austin replied. "That's very generous."

Roman smiled. "I'm in a generous mood. I just found out last night that I'm going to be a father."

"Och, that's grand." Connor shook his hand. "But I thought ye had stopped trying because of the . . . problem."

Roman's smile faded. "Apparently, our first attempt worked."

A vampire fathering a baby? Austin gave Darcy a questioning look.

"I'll explain later," she whispered.

Austin glanced at Roman and Connor. They looked more worried than happy. "Congratulations." Austin extended a hand.

"Thank you." Roman shook it, his smile returning. "You'll enjoy working for Angus."

"Who is he?"

"The owner of MacKay Security and Investigation," Connor explained. "And coven master of the United Kingdom."

"Oh." Austin swallowed. He should have realized he'd be working for a vampire organization.

Connor's eyes twinkled. "How soon can ye start?"

"Ah, we need a few weeks. We need to get married."

"You can have the reception here, no charge," Roman offered. "And I have an apartment in Paris you can use for your honeymoon, if you like."

"Thank you." Austin realized that even though he and his future wife were mortal, their life would still revolve around vampires. "Darcy and I need to make a few trips first."

"Trips?" she asked.

"One to Wisconsin to see my family. And the other—"

She gasped. "*My* family?" She glanced at Roman and Connor. "Is that all right?"

Connor shrugged. "As long as ye have a good explanation."

"Don't worry," Austin assured her. "I'm an old pro at cover stories. We'll just say you were in hiding from some bad guys, and now that the bad guys are dead, you're able to resume your old life."

She looked skeptical. "You make it sound so simple."

"The simpler stories are the best," Austin said.

She smiled. "Then I'll also tell them you were the hero who rescued me."

"Well, if you insist."

She took a deep breath. "Everything's perfect now."

Austin kissed her brow. "We have each other."

She smiled at the men surrounding her. "Mortal and vampire." She squeezed Austin's hand. "I have the best of both worlds."

Coming in June from Avon Books—
four fantastic love stories by four
amazing authors

She's No Princess by Laura Lee Guhrke

An Avon Romantic Treasure

What happens when Sir Ian Moore, London's most proper diplomat, has to play matchmaker for the daughter of a notorious courtesan? He wants to get her married off as soon as possible. . . but finds himself tempted by the lady herself!

Almost a Goddess by Judi McCoy

An Avon Contemporary Romance

Kyra, the Muse of Good Fortune, hasn't been doing a very good job over the past hundred or so years. . . so she's sent down to Las Vegas to make a difference in the life of unsuspecting Jake Lennox. But if she falls in love all bets are off. . .

Sinful Pleasures by Mary Reed McCall

An Avon Romance

Once Lady Alissende and Sir Damien were passionate lovers, until she had to turn her back on him, shattering his heart forever. Now, his life endangered, she will do anything to protect the man she still secretly loves.

How to Seduce a Bride by Edith Layton

An Avon Romance

The Viscount Haye wants to know everything about Daisy Tanner, the ravishing, secretive woman luring his best friend into marriage. He finds himself falling in love with the beauty himself—but what are the secrets she hides?

Avon Romances

the best in
exceptional authors and unforgettable novels!